PRAISE FOR

'Clever, twisted, and dark as m. . . .ll

'Marrs is brilliant at twists.'

—Peter James

'Whatever you do, don't read this in the dark . . .'

—Cara Hunter

'John's thrillers never fail to keep me furiously turning the pages.'

—Sarah Pearse

'John Marrs is a master of suspense.'

—Jeneva Rose

'This one will leave you with paper cuts.'

—C. J. Tudor

'Tensely plotted and terrifyingly imagined.'

—Harriet Tyce

'A smart, gripping and scarily believable story.'

—T. M. Logan

'What a twisted sinister book that was. Loved it.'

—Peter Swanson

'One of the most exciting, original thriller writers out there. I never miss one of his books.'

—Simon Kernick

THE STRANGER IN HER HOUSE

ALSO BY JOHN MARRS

When You Disappeared
The One
The Good Samaritan
Her Last Move
The Passengers
What Lies Between Us
The Minders
The Vacation
Keep It in the Family
The Marriage Act

THE
STRANGER
IN HER
HOUSE

JOHN MARRS

Text copyright © 2024 by John Marrs
All rights reserved.

Published by Thomas & Mercer, Seattle

www.apub.com

Amazon, the Amazon logo, and Thomas & Mercer are trademarks of Amazon.com, Inc., or its affiliates.

ISBN-13: 9781662506482
eISBN: 9781662506475

Cover design by Faceout Studio, Jeff Miller

Cover image: © Peter Greenway / Arcangel; © PATSUDA PARAMEE © Ivan Popovych © Here / Shutterstock

Printed in the United States of America

For Oscar

'The essence of lying is in deception, not words.'

—*John Ruskin*

PART ONE

CHAPTER 1

CONNIE

I open and close my fists, preparing myself like a boxer before a fight. For the two-minute walk from my bungalow to her house, I roll my shoulders back and forth to try and get rid of the tense feeling that creeps up on me daily. Because when I come to open that front door, I have no idea which version of her I'm going to find.

It could be the one who looks me up and down with caution before reluctantly allowing me over the threshold. Maybe it's the one who can't wait to see me and has been hovering at the window like a child waiting for a parent to return home from work. It could be the angry one who is furious with me for no apparent reason. Or it might be the melancholic version, her cloudy eyes tainted with a pinkish hue, salty tears cutting white lines into clumsily applied foundation. But whomever I'm confronted by, I'm here for her. I'll adapt, I'll handle it. I'm used to it. That's what good daughters do.

I check my watch; it's approaching 7.30 a.m. I've yet to see anyone else. Our village isn't the busiest at the best of times but I've usually spotted at least the newspaper boy zigzagging about on his motorised scooter by now. Heat prickles my scalp as the sun makes its presence felt. The breakfast TV weatherman warned today's temperature is going to break records for May. I'd rather shy away from it and hide in the shade. I can't remember the last time my skin displayed anything approaching a tan. I'm bordering on translucent.

I turn a corner and her house comes into view. Every village has an estate like this, a 1950s build where no thought was given as to how its design might blend in with the existing properties. If you're really local, you'll still refer to it as 'the new estate', despite it having been there for seventy-odd years.

Everything about the property looks tired, I think, including its occupant. I'm sure that in its day, it wasn't a bad-looking house, albeit characterless. Decades must have passed since the wooden garage doors last saw a lick of paint. The faded silver frames of the aluminium windows and the flaking white facias add to its knackered look. The overgrown garden offers an extra layer of neglect. I mow the front and back lawns fortnightly, but I have neither the time, the equipment nor the inclination to dig out weeds from the borders or cut back oversized bushes with swooping branches that overhang the path outside. Some of the neighbours have mentioned they struggle to get past the house without walking on the road. I guess I should take the hint and get someone in to do it.

The views from the back garden are enviable, though. Well, I imagine they will be once the huge hedge at the end is cut right back and we can appreciate the acres of fields behind us. Some local by-law forbids the council from allowing developers to cover it in identikit homes. Not that it makes much difference to me. In all likelihood, I'll sell this place eventually, when . . . well, you know. I'm sure it'll be snapped up by a DIY enthusiast with time on their hands.

I make my way up the drive, but she's not at the window and the curtains are still closed. I take the key out of my pocket, ring the bell to alert her I'm here and unlock the door.

'Mum, it's Connie,' I shout, dropping my handbag to the floor.

There's a sour smell in the air and I can't quite put my finger on what it is. I find her sitting in her armchair in the lounge. The smell is stronger in here, and as soon as I see her, I spot the damp patch on the front of her trousers. She looks both confused and ashamed.

'I've had an accident and I don't know what to do,' she apologises, and my heart breaks for her.

'It's okay,' I say softly and pat her hand. 'Let's get you cleaned up, then we'll find you a fresh pair of trousers.'

Her balance and coordination come and go like the tide, so I help her out of the chair and slip my arm around her waist. Some days she's flitting about the house like she's in the cast of *Riverdance*; on others, she's like a newborn foal taking its first steps. She's lost weight over the last few months; her ribs feel like piano keys. I notice dampness on the raised cushions she sits on that help her get up and out of the armchair. I'll put them on a fast cycle later. 'It's like raising the *Titanic* trying to get you up!' I joke.

'I quite fancied that Leonardo DiCaprio,' she replies.

'I think you're a bit old for a toyboy.'

She suddenly looks anxious. 'Do you think it's the Covid?' she asks. 'Have I caught the Covid? Is that why I had my accident?'

'No Mum, it was an accident.'

'But how do you know? You're not a doctor.'

'Because Covid doesn't make you pee yourself. Besides, you're up to date with your jabs.'

'Am I?'

'Yes, we went to the surgery in March. The nurse gave you another booster. Do you remember?'

Of course she doesn't remember it. There are days when she can barely recall what she ate ten minutes ago.

'But Covid killed Felipe, didn't it?'

'Who?'

5

'Felipe González. The man who lives in the villa with the avocado trees. He's married to Gwen.'

'You're Gwen.'

'I know that,' she huffs. 'I'm not the only Gwen in the world.'

Fair point. 'Did he live near your old house? I don't think there's a Felipe González in Avringstone?'

'Not anymore, he's dead. He caught the Covid.'

I take the first of many deep breaths I'm sure I'll be taking today, and allow the conversation to reach its natural conclusion.

We walk slowly up the stairs together, her considering each step as she grasps the banister. I stand behind her in case she loses her footing and slips. She has stumbled in the past, and once she almost knocked me down like a ten-pin bowling skittle. Upstairs, I lead her into the bathroom, helping her remove her trousers and underwear. I open a pack of wet wipes so that she can clean herself up, then I pass her an open bottle of talcum powder and a white cloud appears as she pats it into skin that sags like melting wax.

'I'll be back in a minute,' I say and choose a fresh outfit from her wardrobe. Everything is crammed in here. There'd be a lot more room if she cleared out his clothes. Jackets, shirts and trousers are gathering dust as each day passes. By the time I return to the bathroom, she's moved into the spare room and is standing in front of the window in just her bra, the net curtain pulled to one side. I can't help but laugh, bless her.

'Mum!' I say. 'Stop flashing your bits to the neighbours!'

'Oh,' she replies, suddenly remembering she's undressed. She turns and takes the trousers and underwear from me. 'I could start an OnlyFans page,' she jokes.

'How on earth do you know about OnlyFans?'

'They were talking about it on *This Morning*,' she replies, dressing herself. Aside from myself and the village church on a Sunday morning, television is her closest friend. Sometimes the soundtrack of magazine programmes, advertisements, quiz shows and old movies makes her muddled. Once, she swore blind that she lived in Albert Square and that the cast of *EastEnders* were her neighbours.

'People make a lot of money from getting their bits and bobs out on the interweb these days,' she continues. 'There's a market for everything.'

'I think you might end up offering lot of refunds.'

'Oi, I'll have you know I was quite a catch in my day.'

'As you remind me, often.'

'I could have had my pick of any of the lads in the clubs where we went dancing. All it took was a bullet bra and a plunging neckline and I'd be swatting them away like flies for the rest of the night.'

'Is that how you caught Dad's attention?'

'No, that's a completely different story. As soon as I clapped eyes on him, I knew he was going to be mine, despite the circumstances.'

'And what were they?'

'What were what?'

'The circumstances?'

She doesn't answer. 'I miss him,' she says instead, and we both go quiet. It's been fourteen months since he died, a drop in the ocean compared to the sixty years they spent together. Yet I bet to her it feels like an eternity.

'We all do,' I add. 'Why don't we go back downstairs and I'll make us some breakfast? I think we have some croissants left in the breadbin.'

'I'm not trying any of that foreign rubbish,' she replies, dabbing at a tear in her eye with her finger.

'Didn't you and Dad live in France for a while?'

'Did I?'

'That's what you told me. You must have eaten French food there.'

'Marmalade on toast will do me.'

'Marmalade on toast it is then.'

We make our way into the kitchen, where she sneezes and wipes her nose with a patterned cloth handkerchief tucked under her sleeve. It's part of the uniform for women over a certain age. 'Do you think I have the Covid?' she asks.

'No Mum, I think you're fine,' I say. I ask Alexa to choose a random playlist of 1950s music. Nothing relaxes her more than humming along to tunes from her teenage years. I leave her alone for a moment, pick up my handbag from the floor and remove the two framed photographs I've brought with me. In one, I'm a young girl sitting on a yellow bike with stabilisers attached to the rear wheel. I'm a teenager in the other, dressed in an oversized East 17 T-shirt and ripped jeans. I place them among the pictures arranged on the console table in the hallway. Apparently it helps to have familiar faces surrounding her. Some of the others I've already framed are holiday snaps taken in various European cities, others are from her wedding day and many are from their early years of married life. They look so relaxed in each other's company.

It saddens me to think it's unlikely I'll ever experience a love like theirs. I know that, at forty-two, my life is hardly over, but as the years march on, the opportunity to find happiness with a like-minded soul is slipping further from my reach. I don't have the time to offer anyone else my attention even if they did come along. As her vascular dementia and Alzheimer's continue to tighten their grip and she forgets who I am, it would be nice to have at least one other person in this world to care for me like I care for her.

CHAPTER 2

CONNIE

The dog attached to the other end of the lead cocks his leg up against a garden rubbish recycling bin and pees. I inhale from my vaping pen as I wait, puffing out a blackberry-scented cloud while I savour the gentle buzz from the nicotine. It's my one remaining vice.

This wiry ball of white fur and I have already completed two laps of the village playing fields and one around the churchyard, and now we're making our way back to his home. Walking the neighbours' dogs won't make me my fortune, but as I don't have much in the way of an income at the moment, beggars can't be choosers. I have four more regular clients, and they, along with doing some of my other neighbours' ironing, keep me ticking by. Only just, though. Once the bills are taken care of, it leaves little in the pot for luxuries, short of a few vaping cartridges and the occasional bottle of supermarket wine. You'll never meet a rich carer.

With the dog dropped off and after a quick chat with Walter, his owner, I approach Gwen's house and spot a van parked on the drive. It's a plain white one; well, it might be closer to grey as it hasn't seen a car wash in a while. Some joker has written in the muck on the passenger door, 'I wish my wife was this dirty'. It must've amused the owner or they'd have wiped it off by now.

A man appears from behind the vehicle carrying a metal ladder. I've not seen him in the village before and I'm sure I'd remember him. He must be over six feet tall, has a rugby player's build and is wearing a fitted black T-shirt, blue cut-off jean shorts and workman's boots. His hair is cropped short, and both it and his stubble contain salty flecks. He's probably around my age only he's carrying it better. He has a handful of deep-set lines etched into his tanned forehead, like many men do who spend the majority of their lives working outside. I realise I've been staring at him for too long. But he's hard to stop looking at. The closer he gets to me, the more piercing his blue eyes become. Goosebumps skitter across my back and shoulders.

I clear my throat. 'Can I help you?' I ask, but he doesn't reply. Instead, he nods, then walks right past me. Hello? Am I invisible? His rudeness takes me aback until I spot the white plastic casing of headphones embedded in his ears. He's listening to something.

He leans the ladder up against the wall, climbs it, removes a bin bag from his pocket and starts to fill it with leaves and silt he fishes out of the gutters. I raise my voice and ask him to stop for a moment but he doesn't hear me. Only when I wave both hands, like I'm flagging down a cab in a dark street, does he finally come to a halt. He raises his eyebrows and pulls out one of his earbuds.

'Can I help you?' I ask again.

'You can keep the ladder steady if you like?' he says.

It takes me a second to realise he's joking. 'I meant what are you doing in my mum's garden?'

'Well, if I'm not mistaken, I'm cleaning out the gutters.' He grins, and I'm not sure if he's expecting me to reciprocate. I offer a fleeting smile that disappears as quickly as it arrives.

'Who asked you to do this?'

'The man upstairs.' He looks above him into the sky.

'What?'

He signifies the conversation is over with a wink, slips his headphones back in and returns to the job in hand, leaving me standing there like a lemon.

I'm simultaneously patronised, curious, and suspicious of him. The mix of all three is my default setting. 'Guilty until proven innocent' is my motto. I'd never make it past the selection process for a jury.

I hurry along the path, tripping over the wooden handle of a rake he has left lying there. I turn quickly in the hope he hasn't seen my slapstick clumsiness. But of course he has, and it's amused him. My cheeks blush and I feel it spread to my chest and neck.

'Mum,' I shout as I enter the hallway. 'Who's that man in your garden?'

I find her in the kitchen, arranging biscuits in a circle on a plate. They're the posh Waitrose cookies with the chunks of white chocolate and cranberries I left here for us as a treat. I watch as she pours water from a kettle into a teapot. There's no steam coming from it so I assume she's forgotten to boil it again.

'It's Paul, isn't it,' she says matter-of-factly, as if he's here daily and I'm the one with dementia, not her.

'Paul who?'

'Paul Whatshisname.'

Something catches in my nostrils. I think it's perfume. I inhale with a little more effort. Yes, she's definitely wearing perfume. Something light and lavender-like. I can't remember the last time I smelled a scent on her that wasn't shower gel or Deep Heat. I look her up and down and realise it's not the only change. She's pencilled over the gaps in her eyebrows, and put a little blush on her high cheekbones and foundation on her forehead and chin which has taken away her ghostliness. It's enough to make me forget what she's become. She was beautiful once, and still is a very striking woman. I'll never know what it's like to rely on my looks to get by.

I take the kettle and refill it, then flick the switch to boil it. 'Why is he cleaning out the gutters?'

'The vicar asked him to. Reverend Edwards said there was a charity that matches handymen and women for odd jobs and gardening work that people like me need doing.' She trails off and taps at her head. She hates saying either 'dementia' or 'Alzheimer's'. Instead, it's referred to with a gesture. 'I said yes, he should get in touch with them. I must have forgotten to mention it.'

Since I moved here to look after her, I've become used to being relied upon to do everything. It's just me and her, living in our own little bubble. So I should be grateful that the gutters will be one less thing to worry about. Yet I feel a little irked that it's being done without my prior knowledge, and I'm treating Paul's visit as a failure on my part. I need to snap out of it.

I drop a fresh teabag into the pot, pour in some boiling water and swap my good biscuits with her plain digestives before carrying them out to him. She follows closely behind me.

I wave to get his attention again and leave the tray on the wall. He replies with the tipping of an imaginary hat and my goosebumps return. What kind of effect is he having on me! I shake my head in the hope that it'll dissipate the blush from my cheeks. I can't deny that he's handsome, but then, I doubt he would deny it either. I've learned the hard way that you can never trust a good-looking man who knows the power of his own appearance.

CHAPTER 3
ZAINAB JENKINS, NEIGHBOUR

Come rain or shine, umbrella or shorts, nothing stops me from lacing up my hiking boots for my daily walk. I'm slathered in sun cream – factor 50, after that scare with the mole on my arm – and I'm wearing my eldest daughter's baseball cap to protect my head from the sun.

The end of my hike is in sight and I'm walking the river-bank route back towards the village when I spot Connie leaving the Village Hopper at the bottom of the hill. That minibus is a lifesaver, travelling from village to village, dropping people off at libraries, supermarkets or in Buckingham town centre. I count six bags of shopping in Connie's hands and they're dragging close to the ground. I cross the road and offer to share the load.

'Oh, thanks Zainab,' she says gratefully as I take three. I steal a quick glance inside. They're crammed with inexpensive, own-brand tins of soup, vegetables, beans and fruits.

'It's a cheaper workout than joining a gym,' I joke as we begin our ascent up the steep hill. As much as I enjoy my walks, my knees start to ache by the time I reach this bit. 'Have you tried online deliveries?' I ask. 'We started using them during the last lockdown and I've yet to return to a supermarket.'

'The places we shop don't deliver,' Connie replies, and I realise the insensitivity of my question. She can't afford Sainsbury's. 'And my car is back in Italy,' she continues. 'So until I get the chance to return and drive it back here, it's public transport for me.'

'How long has it been now since you moved here?'

She thinks for a moment. 'Well, Mum and Dad came here sixteen months ago, then Dad died two months later, and I returned to England soon after that.'

'It was a terrible shame,' I tell her. 'I only met your dad a handful of times, when they joined the bowling club, but I remember how funny he was. And you could tell, even after all their years together, he and your mum were still besotted with each other.'

'They were very lucky.'

I quietly recall the first time I met Gwen and how, a few minutes into our conversation, I knew that there was something about her that looked a little bit – well, I'm not sure how to describe it – *uncertain*, perhaps? Like she was trying to mask an anxiousness. It reminded me of an aunty I had back home. Like Gwen, her expression sometimes froze mid-conversation and you couldn't be sure if she was disinterested or deep in thought. They didn't have the experts or the diagnoses we have today and so doctors dismissed it as 'the brain sickness'. It was only after Bill died that I learned Gwen had vascular dementia and Alzheimer's. I only see her now when Connie walks her to church on Sunday mornings.

'Do you still need me to sit with her on Friday afternoon?' I ask.

'If you don't mind,' Connie says. 'I shouldn't be more than a couple of hours. I have a few loose ends to tie up work-wise.'

'You must miss living in Italy.'

'Oh I do,' she replies. 'Good food, good weather, good friends.'

'Where were you living?'

'The Amalfi Coast. Do you know it?'

'I've only been to southern Italy once, a long time ago. What line of work were you in again? I want to say something to do with weddings?'

'Yes, I was a wedding planner.' Her brown eyes light up as if, by mentioning it, she has been transported back there. 'My clients were British couples who wanted the Italian wedding experience but weren't sure where or how to go about organising it. I'd give them a list of suggested locations, I'd FaceTime them from each place on their shortlist or send them videos, and once they made their decision, I'd do everything from applying for the right licences to booking hotels and villas.'

'And you gave it all up for your mum.'

'At least for the time being, anyway. I've handed most of my clients over to other planners I know over there, but there were a few soon-to-be-wed couples I couldn't find a replacement for and I can't let them down. So I'll have to spend a few more weeks there later in the summer.'

'And is there a young man waiting for you over there? Or a young woman? Sorry, I never know what I can or can't ask these days.'

'It's fine, and no, there's neither. Just me.'

'Do you think you'll eventually go back and live there full-time again?'

'You mean after Mum dies?'

'Oh no, I didn't mean . . .' My voice fades because that's exactly what I meant. I must engage my brain before I open my mouth to speak.

'It's okay,' Connie says. 'I've sublet my apartment, so we'll see what happens. Everything feels a bit up in the air at the moment.'

My arms are growing weary so I throw my shoulders back. 'And how is Gwen doing?'

'So-so. Lately I've found myself having the same conversations with her time and time again. But at least it means we never run out of things to say.'

I feel sorry for Connie. It's no life for a woman of her age. It must get lonely spending all her time cooped up with Gwen.

'To be honest,' I say, 'I didn't even know she had a daughter until you moved here.'

Her laugh is dry. 'A few people have said that. I've had to put up photos of myself around the house to remind her, because sometimes she forgets who I am. And Dad too – she can't remember he's passed. She wanders around the house searching for him. It's heart-wrenching, really.'

'It must be. And it's got to be tough on you too.' When she shrugs, I continue, 'Gwen's very lucky to have you. Everyone in the village has nothing but good things to say about you.'

Connie hesitates, and for a moment I think I might have said something wrong again.

'I know I shouldn't expect praise or gratitude,' she says. 'But sometimes, it's nice to hear I'm doing okay. So thank you.'

We reach the top of the hill and make our way to Connie's house. It's one of a handful of red- brick semi-detached bungalows facing on to a small grassy area. I help her inside with her bags. It's the first time I've been in here, and I'm immediately struck by how sparsely furnished it is. 'The rest of my stuff is still in Italy,' she says, as if reading my mind.

She thanks me again, and as I leave, I make a mental note to check in on her more often. Things are going to get a lot harder for mother and daughter. Unfortunately, bad things have a habit of happening to good people.

CHAPTER 4

CONNIE

The heat from inside and outside her house has me sweating buckets. Thursday is my day to clean this place from top to bottom, but by mid-morning, I've only finished the lounge, the dining room and the kitchen, and I'm ready to throw in the towel I'm using to mop my brow. I rifle around in the overnight bag I keep in the spare room for emergency sleepovers until I find a can of anti-perspirant. The shock of the cold blast under my arms takes me by surprise but I follow it up with a generous spray across my chest before it's time to change her sheets.

My throat is as dry as the Sahara so I make my way downstairs to refill my drinking bottle with iced water from the fridge. Only then do I realise why it's so stifling in here – she has closed every window and door I opened when I arrived.

'Mum, this house is like an inferno!' I complain. 'Why have you shut everything?'

'I thought you did?' she says without looking up from the television.

I open my mouth but decide I can't be bothered to argue, so I head into the dining room to slide open the patio doors again. The sideboard, where she stores her best crockery and cutlery, is covered by more than two dozen porcelain figurines of cats. I don't see the appeal but she adores them and has named almost all. Even when she's having one of her bad days, she can identify each one. Her favourite is the tall, jade-green Siamese cat ornament, but it's also the one I dislike the most. It's about a foot tall and towers over the rest with its elongated upper back and neck. It wears a conceited expression and sometimes I want to accidentally nudge it to the floor with a feather duster, then gladly watch as it shatters.

I return to the lounge with today's dose of medication in the palm of my hand.

'What's this for?' she asks suspiciously.

'The Reminyl is for your . . .' I tap the side of my head so she doesn't have to hear me say the 'D' or 'A' word. 'The rest are your aspirin and happy pills.' She hates it when I call them anti-depressants. 'It makes me sound weak,' she often reminds me. 'I'm not weak.'

She eventually obliges, swallowing them with a swig from my water bottle.

Outside, a vehicle catches my eye. It's that handyman's dirty white van reversing up her drive. Before I can say anything, she's up and out of her armchair faster than Usain Bolt and is darting towards the front door like it's a finishing line. So much for her balancing issues. She closes it behind her and she and Paul begin a conversation outside. I'm being nosey and stand behind the net curtain wishing they'd either speak louder or I could lip-read. She smiles a lot at what he has to say and if I didn't know better, I'd swear she was blushing. I'm in the hall when she returns a few minutes later.

'Why is he back?' I ask.

'Who?'

'Paul. The man you were just talking to.'

'Oh, is that his name?'

I look away to an imaginary camera filming my frustration. 'Yes,' I say. 'So why is he back?'

'I thought you'd asked him.'

We could go around and around in circles like this for the rest of the afternoon so I cut out the middleman and ask Paul myself. He has already let himself in to the back garden via the open gate and scaled a tree, and is sitting astride a branch as thick as his thighs, a saw in his grip. His T-shirt lies on the grass and he catches me checking out his broad chest and the tribal tattoo wrapped around his bicep. All he needs is a can of Diet Coke.

He grins. 'Enjoying the view?'

I hope the heat of the day and my already reddened face will mask the fact that yet a-bloody-gain, I'm flushed in his presence. 'I thought your last visit was a one-off?' I ask, not bothering to disguise my suspicious nature.

'Gwen asked me to shape her walnut tree,' he replies. 'Which isn't a euphemism.' This time I find his smile disarming. But the sound that leaves my mouth is part pig-like snort and part-laugh. Its volume takes us both by surprise.

'And when I'm done,' he adds, 'she wants me to level and jetwash the paving slabs and clean out the old pond at the end of the garden.'

'Old pond?' It must be very overgrown because I didn't realise we had one. 'Oh, right,' I say. 'And who is paying for all this?'

'It's voluntary. Can't let an elderly woman struggle alone, can I?'

I fold my arms. 'She's not alone. I look after her.'

'Oh yeah, she said you do a bit of cleaning sometimes.'

I'm about to defend myself and tell him that I do more than just 'a bit of cleaning' when he flashes me another grin. He's joking. Either I need to lighten up or he needs to stop being a dick.

'Nope, not today,' I reply. 'I'm not going to bite.'

'That's a shame, I like a little biting.'

He winks, jumps down from the tree and I beg my face not to give me away. I think he might be flirting but it's been so long since anyone has paid me that kind of attention that I can't be sure. I'm certainly not feeling like much of a gift to the opposite sex right now. I'm carrying a few extra pounds, all my clothes were bought on the cheap at supermarkets or discount stores and I can't remember the last time I had my hair cut or coloured at a salon and not by yours truly. I've tried telling myself my grey streaks make me distinguished, but in truth I'm one streak away from Cruella de Vil.

I steal a glance at Paul's wedding ring finger and it's bare. But once again, he catches me out and holds up that hand and waves it at me.

'So how's Gwen today?' he continues.

'She has good days and bad days. You're aware of her situation?'

'Yeah, the charity tells us who we're being matched with and why. A lot of my girls are like her. Life can be a bastard, eh?'

I can't argue with that. Maybe it's because new people come into our lives rarely that I find myself offering Paul our potted history without him asking first. But he seems really interested. He doesn't extend me sympathy or pity; he just listens and asks lots of questions about her and the ways I help. We discuss how her memory ebbs and flows, what makes her happy, how I relax her when she's anxious and what makes her sob like a child. We laugh at the absurdity of the time soon after I moved here, when she took the family car out somewhere and returned by foot. And how, to this day, we still have no idea where she left it. I've checked all the car parks in the surrounding villages. I live in hope I'll come across it one day, waiting for me. Then my bus travel days will be over. I tell him how her medication helped to a point but how I'm seeing another decline. When I realise more than an hour has passed, I apologise for offloading and tell him I should leave him to continue his work. But I find myself not quite ready to go. I've enjoyed his company.

'I thought I might drop into the garden centre later in the week and pick up some bedding plants to brighten the borders up,' he adds. 'What's your favourite colour?'

'Red.'

'And your mum's?'

'Yellow.'

'I'll see what I can do.'

As I'm returning to the house, I realise I haven't thanked him so I turn to do so. I think he has an in-ear headphone inserted at first and is miming along to a song. But he hasn't. He's just muttering away to himself and he doesn't look best pleased. Then he takes a hatchet and whacks at a sawn branch lying on the ground. I don't interrupt.

Closer to the house, I spot a figure lurking behind the patio doors. Now it's her turn to be nosey. She'd been watching us before she starts shuffling away, believing that I haven't seen her. I almost feel guilty. I think she wants to be the prime focus of Paul's attention, and now I've taken it away from her, when she's already been left with so little.

Soon after, I'm running a wet cloth over the front door when the postwoman greets me with a friendly smile. Between a handful of envelopes wrapped in an elastic band is one addressed to me. I wait until she leaves before I tear it open. Thank God for that. After weeks of waiting, it's a letter confirming that I've now been awarded a Carer's Allowance. I open a second letter, this time addressed to her, and discover she will be receiving a regular Attendance Allowance. Together, these payments total around £145 a week. It's not much, in fact, for an entire day's work; if you break it down, I'll be earning the equivalent of an hour and a half of the minimum wage. But it's better than nothing and will ease the financial pressure for a while. There have been times when I've been forced to use her debit card to keep myself afloat. I'm not proud of myself, but then pride always comes before a fall and I've had so many of those, I should have bought my own crash mat.

CHAPTER 5

CONNIE

'Mum, do you want a biscuit with your tea?' I shout. She doesn't answer.

She's where I left her a few minutes ago, sitting in her favourite armchair. A deck of playing cards is spread across an occasional table in front of her, alongside the chair I was sitting in. We played her favourite card game, poker, for about twenty minutes until she began to forget the rules and started laying down any old card.

'I made $5,000 in one night playing Texas Hold 'Em at Circus Circus when your dad and I were in Las Vegas,' she told me. 'I beat every man around that table until the final hand, when I lost it all to a bloody German. Easy come, easy go.'

I struggle to reconcile this carefree version of her with the one who is now staring blankly into a fan that blows recycled warm air into her face.

'Mum, did you hear me?' I repeat. 'I asked if you wanted a biscuit with your cuppa?'

Her eyes meet mine and taper. 'Who are you?' she growls.

Oh here we go. Once, she was so convinced I was one of TV's *Loose Women*, I ended up playing along and answered to the name Coleen Nolan for the rest of the morning. 'I'm your daughter, Connie.'

'I don't have a daughter.'

'Yes you do, Mum, I'm the girl you and Bill had.'

'Bill who?'

'Your husband.'

'I'm not married.'

'You were for sixty years but now you're widowed.' I leave the cup on the arm of her chair, pick up two framed photographs from the console table in the hall and return to her. 'This is me as a little girl on my bike,' I say, pointing to one. 'And this is you and Dad on your wedding day.'

'I know who she is,' she says, pointing to her younger self. 'That's Meredith.'

'No, it's definitely you.'

She shakes her head, adamant that I'm lying.

'Why don't you finish your tea and we'll talk about it later,' I suggest.

She looks at the cup, and before I can do anything about it, she swipes at it with such gusto that it flies across the room and smashes into the wall, leaving tea and porcelain everywhere.

'Mum! Why did you do that?'

Leaning forward in her chair, she shakes her finger at me. 'I don't know who you are but I want you out of my house now!'

'I'll find a tea towel to clean this up.'

'No!' she shrieks. 'Get out! Get out! Get out!'

She's never lost her temper on this scale before. Her rage moves at such speed I'm surprised neither of us have whiplash. She pulls herself up to her feet but she's unsteady and I worry she'll fall. I move towards her, completely unprepared for the slap she gives me. I clasp my cheek; it stings like hell.

'Mum!' I shout, then realise my tone is likely to make the situation worse. I need to calm her, not rile her. 'Listen to me . . .'

'Stop calling me that,' she shouts, and this time, she loses her balance and falls to the floor. I scurry over to help her up but, clearly thinking I'm going to hurt her, she launches herself at me again. The palm of her hand misses me but her fingernails connect with my skin as she scratches the cheek she just slapped. And now she's shouting too. 'Help me! Help me!' she screams and covers her face with her hands.

I try and grab her arms to help lift her up but now she's curling herself into a ball, like a child might, and I can't get a grip of her. 'Mum, please,' I shout but she's not listening.

'Can I help?' a voice comes from behind. I turn quickly; Paul's at the doorway, putting his phone in his pocket. I'm embarrassed, awkward and frustrated all at once. What will he make of this madness?

She speaks first. 'She's been hitting me; she's trying to kill me. You've got to get her out of my house and call the police.'

He looks to her and then me. 'Why don't you give us a minute?' he says. He sounds composed, his demeanour unruffled.

'No, I've got this,' I reply stubbornly. But it's clear to us both that I haven't.

'You're bleeding.'

I reach to my face and realise her fingernails went deeper than I thought.

'Go and clean yourself up and let's see if she'll listen to me.'

I swap places with him and hesitate, remaining under the doorway, watching as he approaches her like he would a frightened, wounded animal. 'Who am I, Gwen?' he asks.

'I . . . I don't know,' she says. The rage has passed and left bewilderment in its wake.

'I'm Paul, do you remember me? I've been tidying your garden. Why don't you come outside and I'll show you what I've done?'

She offers a succession of small, almost imperceptible nods, and he helps her to her feet. He waits until she's stable and clinging on to his arm before he walks her through the patio doors and into the rear garden. Then he moves a plastic chair from under the kitchen window and positions it at the end of the garden so that it overlooks the fields. He's cut down the hedges, so she has a view for miles. He helps her to sit down, then kneels as he rubs her arm and says something. She appears relaxed.

I peer at my red, raw, bleeding cheek in the cloakroom mirror, then splash my face with cold water. I can't hold back from bursting into tears, and cry into the hand towel I was using to pat my face dry with. I'm failing miserably at being the strong one here. This is so much harder than I ever imagined.

'It's not your fault,' Paul says as he returns and finds me in the kitchen. 'Honestly, I've seen it happen with all the girls I've volunteered for. One day they know who I am, the next, it's like they've never seen me before and want me off their property. Confusion and violence are part and parcel of the disease.'

'Sometimes I'm convinced she hates me,' I say.

'She directs her pain at you because she has no one else to take it out on.'

'I'm trying my best . . .' I can't finish what I was going to say because I choke up again.

'And you're doing a great job,' he adds, then pulls me in to his chest. I'm so close that I feel his heartbeat against my cheek. I don't know to respond. I'm so unused to this level of physical interaction that it's alien.

25

'Leave her with me for the afternoon,' Paul suggests as he lets me go. 'Go home, chill out, read a book, enjoy a few hours of you time. And I bet when you get back, she's as right as rain. And why don't you and I go out one night? When was the last time you went out of an evening?'

His offer and question fluster me. 'I . . . I don't know.'

'Can you find someone to sit with Gwen?'

'Yes, probably.'

'I'll leave it in your hands then. Just let me know when.'

'Thank you,' I reply, thrilled with his offer.

When I return later that afternoon, they are still out in the garden and they're sitting at the table playing poker.

'Oh Connie, have you met Paul?' she asks when I approach them. 'He's volunteered to tidy our garden.'

I smile. 'What a kind man,' I say.

'What a kind man indeed,' she replies.

CHAPTER 6

CONNIE

What is wrong with me? I hold my left hand out far enough to register that it's not my imagination, it's actually trembling. Am I really this nervous? No, it must be the vibrations coming from Paul's van. I move my hand back quickly before he sees what I'm doing. But his eyes appear firmly fixed on the road. I need to chill out. It's only a dinner, I remind myself.

We've chatted a lot on our way to the restaurant, and once inside, the conversation flows just as smoothly until we pause to pick from the menu. He picks an antipasti board for us to share as a starter and opts for a smoked-salmon penne main for himself, while I choose the chicken alfredo tagliatelle. I become tongue-tied and struggle to pronounce the tagliatelle part. Instead, I say titty-telly and die a little inside. I have a glass of red wine; he has an alcohol-free beer.

'You must be a connoisseur of Italian food,' he says and I look to him, a little confused. 'After all that time you spent working there,' he prompts.

'Yes, sorry.' I laugh awkwardly. 'Although it's not so great if you're on a no-carb diet, as pasta comes with everything.'

'So are you a dab hand at cooking Italian too? I don't see you as a frozen meal or Pot Noodle kind of girl.'

'I don't get the opportunity to cook nice meals very often. She won't eat anything other than plain, British food nowadays. When I tried to give her a croissant and a pain au chocolat for breakfast she looked at me as if I was trying to poison her.'

'Ah yes,' he says. 'She was in Germany and Spain for a while, wasn't she?' I don't remember telling him about that. 'Gwen mentioned it when I sat with her the other afternoon,' he adds.

'She and Dad travelled around a lot.'

'Which I suppose is where you get your love of travel from.'

'I guess so.'

As we eat, Paul asks me more about my work in Italy, about the couples I planned weddings for and when I hope to return. He asks me if it was a difficult choice to give it all up and become a carer instead of finding a suitable nursing home to put her in. 'I couldn't do that,' I tell him. 'I know a lot of children do when their parents get sick and I absolutely don't judge them for that, but it's not what I want for her right now.'

'Don't you get lonely?' he asks. 'Spending all day, every day with her. Putting your life on hold for her.'

I can't deny that yes, it's exactly how I feel. Unseen and unnoticed. Which is why I was a little taken aback when he asked me out for dinner. Someone had noticed me beyond the role I play. 'As a carer, there are times when I feel invisible to the world,' I explain. 'It's not a nine-to-five job, there are no holidays, there's rarely any support and never any thanks. You just get on with it because that person you're caring for is wholly reliant on you and you don't want to let them down.'

'It's admirable,' he says and toasts my glass with his bottle. For a split second, our little fingers connect and I swear there's a spark of electricity.

We talk more about me, my life before and after moving to the village, our mother-and-daughter relationship and what she was like pre- and post-diagnosis. It's a cliché, but he and I are literally the last people in the restaurant by the time we realise they're waiting to close.

And as he drives me home I can't remember when a date last asked me so much about my life instead of talking over me about theirs. Then it dawns on me that I've asked very little about him. Now I'm worried I've blown it and this is destined to be a one-off. Because I've very much enjoyed myself and I'd like to see him again.

'You did say you wanted dropping off at Gwen's didn't you?' he asks as the van makes its way up her road.

'Yes, I won't sleep until I've seen she's okay.'

'You should get one of those nanny cams in her room so you can check up on her.'

'She needs a good night because we have an early start in the morning. Doctor's appointment. Just routine though.' We pull over. 'Thanks for a lovely night,' I say. 'I know I didn't ask much about you, which is bad of me.'

'Honestly, it's been great. I'll tell you about me next time, if you want a next time?'

'Sure,' I reply, desperately trying to play it cool.

Then the moment I have been waiting for happens. He leans over slowly towards me, his hand reaching out to cup my face. I move towards him, close my eyes and place my lips on his. Only, when we connect, they don't feel like his lips. I open my eyes and I realise I've got them wrapped around his nose. And the worst thing is that they are still there. I haven't pulled away yet. What the hell am I thinking! I push back quickly and he pulls his arm away.

'The handle is a bit stiff,' he says, and I realise he was reaching for the door, not my face.

I don't believe it is possible for anyone to feel more embarrassed than I do. Once again, there is a good chance I might just die, here and now. Perhaps the only way to get mouth-to-mouth is to do just that.

CHAPTER 7

CONNIE

I wake up with a start, convinced someone is behind me in the doorway of my bedroom, watching me sleep. I'm lying on my left side, facing the window and covered only by a thin sheet. I'm vulnerable, rigid and frightened. I clench my fists, ready for fight or flight. The top window is open, so if my intruder attacks, I can scream and there's a chance a neighbour might catch it and help me. I don't know how much time passes but I hear nothing that indicates I have company. Eventually I pluck up the courage to turn, and to my relief, the door is as I left it when I went to bed last night. My subconscious mind must've been playing tricks on me again.

I remove my phone from the charger and check the time. 'Shit,' I mutter when I realise I forgot to set the alarm for 7 a.m. It's now approaching eight-thirty. I throw the bedsheet aside, hurry to the shower, the movement making my head pound. I didn't think I had that much to drink last night with Paul, until I realise I polished off a bottle and a half of wine myself while he drank non-alcoholic beers. No wonder my tongue feels like sandpaper.

She has a doctor's appointment in an hour and a half and my sleep-in means we will be cutting it fine. It'll set me back with my dog walks too. I've been awake all of ten minutes and, already, this day has gone to buggery. As I towel-dry my hair, I glance in the mirror and note the scratch marks on my face from Gwen's tantrum earlier this week. I'll need to put on more concealer to hide the darkening brown scabs. I still look as if I've been attacked by Freddy Krueger.

She'll probably be famished by now and will need breakfast first, so I hurry things up. Even though each night by her bed I leave a flask of orange juice, a handful of Ritz crackers and some soft cheese squares, she's been known to forget they're there, and on a few occasions, has gone wandering. Once, she ended up in the garden, confused about how to get back inside. She has also turned up in the middle of the night at a neighbour's house knocking on their door and begging for food because she forgets she's eaten.

A couple of minutes later and I can't stop the smile from blooming across my face when I see Paul's transit van parked on the drive. He's early, as he doesn't normally arrive until about ten-ish. Maybe he hoped to catch me before she woke up? Aside from last night's nose-sucking incident, I think our date went well. I guess he thought so too as he suggested a second one.

He has been here most days this week since Meltdown Monday, as I'm calling it. He's spent more time keeping her company than doing the garden, which has really taken the pressure off me. She's certainly enjoyed the attention and I've watched her become giggly and, dare I say it, flirty with him. But as sweet as it is, it can also be a little irritating. She wants to be around him all the time, which makes it that much harder for us to get to know one another. I became snippy with her on Monday when she gave him a bottle of wine I'd bought and left in her cupboard. She told him it was a thank you for his hard work, but we both know that she was trying to impress him.

I give the garden a quick once-over as I make my way up the drive. I must hand it to him, he's done a really thorough job. And for the briefest of moments, I surrender to a pang of sadness as there isn't much left for him to do. I've grown used to him being around. He's shown interest in both of us and he's a good listener.

Music from the 1950s wafts out of the kitchen and reaches me in the hallway. It's the decade she adores, and above it, I overhear her and Paul laughing. I hesitate in the doorway. They sit either side of the table, separated by a steaming teapot, plates with crumbs and two empty paper bags from La Patisserie in town. I'm surprised to see she's dressed, her hair is almost in place, and once again, she's wearing make-up. She reminds me of one of those glamorous movie stars from the 1960s you haven't seen in years before suddenly they turn up on the red carpet for some movie event and you can't believe how incredible they look for their age. Paul is certainly bringing out the best in her.

They are too engrossed in conversation to notice me. So I take a mental snapshot of a lovely moment.

'Good morning,' I eventually say.

She turns her head. 'Hello, Connie,' she says, puzzled. 'I wasn't expecting you today.'

'I'm here every day, Mum. Hi Paul.'

She doesn't give him a chance to respond. 'Did you notice the flowers when you came in?' she asks. 'Paul's filled the borders with begonias. Aren't they beautiful?'

Outside are rows of carefully planted yellow flowers, her favourite colour. There are none of the red ones that I like, though. Never mind, I guess they were out of stock.

'And look what Bill's brought with him . . . croissants,' she continues. 'I used to eat these all the time when we lived in France. And they're absolutely delicious.'

I refrain from reminding her of the number of times she's refused to even try a bite of the ones I've bought her before, or that her breakfast partner's name is Paul and he's not the man she married. My attention again returns to him and I realise he has yet to acknowledge me. Is there a dip in the room temperature or am I imagining it?

'What are they in aid of?' I ask him.

'No reason. I just prefer not to eat alone,' he says. 'And neither does Gwenny.'

Gwenny? That's new to me. I let it pass. 'She doesn't normally have breakfast on her own,' I reply, 'but I forgot to set my alarm this morning. Anyway, Mum, we need to get going. You have your doctor's appointment soon and the Hopper will be picking us up in twenty minutes.'

'Not to worry, Paul said he'd take me.'

'Oh wonderful, thank you, Paul,' I say. 'Shall we get going?'

'It'll just be your mum and me I'm afraid,' he replies. 'I can only get two people in the van.'

'It has three front seats, doesn't it?' I ask.

'One of the seatbelts is broken. And I don't want to risk anyone's safety. Don't worry, I'll look after her.'

Paul still hasn't looked at me today. Not once. Have I done or said something to upset him? I think back to last night's conversations, but we were mainly discussing her and my life in Italy. I don't think there was anything I said that could've offended him. Or maybe it was the disaster of a kiss. Have I totally misread him?

'There are things I need to talk to her GP about,' I say, 'so it's best if I take her.'

'I found the note you left in the bureau to remind you of what you need to discuss,' he says. 'So I'm sure we'll be okay.'

He *found* the note? How do you find something that wasn't left out to find in the first place? What was he doing looking inside the bureau?

33

'Thank you again for offering to help,' I say, 'but I really don't think it's a good idea.' I'm polite but firm. 'I've been taking Mum for the last year and Dr Chambers knows me. So Mum, let's get your handbag or we'll be late.'

'Stop telling me what to do!' she shouts. Her outburst is swift and sudden. I jump but Paul doesn't flinch.

'Mum, don't stress yourself,' I say.

'I wasn't stressed until you arrived. I want Paul to take me.'

A stand-off ensues, none of us saying a word. I'm the first to back down.

'Fine,' I huff. 'Do what you want, but don't complain to me when you can't remember anything the doctor tells you.'

Paul looks at her and taps his temple with his forefinger. She and I do the same action to one another when we don't want to mention the dementia word. I recall telling him about it. 'Don't worry, Gwenny, I'm like an elephant, I never forget anything. I'll remember for the both of us.'

Only now does he turn his head to make eye contact with me. 'Why don't you take another day for yourself.' He doesn't phrase it as a question. He's telling me what's going to happen. 'I'm sure I can keep your mum entertained.'

'Mum?' I ask one last time, hoping she'll intervene. She doesn't reply. She is too busy cooing over Paul to listen to me.

I turn on my heel and spot her purse lying on the side of the kitchen worktop. The clasp is open and the section where she keeps her debit cards is empty.

'Where are your bank cards?' I ask.

'I don't know,' she says.

I glare at Paul. He sips his tea like a buttered croissant wouldn't melt in his mouth. 'I put them away in her bureau for safekeeping,' he says. 'You shouldn't leave them lying about. You can't trust anyone these days, can you?'

I honestly don't know what to say. What the hell is happening here? How have I just been frozen out of a routine GP appointment? I slam the front door behind me, cursing them both, but especially Paul.

Why is the man who I spent the last few days opening up to behaving like he's made of ice? He is like a completely different person.

I've met his type before, men who are drawn to women they believe are lacking love and craving affection. They lavish them with attention, and once they're reeled in, they begin to antagonise them, knock their confidence and ensure they never really know where they stand. Does Paul think I'm like that? Is that the image I portray of myself? Well he's wrong. Nobody gaslights me. Nobody.

I'm about to pass his van when I slow my pace. I open the passenger door and lean inside. I tug on the strap of the middle seatbelt. Aha! Just as I thought, it's not stuck. I keep pulling it further and push the metal part into the buckle. It slips in with a simple click. So he *was* lying.

I'm about to close the door and return to the house to confront him when the belt unclicks itself and falls open.

So Paul is not a liar. He's still an arsehole though.

I turn to check he's not watching me from the window – he isn't – and the open garage door catches my attention. I glance inside. It used to be almost empty, but now it contains spades, forks and a wheelbarrow, along with ladders, a workbench and tools.

I assume they belong to Paul, but why has he left them here? And how did I miss it?

CHAPTER 8

REVEREND EDDIE EDWARDS

'Morning Connie, how are you?'

'Oh hi, Reverend Edwards,' she exclaims, as if only just noticing me. Moments earlier I spotted her reflection in the thick plastic counter screens at the post office in the village supermarket. She appeared to be hovering in the aisle, as if waiting for me to finish sending my parcel before approaching me. 'I'm good thanks,' she continues. 'And you?'

'Can't complain,' I say. 'Well I can, but then you might be here all day.' We both chuckle but I suspect neither of us actually found it that funny. 'And it's Eddie, please. How's your mum? She was in good voice at Sunday's sermon . . . singing her heart out to "How Great Thou Art" without even opening the hymn book.'

'This week feels like a positive one.'

'Absolutely. And perhaps one day we might even see you in our congregation.' I make sure to smile so that she knows I'm kidding. As much as I enjoy seeing every new face under our roof, I'm not one to guilt-trip anyone into attending. We all believe in something, whether it's ourselves, a loved one or Him.

'I'm afraid organised religion isn't my thing,' she tells me. 'But I appreciate how much it means to so many, like Mum.'

'As long as you're aware that you don't need to be a Christian to come and talk to me if you ever need an ear. I know from witnessing other parishioners' families and carers on the same journey as you and Gwen are on, just how tough it is. My door is open any time you'd like to chat or just to raid the biscuit barrel.'

She thanks me with a nod and a half-smile. There's a brief pause in the conversation as I await the real reason she's engaging me in conversation.

'I've been meaning to say thank you for introducing us to Paul,' she says.

'Paul?' I reply, trying to place the name.

'Yes, the man from that charity who's been tidying up Mum's garden for the last fortnight.'

'Oh yes. I'm glad he was able to help. He's done wonders, hasn't he? You don't need to cross the road to use the path anymore.'

'Actually, he's still here,' she continues. 'Just when I think he's about to finish, he finds something else that needs doing.'

'Oh really? Gwen said she wanted someone for a few light gardening duties.'

'Yes, but he's very keen. Have you used him before?'

'Not for any of my parishioners, but he comes highly recommended by the charity.'

'What's it called again?'

There's a subtext to Connie's questions but I'm struggling to find it. 'Help for Homes,' I reply. 'They're a non-profit organisation.'

'I suppose they must really vet the volunteers they recommend. There are a lot of cowboys out there.'

'That's why we use them. We can't take any risks with vulnerable people like your mum.'

'Out of interest, what kind of checks might they include?' I think she intends the question to be casual but it comes across as rehearsed. 'I'm thinking of volunteering,' she adds.

'I can't say for sure, but I assume they check criminal records, probably trading standards too, to see if there have been complaints made against them. I think they even look at places like Checkatrade and online reviews. I can put a call in and find out for certain, if that'd ease your mind?'

'No, no,' she backtracks and holds up two conciliatory palms to her chest. 'No need at all. It's something I'm considering in the future for after, well, at some point when . . .'

She struggles to finish her sentence and my eyebrows knit. 'Connie, is there something I can help you with?'

She hesitates and then slowly opens her mouth. 'Are you sure . . . Paul can be . . . trusted?'

'Well, we've used that charity on many occasions and never received a complaint. I very much doubt you have anything to worry about.'

She hesitates again before she paints on a smile. 'I'm sure you're right,' she says. 'I just get very protective over Mum, as I'm sure you understand. Anyway, I've taken up enough of your time already. Have a lovely day.'

Connie doesn't wait for me to bid her farewell before she hurries out of the post office without buying or sending anything. I wish I could say that I was able to put her mind at ease. But I suspect I might not have succeeded.

CHAPTER 9

CONNIE

The night is drawing in with ribbons of purple and orange. This is normally my favourite part of the day, sitting out here in her garden, alone, staring into the quiet horizon. But this evening, I'm too preoccupied to enjoy it. Paul is playing on my mind.

I take a puff from my vaping pen but the nicotine is slow to reach my brain. Then I inhale too deeply with the next drag and cough when it hits the back of my throat. Neither this nor the wine by my side is doing its job and helping me to relax. I suppose I should return to my own home soon. But I'm reluctant to leave her on her own.

I'm suspicious by nature, I know that. Paul has been a presence for a month now and I've seen two sides of him. And it makes me think he has a hidden agenda. It could only be money. 'You can't trust anyone these days,' he said when he told me he'd moved her bank cards from her purse and into her bureau. Was it friendly advice or a warning of what he could do if he wanted to? Her vulnerability is precisely the reason why, when I moved to the village,

I helped her to make a will to protect both of our interests. Over my dead body will I allow anyone to interfere with that.

Since he said that, I've been regularly checking her banking apps on my phone but there have been no unaccounted-for withdrawals. Just in case, I hid the cards elsewhere in the house, between the pages of the novel *The Talented Mr Ripley* that sits on a shelf among a hundred other books. I haven't seen her read any of them and I assume it's another pleasure that dementia has robbed her of.

Even if I'm wrong not to trust Paul, something has definitely shifted between us. We've barely spoken in the last week. Each time I've tried to make conversation, I've been shut down with monosyllabic responses and complete disinterest in anything I've had to say. So I've stopped bothering. I don't know how you can ghost someone when they're standing right in front of you, but he's doing it pretty well.

It's only as I replay our conversations that I'm wondering if there was a motive behind the time he spent with me and how much of it was given over to discussing her. He steered the conversation the whole night and I was only too happy to spill my guts to a good-looking guy who'd asked me out. And only now does that level of interest in us concern me. As do the tools he's storing in her garage, which are multiplying each day like mechanical locusts.

Reverend Eddie must have sensed something about Paul was on my mind because he dropped by the bungalow last night. He'd been in touch with Help for Homes despite me telling him he needn't bother. Apparently they assured him Paul was a trusted, valuable volunteer. The last two mornings I've again woken up early with a jolt, utterly convinced there's someone in my room, watching me. Then I've realised it's a Paul-shaped cloud hovering over me.

The grandfather clock in her lounge chimes nine times. She's been upstairs asleep for about an hour now. I don't know what

I'm scared might happen if I go home. It's not as if Paul is going to swoop in like a vampire the moment darkness falls, to carry her away. But there's something making me feel protective of her right now. Tonight, I made her supper, helped her up the stairs, bathed her, got her ready for bed and sat in the armchair next to her until she drifted off. And what was the last thing she said to me? It wasn't 'goodnight' or 'thank you'. It was 'What time is Paul coming tomorrow?'

I know I'm petty for allowing this to upset me. But I'm the one who has given my life to taking care of her. I've spent hours researching what her diagnosis means for both victim and carer. I've joined online dementia family support groups to get a better understanding of what she's going through. I suffer her confusion and I put up with her tantrums and outbursts. And what do I have to show for it? Faint scratch marks on my face while Paul rides in like a knight in a shining Ford transit van, and it's his backside the sun shines out of.

I watch as she changes every day around him. She sheds the skin of dementia and replaces it with the vibrancy of a long-departed youth. She's begun choosing her own clothes instead of relying on me to pick out her wardrobe; she has started styling her hair again and I hate to admit it, but she is better presented than me. I also can't deny that she is a little more focused in her conversations when he is here. The television isn't playing all day long, and instead, she spends more time sitting outside in the garden under the shade of a parasol wearing her oversized tortoise-framed sunglasses, like the ghost of Jackie O.

Perhaps she's behaving like this because Paul gives her purpose; there's clearly something about him that's rejuvenating brain cells yet to be decimated by her disease. And maybe I do the opposite. Maybe I dampen her spirit and remind her of the inevitable. I could have that effect on everyone and it's why I'm heading towards my fifties and still single. He brings her happiness so I can't get rid of him, and I don't want to leave them alone because I don't trust him.

Perhaps a better person would be encouraging her and Paul's May-December friendship, and not allow trivial jealousies to breed resentment.

Clearly, I'm not a better person.

I shake my head. I need to think about something else, so I try and refocus on the sunset. I've always assumed that when the inevitable finally comes, I will sell this place and find somewhere of my own choosing. But now I'm considering staying here. I could do a lot worse than spend my summer nights with this view. I even begin to visualise the changes I'd make outside. Right here, for example. This would be my patio area, with grey flagstones under my feet. And above me, I would train vines and colourful clematises to climb up the posts and across the beams of a newly constructed pergola.

But I can tell you this for nothing, I won't be asking Paul to lay or build any of it. The sooner he runs out of work here and pisses off to someone else's house, the better.

CHAPTER 10

CONNIE

There's been an unspoken rivalry between Paul and me of late as to who can reach her house the first. If I arrive earlier than him on a Monday, he will be there before me the next day. If I reach hers at an even more ungodly hour on Wednesday, he will be waiting for me there on Thursday. If it continues like this, we'll be camping overnight in tents on her lawn to cut our journey times.

Today, however, I'm late. I couldn't get away from a chatty Walter, which set me back taking his dog for a walk. He was trying to tell me something about his bitcoin and cryptocurrency investment that I didn't understand. For a man of his age, he's very clued up about technology. Oscar only gets one lap of the playing field today as I need to get to her house quickly. And instead of dropping him home early, I take him with me. He can play in her garden for a while and wear himself out.

When I arrive, as I both feared and expected, Paul's van is parked on her drive. He has won today's round. I open the latch on the gate to the back garden and find her sitting at the table at the end of the garden under her parasol. She turns her head and glares at me, puzzled, before registering who I am.

'Oh, hello Connie,' she says and waves. She's wearing a silver bangle on her wrist that I haven't seen before, and a matching necklace.

'You're up early,' I reply.

'Bill helped me.'

'You mean Paul.'

'Oh yes, Paul.'

'What did he do to help you?'

'The same as you.' She smiles, then points to a plate with a half-eaten croissant. 'Look,' she says. 'They're French.'

'What do you mean he helped you the same as I do, Mum?'

'Paul helped me out of bed and to get dressed, then he brought me here and made breakfast.'

What did she just say? She must be misremembering. 'Are you sure he helped you get dressed?' I ask.

'Of course! I'm not daft.'

'How did he get into the house?'

'I gave him a key.'

What the actual fuck! I try and measure my tone. 'Why would you do that?'

She frowns as she thinks. 'I'm not sure.'

The rage rises inside me like lava reaching the rim of a volcano. Paul helped an elderly woman he barely knows to get washed and dressed? How dare he do that! And now he has her front door key? He has crossed a line, and as soon as I get him out of here, I'm reporting him to that charity and getting him cancelled.

'Where's Paul now?' I snap, looking around the garden.

Her face lights up. 'Paul? Is he here already?'

'His van is on the drive.'

'He must be in the house then.'

'Can you keep an eye on Oscar, please?' I say, and hand her the lead without waiting for an answer.

I hurry across the garden, and as I enter the kitchen, I spot Paul in the hallway. He is dressed in paint-splattered white overalls and is pulling off strips of wallpaper. He's also quietly muttering to himself. He looks displeased, but I can't understand what he's saying. He notices me and my appearance seems to ever-so-briefly fluster him. A split second later he's returned to form. It's unnerving.

'What the hell are you doing?' I ask.

'It's called redecorating.' This time, there's nothing disarming about his smile. I just want to slap it from his face.

'Who told you to do it?'

'Gwenny.'

'What did she say, exactly?'

'Um, let me think . . .' He exaggerates placing his finger to his chin as if deep in thought. 'Something like, "Paul, could you redecorate for me?"'

'And what do you think you are doing letting yourself into her house, getting her out of bed and changing her? Do you know just how inappropriate that is?'

'She'd fallen out of bed and was struggling to get back on her feet,' he replies. 'Would you rather I'd have left her there until you arrived?'

'Well, no, but —'

'And I stood on the landing while she showered with the bathroom door closed, then I led her back into her bedroom where she got ready – alone. The key she gave me is to the garage door so I can get to my tools, which Gwenny's kindly let me store here for now.'

'You should have called me. You have my number.'

'I tried but you didn't answer.'

I remove my phone from my pocket and realise it's turned off. We remain in an awkward stalemate until it comes to life, and I see

I have three missed calls from him an hour ago. He has me over a barrel. What can I say if I report him to the charity? That he helped one of his clients back to their feet after she had a fall? That he fed her breakfast? Hardly Dr Harold Shipman, is he?

I don't offer him any more satisfaction than I've already given him so I exit, licking my wounds. I return to the garden, where Oscar is lying on his back, paws in the air, while she is stroking the white fur of his belly. 'Why is Paul redecorating?' I ask.

'It's exciting, isn't it?' she beams.

'Did he talk you into it? Did he persuade you to say yes?'

'Of course not!'

'Has he taken any money from you?'

'No.'

'Why didn't you discuss it with me first?'

'I was telling him how Bill and I didn't have time to make this place our own before he died and how I'm living in a house surrounded by someone else's taste. Paul offered to freshen it up.'

I bet he did, I think. I bet he practically bit your hand off for the work. She may not have given him any money yet, but it'll happen and he will charge her an arm and a leg for it. This is how predators like him operate. He lures people in with his smile and twinkly eyes, and because he's done such a good job with the voluntary work, you trust him to do other things. And that's when he stings you with the big-ticket work. He's a conman, I just know it. But how far will he go? What's his ultimate goal?

'At least reassure me he's only redoing the hallway?' I ask.

'Oh no, he said he might as well do all of downstairs too while he's here. He has tradesman discounts all over town.'

'That'll still cost us a fortune!'

'*Me*, not *us*,' she huffs. '*I'm* paying for it.'

I want to remind her that it's not going to be her money forever, that one day it will make up a part of my inheritance, and how

46

unfair it is that I have to scrimp and save and live off bargain own-brand foods, state handouts, and a few quid here and there that I withdraw from her account when I'm absolutely broke. And all so that I can afford to take care of her. 'It's your rainy-day money,' I say instead.

She reaches out and takes my hand in hers. 'Look at me, Connie. Almost every day there's a rainstorm in my head. I don't know how many more dry days I have left. So let me enjoy them.'

Reluctantly, I nod. How can I argue with that? Sometimes she says so much about how she feels in even the briefest of sentences.

CHAPTER 11

CONNIE

My laptop is taking forever to fire up. It's so old that it's a decade's worth of operating systems behind the latest version. I refill my vaping pen while I wait for a screen to appear, then pour myself a glass of red wine.

I'm staying at hers this evening and have done so for the last three nights. I hate that Paul has a key to this house, even if only to the garage door, because that leads to another door in the utility room. It means he can get into her house whenever he likes. He hasn't done it yet to the best of my knowledge, but it still makes me very uncomfortable.

When I'm finally able to access next door's unsecured wi-fi, I begin by googling the name 'Paul Michael'. But with two generic names like this, it's no surprise when 5,620,000,000 results appear. I add '& Buckinghamshire' which whittles it down to 11,500,000, but that's still a drop in the ocean. I throw in words like 'gardening', 'decorating' and 'handyman' but the results aren't narrowed down by much more.

The list of men who share his name on Facebook and LinkedIn is also immense. But I have to start somewhere so I begin trawling through page after page of thumbnail photos. It takes me an hour and I still haven't found a profile that I believe, with certainty, belongs to him. I also can't find a trace of him on Twitter, Instagram or – although it's a long shot – TikTok or Snapchat. I might get a concussion with the number of brick walls I'm hitting. Paul Michael is either buried deep somewhere among all these others, or he is as absent online as I am. And that does nothing to alleviate my suspicions. Why and what is he hiding?

It's approaching midnight and, mid-involuntary yawn, an idea hits me, an alternative way to search for him. I return quickly to Facebook, and it turns out Help for Homes has its own page. There's not much to it and it's rarely updated but I stumble across what I'm looking for after scrolling back four years.

It's a photograph of a group of people, and according to the caption, they're working on the completion of a room in a daycentre in Buckingham for carers and their families. Some volunteers are perched on scaffolding and ladders and others hold paintbrushes or power tools. Paul's head is only a few millimetres in size but I recognise him immediately. His hair is a little longer and he's clean-shaven, but the tattoo around his bicep gives him away. A dozen comments have been left beneath the photo, praising the team's effort and Paul in particular.

Great work guys, reads one. *Paul, you're a star!*

Thanks to all of the team, reads another. *You did a fantastic job. Thank you Paul for going that extra mile.*

Huge thank-you to Paul and the team for all they've done. I didn't believe in angels until I met you.

I deflate like a leaking balloon with each line of praise. Either he has brainwashed all of them or I'm the one who has got it hopelessly wrong. Maybe I'm projecting. Not everyone is a liar, not everyone has a hidden agenda, not everyone is going to stab me in the back like Caz did.

Wait, what's this? I sit up straight when I reach the penultimate post.

Don't let Paul pull the wool over your eyes. He's fooled you all. Beauty and the devil are the same thing.

I read it again and again, wondering what Paul has done to elicit an accusation like this. I guess there's always a troll under a bridge somewhere with an axe to grind. However, this is the only like-minded person I have found so far so I can't dismiss it just like that. The comment was added three years ago. I can only assume the charity missed it and failed to delete it.

I study the user's profile. Their name is clearly fake – it's spelled Ann On – and the picture they've used is of a red poppy field emblazoned with 'Lest We Forget'. The rest is set to private so it gives nothing away. I take another sip of wine before clicking the messenger symbol and think about what I want to write. I keep it simple.

Hello. I read your post on the Help for Homes Facebook page regarding volunteer Paul Michael. Can I ask what you meant by it? I'm worried for my mum. Thanks.

If this were a film, a reply would appear in seconds, but it doesn't. I'm still holding out a little hope when, after two hours of silence, the laptop battery dies and I close the lid. I drain the rest of the bottle of wine, and as I make my way to my bedroom, I know that even if that Facebook poster doesn't reply, at least I'm not going mad. I am not the only person who believes there is something about this man to be wary of.

CHAPTER 12

WALTER CLARK, NEIGHBOUR

'What's troubling you?' I begin.

'Nothing,' Connie says, a little too breezily. You can't pull the wool over this old codger's eyes. I save the spreadsheet on my laptop and close the lid.

'Is it Gwen? Has something happened?'

'No, it's nothing like that.' She lets out a sigh as long as my sideboard.

'In the cupboard above the stove is a box of lemon slices,' I say. 'Put the kettle on, then we'll sit down and you can tell me what's making you a mardy Mary.'

Even when her mum isn't at her best, Connie always arrives with a smile on her face and ensures I'm okay before she lets Oscar off his lead, tops up his water bowl and leaves. The second stroke left me less mobile than I once was, my left side far weaker than my right, which is why she helps when she can. But today, her smile is thin and forced and I get the feeling she might like to talk about it. And to be honest, I'd like her to stay a little longer because I enjoy her company.

Ten minutes later and Connie returns with two mugs and a plate of cakes. I don't tell her it's the crockery I usually save for best or I'll sound like Hyacinth Bucket and her Royal Doulton with the hand-painted periwinkles.

'I think Mum's being taken advantage of by someone,' she says carefully.

'Who?'

'There's a man who's been helping us tidy the garden and do some odd jobs.'

'And . . .'

'And I can't put my finger on what it is about him, but there's something I don't trust.'

'Are you talking about Paul?'

'Yes. Do you know him?'

'Once seen, not forgotten in a hurry,' I reply. I use my hands to pretend to cool myself with an invisible fan. 'He works for a charity, doesn't he?' She nods. 'He's been going house to house asking us oldies if there's any work we need doing. Storm Michael almost ripped the satellite dish off my chimney pot, so he reattached it. And Samesh, two doors down, said Paul replaced a cracked pane of glass in his bathroom.'

'Oh. What did you think of him?' Connie asks.

'I thought he was a lovely lad; he did my job straight away and didn't want paying. He did some pointing work on a wall for George and Betty Harris too. Didn't charge them either.'

She puts her half-eaten cake back on the plate like she's lost her appetite.

'Can I be honest with you, Walter? It feels like he is slowly edging his way into Mum's and my life. I don't really know the first thing about him, yet he's in her house almost every single day and has been for weeks. This might sound ridiculous, but I'm sure he's flirting with her. And she does the same back to him.'

'He did the same with me. But I think that's just his way. Nothing is ever going to come of it, is there?'

'I suppose not.'

'There's no "suppose" about it. Trust me, when you get to mine and your mum's age, you'll relish a cheeky wink and a bit of chit-chat with a hunky handyman. A little playful banter never did anyone any harm. And to be honest, I'm thinking of finding more stuff to break around the house just so I have an excuse to ask him back.'

'But he keeps coming up with jobs that were never on our to-do list. And now I find him redecorating Mum's house without asking me first.'

'What's upsetting you most, the flirting or the making decisions without consulting you?'

'Both, I think.'

'And you're worried about what, exactly?'

'That he's trying to rip her off.'

'Do you have any proof? Is he charging her over the odds for the work?'

'No. I've seen the receipts for what he's already bought and compared them to online shops and his are cheaper.'

'Connie, be honest with me, are you a little, how do I put this . . . envious?'

'Of what?'

'Of Gwen? And that Paul's paying her more attention than he is you?'

'No! Of course not.'

Her gaze sinks to her trainers, which suggests she might be being a little economical with the truth.

'So . . . what do you think he's up to?'

'In my experience, people don't go the extra mile for you without a reason.'

'In-ter-esting,' I say.

'Why are you saying it like that?'

'Because you do exactly the same as Paul does.' I let that hang mid-air for a moment. 'Look at how you help me. I pay you to walk

Oscar but not for you to feed him, fill his water bowl, take him to get his fur trimmed, or call and check up on me if you haven't seen me around at the weekend. And I don't ask you to draw all the curtains on the dark nights or to push my wheely bins up and down the driveway on collection day. But you do it anyway, don't you?'

'I guess so.'

'And what about the other crumblies in the village? How many drives and paths did you clear after that snowstorm in February? Who swept out Iris's stables each night when her husband fell ill? Was there a hidden agenda as to why you went the extra mile for them?'

'No.'

'So why should Paul have one? You do it out of the goodness of your heart because that's the kind of person you are. And look at what you're like with your mum. You waved *arrivederci* to your fancy-pants jet-setting life in Italy to move to this little village in the arse end of nowhere because Gwen needed you. So I wonder if the problem isn't Paul, but *you*? You're so used to doing everything for other people that when a stranger comes along and shows you both some kindness, you find a reason to mistrust them. You say you know nothing about Paul, so change that. Try to get to know him better.'

'I have done.'

'Then try harder.'

Connie mulls over my advice for the length of time it takes to eat the rest of her lemon slice.

'Trust me,' I add. 'You don't get many things in life for free, so when someone wants to help you, grab it with both hands. And if you're still not convinced, tell him you're grateful for what he has done so far but you won't be needing him anymore. Then send him around here. Preferably on a day that's too hot for him to keep his T-shirt on.'

When she rolls her eyes and smiles, I know she's taking my advice on board.

CHAPTER 13

CONNIE

I've given a lot of thought over the last few days to Walter's suggestion about getting to know Paul better. So I've invited him to dinner with us tonight. It doesn't mean I'm giving him the benefit of the doubt – precisely the opposite, in fact. It's because I don't trust him and I want to get more of an idea of who he really is and what he wants from us. And the best way to do that is to get to know him better. Sooner or later, every mask slips.

I keep thinking back to the Help for Homes Facebook post. *Don't let Paul pull the wool over your eyes. He's fooled you all.*

You don't post something like that on a public forum without reason. Its author still hasn't returned my message; in fact the bloody thing has since been deleted. I wonder if my message scared them off?

While I took the Village Hopper into town to buy food for tonight's meal, I reluctantly left her alone to ogle Paul as he sanded and painted the banisters. I used her debit card to pay for a nice bottle of Italian red, a garlic baguette, a microwavable lasagne and three raspberry panna cottas. Paying for it myself would have used up half my weekly food budget, and I'm not starving myself for Paul's sake. I've banished them both from the kitchen as I now remove the cooked food from its packaging and place it into her serving dishes to pass off as my own.

My hackles rise when I find them in the lounge playing poker again. That's *my* game to play with her, not his. The song 'Let It Go' from that Disney movie starts playing in my head, so I usher them into the dining room. They're cosying up together sitting side by side when I bring in the food and arrange the dishes on table mats.

'Mum,' I begin, 'you forgot to put the cutlery and serving spoons out.'

She looks around the room as if unsure of where to find them.

Without missing a beat, Paul takes them from the correct sideboard drawer. I hold back from asking him how he knew where they were.

'Smells good,' he says, inhaling the lasagne. 'Which supermarket is it from?'

'It's homemade,' I lie.

'I assumed, from the empty boxes at the bottom of the recycling bin, that you got it from Waitrose.'

The hairs on my arms bristle. 'That's a different meal for later in the week.' He knows I'm lying.

I'm about to plate up her food when she stops me. 'Paul can do it,' she says. 'He's closer and I don't want you dripping sauce on the tablecloth.' She turns to him. 'Meredith can be very clumsy. It's her big hands you see. They're like snow shovels.'

She's mentioned this Meredith woman before, but every time I ask who she is, the shutters drop. Either she can't remember who she is, or she doesn't want to elaborate. Paul's sleeve rides up when he reaches for the silver serving spoons and I recognise a familiar object affixed to his wrist. It's a watch with a blue face, silver hands and a thick, matching strap.

'Is that Dad's watch?' I ask, pointing to it.

She smiles. 'Yes.'

My toes curl but I can't let my anger boil over in front of him. 'And why is Paul wearing it?'

'I'd forgotten I had it until Paul found it,' she explains. 'It was just sitting in a box in the wardrobe on the shelf.'

I swear she says 'on the shelf' pointedly.

'What were you doing in the wardrobe, Paul?' I ask, my voice deliberately singsong-like.

'Gwenny asked me to help her empty it before I started decorating her room.'

'Bill wouldn't have wanted it to go to waste,' she chips in.

I resist ripping it off Paul's wrist and putting it back where it belongs. And the dark cloud that so frequently hovers above me when I think of him returns.

'Where did you learn to cook?' he asks.

'Italy,' I reply. He knows this, we already had this conversation when we went out for dinner.

'Ah, yeah, that's right. Where were you living?'

I take a mouthful of my lasagne. It's too hot and it burns my mouth as I swallow. I don't let on. 'Costiera Amalfitana,' I say and take two long, cooling gulps of wine.

'That's a big area. Where, exactly?'

'I worked all over the region, depending on where my clients were getting married.'

'So, Cetara, Minori, Vietri sul Mare, Mongibello? Places like that?'

I nod as I blow to cool my next forkful. Gwen is listening intently as if she's hearing me talk about work for the first time.

'Oh wait, Mongibello is that fictitious town in *The Talented Mr Ripley*, isn't it?' Paul adds.

He is telling me two things here. First, that he doubts my working credentials, and second, he knows where I've hidden her bank cards, in the Ripley book on her shelf. He is using my invitation to dinner to do to me what I'm trying to do to him – wrongfoot him.

'It's an easy mistake to make,' I reply calmly. 'They filmed much of the movie adaptation on the coast in Positano, so I understand why you've mixed up fact with fiction. There are also many towns and villages a few miles inland which claim to be a part of Amalfi when they aren't. They do it for the kudos and the tourism. I couldn't pretend to do that.' I stare him in the eye. 'Be something I'm not. For money.' He doesn't flinch.

I use his attempt to discredit me as a springboard. 'Do you know Italy well?' I continue. 'Have you travelled much or are you more of a homebird?'

'I can be both.'

'And where is home?'

'Just across the county.'

'Which direction?'

'Northants.'

He drains his glass and reaches for the bottle of wine he brought with him. He chose it deliberately: it's the one that belonged to me that she gave him a few weeks ago as a thank you. 'Shall I open it?' he asks, but he's already unscrewing the cap. He leans towards her to fill her glass up.

I hold my hand over the rim. 'She can't drink because of her medication.'

'Will one glass really do her that much harm?'

'Then what, shall we give her some fireworks and a box of matches to play with? Alcohol can make her angry or confused and stop her from remembering.'

He turns to face her and gives her a wink. 'And do you always play by the rules, Gwenny? I bet you could be a naughty girl in your day.'

She taps her nose and she chuckles. 'What happens in Geneva, stays in Geneva.'

I have no idea what she's referring to.

'Come on, Connie. I'm sure one glass won't hurt,' Paul continues. And before I can protest again, he pours her glass up to the halfway mark. She sips it and her face lights up, like a child discovering sugar for the first time.

'So Paul, what else do you do when you're not so generously donating your time to others?' I ask. 'Do you have a full-time job?'

'I'm self-employed.'

'As what? There's no business name on your van.'

'I work on the railways . . . maintenance . . . that kind of thing. And you? Does it bother you always being the bridesmaid and never the bride?'

'I'm a wedding planner, not a bridesmaid. And I took over a friend's business when she left,' I explain.

'Which friend was that again?' she asks.

'Martine. We were in sixth form together.'

'Have I met her?'

'Many times.'

'And what did you do before that?' Paul continues.

'A lot of things. Too many to list.'

'I'm sure you made your mum very proud,' he says and turns to her again. 'What do you say, Gwenny? Did Connie make you proud?'

She thinks carefully before answering. 'I suppose she must have.'

'What was she like as a little girl?' he persists.

She frowns. 'I'm not sure. I . . . I think . . .' She has lost her thread.

I take the opportunity to turn the tables. 'You must like vulnerable people. I hear you've been badgering the neighbours for odd-job work while you've been in Avringstone. Flirting with a few of the ladies, eh?' I add cruelly. His jaw tightens.

'Have you been asking around about me then?' Paul's smile doesn't reach his eyes.

'You know what small villages are like. People like to chat.'

'And gossip.'

'People only call it gossip when they've got something to hide.'

'I'm an open book.'

'Talking of books, I stumbled on Help for Homes' Facebook page recently. I spotted you in a photo.' He looks at me sharply then softens his gaze a little too late. 'You were helping create a room for autistic children in a daycentre,' I go on. 'Do you have any family? Any kids from a previous relationship?'

'No, not that I'm aware of. But you never know, eh?' He nudges her arm and she giggles.

'Any brothers or sisters?'

He shakes his head. 'Like you, I'm an only child. I prefer it that way.'

This meal – or more accurately, this endurance test – continues along these lines for another fifty minutes. It's as if we are amidst a tennis rally, neither of us ready to flag and lose a point to the other. And it solidifies what I was already convinced of before tonight – I cannot trust this man. Our deadlock is only broken when I clear the table of dirty dishes and prepare to return from the kitchen with the raspberry panna cotta desserts. I hover by the door when I overhear them talking quietly. 'I won't say a thing,' she whispers, then puts her finger up to pursed lips. I don't catch his response.

'What have I missed?' I ask as I enter the room.

'Nothing,' they say together, and I realise Paul isn't the only one keeping things from me. He has her doing it too.

CHAPTER 14

JOE LAWSON, NEIGHBOUR

When the bell rings to the tune of 'Greensleeves', I open the front door and see Gwen's daughter Connie. She looks anxious. We have spoken if we've bumped into one another in the village shop or while she's walking her mum to church on a Sunday morning, but she's never been round to the house before, so this appearance is a little unexpected. And it's not great timing, if I'm being honest. I have a round of golf booked this afternoon. My clubs are already in the boot of the car.

'I'm really sorry to bother you . . .' she begins, but gets distracted by Mary's appearance behind me. She's drying her hands with a tea towel.

'Hi luv,' Mary says. 'Joe, where are your manners? Don't leave the girl on the doorstep.' I move to one side. She follows Mary into the lounge. 'Now, how can we help?' asks Mary.

'Have you seen Mum today?'

'No, but then I don't see her very often these days,' says Mary. 'What about you, Joe? Nothing escapes your beady eye.'

It bothers me whenever she makes me sound like a curtain twitcher. I've reminded her many times that I take my job as Neighbourhood Watch coordinator seriously and that means knowing other people's business. 'No, I haven't seen her,' I tell Connie. 'Isn't she at home?'

'No,' she replies. 'I was there at a quarter to seven this morning but the house was empty. I've been searching the village ever since. But there's no sign of her.'

I take a sideways look towards the carriage clock on the fireplace. It's approaching eleven and I really should be on the road by now. I'm sure Mary can deal with this on her own.

'She's wandered off before, hasn't she?' Mary recalls. 'I think someone said you found her in the bowling club car park once, looking for your dad. Perhaps she's gone for a walk and has lost track of time?'

'I bought her a mobile phone to take with her if she goes out,' Connie explains. Her hands are trembling. 'I put that app on it where you can track where a person is. But either she's forgotten to switch it on or she hasn't recharged the phone, because it keeps going to voicemail. She's taken her handbag with her but she's left her debit cards.'

'Might she have gone into town on the Hopper?' I suggest.

'I've already called the driver and he hasn't seen her. And she never lets me book her a taxi because she thinks they're all going to overcharge her.'

'She's not wrong there,' adds Mary.

'Hmm,' I say as I think. 'If she's got herself lost, can she communicate well enough to ask for help?'

'Yes. But what if she's gone wandering through the fields at the end of the garden? She had the bushes cut down, so she could've left through the gate. If she's gone that way and she's made it right to the back, there are miles of forests she could get lost in.'

Connie's welling up, so Mary comforts her with an arm around her shoulders. I look at the clock again. The club is a stickler for punctuality, and if I miss my tee-time, Francis and I won't get another one today. 'Look, I'm sure Gwen will be fine and she'll be home in no time,' I say and begin to make my way towards the front door. I expect Connie to follow, and grit my teeth when she doesn't.

'She's been getting worse lately,' she continues. 'I think part of her brain is regressing into her teenage years.' Her face hardens. 'She won't leave Paul alone.'

'Paul?' I repeat.

'The gardener and odd-job man.'

'He's the lad who cleaned the leaves out of the gutters for us,' Mary adds.

'Ahh of course,' I say. 'Very friendly young man. He said if we ever need anything doing in the garden to let him know as he'd be happy to help while he's around.'

I think I spot Connie's teary eyes narrow ever so slightly, as if praising Paul isn't something she wants to hear.

'He's been spending a lot of time at Mum's house,' she says.

Mary tilts her head at this. If I'm the village busybody, she's the village gossip. The world and his dog will hear all of this by the end of the day. 'What do you mean?' she asks.

'She's becoming dependent on him being around and it makes her confused. Half the time she thinks he's Dad, which isn't good for her. And it doesn't help that he's always there, creating more work for himself.'

'And he hasn't seen her either?' I ask.

'I haven't seen him.'

'Joe, I think you should call the police, just to be on the safe side.'

I grit my teeth. That's my plans for the afternoon kiboshed.

'But what if they think I'm overreacting?' asks Connie.

'Joe has contacts there who he reports his Neighbourhood Watch gripes to, so they'll listen to him. If it was my mother out there on the streets I'd be worried sick too.'

I reach for my glasses and flick through the pages of my address book. 'I'm going to organise a search party until the police arrive, and get a head start on finding her,' I say. The right thing to do, certainly, and my playing a visible role in finding Gwen won't do me any harm in my campaign to be elected chairman of the parish council this winter when Ken steps down. 'If you're happy that you've searched the village thoroughly, then we'll start with the fields.'

I suppose I should try and comfort her but I'm not good at that sort of thing. Mary is, though, and puts her arm back around her.

'I'm sure she'll be okay,' Mary says. 'Mark my words, Gwen will be back before you know it.'

I hope we find her too. But perhaps not straight away. Not until I've been seen doing my bit.

CHAPTER 15

CONNIE

I hate her for doing this to me. I perch on the end of the bed in her room, angry, shattered, hungry and worried sick. I'm constantly on edge but I know it's not her fault. She is my responsibility, and it's on my watch that she's gone missing. So this is on me, not her.

A day and a half has passed since I turned up here to find her house empty. But it's hard to know for sure just how long she has been missing. Even moments after I left her the night before, she could have found her keys, unlocked the front door and vanished. Before the police arrived to search the house, I found all the pills she was supposed to have taken, wrapped in tissue and tossed in the bin. They included the sleeping tablets I've been adding to her cocktail of meds. Dr Chambers prescribed them to me but I started slipping them to her because it was taking her longer and longer to settle at night. I didn't mention it to the detectives as I don't need anyone else pointing the finger at me when I know I'm to blame.

Through her window I count a dozen uniformed and plain-clothed police officers making their way around the village streets conducting house-to-house enquiries and handing out flyers with her face, name and description splashed across them. They're asking everyone to check their gardens, garages and sheds in case she is locked inside one, like she's a missing cat. I also heard the humming of two police drones circling the skies above the village before making their way towards the fields and forest. Their thermal image cameras can locate people in undergrowth and woodland but have so far failed to pick up her body heat. To date, two neighbours think they might have spotted her shortly before I arrived at the house. Both say she was walking down the steep hill out of the village and towards the riverbank. But neither sighting has been confirmed. I'm told they won't send divers to search the river until they have good reason to believe she might have fallen in.

The search began yesterday, soon after Joe contacted the police. Dozens of villagers started scouring the fields for her before the officers arrived and helped to coordinate and expand it further. I joined them this afternoon and my throat is still hoarse from shouting her name as we made our way through the forest. She's known by more people than I thought because of her weekly church appearances. And I'm touched by how this kind, thoughtful community is bending over backwards to help us. It doesn't matter that she and I haven't lived here long; they consider us their own.

I move downstairs and take a cigarette from the packet I left on the kitchen worktop, lighting it from the gas hob. I ignore the photograph of the diseased lung on the front of the sleeve. I'm in no mood to be lectured. I promised myself I'd stick to vaping when I moved here, but last night I caved in and bought a packet. I'll add it to the tally of other promises I've broken.

As well as her disappearance, there's been neither hide nor hair of Paul. For weeks he's been an unwelcome but constant presence I can't shake, like a poltergeist or some other evil spirit. It's too coincidental that the two of them vanished at the same time. When I told this to Detective Sergeant Krisha Ahuja, who has been appointed my family liaison officer, she wanted to know everything I could tell her about Paul which, despite my best efforts, wasn't much. We searched Gwen's address book, but his number wasn't listed under P and the page for surnames beginning with M, which may have included Paul's surname, Michael, had been torn out.

Instead, I pointed her in the direction of the charity who inflicted him upon us. They must have his home address or a record of his van's registration number so that roadside cameras might pick it up if he passes them. So far Krisha hasn't let me know one way or the other.

'Are you treating him as a suspect?' I asked.

'We don't yet know if a crime has been committed,' Krisha replied. 'It's relatively common for people with dementia to wander. Something like sixty per cent go walkabout at least once.' She couldn't – or wouldn't – tell me how many returned safe and well. 'Do you have any idea what sets your mum off? Because it's often triggered by something. Boredom, confusion over time, it can also be a mechanism to alleviate stress or they can just be searching for something from the past.'

'I just accepted it was one of those things people with dementia do. Perhaps she's searching for Dad?'

It makes sense. Much of her behaviour is triggered by having lost him. There are days when she doesn't remember he's dead, days when she does, and days when she can't process what death is but fears she won't be seeing him again.

My fingers suddenly start to heat up and I notice I've smoked the cigarette down to the filter, so I stub it out and suck on two extra-strong mints. I realise that of all the scenarios I've played out in my head in which something horrible happens to her, vanishing into thin air wasn't one of them. And I have to face facts that this really might be it. I might never see her again. I begin planning her funeral in my head. She has put some money aside with one of those firms that organise it for you. She told me she wants a small ceremony in the village church with two hymns and a Bible reading. She also wants to be buried in the space next to the only man she ever loved. Reverend Eddie directed us on how to buy a plot.

I shake my head. I need to snap out of this. I need to be positive and not stand here imagining the worst. However, even though the light summer nights allow the hunt to continue longer into the evening, with each passing hour the odds of her safe return are rapidly shrinking. Krisha has tried to keep my spirits up but I can tell her positive energy is also beginning to wane.

There's a knock at the open front door and I turn. Speak of the devil, it's Krisha letting herself in. Behind her is a woman holding a grey boom microphone with a furry cover and a man with a television camera under his arm. My stomach cinches. I know why they're here.

'This is the team from Anglia News, Connie,' Krisha begins. 'As I explained this afternoon, the appeal will only take a few minutes to record.'

She directs them into the lounge to set up their equipment and then joins me in the hallway. I have been dreading this. My heart couldn't beat louder or faster if it tried.

'Is there any other way?' I ask. 'I'm really uncomfortable being in front of a camera. I'm going to make a mess of it. Won't it sound better coming from you?'

Krisha offers me a sympathetic but firm smile, one that suggests she isn't going to let me off the hook. 'I'm sure most people would feel the same as you but it'll take just a few minutes. They'll broadcast it tonight and then again on tomorrow's breakfast news and it'll go online too. It's our best chance at getting the public to keep a lookout for Gwen.'

I want to tell her no; that I've spent my life living in the margins and I want no place in the centre of the page. But I can't. I have to do this. For *her* sake. So as the film crew set up, I put on a little lipstick, change my top for one in my overnight bag upstairs, brush my hair and return to the lounge as they are adjusting the lighting.

The cameraman directs me to where to sit while the reporter holds the mic in one hand and her notebook in the other. Krisha returns from the hallway with a framed photograph of Gwen in her hands and asks me to hold it facing the lens. I take up my position as the cameraman turns on his device and begins to record.

Just as the reporter opens her mouth to ask the first question, we are distracted by the front door opening.

And seconds later, there she is. Alive and well, but baffled as to why there are so many strangers in her house.

'Mum,' I gasp, and seconds later, Paul follows her into the hallway.

CHAPTER 16

CONNIE

I'm speechless, my eyes fixed upon her and then Paul. I feel everyone else's gaze shift from them to me as I clamber to my feet and hurry over to her. I catch the reflection of the camera in the mirror. It's focused on us. I hug her as tightly as my arms and body will allow and only stop when I worry I might be hurting her.

'Where have you been?' I ask, then take a step back and look her up and down. She seems perfectly fine. 'We've been so worried about you! Are you okay?'

'Of course, why wouldn't I be?' she says. 'Who are your friends? Are we having a party? I used to love parties. Should I put on a dress?'

'Mrs Wright,' says Krisha, equally as surprised as me. 'There are a lot of people out there looking for you right now.'

'Me?' she asks with genuine disbelief. 'Whatever for?'

'Because you've been missing for almost two days!' I exclaim.

Her face is blank. 'But I haven't been missing, I've been to Clacton-on-Sea, haven't I?' She delivers this as if it's perfectly obvious where she has been.

'Clacton-on-Sea,' I repeat. 'What the hell were you doing there?'

'Paul took me. It was a surprise.'

'Your mum said she hadn't been there for years so we took a road trip,' Paul adds matter-of-factly.

'It was really quite charming,' she continues. 'The pier looks wonderful when it's all lit up at night.'

I don't know who I want to throttle the most, Paul or the woman I've been beside myself with worry over. It's only the presence of Krisha and the Anglia News team that prevents me from exploding into a fit of rage. Meanwhile Krisha calls her colleagues and asks for a medic while I attempt to compose myself.

'Did you see the police when you drove back into the village?' I ask as calmly as my voice allows. 'There are search parties everywhere. We thought you'd got lost or were lying dead in the woods somewhere.'

'Why ever would you think that?' she replies. 'I've been to Clacton-on-Sea. Paul took me. The pier looks wonderful when it's all lit up at night. Now, whose party is this? Should I have bought a gift?'

Krisha apologises to the news team but reads my expression when they ask if they can record some extra footage of us being reunited. She politely declines their request and ushers them out of the house. As soon as they leave, I can no longer hold my tongue. Paul is getting the brunt of my fury as Krisha returns.

'What the hell makes you think it's acceptable to take an elderly woman away from her daughter for two days without asking first?'

Paul shrugs. 'She said she'd texted you.'

'Of course she hadn't! She doesn't even know how to fucking text! And why wasn't her phone on? I've been calling for two days and it's been switched off.'

'I bought her a new one.'

'What? Why?'

'I got a buy-one-get-one-free deal on mine. She has a new number too.'

71

'And how was I supposed to know that?'

'I wrote it down for you and left it in the dining room, propped up against the cat ornament.'

'Which one?'

'The green one with the eyes that feel like they're staring at something.'

Krisha moves to verify his claim and returns with a yellow Post-it note with a number scrawled upon it. 'It was under the sideboard,' she says.

'Perhaps the wind blew it when you opened the patio doors,' Paul suggests.

'Bullshit.'

'I also emailed it to you along with the address and contact details of the hotel where we'd be staying.'

'I didn't get any email from you.'

'Have you checked your junk folder?'

I whip out my phone and scroll through it. Sure enough, the junk folder contains an email from Paul Michael dated two days ago.

I turn my head towards Krisha in disbelief. 'Do you see what he's doing?' I ask. 'First he kidnaps her and makes sure she's uncontactable. Then he tries to make it look like I'm the one in the wrong.'

'Kidnap?' Paul cocks his head and looks at me as if I'm mad. 'Why would I want to kidnap Gwenny?'

'Stop calling her that!' I yell, even though I know that by losing my temper I'm playing into his hands. He wants to goad me, to remind me it's a name for her that only he uses. 'I know exactly what your game is,' I accuse, prodding him in the chest. 'You're trying to worm your way into her life for her money, and I'm not going to let it happen.'

Krisha inserts herself between Paul and me. 'Connie,' she says, calmly but firmly, 'perhaps we should have this conversation away from Gwen.'

The holiday glow she had moments earlier has been replaced by fear. She is scared of how I'm reacting. Her hands are pressed upon both cheeks like that painting *The Scream*. I feel awful.

'I think it might be a good idea if you took a few moments for yourself in the kitchen,' Krisha continues. 'It's been an extremely stressful two days but let's not lose sight of the fact that we have the best possible outcome here. Your mum is alive and well, which is what everyone wanted.'

I let out a huff as I leave the room just as more police officers come in through the front door, along with paramedics. I hesitate and watch as two officers and Krisha escort Paul outside into the front garden. Alone in the kitchen, I light up another cigarette as my pent-up tears flow faster than Niagara Falls.

Thirty minutes pass before Krisha returns to the kitchen and closes the door behind her. She asks me to take a seat and I know I'm not going to like what she has to say because she isn't focused on me, but on a small black pocket notebook she lays out on the table in front of us.

'Okay,' she begins. 'We've spoken to both Gwen and Paul separately and their stories match. Your mum had apparently mentioned to Paul that Clacton-on-Sea was where she and your dad had their first proper holiday and that she wanted to go back one day. He thought it would be a good idea to take her there to relive some old memories while she still has—'

'I don't believe him,' I interrupt. 'There is more to that trip than he is telling you. I feel it in my gut. They flirt with one another and then he whisks her away for a weekend where it's just the two of them. It's not right. You can see that, can't you?'

'Paul claims that nothing untoward has ever happened between him and Gwen and that they had separate rooms at the bed and breakfast hotel where they stayed. He showed us a receipt to prove that two rooms were paid for.'

'By whom?'

'By him. He also showed us a bank statement to confirm this. One of my colleagues has also contacted the premises and confirmed your mum appeared happy and relaxed. There's nothing to suggest she'd been taken there against her will.'

'Then why didn't he ask me if it was okay that he took her there first? Because he knows I'd have told him no. And as for that note falling off the sideboard . . . surely you aren't buying that?'

'Paul had no reason to disbelieve Gwen when she told him that she'd texted you on her new phone to tell you where she was, and he assumed he had done the right thing with his note and the email. But he admits that it slipped his mind to give his new number to Help for Homes. He also accepts that while he should have spoken to you in person, he finds it difficult to communicate with you since your previous encounter.'

'What previous encounter?' I ask, puzzled.

'Since he made it clear he was not interested in you. Romantically.' My throat tightens as she continues to read from her notebook. 'Paul claims you have made several passes at him, each of which he has politely declined. He says that you then became stand-offish with him and hard to approach.'

A humourless laugh escapes me. 'Oh my God, the nerve of that man! That categorically did not happen. He's lying.'

'To be honest with you, Connie, that's between you and him. But we are satisfied Gwen was not kidnapped or coerced and so we won't be investigating this any further or making an arrest. However, Help for Homes will likely want to talk to Paul because, as a volunteer, this would be regarded as a safeguarding breach.'

I shake my head. 'This is insane. Am I the only one who can see there's something not right about that man?'

'As I said, there is no evidence to suggest Paul has committed a crime.'

'Gwen is mentally impaired! She doesn't know what she is doing or saying from one day to the next. He's taking advantage of her.'

'How, exactly?'

'I don't know!'

'And until you have proof, our hands are tied. I'm sorry but he hasn't broken the law.'

'So I have to wait until he hurts her or robs her blind before you'll do anything?'

Krisha removes a card from her wallet and leaves it on the countertop as she rises to her feet. 'This is my direct line and mobile number if something else happens and you need to contact me. Look, I'm sorry I can't give you the solution you're looking for. What you can do is contact the local Alzheimer's Society to see if they can arrange a home visit and offer you and your mum some support. But for now, try and focus on the positives. Your mum is alive and, dare I say it, happy. I've seen many, many outcomes a lot worse than this.'

I can't look at her as she leaves the room. Meanwhile, Paul has taken Krisha's advice and crawled back into whatever hole he calls home. Shortly after that the front door closes and the only people left in the house are me and her. I lead her up the staircase and into the bathroom to get changed.

'I've been to Clacton-on-Sea,' she says as she slips her nightie on over her head. 'Bill took me. The pier looks wonderful when it's all lit up at night.'

I don't reply as I help her into bed, then close the curtains.

'And when you speak to Meredith, don't forget to tell her I have Tom.'

She gives me a little smirk when she says 'Tom' but I have no energy left in me to ask who Tom and Meredith are. And frankly, I don't give a shit. I don't even wish her goodnight before I make my way back downstairs and sit in the darkness of the garden, and light up yet another cigarette.

CHAPTER 17

CONNIE

God, I ache. All these nights of sleeping on the world's lumpiest mattress in her spare room have left me with a neck, back and hunched shoulders that throb like I'm suffering whiplash. As reluctant as I am to leave her this morning, I just cannot function unless I get some help. So I've booked an appointment to see an osteopath who can manipulate my knots and niggles until I feel human again. I can't afford it, so I'll charge it to her debit card. Perhaps I shouldn't, but it's the least she can do after the worry she put me through with last week's vanishing act.

I leave her in Mary's capable hands and hope she can distract her from tunnelling her way out to freedom in another great escape. If I'm forced to hear one more time how beautiful Clacton-on-Sea's pier looks when it's illuminated, I might go there and illuminate it myself with a box of bloody matches.

The Village Hopper trundles along the dual carriageway and I wonder where Paul is. It's been six weeks since he first appeared in our lives and six days since he vanished after their jolly. He can pretend to the police all he likes that it was *Gwenny's* idea and that he was trying to do something nice for her, but I wasn't born yesterday. And it's annoying that no one will believe me when I keep telling them he has a hidden agenda.

I wonder if he's staying out of the way because he knows how far he stepped over the line? Especially now he's on the police radar. But what did he expect would happen? He must have known when he whisked her away that I'd contact the police. So I can only assume he wanted to make a fool of me in front of them with the missing Post-it note and his email going straight to my junk folder. I googled how he could know my mail provider would decide his message was spam and it's easier than I thought. If someone sends me an email that I then mark as spam, any other message from them will likely end up in my spam folder too. A week earlier I'd received a junk email from Paul that I'd moved to my spam. So he knew the next message containing the address of the hotel would also find its way in there.

But what I still can't figure out is his motive. Because as far as I can see, all he's succeeded in doing is upsetting an already confused woman. Her moods have been swinging like a pendulum since he's stopped coming around. One minute she's recounting stories about their walks along the pebbled beaches, the fruit machines and their fish and chip suppers, and the next, she's wandering around the house and garden looking for both Bill and Paul and asking what time they'll be home. She's anxious and restless and I'm concerned it might prompt her to go wandering again. Hence me having little choice but to leave her with a babysitter when I'm not there. I've also upped her medication by another half a sleeping tablet a night, only now I watch and wait until she swallows it. They've been knocking her out for twelve hours at a time. Like today's use of her debit card, perhaps I shouldn't be doing it, but it's twelve hours less I need to worry.

There's something else that's pressing on my mind, but this time, it's nothing Paul's done. In a few weeks' time, I'll be leaving her to fend for herself.

'It's my busiest period for weddings in Italy,' I explained to Walter when I told him he'd need to find a temporary replacement to walk Oscar. 'I have several lined up over a few weeks that I can't get out of. I've subcontracted everyone else to local planners but I've been living off what the remaining couples have already paid me. So I have no choice but to be there. If there was any other way then I'd stay here, but there's not.'

'How long will you be?'

'About eight weeks in all, I think.'

They might just be the longest few weeks of my life. A private care agency is going to provide a temporary carer to visit her twice daily. Gwen will have to foot the bill for that though, as it's way beyond my means. They'll help get her in and out of bed, ensure she's fed, and keep on top of her personal hygiene. And her neighbours and Reverend Eddie said they'd keep an eye on her. It's by no means ideal, but it's the best solution I can come up with until I return.

The Hopper is one stop away from the town centre when we come to a halt at temporary traffic lights. I'm gazing out of the window when a vehicle on the other side of the road catches my eye. It looks like Paul's van, only cleaner. A cloudless sky and the sun shining in my direction means I can't see who's behind the wheel. But there must be thousands of identical vehicles on the road. Eventually, the lights on that side switch to green, the van pulls away and I finally catch a glimpse of the driver.

What the . . . No, it can't be. Is that him? No. Is it? Sleep deprivation from that bloody mattress is making my mind play tricks on me. Or is it Paul? A clenched fist appears in my stomach and starts trying to punch its way out. I turn my head quickly and the pain in my shoulder extends up into my neck and the base of my skull. Whoever it is, they are driving in the direction of our village. What the hell am I going to do? I can't risk it, I just can't. I need to get back to her house now.

There are no more stops planned so I'll have to wait until the bus reaches the town centre and turns around again. I look at my watch: I can be home in twenty minutes. He can't do that much damage in such a short amount of time. Besides, Mary is with her.

It's our turn to go but we aren't budging. I anxiously glare out of the front windscreen and spot a car three vehicles ahead that isn't accelerating. The light turns to red again. 'Shit,' I mutter aloud. I wait and wait and wait for it to turn green again, and when it finally happens, I'm dismayed to see the car ahead still hasn't budged. It's like a bad dream where I'm running as fast as I can but my feet are trapped in thick mud. Horns are blasting and the car's hazard lights start flashing. Drivers as frustrated as me are exiting their vehicles to help that car owner push his vehicle to the side of the road. *Come on, come on, come on.*

I've got no choice but to sit and wait. I try and talk sense into myself. *It's in your imagination, you didn't see Paul, you saw what you wanted to see.* I desperately want to believe this.

And even if I did believe that, it doesn't matter because she is with Mary. She won't have let him in, will she? She knows the chaos he caused when he took her to Clacton-on-Sea.

By the time the Hopper reaches its destination, I'm trying to message Mary but it won't send. My phone has no signal. I'm still waiting for the bus to fill with customers before we are on our way.

By the time we reach the hill at the bottom of Avringstone, forty-five minutes have passed since I saw that van and I'm crying in sheer frustration. I don't care that other passengers are looking at me as if I'm a madwoman.

I half walk, half jog as fast as my legs, inflamed back and neck muscles will allow. It's just as I arrive in her street, wiping the sweat blooming across my brow, that I spot it. Paul's van, on Gwen's drive. None of this was in my imagination. It's very much real. He is back.

CHAPTER 18

CONNIE

Calm, Connie, stay calm. Just stay calm. Even when I stop repeating this in my head and start saying it aloud, I'm not listening. Instead, I'm a bag of nerves for what I might find in her house, and livid that Paul has the audacity to return here.

I scan the front seats as I hurry past his van, then glance across the garden, but he is nowhere to be found. The first things I spot when I open the front door are five bulging suitcases lying side by side at the top of the staircase.

I grab some tissues from a box on the hallway console table and pat my forehead and armpits dry on the way to find her sitting in front of the television watching a black-and-white movie. She's alone.

'Where's Mary?' I ask without pleasantries.

'Paul's here!' she exclaims.

'But Mary's not.'

'I told her she could go home.'

I'll have words with Mary later. 'And who do the suitcases belong to?' I'm praying for the answer I'm not expecting.

'They're Paul's,' she says with a grin so sudden that the top row of her dentures slip. She readjusts them with her fingers.

'And what are they doing here?'

She pauses for a moment and cocks her head to one side. 'I'm not sure,' she says, then corrects herself. 'Oh, that's right, he's coming to stay for a bit.'

'Over my dead body he is.'

Without giving her the opportunity to reply, I storm out into hallway and march up the stairs. I find Paul, dressed in his decorating overalls, painting the landing's skirting boards an off-white colour. He hums along to a station playing dance music. I kick the switch on the plug socket to turn it off.

'Ah, Connie,' he chirps. 'It's been a while. How have you been?'

'Why are your suitcases here?' I demand.

'Are they in the way? I'll put them in my room once I finish this coat.'

'You don't have *a room.*'

'Well I can't sleep on the landing.'

'Why do you need to be here?'

'Gwenny kindly invited me while I'm in between homes. I haven't been around for a few days because I've been packing up and selling my house. But I won't be exchanging on my new place for a couple of weeks.'

'You're not moving in here. No way,' I say and shake my head. 'You can't be trusted around Mum.'

His show of offence is as phoney as his need to stay here. 'I'm sensing a little hostility,' he says.

'You're taking advantage of her and we both know it. Half the time she doesn't even know who you are. She thinks you're my dad.'

I swear he is the only person who can fire me from nought to sixty in a heartbeat. I snatch the paintbrush out of his hand and hurl it on to the plastic sheeting covering the carpet. 'I'm only telling you this once. Get the fuck out of my mum's house. Now!' I square up to him, almost daring him to retaliate. If he does, I will be straight on to the police. But instead he gives me a sour smile, then looks over my shoulder.

'I don't know who you think you are but I'd like you to leave right now,' comes a frail, trembling voice behind me.

I turn around. Gwen's brow is taut, her lips pursed. 'Mum, I'm your daughter.'

'You're not—' I know what's coming next as she's said it dozens of times before, so I cut her short.

'He's a conman. You can't trust him.'

'Don't talk about Bill like that!'

'He's not Dad, he's Paul,' I snap. 'And he's not staying here.'

'But he's my friend and this is my villa, not yours.'

Paul interrupts. 'Thank you, Gwenny, but I don't want to come between the two of you.'

Like hell he doesn't. His focus locks on to her and her cheeks flush. A twinkle appears somewhere deep in those milky eyes. And not for the first time, I have a bad, bad feeling about this.

'Please leave my house,' she directs to me, more firmly.

'Mum!' I protest.

'You have no right to call me that,' she says. 'Bill, tell her to go.'

'Let's go downstairs and talk about this in private,' I say.

'I don't need to talk about anything. If you can't accept my friends then you're not welcome here.'

I take a deep breath and glare at her. I know her well enough to recognise there's no use in trying to talk her around to my way of thinking when she is in this mindset. I'd normally give her space, let it run its course, and later, she'll have forgotten why she was so angry in the first place. But if I do that now, I'll be leaving her with Paul. That's the last thing I want. 'Mum?' I say again, but she's not listening. To her, he is the only person in the room.

So with no choice but to leave, I do just that. I make my way back downstairs, but before I go, I open the cupboard doors at the bottom of the bureau in the lounge and remove a concertina box of files. Among her bills, insurance policies, the deeds to the house and pension is her most recent will.

I open the envelope and make sure the document is still there. But instead of replacing it, I slip it into my pocket to take home with me. With Paul around, I don't just need to protect her, but my own interests too.

CHAPTER 19

CONNIE

When my roles as next of kin and carer come to their inevitable conclusion, I'm thinking of offering my services to Steven Spielberg. Because over the last ten days, I've been putting in an Oscar-winning performance following our falling-out over her invitation to allow Paul to stay at her house. But if the only way I can safeguard her is by pretending to regret my outburst, then I've no choice but to keep my mouth shut. If there was another confrontation, I fear she'd again choose him over me.

Neither Paul nor I have made reference to our fight, but it hangs so heavy in the air it sticks to my clothes like glue. He's under no illusion how deep my hatred for him runs. He's a malignant presence, a cancerous tumour I need to remove before it becomes terminal.

I'm not exaggerating when I say he's a permanent feature in her life now. The fox in the henhouse slinks from room to room, leaving behind him the stench of gloss paint and wallpaper paste. He might as well be pissing up the walls to mark his territory. He finished redecorating the landing yesterday, and this afternoon, he announced his next projects will be the lounge and dining room.

Of course she readily agreed when he told her he wants to paper a feature wall and affix wood panelling to another. But it's far too contemporary for someone her age and I'm sure it's more his taste than hers. And wasn't the point of doing all this work to make the house feel more like hers than the previous owners? I can only hope that he can't keep this pretence up forever and that I'm here when he reveals his true colours.

After May and June's relentless heatwave, at least July is behaving as a British summer should. I look up to the sky, grateful the morning has begun with darkening clouds. At least I won't be sweating quite so much when I start cleaning her house after dropping Oscar back to his owner. I politely decline Walter's offer of a cold glass of fruit squash as I'd rather not leave Paul alone with her any longer than necessary. He already has her to himself in the evenings and God only knows what lies he's been poisoning her fragile mind with.

I arrive at her house but the door is locked, which is unusual because Paul's van is here. I slip my key into the lock but it won't turn. I try again, twisting it at all angles, but it absolutely won't budge. I make my way to the gate to let myself into the back garden but the latch won't open either. Then I realise there's a new lock fixed to it that requires a key.

I've been slow to catch on, haven't I? Paul has changed the bloody locks without telling me.

Stay calm, I tell myself, a mantra I'm repeating many times daily. I return to the front door and go to press the bell, but it's missing. It's been replaced by an electronic device with a built-in camera enabling you to see who is on your doorstep by phone. I hold back from pounding the glass with my fists. Instead, I remind myself he will win again if I allow emotion to cloud my judgement. After a time, she opens the door a crack.

'Connie,' she begins. 'Paul said you weren't coming today.'

That's news to me. 'It's cleaning day, isn't it?' I reply, and I don't wait until she invites me in. I push past her and pretend as if everything is normal and that I haven't just been locked out of her house.

Passing through the hallway, I notice that about half the framed photographs that were positioned on the console table have vanished. Her wedding pictures are no longer there, along with the two photos of me I put there myself.

She follows me as I remove the caddy of cleaning products I keep under the sink. 'What's happened to the front door?' I ask breezily. 'My key isn't working.'

'Paul installed new locks for me.'

'That's good of him,' I reply through gritted teeth. 'Why did he do that?'

'Because I was frightened when he told me there've been burglaries in the village and they've been targeting pensioners. He said new locks would make the house safer.'

'Well, aren't we lucky to have him around?' The sarcasm is lost on her. 'And the camera on the door?'

'It's amazing, isn't it? Paul can use his phone to see who it is every time someone comes.'

Paul's voice comes from behind me so suddenly, I jump out of my skin.

'You never know who might find their way into your house when your back is turned,' he says pointedly. He is clad in just a towel around his waist. His hair is wet and he is in no hurry to cover himself up. I force myself not to give him the physical attention he craves. 'Gwenny, I thought from now on only I was going to answer the door?'

'Sorry, I must have forgotten.'

'We've got to be careful, haven't we?' He looks me in the eye. 'There are a lot of people out there who don't have your best interests at heart.'

I ignore the jibe. 'Where do you keep the spare keys?' I ask.

'We don't have any,' Paul says. 'I need to get some cut.'

'I'm going into town later; I'll get it done and save you the trouble.'

'An ordinary locksmith can't supply them. They need to be custom-made by specialists.'

If I bite my tongue any harder, I'm going to sever it. I don't believe him for a second.

'Well, where do you want me to start today?' I direct to her. 'Upstairs or downstairs—?'

'You'll be wasting your time,' Paul interrupts. 'Sanding the floorboards threw up a lot of dust and it'll only get covered again when I finish the rest tomorrow.'

'I thought you hated bare floorboards, Mum? You said they reminded you of your childhood, when your parents couldn't afford to buy carpets.'

'Did I?'

'Well, it's lovely to see you, as ever, but we're heading out soon,' Paul says. 'And you don't have a key to lock up after you.'

I am not budging.

'It's okay,' I say. 'I'll take my time and stay until you return. Best to have someone here with all those burglaries going on, isn't it? Where did you say you were going, Mum?'

'The garden centre for brunch,' she says and turns to Paul. 'That's right, isn't it? I've never had brunch there before.'

She has. I've taken her before. And for a moment, I'm jealous that he gets to spend the morning with her and I don't. But there's an opportunity here, isn't there?

'Well, have a lovely time,' I say. 'Bring me back a doggie bag.'

Paul returns upstairs to change into his clothes, and soon after, when his van pulls off the drive and I'm alone, I get to work. Not cleaning, but snooping. His suitcases are stacked up in the corner of his room. I look inside but they're all empty. Does he really need to hang everything up if he's only staying for a fortnight like he claims? All he wears are shorts and T-shirts anyway. I move to his chest of drawers instead, but that's empty too. It's the same with the wardrobe. There is nothing inside the bathroom cabinet either. I'm confused. What game is he playing now?

It's then when the nauseous feeling that so frequently appears when I think of him returns. I walk hesitantly towards her room and slide open the mirrored wardrobe doors. Three-quarters of her rails are filled with *his* clothes. He's also filled most of the drawers. Many of her clothes have been stuffed inside black bin bags in the corner of the room. Inside her en-suite, his electric razor and toothbrush are plugged in and charging. I look to the bed. It's made, but both pillows have head indentations.

I need a timeout here to unpack what I'm seeing. This can't mean what I think it means, can it? I want to come up with other explanations, but there is only one. They are sleeping together. An eighty-two-year-old woman and a conman half her age. Oh dear God.

My legs threaten to buckle beneath me so I sit on the side of the bed.

There's a brand-new Samsung mobile phone on her side. It's the first time I've seen it and I assume it's the one he gave her. I switch it on. He hasn't put a code on it, probably because she's unlikely to remember it. I scroll through it. They have been texting one another: dozens and dozens of messages, beginning on the day they returned from Clacton-on-Sea. Paul tells her what a wonderful time he had, how he wishes they could have stayed away for longer and how he'll never forget their first kiss by the beach.

I realise now that even though he wasn't physically here for almost a week, they were still in regular contact. She texted him the moment I left the house for my osteopath appointment, to ask him over.

I read on. Paul confesses to how deeply he is falling for her, how special she is to him, how much he misses her. While her replies are less frequent and littered with spelling errors and very few spaces, I get the gist. She feels the same as him.

I'm just as shocked at this clandestine relationship as I am that she knows how to send a message until I see his handwritten instructions written in marker pen on the back of the phone. There have been many long calls between them too, all incoming and some lasting way into the night. She must have been talking to him while I thought she was asleep. She can't have been swallowing the sleeping tablets I was giving her.

It's like a car crash that I can't take my eyes off. My heart sinks when I read her telling him that she loves him too. He begs her to keep their relationship a secret from me, explaining that I can never understand what they have together and that I will try to keep them apart. He reminds her I've already tried to do it once by calling the police during their trip to Clacton-on-Sea, and he fears that I'll put her in a home if I find out about them. She agrees not to say anything.

When there are no more messages left to read, I return to his bedside cabinet – I hate the fact I'm even calling it *his* – but there's nothing personal here, no wallet, no credit cards, no bills, no receipts, nothing. I search the clothes in his wardrobe but he's been careful not to leave anything in the pockets. It's as if he only exists on his own terms.

And then I'm struck by something. Despite what his messages say about wanting to keep their relationship a secret, he's done little to hide this evidence. And I realise Paul has left all this for me to find on purpose. If he hadn't, his clothes would be kept in the spare room and her phone hidden. He wants me to know they're together. He is taunting me because he believes there's not a damn thing I can do to stop him.

He doesn't know me very well. Because I won't give in just like that.

CHAPTER 20

SARAH COGGINS, SOCIAL WORKER

I assume the woman poking her head around the café door is Connie. I sense her anxiety from all the way across the room. Her head slowly swivels, trying to locate someone she has only ever spoken to by phone. I wave my hand and she makes her way towards me.

'Hi, I'm Sarah,' I begin, rising from my seat and offering my hand to shake hers.

'It's nice to meet you,' she replies, and hangs her handbag over the back of the other chair. I have a pot of tea and two cups waiting for us and I begin to pour. I unapologetically drop three sugar cubes into mine. Our days are long, our weeks endless and our staff is short. I need a sugar rush whenever the opportunity arises.

I feel her gaze boring through my skull, trying to pre-empt what I'm going to tell her. There are some parts of my job that I enjoy, and some, like this afternoon, that I'm not so keen on. Meeting the needs of everyone in this job is impossible. So I've become used to being let down and letting other people down.

I recall my conversation with Connie eight days ago, when she first called the office in a highly emotional state. Safeguarding vulnerable people in the community is one of my many roles and her elderly mother's dementia potentially fell into that category. I made notes as she recalled how a stranger had befriended Gwen and, in a very short space of time, had insinuated himself into her everyday life. Connie was also convinced they were in a sexual relationship.

'I'm really worried about her,' she wept. 'I am sure that he's manipulating her, coercing her to lie to me and trying to come between us. The police can't do anything because he hasn't broken the law, and when I went to see her doctor to tell him I thought Mum was becoming a danger to herself, he told me she'd withdrawn her consent for him to talk to me and replaced me with Paul. However, he said he'd already contacted social services as a potential safeguarding issue.'

I've been trained to be non-judgemental when a case like this first comes to my attention. It's not my job to form an opinion until I meet everyone involved, and only then will I achieve an informed view. At least that's what I'm supposed to do, in theory. Because in practice, it can be easier said than done. I'm human, after all. If someone tells me a forty-two-year-old man is sleeping with someone almost double his age and with dementia, then of course I'm going to question his motives.

Today, I place my notebook on the table and flick through it until I find the right pages.

'As you're aware, earlier this week I visited Gwen's house unannounced and I had a long conversation with her on her own, away from Paul Michael,' I begin. 'I asked some quite personal questions that she was willing to answer.' I remember getting the impression she was keen to share her relationship with someone, as she couldn't stop smiling. 'She admitted that she and Paul were "courting" but apparently they chose not to tell you because they didn't think you'd approve.'

'Of course I wouldn't!' says Connie. 'Would you?'

I recall how Gwen's face lit up every time she spoke of Paul, how she explained that he made her feel like a young woman again and not 'old and worthless'.

'Who did you say sent you to check up on me?' Gwen asked me.

'I can only tell you it was someone who was concerned for your welfare.'

'But I'm perfectly fine, apart from the obvious. And now, when the bad days appear, Paul helps to make them go away.'

'And do you have a lot of bad days?'

'I'm in my eighties and I'm being driven by this thing,' she smiled as she tapped her head with her finger. 'So what do you think?'

'Can you tell me a little about your family?'

'There is none. My husband died and we didn't have any children.'

I frowned. 'None at all?'

'Oh, Connie,' she corrected herself. 'Yes, Connie. Of course.'

'And do you see her very often?'

'I don't know if I do. I think I might.'

'Do you understand why people might be concerned about you?'

She nodded. 'When I lost Bill, it didn't cross my mind for a moment that anyone else would show any interest in me again. All I knew was that my *problem* was going to slowly eat away at me until . . .' She didn't finish her sentence. 'But then I met Paul and he's given me a new lease of life.'

I hold back from mentioning any of this to Connie, as it would be breaking privacy regulations. Instead, I look to her and quietly take a deep breath. This is the part she's not going to like. 'To safe-guard someone, we have to be sure abuse or neglect has occurred,'

I continue. 'And from what I observed, Gwen doesn't fall into any of the "at risk" categories she would need to be in.' Connie rises in her seat.

'Of course she is!' she protests. 'She's got bloody dementia! How much more at risk could she be?'

I continue regardless. 'She is nourished, her hygienic needs are being met and she does not appear distressed. You admitted in our call that you have no evidence to suggest she's being taken advantage of financially, and that there are no signs of physical, sexual or psychological abuse or coercive control. Even though Gwen is quite rightly considered vulnerable, she's presently still capable of making her own decisions, and we have to respect she has the right to make choices, even poor ones. Taking all of that information into account, it makes my powers to intervene very limited.'

Connie's face has collapsed. This is not what she wanted to hear. No child with an elderly parent would. I really feel for her.

But she isn't ready to give up. 'You must have caught her on a good day,' she insists. 'Go and visit her again, please. She's not like that all the time. She holds her glasses case to her ear because she thinks it's her phone. I've found her hiding loaves of bread in the greenhouse. Many times I've caught her in tears and she never knows why. And I told you she has gone missing several times before, didn't I?' She leans forward. 'I read up about it online. A court can issue an "occupation order" to stop Paul living in that house. Who do I speak to to organise one of those?'

'They will only grant it if he is a risk to her.'

'But he is. You spoke to him too, yes?'

'I did.'

'You must have seen through his bullshit.'

'I'm not allowed to go into detail about our conversation.'

I remember the last thing Paul said to me when I spoke to him alone. 'Age is nothing but a number and I don't expect everyone to understand that. Gwenny and I are always aware that because of her illness, our happiness is against the clock. So we make the most of every minute. Why would anyone begrudge us that?'

I've done this job for close to seventeen years, so I believe I can read people well. And I remember thinking how well rehearsed his answer was, as if he had expected someone like me to appear unannounced one day on his doorstep. 'Gwen's age isn't what concerns us,' I told him. 'I have to be sure that no one is taking advantage of her condition.'

'Do you think I'm after her money?' he asked, then shook his head and laughed. He removed a phone from his pocket, opened a banking app and showed me the balance. It contained more than £460,000. 'I pay my own way,' he boasted. 'I don't need Gwenny's money.'

Satisfied as I could be but still far from feeling comfortable, I was escorted out by both him and Gwen, who saw me off with a wave. But just as the door began to close, I overheard Gwen ask him, 'Was I alright?' I hesitated, the hairs on the back of my neck prickling.

But by law, Gwen's words still weren't enough for me to take this any further. It's what my supervisor reaffirmed later that afternoon. I don't mention this to Connie.

She looks me dead in the eye. 'So what happens now?'

'Well, I'm afraid nothing happens now,' I say. 'There is no evidence to suggest any wrongdoing. And until there is, my hands are tied. I'm very sorry this isn't what you want to hear.'

Connie slumps back in her chair.

'But I'm losing her, Sarah,' she says. 'I was prepared for the dementia to take away a little bit more of her every day. But I didn't expect another person to rob me of her.'

I wish I could help her. I wish I had seen something concrete that concerned me enough to take this further through the correct channels. But I didn't. All I saw was a happy, elderly woman making the most of her declining years in the face of extreme adversity.

'What about when I go back to Italy for a few weeks?' Connie asks. 'I found out yesterday that Paul cancelled the care worker agency I'd organised to visit her each day, claiming he'll be looking after her. Some of the neighbours have promised to look out for her. What else can I do?'

'You're free to give them my direct line if that might put your mind at rest.'

'Thank you,' she says. 'Do you think I'm wrong to be worried? Is this all in my head?'

I choose my words carefully. 'Your mum is very fortunate to have someone looking out for her like you are. I see many, many people like Gwen who don't have anyone on their side. You might not believe this, but she is one of the fortunate ones.'

I rise to my feet but Connie remains where she is, visibly deflated. We say our goodbyes and, as I cross the road outside, I turn to look over my shoulder and catch her through the window. Her head is in her hands.

I desperately hope Connie is wrong and that Paul can be trusted to care for her mum. But my gut instinct tells me she has every reason to be worried. And I hate my job for allowing me to only act on the facts.

CHAPTER 21

CONNIE

'They're in a relationship,' I tell Mary. 'He has moved his stuff into her bedroom. His clothes, his toiletries. I'm at my wits' end. I don't know what to do.'

Our neighbour is literally my last hope. The tears stream down my face as I stand on her doorstep waiting to be asked to come inside. But the invitation doesn't arrive. Mary is normally friendly, but no more than one rung past a pleasant acquaintance. But today, there's a coolness about her. She's curt when she speaks.

'So it was you who reported them to social services?' she asks.

I think I've misheard. How could she know about that? 'Pardon me?'

'Paul told us someone had been sent to interrogate them. And that it was probably you.'

'Well, yes . . . Wait, so you know about him and Mum?'

Mary's face gives her away. Of course she already knows this. Nothing happens in this village without her then telling everyone about it.

'It was a very distressing experience for Gwen,' she says. 'I saw how scared she was.'

'When?' I say.

'Gwen and Paul dropped by soon after it happened,' Mary continues. 'The poor woman was petrified social services were going to take her away and put her in a home. She couldn't sleep properly.'

I shake my head. 'No one wants to take her from her home. Paul may just have put that idea in her head because that's what he does, he manipulates people.'

She and Paul have yet to acknowledge the visit in the thirteen days since it happened. I'd expected it to have slipped out by now, from her though, not him. He's too clever to make mistakes.

'Paul brought your mum around here because he knows I don't judge,' Mary says. I hold back a snort of laughter. 'He hoped I could convince her she was safe while they were together.'

'Which of course you told him was wrong because they shouldn't be together.'

'I did no such thing. What people do behind closed doors is their own business.'

'It's disgusting!' I say. 'You must see that.'

'Like I say, I'm not one to judge.'

'But that's precisely what you're doing to me. Only, you're judging me for wanting to protect Mum.'

She folds her arms and I have to stop myself from grabbing her shoulders and shaking some sense into her. It would do no good. Paul has launched his charm offensive and Mary has bought into it. At home his behaviour has been even worse. He has been finding new, subtle ways of creating more distance between her and me. He now does their shopping and washing, he cooks her meals and he's organised a weekly cleaner, all of which gives me fewer reasons to be at her house. My only role in her life now is as a daughter. And lately, when I appear at her door, I don't get to see her. He claims

97

they're just about to go out somewhere or that she is napping. On occasions, he doesn't even bother to answer in person and we speak only through the doorbell camera.

'What other lies has Paul been telling you?' I ask Mary.

'I don't like to gossip.'

Like hell you don't, I think. I try a different approach: flattery, like Paul has obviously used on her.

'Mary, people around here listen to what you have to say and I know Mum does too,' I persist. 'Do you think you could sit her down and talk to her on her own? This so-called relationship is a disaster waiting to happen, and I know deep down you can see that.'

Mary shakes her head firmly. 'I don't think so, no.'

'But it's not right, is it? He can't be trusted.'

She raises an eyebrow. 'Paul mentioned that before he moved in, you were apparently sedating her with sleeping tablets.'

I tense up. 'What?'

'He told me he found several packets of prescription tablets in your name in the house. He can only assume you were giving them to Gwen.'

Damn it. I thought I'd removed them all but I must have left one behind. I must defend myself. 'They were to keep her safe. You know that she goes wandering at night. What else has he told you?'

'He said he once caught you yelling at Gwen for falling over. She was on the floor, cowering, while you screamed in her face.'

'That's not true.'

'I've seen the video.'

'What video?'

'Paul took it shortly before he had to intervene.'

Now I remember him slipping the phone back in his pocket before he offered to help pick her up. I didn't think for one moment that he'd been recording us. 'She lost her balance and fell,' I protest. 'I was trying to help her back up when she attacked me.'

'He says that you have a grudge against him because he has a connection with Gwen and not you. That you're trying to sabotage their relationship.'

'Mary, please listen to yourself. Are you really taking his word over mine?'

'The evidence speaks for itself, doesn't it? He and Gwen made several attempts to tell you they were going on a trip to Clacton-on-Sea, but you told the police he'd kidnapped her.'

'That's not evidence!'

'What about her cash cards? Paul says you've been spending it in fancy supermarkets and on massages.'

'Well yes, but not in the way he's making it out. It was for one meal, that *he ate*. It wasn't a massage, it was to see an osteopath . . . Oh, it doesn't matter. He's twisting the truth to suit himself.'

'Paul says there have been large amounts withdrawn in the last few days . . . hundreds of pounds at a time.'

I'm close to shouting my responses now, as she just isn't listening. 'Well not by me.'

'He showed me the statements on his phone. Clothes bought at a woman's boutique in town, spa day vouchers, even a car purchased in Italy in somewhere called . . . what was it now . . . Mongibello.'

'That place doesn't even exist! He's making this all up and you're falling for it!'

'How could you do that, Connie?'

Mary's husband Joe appears behind her at the kitchen door. As soon as he spots me, he backs away, hoping not to have been seen.

I shake my head, exasperated. 'And you, Joe. I thought better of you,' I say and turn to leave. 'You're mugs.'

My hands are trembling as I head back up the street, digesting all I've been accused of. Paul has deliberately targeted the village gossip in the hope – or expectation – that she has spread this far and wide. What must everyone else think of me? Clearly it's not enough for him to only separate us, because now he wants to ostracise me from my own community. And why does no one but me care that they're in a relationship? Has the world become so damn woke that people are too scared to stand up and say what's right and wrong?

I open the banking app on my phone and try to log in to the account in question, to see if there's any truth at all in what Paul's told Mary. However, each of my three attempts fail and it locks me out for twenty-four hours. I make my way to the supermarket and slip Gwen's card in the cash machine to check the balance, but the display screen tells me it won't be returning my card and to 'contact my service provider for further assistance'.

This is Paul's doing. He has cut off all my access to her accounts.

Once again, he has the upper hand. And I have never felt more alone.

CHAPTER 22

CONNIE

It's approaching 3.45 a.m. and I'm wide awake again. After much tossing and turning, I must have finally drifted off in the early hours, only to wake myself up mid-dream. It was another one about Paul.

Tonight, he was walking across the fields behind her house, his arm entwined around 'Gwenny'. Only she didn't look as she does now, but back to how she was in the old photographs she's shown me – perfectly primped, stylish and eye-catching. He turned his head to wink at me and I began shouting 'Mum! Mum!' as if to warn her she was making a terrible mistake. But then she started dancing, twirling around in circles, holding the hem of her skirt up to her knees and laughing so joyously in a way I'd never heard her laugh before. I called her name again but she was too caught in the moment to hear me. But when I tried to chase after them, I couldn't move at all. My body was paralysed. Other nights I've dreamed Paul has her locked in the back of his van. She's banging on the rear window with her fists and begging me to free her. The closer I get, the more sunken her eyes and cheeks become and I know that I must reach her before she withers away into dust before my eyes. But as soon as I'm within touching distance of the vehicle, Paul speeds away. It doesn't take Sigmund Freud to interpret what any of this means.

I prop myself up in bed and sip from the glass of last night's wine. It's too late to take a full sleeping tablet, so I break off and swallow only a quarter. And as I wait for it to work its magic, I fixate on Paul again. I've never felt more hatred and more disgust towards anyone in my life than I do towards him. And believe me, I've met some bastards in my time. The worst part of the lies he's been spreading about me throughout the village is that I can't call him out on them or go on the attack, because he'll find a way to use it against me and cut me off from her completely. I'm sure that's part of his long-term strategy anyway. But I don't want to give him an excuse to make it happen sooner rather than later. Especially with me going away soon.

I've put off packing my suitcase, but my leaving date is fast approaching so I'll need to make a start. It's come at the worst possible time, and if there was any way to get out of it, I would. My only hope is that the neighbours who have turned against me will at least keep an eye on her until I return. Even Walter, the one person I thought would be on my side, seems wary of me. Our conversations are briefer, and when I bring up Paul's name, he changes the subject.

Another result of Paul's lies is that my money is tighter than ever. Two of my regular dog walks have cancelled with no explanation, along with half of my ironing clients. Mary and her tittle-tattle are to blame for this, I'm sure. I'm still appalled by how fast she sided with Paul. Why do some women always take the word of a man over another woman? When the truth comes out – and I hope to God it will soon – I want to see that old cow on her knees and begging for my forgiveness.

I yawn so widely my jawbone clicks. The tablet is finally kicking in and it's not long before I nod off. But my second round of sleep doesn't last for long as a persistent banging rouses me. It's only when I hear shouting that I realise someone's at the front door. I slip on my dressing gown and walk cautiously towards it, being careful to leave the chain on when I answer. To my surprise, it's Mary. She appears flustered. I unhook the chain and open the door wide.

'It's your mum,' she pants. 'There's an ambulance at the house.'

'What? Why?'

'I don't know, but you'd better hurry.'

I don't bother to change out of my nightclothes. Instead, I slip on a pair of trainers lying on the doormat and run. A first responder's yellow and green vehicle is parked by the verge and an ambulance is behind it. The lights are on inside her house and I hurry up the path and in through the open door. I hear Mary following me and turn to glare at her before I slam it shut in her face.

'Mum?' I shout as I enter the hall and spot a kitchen full of people. She is sitting on a chair and a rush of relief spreads through me. She's alive. She is wearing the pale yellow nightie I bought her from M&S for Christmas, but only one slipper.

I last saw her this afternoon and she seemed perfectly alright, alert and chatty. But this version of her is completely different. Her stare is manic. At first I struggle to understand what she's saying until I realise she is hurling abuse at four paramedics. I've never heard her swear like this before, even when she loses her temper with me.

'Mum, what's going on?' I ask just as she changes tack and begins spewing racist bile at the only person of colour in the room, a mixed-heritage paramedic. I'm about to apologise and explain she doesn't normally behave like this when he raises his hand as if to say it doesn't matter, he knows she's not in her right mind. I'm still embarrassed for her though.

Paul stands the furthest away, his shoulders resting casually against the fridge door as if this is all perfectly normal. 'What have you done to her?' I snap.

'And who are you?' asks a paramedic.

'A family friend,' Paul says before I can respond.

'I'm her daughter,' I say, then wheel back on Paul. 'You are nobody. Get out of her house.'

The paramedic ignores whatever is going on between Paul and me. 'Your mum appears to be having a psychotic episode,' he informs me. 'Once we've calmed her down, it might be wise to take her to hospital for a full assessment.'

For the first time, I notice the scratch marks on Paul's forearms and what I think is a bite mark on his hand. He knows I've spotted them. 'They say you only hurt the ones you love,' he says. 'Anyway, she doesn't need the hospital. I can look after her here.'

'With the best will in the world, I'm not sure you can,' the paramedic replies. 'She needs a thorough examination and tests.'

'It's happened before and it passes. If you take her into hospital, it'll only stress her out more—'

'I've never seen her like this,' I interrupt.

'You're not around much these days.'

'Because you don't let me see her!'

'And how long did previous episodes last?' the paramedic continues.

'Not long,' Paul replies vaguely. 'Usually twenty minutes, maybe half an hour. But this one's been going on for a few hours now.'

'Why didn't you call me?' I ask.

'There was no need to get anyone else involved.'

'I'm not just anyone else though, am I? I'm her daughter. I need to know when she's unwell.'

'Have there been any recent changes to her medication?' the paramedic asks me. And to my shame, I can't answer. I no longer know every aspect of her life like I once did. Instead, Paul rattles off a list of what she takes while I feel utterly helpless, watching as they locate a vein in a pencil-thin arm and sedate her with a syringe. Ten long minutes later and she's finally calm.

'What are all these people doing here, Bill?' she asks Paul.

'He isn't Dad,' I say quietly.

'They're here to help you,' Paul says as he kneels down by her side. 'You've had a funny turn.'

'Another one?' she asks.

'Yes, but for this one we needed a little help. You're okay now.'

He cups her face with his hands and draws it towards him. He plants a kiss on her lips and I'm too fixated by the car crash to look away. Eventually, I look to the paramedics to gauge their reaction but they aren't acknowledging it. I suppose they must've seen it all in their job.

'I'm staying here tonight,' I say firmly.

'Not necessary,' Paul replies and shakes his head.

'She's my mum and I know what's best for her. I have a change of clothes upstairs and my toiletries are in the box room.'

'Oh, were they yours?' he asks. 'Sorry, we threw them away when we were having a clear-out. I assumed they were junk.'

'Then I'll bring some new ones over.'

She finally turns to me. 'It's not necessary, Meredith,' she says. 'I just need to sleep.'

That name again. Who is Meredith?

'See, she's fine,' Paul adds.

'A few minutes ago she was hurling abuse at you all,' I remind him. 'She is not fine. She doesn't even know who I am. Are you taking her to hospital?'

'We'd rather not add to her confusion by taking her out of her home, so only if we have to.'

'Then I'll wait here until you make a decision.'

'Stop smothering me!' she says suddenly. I think she meant to shout it, but she's stymied by the drugs.

Paul offers me a fake sympathetic look. 'Probably best you do as you're told,' he says. 'You don't want to make her any more agitated, do you?'

I have no choice but to leave, defeated.

I reach home and know there will be no more sleep for me. Just anger. Absolute, undiluted anger.

CHAPTER 23

CONNIE

I've been dreading today more than anyone can possibly know. If I had any choice in the matter, I'd stay. But I really don't. My suitcase is packed and waiting for me in the hallway. I've booked a taxi to pick me up this afternoon and drop me at the coach station. And all the time I keep asking myself, what kind of person am I to leave her like this? Especially only a week after her episode. The paramedics didn't take her to hospital but her doctor did visit the next day. Neither he nor Paul would tell me what was said.

I have told Paul in no uncertain terms that I'll be coming over to visit her this morning and not to make any plans. Only, now I'm at the door, he informs me through his camera that she is asleep upstairs and that it's probably best I don't disturb her.

'If you don't let me in right now, you'll spend the rest of the day clearing up every window I have smashed to get in there,' I warn him.

He must be watching me, because when I pick up a large stone from the rockery and raise it above my head, he appears at the door and allows me inside. I'm tempted to put the stone to good use and beat him around the head with it.

I do a double take when I reach the top of the stairs and notice that while her bedroom door is open, he has fixed a padlock to it. 'She wanders a lot at night,' Paul says casually, as if locking a pensioner in her own room is normal. 'It's to make sure she doesn't hurt herself.'

'How is that any better than me giving her sleeping tablets?' It's the first time either of us has mentioned the pills. So now he knows for certain that I'm aware of the stories he's spread through the village about me drugging her. 'And besides,' I continue, 'I thought you shared that room?'

'Some nights I need a break.' He shrugs. 'The lock ensures she can't do herself any damage. You've seen how violent she can get.'

Her decline over the last few weeks has taken me by surprise. I assume she's displaying what the experts call the behavioural and psychological symptoms of dementia. There's more shouting, screaming and agitation. And it's awful of me to admit, but I'm a little pleased that Paul is bearing the brunt of these incidents, not me. I'm hoping that any day now, he'll think 'Sod this' and move on to his next sitting duck.

He leaves us, and for the first time in ages, I have her all to myself. 'Mum?' I whisper. She is asleep on her back and snoring gently. I notice for the first time how sunken her cheeks are becoming. That's another sign of dementia's progression. I approach the bed, kick off my trainers and lie next to her, curling up into a foetal position. My hand clasps hers. She is lukewarm and her skin is paper thin. I hate to think what state she might be in when I return.

I've already told her that I'm returning to Italy to work for a few weeks, but I doubt she remembers. I'd hate it if she thought I was abandoning her. Then she unexpectedly opens her eyes and stares at me. 'Connie,' she says and I smile at her, delighted she's recognised me. She smiles back and a warmth spreads across my chest.

'Hi Mum,' I say. 'How are you feeling?'

'Tired,' she says, 'I'm sure after a good night's sleep I'll be right as rain in the morning.'

'It is the morning,' I say.

'Is it really? Oh. Perhaps I should get up. Bill's driving me to Saint-Tropez.'

She pushes herself to the edge of the bed and tries to swing her legs over the side but she doesn't have the strength. I position myself next to her and place an arm behind her back for support. She starts to move again, then stops herself. And I remain where I am, just holding her. Our physical connection chokes me and I push my tongue against the back of my teeth to try and hold the tears back. It doesn't work. I turn my head to look at her and she rests her cheek on my shoulder.

'It'll be okay,' she says softly. 'Everything is going to be okay. It always is in the end.'

For the first time since I became her carer, she is the one caring for me. And I feel every bit as vulnerable as she does. I cling on to her and don't want to let go. But a presence behind us shatters the intimacy.

'Dr Chambers said she needs bed rest,' Paul says.

He makes his way towards her and I reluctantly move to one side. He lifts her legs up, manoeuvres her body around and tucks her under the duvet with the efficiency of someone who has done this many times before. Defiant, I remain where I am until he has left and she closes her eyes again and begins to drift away. I lean over to kiss her on the forehead, stroke her hair and tell her that I love her.

'Don't forget to let Meredith know that I have Tom,' she whispers, eyes still shut.

Once again, I have no idea who she's referring to. 'Who are Tom and Meredith?' I ask.

Her fingers move until they connect with my sleeve. She tugs it. 'Will you do that for me? It's important she knows.'

'Of course,' I say.

I might be mistaken but it sounds like she's just given a short, sharp laugh. Sleep follows quickly and I stroke her hair again before I'm back on my feet.

The window catches my attention. There's something different about it. Only when I move closer do I realise that Paul has affixed a reflective film across it. I can see out, but I assume no one outside can see in. I head downstairs with him following behind me and realise every room that can be overlooked by the street or by a neighbour's home has been sealed from the view of the outside world. I think I want to be sick.

'Why have you done this?' I ask.

'For security.'

'You mean to stop anyone from seeing what you're up to.'

Paul shakes his head in mock offence. 'Where do you get your suspicious nature from? It's certainly not from Gwenny.'

'I didn't have one until you came along.'

'And remind me, how long did you say you'll be in Italy for?'

'Not long,' I reply. 'But the neighbours will be checking in on Mum regularly.'

'How about your social worker friend? Will she be coming back?'

He hasn't mentioned that visit before but I don't see the point in denying I reported him. 'I have her number,' I say. 'She takes the safeguarding of vulnerable people seriously, as do her colleagues.'

'Be assured, you're leaving her in very safe hands.'

I wish I could sound more authoritative, more threatening, but my voice betrays me and cracks mid-reply. 'If there is any decency in you whatsoever, you will look after her,' I say. 'Just be kind to her.'

'You can trust me,' he says, but his disingenuous smile is designed to unsettle me. This man is as far from trustworthy as you can get, and the only two people who know it are him and me.

CHAPTER 24

SIX WEEKS LATER – REVEREND EDDIE EDWARDS

I'm in the kitchen at the back of the church drying the dishes Mrs Kelly washes when my mobile phone rings. I flip open the leather case and the name 'Joe Lawson – Neighbourhood Watch' appears. I answer immediately, but I instinctively know what he's going to tell me.

'She's back, isn't she?' I say first.

'There's a taxi dropping her off outside the bungalow right now.'

I imagine Joe has spent the last few weeks in his lounge, perched by the window, curtains twitching, preparing for this moment. 'Okay,' I say. 'I'm only at the church, so I can be there in a couple of minutes.'

'Do you want me to delay her?'

'Only if she leaves the house and I'm not there. I'm setting off now.'

I apologise to Mrs Kelly and ask her to finish clearing the detritus from the coffee morning, then I hurry through the church grounds, September's leaf fall crunching underfoot. I really hope I can reach Connie's bungalow before she sets off for Gwen's. I half walk, half jog, and in my head I'm running through what I'm going to say. This has been my vocation for the best part of thirty years and there's not much I haven't yet encountered, but these circumstances have added complications I've never experienced before.

I catch Connie just in time. She's exiting her house and locking the front door. I know where she's headed. She is casually dressed and her hair is tied up over her head. She looks pale and drained and I can only assume the flight back from Italy wasn't an entirely pleasant experience.

'Hi Connie, have you just got back?' I ask.

'Hello Reverend Eddie,' she replies, surprised to see me. 'Yes, I landed a few hours ago.'

'And are you well? How was Italy?'

'It was busy, thanks. Look, I don't mean to be rude, but I'm just about to visit Mum . . .'

'That's why I'm here. Do you have a moment?'

She cocks her head to one side and stares at me, as if trying to read me. 'Why, what's happened?'

'Could we perhaps go inside?'

She hesitates. She must know I'm not here without a reason. We make our way into her lounge but she doesn't offer me a seat.

'I'm so sorry to be the one to tell you this, Connie, but I'm afraid Gwen died while you were away.'

She holds a hand up to her mouth and steadies herself against the arm of the chair. I move towards her to offer my support but she holds her palm out in front of her. 'What . . . what happened?'

'It was an accident. It appears that Gwen had a fall down the stairs one evening and hit her head on the radiator.'

'Wh . . . when?'

'About a fortnight after you left.' She shakes her head. 'A few of us tried calling the number you left us, but it doesn't appear to work.'

'Was she in pain?' she asks.

'I don't think so. From what we've been told, Paul found her in the morning and called an ambulance.'

'The morning? You mean she was there all night? Where the hell was he?'

'I don't know.'

'He was supposed to be looking after her.'

Within a heartbeat, Connie's mood has shifted from shock and grief to anger. She moves quickly to the front door and is out of the house before I can stop her. Now I'm trying to catch up with her in the street, calling her name and asking her to slow down. But she either can't hear me or is deliberately ignoring me.

'I don't think this is a good idea,' I call to her, aware of how weak it sounds, but I know what's ahead and she doesn't. 'Connie, please, just give me a minute.' She doesn't. She only stops when she reaches Gwen's house.

The curtains are closed and there are no vehicles on the drive-way. There's a prolonged silence while I await the sound of the penny dropping. It's a painful interlude. Eventually she spots what the rest of us have been seeing every day since it first appeared.

A For Sale signboard in Gwen's front garden.

CHAPTER 25

CONNIE

I'm like a cartoon character when I double-take the For Sale sign hammered into the lawn. All I'm missing are stalks attached to my eyes.

'I wanted to warn you before you saw it for yourself,' apologises Reverend Eddie.

He continues talking but I've tuned him out. I'm trying to make sense of what I'm looking at. 'Who put Mum's house up for sale?' I ask, eventually.

'We don't know for sure, we can only assume it was Paul.'

'But he can't do that. It's not his house.'

'Apparently his name was added to the deeds of the property some weeks ago by way of a gift.'

A familiar rage flares up inside me as I make my way to the front door and turn the handle. It's locked. I bang on it with my fists. 'Paul!' I yell. 'Paul! Open this fucking door right now!'

'Connie,' pleads the reverend, but the look I shoot him warns him off. I'm in no mood to be placated.

I bang again a few more times but there's no answer, and my attention turns to the doorbell with the camera in it. I press the button several times and push my face up close to it but he doesn't respond. My gut tells me that wherever he is, he's watching me. So for his benefit, I mouth 'You won't get away with this' into the lens.

I peer through the windows but the one-way film he attached to the inside means I only catch my own haunted reflection. I move around the side of the house to the gate that leads into the back garden. The padlock he fitted remains attached and he never gave me a key. But that's not going to stop me. I pick up the same rock I wanted to hit Paul with weeks ago and use it to smash the lock with a thwack.

'Oh, Connie, I don't think you should be doing that,' Reverend Eddie says nervously.

'It's my house,' I snarl.

It takes five more blows before it snaps in two and falls to the ground. I push the gate open and head towards the back door of the house, but that's also locked. There's no film on these windows but all the curtains are shut and the windows are closed.

I turn and see the vicar has been joined by Joe, Mary, Zainab and Walter. The beat from Mary's jungle drums has travelled quickly.

'Where the hell is Paul?' I direct to them all.

'We haven't seen him since a few days after Gwen died,' Mary says.

'His van hasn't been here either, but I've been looking out for it,' Joe adds keenly.

Think, think, think. But I don't know what to do next or where to start. Instinctively, I reach into my pocket for my cigarette packet but it's not there. I've left them in my handbag in the bungalow. It only adds to my anger.

'He's killed her,' I say adamantly. 'I am telling you, Paul has killed my mum. You were all supposed to be looking out for her.'

'It was an accident,' Mary says. 'She fell.'

'And you know that for sure do you, Mary?' I fume. 'Were you there? Were you standing at the bottom of the stairs when she hit her head? Because if you weren't, then yet again, you're taking Paul's word for it.' She takes a step back and clings on to Joe's arm. She knows she backed the wrong horse. She's scared of me and I like it. It's the only bit of control I have over anything right now. 'Just why do you keep taking Paul's side?' I continue. 'Do you have a little thing for him yourself? Now that you know he's into pensioners, do you hope that when Joe snuffs it, Paul might make a move on you?'

'Connie,' Walter interjects, 'I know you're in shock, but I don't think—'

'No,' I say with force. 'You don't get to have an opinion, Walter. Any one of you who defended that bastard does not get to have an opinion.'

Now it's Reverend Eddie's turn to feel the brunt of my rage. 'How the hell was Paul able to put the house on the market? It isn't his to sell. And probate can take months.'

'This is beyond my area of expertise.'

I shake my head. 'You're all useless,' I mutter. 'You told me you'd keep an eye on her. You promised.'

I take a photo of the sign so I can contact the estate agency and tell them they've made a mistake and order them to take it off the market.

My thoughts are bouncing from one invisible wall to the next. I suddenly realise that I haven't given a thought to where she is now. 'Where's Mum's body?' I ask. 'Which funeral director is she with?' I turn to Reverend Eddie again. 'You must have their details, because I'll need to start planning her service.'

Mary and Joe look to one another and then at the reverend.

'What?' I ask.

Reverend Eddie briefly loses eye contact with me.

'What aren't you telling me?' I continue.

'I'm afraid the funeral has already taken place, Connie,' he says.

My jaw drops. 'What? When?'

'Three weeks ago.'

'Why didn't you wait until I got back? I told you I was only going to be in Italy for a few weeks.'

'We all tried calling you,' says Joe, 'But we could never get—'

'I don't believe this. You let Paul talk you into organising her funeral? What's wrong with you all?' I shake my head and begin pacing up and down.

'I didn't organise the ceremony,' Reverend Eddie says. 'And Gwen wasn't buried in the village churchyard.'

'But you told her she could be, in the plot next to Dad's? Remember? We had that conversation months ago. It's bought and paid for. That's where she wanted to be.'

'And if I'd had anything to do with it, I'd have ensured her final wishes were adhered to. But I never got the call. It was only when I phoned around the funeral directors myself to see where her body had been taken that I discovered the ceremony had been and gone. It was at a parish in Oxfordshire.'

I look to Joe and Mary. 'Oxfordshire? Why?'

'I don't know, sorry,' says Joe.

'Who went?'

'There was no ceremony or attendees,' Reverend Eddie says. 'And I'm afraid she was buried in an unmarked grave.'

Every possible response I have to this information becomes lodged in my throat. I open my mouth, but for a moment, I can't get a single word out. It wasn't enough for Paul to come between us when she was alive; now, even after her death, he has to keep

117

us apart. And to bury her in an unmarked grave? That's beyond spiteful.

I'm too angry to cry but I need to take my fury out on something. So I storm to the front of the house and begin trying to pull the For Sale sign out from the ground. It's buried deep in the lawn and I almost lose my footing. It takes several more attempts before finally it's out. It's heavy but I find the strength to lift it above my head and start smashing it against the concrete block driveway. After half a dozen attempts, it finally separates into two pieces. More of the neighbours have gathered in their gardens and at their windows to watch the spectacle. They're all either pitying me or they think I've lost the plot. And I just don't care.

The mixture of exertion and frenzy is enough to bring my voice back. 'Why didn't any of you listen to me when I told you Paul couldn't be trusted?' I rage.

I direct my attention towards Reverend Eddie again. 'How can a man my mother barely knows be allowed to bury her and put her house up for sale and no one steps in and calls him out on it? He's not her next of kin, he doesn't have a power of attorney. What he's done is illegal.'

'I'm afraid it's not,' says Eddie.

'Of course it is!'

And just when I think this scenario cannot get any worse, his next sentence makes it so.

'It was legal because Paul and your mother were married.'

CHAPTER 26
CONNIE

Joe is trying but failing to engage me in conversation about the church's harvest festival. He thinks he has a captive audience because he's driving me and it's just him and me in the car. But I'm not really listening. I can't even be bothered to nod or say 'yes' or 'okay'.

He and the other villagers who took Paul's side over mine have been bending over backwards to try and make it up to me, and I've been taking advantage of their guilt. My ironing and dog-walking clients have returned, red-faced and apologetic. I've even gained some more. But I'm not making it easy for them. I know that without Paul around, I'm misdirecting my anger, but I can't stop myself. I'm not ready to offer them my forgiveness.

The appointments Joe has already taken me to today have been as frustrating as they have been pointless. My first meeting was with a useless man at the Citizens Advice Bureau. He barely scanned Gwen's will before he dismissed my claim, informing me that it counts for nothing. Because in English law, her spouse automatically receives everything.

That means Paul can drain her bank accounts and bury her in an unmarked grave and it's all perfectly legal. Murder, of course, is not. But how do I prove that's what he committed?

My second appointment was with the estate agent, who refused to take the house off the market because, and I quote, 'no fraud or deception has been committed'. Apparently, three months ago Paul and Gwen submitted an application to jointly own the house and add Paul to the property deeds. So the house automatically belongs to him on her death – married or not and with no need for probate. Arsehole. So now we are on our way to the third and final meeting of the day. And it's my last hope.

Joe's car slows as we approach a three-storey red-brick building. We are here, at Buckinghamshire Register Office. Yesterday, I logged into my account at the General Register Office's website and tracked down their marriage certificate. I couldn't believe the speed of the ceremony. Just two days after I left, they walked up the aisle. It made no sense, because when I last saw her, she was too tired to even leave her bed of an afternoon. Yet somehow, she found the strength to travel to Buckinghamshire and wed. My only remaining chance to correct any of this is if I can prove their marriage took place under duress. There were also two signatures of witnesses, one whose name I couldn't read, but the other was a Derek Reid. The name is familiar and I remember where I've seen it before. He also signed the form as witness for Paul to his name on the deeds of Gwen's property.

I wonder for how long marriage was part of Paul's plan? Was it always the end goal? Because he must've known for a while. You can't just marry at the drop of a hat; you've first got to give twenty-nine days' formal notice in person to the registrar. Did she know what she was doing when she went with him? Or how about later, on the wedding day itself? How did she keep what they had planned a secret from me? Or perhaps she didn't know anything about it? Is it too far-fetched to believe Paul might have married someone else, someone pretending to be her? I made a note of the registrar's name on the marriage certificate and now we're about to meet in person.

Jan Hudson's warm smile as she greets me at the office door suggests that, even after years of officiating, she still sees her job as a privilege and not a chore.

'You married my mum a few weeks ago,' I begin as she offers me a seat. 'Gwendoline Wright. And to a man much younger than her.'

'Yes, I remember,' Jan says.

I turn the screen of my phone around to face her. 'Is that Gwen?' I ask.

'Yes, that's her.'

'And you're absolutely sure this is the woman who was standing in your office?' I hear the desperation in my own voice. 'There's no possibility you could be mixing her up with someone else?'

Jan shakes her head slowly. 'I've a good eye for faces. It was definitely Gwendoline Wright I married that day.'

I rub at my cheeks with the palms of my hands. 'I'm sorry,' I continue. 'I'm just trying to get my head around it all. You know that she had dementia, right?'

'Yes, she and the groom were quite open about it. She even joked that she would probably forget about her wedding day by the next morning. But I did first speak to both separately – and, as per standard questioning, I asked if she felt that she was being coerced. She was adamant she wasn't.'

'Isn't that what all coerced people say?'

'You'd be surprised. But in your mum's case, there was no suggestion she was misunderstanding why she was there. And during the ceremony itself, she remained in very good spirits.'

'But I don't understand how you can allow someone in her condition to marry.'

'We follow the guidance on a case-by-case basis. It states that we can't refuse a marriage just because family and friends believe it to be an unwise decision.'

'And what training do you have for people in my mum's condition?'

'I'm not sure what you mean.'

'I mean what specific training or qualifications do you have to help you determine the level of understanding someone has when they've got a dementia-related illness?'

'Well, none specifically related to dementia, no.'

'Did she stumble over her words at all?'

'Only once, when she called the groom by a different name . . . what was it . . . Will or Bill, I think. But she quickly corrected herself.'

I close my eyes. 'She thought she was marrying Dad again. Didn't you question their age gap?'

'It's not unique.'

'What about why there were no guests, only two witnesses?'

'Again, that's not unusual. Many people have private ceremonies like your mother's and then hold parties afterwards for friends and family.'

'You know that my mum's now dead, don't you?'

Jan's back straightens. 'Um, no, no, I didn't. I'm very sorry to hear that.'

'I don't believe it was an accident. I think – no, I'm convinced – that Paul killed her.'

'Oh, well, I . . .' She's at a loss as to what to say next. I wonder what her guidance suggests about that. But I like her, so I spare her any further awkwardness by readying to leave.

She touches my arm with her hand as I open the door and she says again how sorry she is for my loss. I believe her. I believe all of them when they tell me that. If only their apologies were worth something.

122

CHAPTER 27

CONNIE

The sky is as dark grey as the gates to the cemetery. Both reflect my mood accurately.

Older people are often obsessed with their mortality and death. I pause to think about the number of conversations we must've had about what she wanted from her funeral. While she often got muddled or forgetful over other subjects, she reminded me a hundred times of exactly what she expected. And I have no doubt she told Paul exactly the same thing. Yet still she has ended up here: a cemetery fifty miles and five bus rides away from where she planned to be, and nowhere near to the only man who deserved to call himself her husband. There isn't anyone close by who can just pop down here with a posy of flowers or to tidy the weeds that surround her plot. Paul has treated her death as nonchalantly as he regarded her life.

It's beyond me why he had her buried when it's twice the price of a cremation. But I'm sure he had a reason. A man like him doesn't act without purpose.

It was Reverend Eddie who stopped by at the bungalow to tell me where to find her grave. And now I'm here, I'm shocked by just how different it is to the one in our village. It is vast and impersonal; there are a handful of trees, no quiet nooks to reflect in, just a smattering of benches to sit upon and no church in sight. Dog poo bins are overflowing with plastic bags; crunched-up beer cans and takeaway cartons have been stuffed into hedges, and plastic flower-wrappers skitter across the ground in the breeze. Behind the metal climb-proof railings that fence us in are three tower blocks for high-rise living and a handful of unidentifiable buildings.

I follow a map Reverend Eddie printed out to locate exactly the spot where she's buried. It contains the names of the nearest headstones to her unmarked grave. It takes ten minutes before I spot a fresh mound of earth. Only when I walk towards it do I realise that I'm trampling over three other unmarked graves, and I find myself apologising to her neighbours. The ground is flat, so I assume they've been here longer than her, and I wonder what their stories are. At least six months must pass for the ground to settle before a headstone can be installed, but I can't see it being on Paul's to-do list. I only wish I could afford to buy her one.

'There you are,' I say aloud. I've been carrying a bouquet of flowers for the two-plus hours it's taken me to get here. The heads of the yellow roses – her favourites – are now looking a little worse for wear, having been brushed against bus seats and my coat. Their leaves are crumpled and some of the petals have fallen off. But at least anyone who passes the unnamed person buried here will know that someone cares. I place them upon the mound of earth.

I torture myself by imagining the night she fell. I can see her in my mind's eye, lying in a crumpled, bloodied heap at the bottom of the stairs, disorientated, in pain and begging for help. As clear as day I can picture Paul standing at the top, arms folded and legs apart. He is waiting for the moment her body gives up fighting to stay alive. Only she's a stubborn old gal, and it makes him impatient, so he turns his back on her, returns to their room and closes the door, leaving her there all night to suffer and die alone. He has taken it all. I shake the thoughts away. Paul has robbed me of my present and my future.

I get down on my knees, unbothered by the moist earth dampening my jeans. I sweep some of the larger pebbles away from the mound with my hand and recall how witnessing a journey through dementia is almost as awful for the spectator as it is the victim. I wouldn't wish it upon my worst enemy, with the exception of Paul. I wish nothing but pain and misery upon that shitty excuse for a man. I know that if I don't eventually find a way through this, I'm heading for a lifetime of bitterness. But if I accept things for how they are, then Paul will have won. And I'm not yet ready to admit defeat. If it's the last thing I do, I'm going to expose him for what he is.

'One day, I'll find a way to get you out of here and moved to where you're supposed to be,' I tell her. 'I promise.'

CHAPTER 28
MARY LAWSON, NEIGHBOUR

That poor girl, I think as she walks like a lost soul past our house and towards Gwen's. Her shoulders are stooped, her clothes are un-ironed, and everything she wears is washed-out and colourless. These days she's always puffing on a cigarette like her life depends on it. You can see it in her face, she's broken. Not only is she struggling with her mum's death, but she's also coming to terms with knowing she'll never see a single penny from the estate. You don't expect what is rightfully yours to be snatched away from under your nose. So I feel for her, I really do. I'd be inconsolable if I was her.

But as I was saying to Joe last night, I think Connie might eventually find Gwen's sudden death a blessing of sorts. Vascular dementia and Alzheimer's and all those brain-related diseases are cruel because they're so gradual and drawn-out. However, as Joe pointed out, it doesn't make the way Gwen died any less than awful. I was saying to Reverend Eddie that I can only pray she was unconscious the moment her head hit that radiator so she didn't suffer. Because if she wasn't, well . . . I'm shivering just thinking about it.

Joe and his network of Neighbourhood Watch volunteers haven't seen hide nor hair of Paul for weeks now. Shortly after Gwen died and before Connie came back, Joe spotted his van parked outside the house. The rear doors were wide open and he and another man, older than Paul and wearing a tartan flat cap, were lugging furniture into the back of it from Gwen's. It went back and forth all day. I thought about going over there to give him a piece of my mind, telling him how wicked he was for the way he buried Gwen without any of us knowing. Honestly, we couldn't believe it when the reverend told us what had happened. But Joe begged me not to get involved. 'It's not our business,' he said. And he was right. I already picked the wrong side when I accepted Paul's version of events about Connie – you know, the sleeping tablets, spending Gwen's money, and so on. I don't know what arrangement Gwen and Connie had when it came to her accounts, but I assumed the worst. More fool me.

But it was an easy mistake to make because Paul was such a convincing character. He had a way of making you feel like he trusted you, and only you, with a secret that he wanted to confide in you. He cared about what you thought. And believe me, that's rare these days. Most young people don't really give a tinker's cuss what people of my age have to say. So I fell for his patter and I understand why Gwen did the same, especially in her vulnerable state. It's not in my nature to admit I'm wrong, but I was about Paul and I hope Connie can forgive me.

But no matter what she says, I'm struggling to believe that Paul killed Gwen. I now believe he's devious and heartless, but not a killer. Or perhaps I'd rather believe that than acknowledge I was taken in by a murderer.

We've all been rallying round to support Connie and I'm not going to lie, she's not making it easy for us. I've popped round to the bungalow a few times to check on her and drop off casseroles and hotpots because she's as thin as a rake. But she always keeps me at the door and never lets me inside. 'Perhaps if you put a bit of make-up on and bought a nice dress you might start feeling better about yourself?' I suggested. If looks could kill, the local funeral directors would've picked me up from her doormat. But I can't take it personally. We all handle grief differently, don't we?

Truth be told, I think her conscience might also be weighing heavy on her. If I was Connie, I'd feel as guilty as sin for not being there when her mum needed her the most. It still doesn't really make sense to me why she'd leave the country for the best part of two months if she was so concerned about Paul's influence over Gwen. I know I couldn't. She accused us of neglecting Gwen, of not keeping an eye on her like we promised. But that's unfair, because how were we supposed to do that when Paul never answered the door or let us in to see her?

I can't tell you the number of times we tried to call Connie when she was in Italy after we learned of Gwen's death. Each time and without fail, we got a voice recording saying, 'The number you have dialled has not been recognised.' Walter remembered her talking about being based on the Amalfi Coast, so Joe tried looking for her on the internet but couldn't find any mention of her. I also asked my granddaughter Katie to try and track her down on the Facebook and that other one with all the photographs with funny filters, but she had no luck there. So eventually we had no choice but to give up.

When Connie finally returned, she told us she'd bought a new phone shortly before she left but had given us the wrong number. She said she'd tried calling Gwen herself dozens of times, but it kept going to her voicemail. I said she could've rung us, Walter or Zainab if she was that worried. And if she didn't have our numbers, then she should've called the church. The reverend reckons he never heard a word from her either.

I really hate to say this because I don't want to knock someone when they're down, but I can't help thinking there's more to Connie's vanishing act than meets the eye. When I mentioned it to Joe, he put me in my place. 'You've already done enough damage to the girl by telling half the village what Paul told you,' he snapped. 'Now give her the benefit of the doubt.'

So for once, I listened to him and I've done just that. I suppose, when it comes down to it, the one thing we can all be certain of is that a daughter has lost her mother in the most awful of circumstances. I can only hope she eventually bounces back from it.

CHAPTER 29

CONNIE

I'm obsessed with her house. Each time I walk the neighbours' dogs around the village, I promise myself I won't go anywhere near it because it kills me knowing she's not inside. She'd be either glued to something inane but familiar on the television or recalling an anecdote I'd heard a dozen times before about a party she'd once been to in Monaco where she'd met Princess Margaret. Or the time Bill and a group of friends with posh names like Binky and Bunny and the like chartered a yacht and they sailed around Capri. How much of it is true, I'll never really know. However, my promise lasts as long as my daily vow to stop smoking. So here I am again, standing in the fields behind the home that I should now be living in, lighting up a cigarette and imagining how different our lives could've been had Paul not destroyed them.

The estate agent has replaced the For Sale sign that I tore down in my fit of temper. But I'm not surprised that it's still on the market as it's hugely overpriced. Paul's being greedy if he expects someone to pay that for a few trimmed hedges and a lick of fresh paint.

If I'm not viewing it on the Rightmove app, swiping from right to left, walking myself through each room, one by one, then I'm glaring at the house in person. I must be feeling particularly self-destructive today because this time, I open her side gate and step inside her back garden. I pause to reflect on how, not so long ago, I daydreamed about spending evenings like this drinking wine against the backdrop of colourful late-summer sunsets, perhaps with a dog of my own by my side or a partner to share it all with. I didn't want much, I just wanted *something*.

I move towards the fire pit he dug out. Scattered across the metallic base are blackened pieces of paper. I can't see the remains of any wood or coal, which suggests he wasn't using this to keep warm, just as a means to burn her stuff.

That's what he does, he destroys things. Possessions. People. Lives.

As I reach the house, out of habit, I turn the handle to the back door. Only this time, instead of remaining firmly locked, it opens. I hesitate. Instead of going inside, I edge along the side of the house and peer through a gap in the fence first. I half expect to see Paul's van on the driveway but it's not there. Either the estate agent has forgotten to lock the door after showing a prospective buyer around, or at some point, Paul has returned here without anyone spotting him.

I should leave right now. That would be the sensible thing to do. So why can't I? Instead, tentatively, I enter for the first time since the morning I said goodbye to her. The first thing that strikes me is the kitchen. There's no longer any pots, pans, cutlery or crockery. The hallway is also sparse, and the lounge has been pared back. Photos on the walls have been replaced with generic Ikea-style prints. There is very little furniture and most of the ornaments and trinkets that decorated the dining room sideboard have disappeared, with the exception of the ugly, tall porcelain cat. That thing remains.

I return to the hall and catch sight of the radiator. The air is forced out of my chest. This is where she hit her head when she fell. I crouch to examine the area more closely. There are no traces of blood from her head wound. The patterned carpet that likely absorbed it has been replaced with a plain one and the radiator has been given a fresh lick of white gloss paint. It's as if she neither lived nor died here.

The upstairs bathroom, second bedroom and box room are all empty. But when I reach her bedroom, something stops me from moving inside it. Instead, I remain at the doorway, recalling the last moments I spent here with her, by her side as she slept. I can see her now, waking and trying to assure me that everything was going to be okay. 'It always is in the end,' she said. Now, her words haunt me. Did she know that was the moment our journey together was at an end? Because if I'm being completely honest with myself, a small part of me thinks that subconsciously *I* might have.

I draw in a deep breath and, hidden between the lingering odours of sanded floorboards and paint, I can just about locate notes from her favourite rose-scented perfume. If I could remember the name she wore I'd buy a bottle to spray it around the bungalow whenever I need to feel close to her. But Paul has thrown everything out.

The external padlock he affixed to her bedroom door has gone too, I note. I rub my fingertips across the paintwork and feel four ever-so-slightly raised bumps where Paul has filled in the screw holes. Then I move inside the room and open the wardrobe doors, recalling the last time I did this and the shock of finding Paul's clothes in there. This time it's vacant.

A cold, sudden shiver runs through me. It's the close proximity of breath on my ear as much as the voice that comes with it that makes me scream.

'Welcome home, Connie,' says Paul.

CHAPTER 30

CONNIE

I turn on my heel to face him, then take a quick step backwards, eyeing him up and down. He looks different, but the same, if that makes sense. A more refined version of himself, almost. His rough edges have been smoothed out. He's wearing dark blue fitted jeans with a black leather Gucci belt, a T-shirt with a small logo I don't recognise and a suit jacket. His cropped hair now has a side parting, and resting on his ears are black-rimmed glasses. Either his tanned skin is making his teeth appear brighter or he's had them whitened. This is where her money has gone. He's used it to reinvent himself.

'You know you're trespassing, don't you?' he asks.

'And you know you're a murderer, don't you?' I respond. 'You killed my mum.'

'Only if you mean I killed her with kindness.'

'What happened the night she died?'

'I'm sure you've already been told.'

'I want to hear it from you.'

He sighs, as if recounting the story is delaying him from doing something more valuable with his time. 'At some point in the night, my wife—'

'Don't call her that.'

'*My wife* got out of bed, lost her bearings and her footing, then fell down the stairs. She hit her head on the radiator valve and . . . well . . . you know the rest. It was quite tragic, really.'

'You didn't call for an ambulance until the morning. So where were you?'

'In the spare room. Asleep.'

'Why?'

'She'd had a few rough nights, keeping me awake all hours. I needed a night to myself.'

'Why didn't you lock her in? Isn't that what the padlock was for?'

He shrugs. 'An oversight brought on by sleep deprivation.'

His words say one thing but his tone and body language tell a completely different story. Every word coming out of his mouth is a lie and he wants me to know it.

'I don't believe you,' I say. 'If you didn't push her, you still heard her down there and left her to die.'

'Earplugs,' he says and taps his ears. 'They block out every little noise – even pitiful cries for help.' I shudder at the twinkle in his eye as he says this.

'I bet you were standing over her body with a calculator, totting up how much you were going to make from this marriage before she was even cold.'

'That's quite the imagination you have there, Connie. But you know a lot about making up stories, don't you?'

I don't get a chance to ask him what he means because he turns and makes his way downstairs. I have too much to get off my chest to end this conversation now and let him off the hook. I need to hear him admit his guilt. I hurry after him, and if I move that little bit quicker, I could probably push him down the staircase myself. It's what he deserves. But that's not who I am.

'You didn't give a damn about Mum,' I continue. 'You saw a vulnerable woman you could take advantage of. She was only ever a meal ticket to you.'

'Shouldn't you be offering a grieving widower a little more compassion?'

'You wouldn't know grief if it slapped you across the face.' We reach the lounge and he stops. I look around. 'Where are all her belongings?' I continue. 'Her furniture, her clothes, her photographs?'

'Her clothes are with the Mind shop, any furniture I couldn't sell on eBay is with the British Heart Foundation, and I think there's still a few bin bags somewhere in the utility room with the rest of her stuff that'll make for fire pit kindling. You should be grateful. My clear-out has saved you a lot of work.'

I run my hands through my hair as I shake my head. 'They weren't for you to throw out or give away, and this house isn't yours to sell. She left it to *me* in her will, not you.'

'The will you encouraged her to make when you first moved here,' he says. 'Yes, she mentioned that.'

'This place doesn't belong to you. You stole it.'

He raises a thick eyebrow. 'Stole?' He laughs. 'You can't steal something from someone when it doesn't belong to them. I have every legal right to this house. I was her husband.'

'Marriage means you didn't have to go through the hassle of taking me to court for a slice of her estate. And why couldn't you have waited until I got back from Italy to arrange her funeral and bury her with Dad like she wanted? Dumping her in an unmarked grave with none of her friends there to say goodbye was heartless.'

'Italy,' he repeats slowly. 'Ah yes. The Amalfi Coast, yes? Don't they have telephones there? Couldn't you have called Gwenny while you were away to see how she was?'

'You bought her a new phone, changed her number and didn't give me the new one,' I counter.

'I thought you'd made a note of it when that copper found it on that Post-it? Or when you were snooping around her bedroom and found the phone next to her bed. I assume you scrolled through it and read our texts. It's what I would've done.'

'I'm not you, I wouldn't,' I lie.

'Do you really believe that? You could also have called the neighbours to see how Gwenny was while you were gone. But you didn't do that either. Why was that, now?'

A sour taste creeps slowly up my throat and into my mouth. He knows something, I'm sure of it. However, he doesn't give me time to read between his lines.

'Was the reason behind your complete silence because you weren't actually in Italy?' he continues. And now his eyes are narrowing to match the shift in his tone. 'You don't have an apartment or a car waiting for you over there and you've certainly never been a wedding planner. Because you've never lived or worked in Italy, have you, Connie? You actually spent those missing weeks in a women's prison in Kent, jailed for fraud. And that's why no one could get in touch with you to inform you of Gwen's "accident". It's why you didn't call. You didn't want anyone to know where you really were.'

He knows. Shit, shit, shit, shit, shit. Shit! How could I have been so naive as to think someone as cunning as him might not have researched me? And if he knows about this, what else is he aware of? I've got to retaliate, but I have nothing in my arsenal to fight back with. I'm throwing flowers at a tank.

'I'm going to the police to tell them that you killed her!' I say in desperation.

He shakes his head again. 'No, Connie, you're not.'

'Yes I am, and you can't stop me.'

'I'm not going to try and stop you. But I know it won't be in your best interests.'

My whole body is shaking now, my brain spinning like a Catherine wheel. I don't want to know the answer to my next question, but I've got to ask it, regardless of the risk. I need to know for sure what he knows. 'Why are you so convinced I won't?'

He throws his head back and gives a deep, unsettling laugh. 'Really, Connie?' he asks. 'Are we still playing this game?'

I swallow hard. 'What game?'

'The one where you turn up on the doorstep of an elderly woman with dementia and convince her you're the daughter she never had. Because she and Bill had no children. They *couldn't* have them. But you made her believe they did.'

CHAPTER 31

CONNIE

I shake my head so quickly it's a wonder my neck doesn't break. *Hold your nerve*, I tell myself. *He's bluffing.* 'Rubbish,' I reply. 'Whatever Mum might've told you, you know she wasn't in her right mind. She could say one thing one day and mean the opposite the next.'

'She told me Bill had caught mumps a couple of years after they married, which left him sterile,' Paul continues. 'I dismissed it at first as she wasn't the most reliable source of information. But another time and in one of her more lucid moments, she recalled how you'd suddenly appeared on her doorstep offering to clean her house, and before she knew it, you'd convinced yourself you were her daughter. But what you don't know is that you weren't the only one taking advantage of the situation. Gwenny was playing along with you because she thought you were lonely and she enjoyed your company.'

'No, Gwen was confused, you know that.'

'It's *Gwen* now, is it? Not Mum?'

'She . . . Mum must have forgotten that she adopted me when I was a baby.'

'Why are there no records to prove it? And you must know I've looked far and wide for them.'

'It was an informal adoption,' I counter. 'It was through a friend of a friend.'

'Can you explain why there are no records at all for a Connie Wright with your date of birth? No National Insurance number, no birth certificate, no anything?'

'Dad worked abroad a lot and Mum moved around with him.' My own voice betrays me, the words catching in my throat. But I fight on for survival because that's what Caz trained me to do. 'I was born in Spain.'

'Interestingly, there *are* records for a Rachel Evans who was born on the same date in Queen's Hospital, Romford. The same Rachel Evans who has also been receiving a Carer's Allowance for Gwen at this address and who is the only benefactor of her will. So I can only assume that's you.'

I'm clutching at straws. 'I changed my name,' I say.

Paul lets out an exaggerated sigh and sits on the arm of the chair. 'Rachel, Rachel, Rachel . . . come on now. Do you really think you can lie to me, of all people? We both saw an opportunity in Gwen's predicament and we grabbed at it. You played the long game whereas I prefer the shorter version. But you and I are the same.'

'We are nothing alike,' I protest. 'You killed Gwen. I haven't killed anyone.'

'Instead, you slowly suck the life out of people like a parasite. It's no different to what I do. Just slower, more drawn-out, and many would say crueller. Your end game was the same as mine: to inherit Gwenny's estate. Only I beat you to the punch.'

I open my mouth to protest again but my words let me down. I hate him for it, but he is right. He's got me. Gwen and I are not mother and daughter, we're not related by blood or in any way. We'd never even met before I turned up at her husband's funeral eighteen months ago.

That was the day I decided that her world would be a perfect fit for someone like me.

PART TWO

CHAPTER 32

CONNIE

I don't know why I bother holding the door open when the breeze returns each puff of smoke I blow outside back into the kitchen. I shiver a little, and notice for the first time the leaves on the lawn have browned as October marches on.

I've long dispensed with the vaping pen, as its nicotine rush doesn't last as long as a cigarette's does. But cigarettes are far too pricey these days so I'm rolling my own like I did during my time in prison. It's only when the remainder of the cardboard roach ignites and singes my lips that I realise this one is spent. I flick it on to the grass where it lies among all the others like a fallen soldier.

Before I close the door, I find myself recalling an afternoon Gwen and I spent together soon after I moved to Avringstone. We were window shopping in Buckingham town centre when she suddenly came out with something that made me question if I'd underestimated her level of understanding.

'I've always wanted a daughter.'

'And you've got one,' I replied.

'I have now,' she said, and winked. And in that moment, I remember thinking three things. The first was, had she seen through me? The second was, if not, how many dreams had she abandoned to remain with a man who couldn't give her the children she craved? And the third was, when it came to our relationship, just who was using who? Was it me, for inserting myself into her life under false pretences, or her, for accepting it so she wouldn't have to spend the rest of her life alone? The only thing I have to thank Paul for is confirming my and Gwen's relationship was mutually beneficial. That makes me feel a little less guilty for the lies I told.

'Oh Gwen,' I say aloud, and the hollowness I've felt in my stomach so often since her death returns. I miss her. I can't help it. I just do. When you spend every day with someone who's reliant on you for an extended period of time, especially when it's as intense and complex as our relationship was, you're going to be hit hard when they're taken away from you. Despite her condition and the circumstances in which we met, she was still more of a mother than the woman who gave birth to me.

Everyone in the village is now aware of how Paul manipulated Gwen and why he did it. I'm sure Mary has also told them all I'm convinced that he killed her. Those who've spoken to me about it assume I've reported my suspicions to the police. And each time I explain I haven't because I've got no evidence to back up my claims. They don't know the real reason why I've kept quiet: that the police wouldn't need to dig deep before they discovered Gwen and I have no biological link, no family or extended family in common, and no history before the day we met. No one can prove I've broken the law, but that, coupled with a string of criminal convictions as long as my arm for scamming and conning people out of money, doesn't make me a reliable accuser. Add to that me being the sole named beneficiary of her will and they'd laugh me out of the interview room.

My need to steer clear of attention and publicity was the reason why I was a bag of nerves when Detective Sergeant Krisha Ahuja, my police liaison officer when Gwen went missing, twisted my arm into agreeing to film a television appeal. I didn't want to be recognised by anyone who knew me from one of my many previous lives. And had the story been picked up by the national press, I'm sure I'd have been ratted out. In the end, the local news didn't bother to broadcast it.

I've also got a lot to lose around here from making accusations against Paul that I can't back up. I currently have my neighbours on side, but their support will vanish with the click of a finger if it becomes common knowledge that she died while I was in prison and we weren't family.

There's a beep, beep, beeping sound coming from behind me; it's my laptop warning the battery needs recharging. I plug it into the mains and wait for the screen to flicker to life before I continue where I left off before my cigarette break. I'm on the homepage of Northampton's *Chronicle & Echo* newspaper. Most people flick through local rags like this for news or events, but for me, it's all about the death notices.

First, I focus on the over-sixties. I scan what's been written about them, paying particular attention to who placed the notice. Was it a family member or the funeral home? I read any names mentioned and their relationship to the deceased. Is there a surviving spouse? Are there children, brothers, sisters or grandchildren? Because the fewer direct family members, the better it is for me. It means I stand more of a chance of slipping into their lives without arousing suspicion. I've been to three funerals in the last fortnight but no candidate's circumstances have even come close to Gwen's. I was lucky with her because she had no one.

She wasn't my first. That honour went to Frederick Elms, a curmudgeonly, three-time widower with terminal cancer and no family, who was looking for a live-in housekeeper and carer. I put up with his racist, homophobic rants and his wandering hands for the six weeks I stayed under his roof. I might have even made him believe there was more to our relationship than there actually was. Perhaps Paul and I aren't that dissimilar. I had high hopes for a mention in the will I was going to help him draft until the selfish old racist keeled over from a heart attack in the kitchen while I was upstairs rinsing out his commode.

Gill Remnant was next, a recent widow with no family but suspicious friends and busybody neighbours who wouldn't give me a moment's peace to properly get to know her. I walked away from that one when I realised I was on a hiding to nothing.

And then the stars aligned when Gwen came along. We were the perfect match. She was going to be my final attempt at making me like everyone else and not who I am. It was a victimless crime. In fact, it wasn't even a crime, just a few mistruths here and there. I'd help her and, in return, she'd help me in the form of a payout when she died that'd set me up for years. I wasn't depriving anyone else because she had no direct family to leave her estate to. Better to give it to me than have the government farm it out to a private company who'd spend a chunk of it trying to trace some distant cousin ten times removed and give it to him. Now the life I wanted is as far out of reach as it ever was.

I unclench fists I didn't realise I'd balled. I've riled myself up again thinking about what I've lost. I should call it a day. My heart really isn't in it anyway. I roll up my next cigarette and promise it'll be the last I smoke until bedtime. I close the back door and pour a small tin of baked beans into a saucepan and heat it up on the electric hob. I drop two slices of past-their-prime white bread into the toaster, and as I watch the sauce bubble and the bread brown, I recognise what a pathetic meal this is. My forty-third birthday is looming, I'm single, I have no savings, I'm behind on my rent, I have no career prospects and I'm eating a meal even most university students these days would shun. My life wasn't supposed to turn out anything like this.

A white box suddenly appears on my laptop screen with a ping. Someone has written to me using Facebook Messenger, which surprises me; I have no friends on there or even a profile photo, as I only use it for researching others.

I take a closer look and my heart almost stops when I realise who it's from. And a flicker of hope ignites inside me.

CHAPTER 33

CONNIE

I re-read who has sent the message, just in case my tired eyes are playing tricks on me. Yes, it's definitely Ann On, the person I messaged months ago after spotting the negative post they'd left about Paul under a photograph of charity work he'd been doing. I remember word for word what they wrote: *Don't let Paul pull the wool over your eyes. He's fooled you all.*

I take a deep breath as I read on. *Who are you?* they've typed. 'Active now', it says at the top of the screen, so I write quickly.

Paul conned his way into my mum's life then married her and stole my inheritance, I write. Three dots appear and I nervously await their response.

Same, comes the reply.

I know what I want to type next but I don't know if I should. They might think me mad. I do it anyway. What have I got to lose?

I think he might've . . . hurt her.

The three dots reappear, but at least two minutes pass before they respond. It's a one-word answer.

Same.

I don't know what to do, I type.

This time, their answer comes quickly: *Find the others*.

What others?

I suddenly wonder if this is actually Paul. I wouldn't put it past him to leave a negative comment about himself just to see if anyone ever responded. It's better to see your enemies than to live in blindness.

No, I think, I'm being paranoid.

The time replaces the dots, indicating the poster has signed out. *What others?* I type again and click the send button, but Messenger doesn't allow it. Ann On has blocked me. Damn it.

I'm distracted by a burning smell. I've cremated the beans in the pan and the tomato sauce has evaporated. But I don't care. I have a more important focus. I leave the computer switched on just in case Ann On has a change of heart, but I suspect they won't. I throw the pan into the sink and return to the back door and light up the cigarette I was keeping for later.

I can't believe I didn't consider it sooner. Why did I assume Gwen was Paul's first victim? Gwen wasn't the first person I tried to con, so it stands to reason she might not have been the first to die at his hands either. I shake my head. That poor woman. What did she do to deserve both of us?

I recall how our paths first crossed. A notice had been placed in the *Bucks Observer* for her husband Bill's funeral, but Gwen's was the only name attached to it.

William Wright, 83, passed suddenly at home. He was a loving husband to Gwen, his wife of 60 years. Funeral to be held at St Peter's church in Avringstone.

Of the many notices I'd read, this was unusually brief. No mention of any family at all, only a wife. Several online searches confirmed the couple had no immediate relatives. It was enough to make me take my black suit to the dry cleaner's, brush my hairpiece, slip on my clear lens glasses to alter my regular appearance and book a taxi to William's funeral service later in the week.

I chose a seat close to the back of the congregation so I'd be partially obscured by a pillar. I counted twenty-one mourners, and in the front row, a woman I assumed to be the grieving widow. Following a brief service, Bill's coffin passed me on its exit into the church graveyard, followed soon after by Gwen. There was something familiar about her. Not the person, but the expression. A simultaneously present yet vacant look. It travelled deeper than grief.

The intimacy of a burial was too risky, so I held back and joined them at the wake later in the village pub.

'The best thing about being a plain Jane like you is that no one will ever remember you in a crowd,' Caz liked to remind me. 'Use that to your advantage.'

So, well practised at blending, I spent an hour or so listening in to conversations to learn all I could about Gwen. Neighbours discussed how she and Bill had moved around Europe for much of their lives, ending up in Spain following his retirement twenty years earlier. They'd returned to the UK only recently after his heart bypass operation. And she'd been widowed within months of moving to Avringstone. There were also whispers of concern over who was going to care for her now, especially with her dementia.

Dementia, I said to myself. That's what I'd seen in her. It should have registered with me straight away. I'd seen many patients just like Gwen in the care homes I'd worked at in my twenties.

Later, it cost me only £3 online to buy a copy of her house's title register, which revealed she and William owned it outright. So far, so good. She was ticking every one of my boxes. And within a fortnight, I was nervously standing on her doorstep wearing a blue tabard and carrying a caddy full of cleaning products, explaining how I'd been sent by the local authority to help with her cooking and cleaning needs. It was the first lie in what would be almost a year and half of them.

'Did Bill organise this before he died?' she asked.

'I believe so,' I replied. She let me in without further questioning.

Over the next few weeks, my visits went from every three days to daily. I dispensed with the uniform and stopped carrying the cleaning equipment after the first visit, so her neighbours wouldn't associate me as her domestic help. I'd spend hours getting to know her and cleaning her house while searching for documents and photographs to build up a complete picture of the life she and Bill shared, and of course, their financial affairs. I learned everything about them, from their taste in music, films and books, to their holidays and hobbies and their lives before, during and after Spain. I had spare keys cut to her front door so I could be the first person she saw when she woke up and the last person as she went to bed. I learned to recognise her more vulnerable moments and began planting seeds in a mind muddied by weeds and thorns about who I really was. It was all leading up to the day when I first called her 'Mum'.

I was walking to her house when I spotted her entering the grounds of the church cemetery, barefoot and in her favourite yellow dressing gown.

'Are you okay Gwen, luv?' I heard a man I later came to know as Walter ask.

'I've come to see Bill,' she replied. 'Where have they put him?'

'She's fine,' I told him. 'You just get a little confused sometimes, don't you, Mum? Why don't we get you dressed and we'll come later with some flowers?'

My heart thrummed as I waited to gauge her reaction to the 'M' word. She didn't dismiss me outright, but neither did she immediately accept what I'd said.

'I didn't know you had a daughter,' Walter said to us both, surprised.

'I've just moved back to the country,' I added. 'I've been living abroad.'

Gwen looked at me blankly for a moment before she replied, 'Yes, you have.'

I could have jumped for joy. Instead, I held my excitement in. 'Right, let's get you home, shall we?' I said. It was as simple as that.

Her neighbours, who hadn't known her well in the short time she and Bill had lived in the village, accepted my explanation of how the nature of her disease meant she often forgot important events, and even that she was a mother. I also told them that sometimes she swore blind she'd never been married. If any of them doubted me, they never admitted it to my face.

Over the coming days, weeks and months, I reinforced Gwen's belief that we were mother and daughter. I showed her photos of us together, ones I'd created using an app to superimpose childhood images of me on old pictures of her I'd found upstairs in albums. I'd invent fake anecdotes about us based on stories she'd told me about her and Bill's life. And because there were times when she remembered very little from one day to the next, it didn't matter if I slipped up or if my stories contradicted one another. I even found myself rewriting our time together as I went along, to create better shared imaginary experiences.

But something unexpected came from all that effort. In Gwen, I was finding what I'd craved my whole life. A mum. And being around her enabled me to create and shape the childhood I'd always wanted. Which is why I miss her so much, even if so much of it was pretend. Without her, I'm back to being me again. Nobody's daughter. And I don't like not belonging to anyone.

My gurgling stomach returns me to the present, reminding me I've yet to eat. Before I search the cupboards for noodles or pasta,

I take one more look at the laptop. Ann On has vanished. But it doesn't matter. I can do what needs to be done next by myself.

If Caz taught me nothing else, it was never to give up even when the odds are stacked against you. I failed to contain the situation first time around with Paul, but now I have an advantage. He thinks that this is all over. I'm getting my second wind.

CHAPTER 34

CONNIE

'Morning Sharon,' begins Leanne as she greets me at reception. It's been a while since I last used this identity, so for a moment, I assume she's talking to someone else. 'How was your evening?'

'Lovely thanks,' I reply. 'A long hot bath, a face mask and an early night.' It couldn't be further from the truth. A bottle of wine, a dozen roll-ups and a barbecue-flavoured Pot Noodle.

'Oh, bliss! I could do with all of those,' she replies.

Leanne and I couldn't look more different if we tried. She is a thick-boned woman with a white streak through the centre of long, auburn hair. Her skin is flawless. I'm underweight, my hair is full of split ends and my skin is pale and blotchy. She's probably around my age and I feel a little reassured that her wedding ring finger is bare. It's become a real habit of mine, glancing at that digit when I first meet someone. It's as if I need confirmation that there are others out there like me.

We exchange pleasantries, and as I don't have an electronic swipe card yet, I follow her into the Help for Homes office. It's been a few weeks since I received Ann On's message and sent the application to volunteer my time to the charity. Today is my fourth on the job.

It's a cramped space that barely fits the three desks arranged inside. Behind us is a window looking out into a larger area with tables and chairs. There is a hot-drink vending machine with an Out of Order sign taped to the front, and a handful of men and women are eating lunches from plastic boxes.

I share this room with Leanne and a man with the name Derek Reid written on a laminated ID card attached to a lanyard around his neck. So this is Paul's friend, the witness at Gwen's wedding, who Paul used to sign the form that got him added to the house deeds. I bet it was thanks to him that the investigation into Paul went no further after Paul took Gwen away to Clacton-on-Sea. I know it was reported to the charity as a safeguarding issue, but as far as I was told they put it down to 'miscommunication'.

However, I can't let on what I know about him in case he says something to Paul. He's chatty, perhaps even a little flirtatious, and at least a couple of decades older than me. There's no ring on his finger, and he's smartly dressed and wears a tartan-patterned tweed flat cap even when he's indoors. Any friend of Paul's is someone I wouldn't touch with a flamethrower, let alone a barge pole.

Yesterday, when I asked him where we keep the files for volunteers and their matches, he tried to stonewall me with talk of GDPR and privacy issues for volunteers, and that because he's staff, he can access them but I can't. But I can smell bullshit from fifty paces. Only he's not here today, he's off sick.

'So you'll be on your own for most of the morning, if you're okay with that?' asks Leanne.

'Sure,' I say, and try not to display my joy at this news. 'Where are you off to?'

'I'm meeting a couple of prospective volunteers for coffee in town. Demand is outstripping supply, so we're desperate for some new faces.'

Leanne told me the same thing when I arrived for my interview at Help for Homes on Monday. 'So as I explained on the phone,' she began, 'we're looking for someone who can help a few hours a week in the office with filing, typing letters, keeping on top of emails and chasing up the criminal record checks for new volunteers. Oh, and thank you for bringing your DBS certificate and references with you.'

'No problem,' I replied. 'I had mine already from a recent temping job.'

It was the first of many lies I told her in a very short space of time. The truth is, it's not hard to buy a forged certificate over the internet that says you have no criminal record if you know the right websites. Only an eagle-eyed expert would realise it wasn't genuine, and I didn't have Leanne pegged as one, bless her. As for my CV, well, the Harry Potter books are more fact-based than what I wrote.

Leanne explained how the charity runs programmes across the Midlands and South East region. 'There are so many cowboys out there and we hate the thought of our clients being scammed,' she added.

And Paul is the biggest cowboy of them all. That's what I wanted to tell her. But I didn't. I know it's not the charity's fault. Though it doesn't stop me from harbouring a little resentment towards Leanne and whoever took him on.

The next day she showed me to my new desk, and this is where I've been ever since. There's a small risk Paul might one day suddenly appear, but it's one I'll have to take. Today, I'm mostly responding to enquiry emails until Leanne slips on her jacket, throws her handbag over her shoulder and tells me she will see me this afternoon.

'I forgot to ask you,' I say. 'Does Paul Michael still volunteer for you?'

'Paul? Yes, he does. Do you know him?'

'I met him through friends a while back.'

'Once seen never forgotten, eh?' There's a twinkle in her eye that suggests she has more than a professional interest in him. 'He's been with us a while, but he's not a regular. He helps out when he's back in the country.'

'Where else does he work?'

'He's often based in Africa, helping famine-hit countries to get back on their feet. We don't see him for months at a time and then he'll suddenly appear. All the ladies love him, and can you blame them?'

'No,' I say through gritted teeth. But I don't believe for a second he has helped anyone in Africa. He's hardly Bob bloody Geldof.

I stare at the clock and wait ten minutes after she leaves. Now it's time to get to the crux of why I'm really here. It takes a while but I finally locate a file on my computer that contains a spreadsheet listing all the charity's clients, along with the volunteers they've been matched with. However, there is no mention of Gwen or Paul's names. But I'm not done yet. I go through every single document I can find – and there are scores of them – until I unearth a file hidden inside a folder titled 'Empty'. It's another version of the spreadsheet, and bingo! This time, I find Gwen's name with Paul Michael's next to it. And there's also a home address for him. I make a note of it on my phone.

I return to the list and count twenty women who Paul has helped over the last five years. Next to each name is a brief description of their situation. It's a shopping list of brain conditions – tumours, strokes, motor neurone disease, Alzheimer's, vascular dementia, Lewy body dementia, mixed dementia and Creutzfeldt-Jakob disease. They all needed practical help just like Gwen did. I wonder how many he took financial and emotional advantage of? I want to be wrong; I want Gwen to have been the only woman he killed. But that Facebook message from Ann On suggests something different.

A voice in the back of my head catches me unawares. *How are you any different to him?* it asks, unfairly I think. 'I haven't killed anyone,' I reply aloud.

But the voice has a point. How *am* I any different? If events had played out as I'd planned, I'd have taken advantage of Gwen's condition just as Paul did. And if I'm being honest with myself, me trying to dig up dirt on him isn't only because I want justice for Gwen. It's also because I want him locked up so I get what I'm owed – her estate.

Does that make me a bad person? *You already know the answer, Rachel*, the voice replies. It can piss off.

Gwen is the last-but-one name listed here. The most recent addition appeared a week after Gwen's death. Her name is Fran Brown. I wonder if that's who Paul is now slowly sinking his claws into.

I print out the names and addresses of all his matches and slip the list into my handbag. I see out the rest of the day before leaving a note to say I've been offered a full-time job elsewhere, and I exit that place for the last time.

Later in the evening and I'm back at my kitchen table, pouring myself a large mug of coffee, rolling half a dozen cigarettes and turning on my laptop. I begin with the address listed as Paul's on the charity's database, but I can't find it online. And according to Google Maps, it doesn't exist. I type in the postcode and address twice more as I have fat fingers sometimes, but I draw a blank each time. I can't deny it leaves me feeling deflated so early on.

Next, I input the names of the women Paul volunteered to help and search the internet for everything I can find about them or their families. Most, to my relief, are still alive, but for others I find death notices and obituaries linked to local newspaper stories. By the time midnight arrives, I have no cigarettes left but I do have three names out of twenty whose circumstances mimic Gwen's.

Eliza Holmes, Lucy Holden and Alice McKenzie.

The women's deaths are spaced a year to eighteen months apart. Each lived in a different county to her predecessor and under a different police authority. According to newspaper reports of their inquests, they died in a similar manner: a rapid decline in dementia-related health, followed by a sudden, accidental death. The first died of exposure after locking herself out of the house on a winter's night. The following two fell down staircases to their deaths.

Cold prickles cover my back, arms and neck like a fridge door has been left open behind me.

As far as I can tell, none of these women had any direct family descendants. But the smoking gun is an online visit to Public Record Search. It costs me £14 per certificate – a sizable chunk out of my weekly budget – but it's worth it when, early the next week, they arrive through the post. It turns out each woman married before she died: one for three months, the rest for less than a handful of weeks. And each certificate contains a different groom's name.

Paul Edwards, Paul Jamison and Paul Field.

The common letters in their signatures are identical. The swirls of the Ss, the loops of the Ls, the dots over the Is.

I check the evidence again and again and again. But I have never been more certain of anything else in my life.

Paul killed at least three women before he murdered Gwen. I am up against a serial murderer.

CHAPTER 35

CONNIE

It's taken me ninety minutes, three separate buses, a maps app and a comfortable pair of trainers, but finally, I'm here. This 1970s-style suburban home is registered in the name of Fran Brown and I already know from my stint at Help for Homes that she is an eighty-six-year-old widow with vascular dementia. She's also the most recent name to have been paired with Paul. Under the 'action required' heading, he'd been tasked with tidying up an overgrown garden, much like Gwen's. And as far as I can work out, the only difference between the two women is that Fran has a next of kin, a son called Jon, but he lives in Dubai. It was he who contacted the charity to organise the help.

I look the place up and down. It's larger than Gwen's, meaning a bigger potential pay-off for Paul. The drive is empty and I can't tell if anyone is inside, as heavy sets of net curtains block my view. What is it with old people and net curtains? I'm too conspicuous standing here, so I find a wooden bus shelter a little further along the road and take a seat inside. I have no idea if I'm wasting my time, but I don't have anything better to do and I desperately want to know if this is a pattern of Paul's – bury one, begin with another. Is he doing this just for the money, or for the thrill of the kill?

I've yet to contact the police with what I've learned because I still don't know enough yet. If I'm about to accuse Paul of being a serial killer, I'll need some pretty damning evidence. I can't risk messing this up and him getting away with it, or I can kiss goodbye to Gwen's estate and getting justice for her.

I pass the next few hours listening to true crime podcasts on my headphones, surfing news websites and, when necessary, taking pee breaks behind some nearby bushes. I also scan my fake dating app profiles, keeping some and deleting others. It's been a while since I've logged on and I find more than two hundred unread messages. I hold back from sending replies even though they've historically been a good way of making a fast buck. I need to focus on one thing at a time.

That reminds me to check the balance again in my bank account. I'm still overdrawn, I see, and it's not getting any better. My earnings from dog walks and ironing are split between keeping the electricity running and a court order to pay back the couple I stole from, which is what landed me in prison. The rest has been spent on utility bills, mobile phone credits, bus fares, etc. There's nothing left over. Last week, I had no choice but to visit the food bank in town for the first time. I'm also two months behind with rent on the bungalow. I've been ignoring the emails and phone calls from the letting agency. I'm aware of my rights and I know they can't kick me out yet. At best, I reckon I have another four months left until a court evicts me. But I should be living better than this at my age.

I keep telling myself that I've endured worse and survived it. You don't have much of a choice if you were raised by the mum I had. *Mum*, I repeat to myself. I liked calling Gwen that. It was the first time I'd got to use the word, as it'd been erased from my vocabulary by Caz, my biological mother, from the start. 'I don't like being reminded of it,' she'd say. 'People see motherhood as a weakness around here.'

A moment from the last time I saw her, back in London, creeps into my head. I can hear her voice as she proudly told me how, even before I was born, I was a criminal. She'd use her pregnant belly as a distraction, and while she asked shoppers in supermarket car parks for directions as they loaded their bags into boots, a friend would steal handbags or wallets from their trollies or inside their cars.

Then, when I arrived in her world, she'd hide clothes, food and bottles of cider from shops in my pushchair – and later, when I started walking, under my coat. And if they set any alarms off, she'd apologise and blame me for taking them when she hadn't been watching. For years I believed it was a moth infestation in our flat that created holes in everything we wore. It turned out it was because she'd cut out the security tags with scissors rather than prise them apart and risk splitting the anti-theft dye capsule. I only have a handful of photographs of myself as a child, and in one of them I was around four or five and on a yellow bike with stabilisers, which she had stolen from a nursery playground she once walked past.

For the most part, it was only ever just Caz and me. When I was old enough to ask about my dad, she'd claim she had no idea who he was, then remind me how lucky I was to be here in the first place. She was seventeen when she discovered she was five months pregnant, and the only reason she didn't have an abortion was because she'd passed the legal cut-off point. 'Besides,' she'd add, 'the government pays for you. So every cloud, and all that.'

Caz made money any which way she could. She'd cash stolen cheques, organise fake Christmas club hamper schemes, sell on credit cards, or fence anything from jewellery to electronics. But targeting the elderly in distraction burglaries was her favourite scam. She'd appear on their doorsteps flashing a fake identification card, claiming to be there to read their utility meters. Meanwhile, I was young and small enough to creep into their houses through open windows and sometimes even cat flaps, and quietly rifle through their valuables. It never ceased to amaze me how often I'd find cash or jewellery hidden in biscuit tins, bread bins and under mattresses.

I suppose I had an inkling what I was doing was wrong, but at that age, you do as you're told and Caz knew best. Also, she was a much nicer person to be around when we had money, even if it was someone else's. If I left a house empty-handed, she'd give me the silent treatment for the rest of the day.

Once, she hooked up with a Polish man called Svaro who taught me how to pickpocket. On Saturdays we'd catch the Tube to tourist spots in Covent Garden, Oxford Street or Camden Market, where I'd move about unnoticed, taking wallets from jacket pockets and purses from unsecured handbags. Svaro was the closest thing I had to a father figure until he stole one too many times and was deported.

I was forced to go solo and put into practice everything I'd learned from Caz and Svaro when she was sent to Holloway Prison. The magistrate didn't fall for her mitigating circumstances – poverty-stricken single parent, alcohol- and cannabis-dependent, struggling to make ends meet, etc. – and jailed her for a year for storing someone's counterfeit cash. Even with time reduced for good behaviour, it would be five months before she was released. She knew from her own experience the hell of children's homes, so she told my social worker I was going to stay with her sister in Devon. She had no sister and no one ever checked. Caz left me with £100 to fend for myself and a note saying: *Time to pull your weight.* I was twelve.

I missed her like anything and was determined to make her proud by surviving without her. Shoplifting and pickpocketing were now second nature to me. Some nights I went without electricity, as I'd run out of money to feed the meter. But on others, I lived like a queen, sprawled across the sofa eating boxes of stolen After Eights mint chocolates and smoking from cartons of counterfeit cigarettes Caz had also stashed away for a friend.

But something about that stay in prison altered her. On her release, it was as if she had ditched her few remaining parental duties and put herself first, completely. She didn't return to the flat to live, and only appeared on fleeting visits to leave me a little money or hide away more stolen goods. Sometimes a fortnight might pass before I'd see or hear from her. There was no way to contact her, and each time I asked where she was spending her time, she'd fob me off with lies about finding a job or looking after a sick friend.

Occasionally she brought one of these 'friends' home with her and they'd disappear behind her bedroom door, only to re-emerge hours later with vacant looks about them, eyelids half-closed and reeking of melted plastic. I knew what she was doing, of course. She tried to hide the blackened pipes from me under the mattress or clothes strewn across the floor, but she gave herself away when she once set fire to her duvet and only just escaped self-cremation.

A vehicle passing the bus shelter catches my eye. It's a grey van resembling Paul's. I peer out and watch as it parks outside Fran Brown's house. My muscles tense as Paul exits. He makes his way to the front door and unlocks it. Then he returns to the van and stretches out an arm to help someone out from the passenger side. An elderly woman grabs hold of it to steady herself before together they make their way towards the house. She is frail and unsteady on her feet, much more so than Gwen was. Then the front door closes and they disappear.

That poor, poor woman. She has no idea what's coming her way. Fran fits Paul's criteria perfectly. It's as if she has been tailor-made for him. History is repeating itself, I'm certain of it.

CHAPTER 36

WALTER CLARK, NEIGHBOUR

I was still in the bathroom when Connie came to pick up Oscar for his morning walk, but I'm downstairs in the kitchen pouring us tea when they return. I open the biscuits she likes and she makes her way to the window and stares out across the garden at the dovecote. White paint is flaking from the roof and the pole it's attached to is rusty. Like me, it's seen better days.

'Do birds ever nest in there?' she asks.

'Not in as long as I can remember. The odd squirrel, maybe. I asked Paul to sand it down and repaint it, but he never got round to it.' *Oh bollocks*, I think. *Why did I bring him up?* But unlike the other times I've spoken about him, today she isn't triggered. Instead, her gaze wanders further into the distance. 'You can see the roof of Mum's house from here.'

Passing it every day must be torturous. 'Come, sit down,' I suggest and she obliges. I place my hand gently on her forearm.

Connie hasn't been the same since her mum died, and who can blame her? She's like a pot of hot water on a hob, constantly simmering but ready to boil over at the slightest provocation – namely the mention of Paul's name. She's convinced he has something to do with Gwen's death but I can't help thinking she's clutching at straws. If she has someone to blame then maybe it will make sense to her. And perhaps – although I'll never tell her this – it might help ease her guilt for not being here when it happened.

Don't get me wrong, I don't think Paul is an innocent party in all this. I mean, who in their right mind marries an older woman with dementia? Someone who wants her money, if you ask me. But do I think Paul killed her for it? No. At least I hope not, because if it turns out he did, a lot of us around here will question just how well we can trust our own judgement.

I already feel terrible for dismissing Connie's concerns when she confided in me months ago that she didn't like the way Paul and Gwen were behaving around one another. I told her that a bit of attention wasn't going to do Gwen any harm. Shows what I know, doesn't it? I suspect Connie harbours a little resentment towards me although she has never said as much.

She looks at me, then down to the table, and back at me again. 'I need to tell you something.'

'Okay.'

'I . . . I don't think Gwen was the first.'

'She wasn't the first what, sweetheart?'

'She wasn't the first woman Paul killed. I think she was the fourth.'

Wow. Okay, well, I wasn't expecting that. I sit up straight and she explains how she recently spent time volunteering at the charity that matched Gwen and Paul, and how she discovered other women on their books who Paul helped. They too later died.

'But that's what we oldies do. We die. Our batteries run out, then we're reduced to our knick-knacks in a car boot sale.'

'You don't all marry Paul first,' she counters. 'Of the twenty or so names listed, he wed four of them, including Gwen.'

Connie reveals how each of them passed: two as a result of accidents and one poor old girl who died from hypothermia. 'And now I think he's getting ready to do it again,' she continues. 'He has a new victim lined up. I saw her myself.'

She explains how she went all Jessica Fletcher and staked out the woman's house until she appeared with Paul. I'm seeing a whole new side to her this morning.

'And you're absolutely sure of all this?' I ask.

'As sure as I can be.'

'Then why has no one cottoned on before and told the police?'

'I think it's because he spaces them apart. One victim lived in Leicestershire, another in Berkshire. Gwen is obviously in Buckinghamshire, and now Fran Brown is in Northamptonshire. If the coroners at their inquests rule no foul play, there are no dots to join.'

I shake my head, but it's no longer because I don't believe her. The truth is almost too shocking to contemplate. 'But he seemed like such a lovely lad.'

'Remember the Hunter family in Stewskbury?' she asks. It's a surname none of us in this county will ever forget. 'Forty kids died before the truth came out. Nobody thought someone like that was capable of such evil.'

I shudder. 'This is awful, just awful.'

'So you believe me? Because you didn't before, when I told you I didn't trust him.'

'I was wrong and I'm sorry,' I concede. 'But you admitted it yourself, you had no evidence he was up to no good, just a hunch. What would you have thought if you were me?'

She doesn't reply, which I take to mean she understands where I'm coming from.

'When are you telling the police what you know?' Her body tenses and she doesn't reply. 'Connie?' I continue. 'You are going to tell them, aren't you?'

'Yes, just not yet. I don't have enough proof.'

'Let them find the proof, that's their job. Just tell them what you told me and they'll do the rest.'

'I have one chance to make them believe me, Walter. If I can't convince them I'm right, they're not going to listen to me again.'

'You don't know that. I'm sure you have enough evidence to make them at least look into it.'

She shakes her head but I don't understand her reluctance. Is there more to what she knows than she's letting on? I suspect Connie is good at keeping secrets. None of us really bought into her excuse as to why she was uncontactable when Gwen died. I have a well-honed bullshit radar, Paul notwithstanding. I spent the first thirty-five years of my life in the closet, so I know when someone is being economical with the truth. 'So what are you going to do then?' I continue.

She takes a long sip of her tea before she answers. 'If I tell you, Walter, you'll try and talk me out of it.'

'Probably, but give me a go.'

By the time she finishes explaining, I'm already waggling my finger from side to side so quickly, I fear I might do myself a mischief.

CHAPTER 37

JON BROWN

I'm at my desk in the office when the phone rings. It's an international dialling code but I don't recognise the rest of the number so I don't answer. Being based in Dubai but having an English- network registered phone doesn't stop me from getting those irritating call centre enquiries telling me I'm entitled to compensation for a car accident I've never had.

As I try to regain my train of thought and type up yesterday's notes on the apartment I surveyed in Palm Jumeirah, the phone rings again. I cancel the call but they're persistent and it happens again. I answer it with an irritated 'Hello'. There's a pause before a female voice begins. It's British and it doesn't sound automated.

'Is that Mr Jon Brown?' she asks. She sounds apprehensive.

'Who's this?'

'You don't know me.'

'Then why are you calling?'

'It's about your mum, Fran.'

Now she has my attention. Something must have happened to her. Mum wears a bracelet with a button that she's supposed to press if she needs assistance after a fall or if she gets ill. The operator has my number, and those of two neighbours who they can call if she needs help. 'Has something happened to her?'

'No, not yet.'

That sounds vaguely like a threat. I pull off my glasses and scratch at the stubble under my chin.

'You recently contacted a charity that provides workmen for the elderly,' she says. 'Help for Homes. Is that right?'

I did. After Mum was diagnosed with vascular dementia following her second stroke, I flew back and tried to talk her into moving into an assisted living home. I'd even found her the perfect place in the same area of Northampton where she lives now, to make the transition smoother. Even though she'd have her own flat, privacy and immediate access to care if required, she was having none of it. I admit the move would've been partly for selfish reasons, as it'd reduce the stress you feel when you live thousands of miles away from an elderly parent. But Mum was – and remains – adamant she'll be staying in the same house where she and Dad lived almost all their married life.

'Look, Mr Brown, there's a handyman the charity has paired your mum with who doesn't have her best interests at heart.'

'What?'

'I've seen him at Fran's house. His name is Paul Michael and he has a history of deception and dishonesty . . . and much, much worse.'

'But the charity has vouched for him.'

'They don't know him like I do.'

'What, is he an ex-boyfriend or something?'

'Absolutely not. I have no hidden agenda here; all I want to do is to protect your mum. I failed to do the same thing with mine, and I believe she's dead because of Paul. I don't want you to live with the regrets that I do. So please, ask the charity to find you someone else to help her before it's too late.'

'Too late for what?' I ask. But there is no response. 'Hello? Hello?'

The line has gone dead. I stare at the phone for a moment and press the redial button. She doesn't answer and the number rings out. If this is supposed to be a joke, it's a sick one.

CHAPTER 38

CONNIE

When the page on the Rightmove app loads, I hit the arm of the sofa with the palm of my hand in frustration. A film of dust becomes airborne before settling again in the same place. Paul has reduced the price on Gwen's house by another £30,000. It's been on the market for weeks now and this is the third time it's been reduced. The estate agent still shows people around it, but Joe Lawson says the number of interested parties has dropped significantly.

I'm convinced my behaviour has got something to do with the price drop. Over the last few weeks, I've made multiple offers and viewing appointments from fake email accounts to suck up the estate agency's time. I've poured live cockroaches I bought from a pet food supplier through the letter box. I've caught mice in humane traps in the fields behind the house and pushed them – gently, I might add – through a cat flap in the back door. And just for good measure, I placed in the borders surrounding the foundations Japanese knotweed roots and shoots that I dug up from outside derelict properties in town. I know it's a fast-spreading weed that, if found, puts buyers off and often prevents banks making mortgage offers.

None of this is going to prevent the sale of Gwen's house forever, but they've been successful stalling tactics. However, at this new listing price, I have a feeling it might finally shift.

I know that I should've walked away from this mess by now, closed the chapter in my life titled 'Paul Michael' and moved on to a new project, leaving him to enjoy his spoils. But my brain isn't wired to give in to defeat so easily.

Two days ago and under a pseudonym, I made a genuine appointment with the estate agent to look around Gwen's place myself. Paul had removed the camera doorbell so didn't know I was there. While the young man occupied himself in the lounge on his phone, I made my way from room to room, eventually finishing in the kitchen and undoing the catch on the back door. Walter had been unimpressed when I told him my plan.

'It's madness,' he warned me. 'You're not thinking straight.'

'About which part?' I asked.

'All of it! You're putting yourself at an unnecessary risk. If Paul knows you're poking about in his business, what makes you think he won't go after you too?'

'Because I'm not an eighty-two-year-old woman with dementia.'

'But he's still potentially very dangerous. You said it yourself, you think he's a serial killer.'

When someone else uses those words, it almost sounds too far-fetched to be true. Books and films would have you believe almost every neighbourhood has its own serial murderer. But in reality, apparently their numbers are infinitesimally small. In fact, there are only thought to be a handful of active ones in the UK at any one time. At least, they're the ones the police suspect. And to my knowledge, they don't suspect Paul of anything.

Walter has a point, but I'm fed up of being taken advantage of. Ironic, I know, given how many people's trusts I've abused over the years. But I need to see this through, even if it's to my own detriment. And Gwen's sofa, with its dusty arms, is where I find myself now, hiding out, taking a break from quietly sifting through every object and scrap of paper Paul left behind after his purge of her belongings.

I've spent much of the last couple of days here, one ear cocked, ready to run the moment I hear a van pull up outside or a key turning in the lock. But nothing has happened yet. I don't know what I'm looking for but I won't be satisfied until I've inched my way through every room like a forensic detective. I've taken a few keepsakes for myself, and this morning I left that horrible jade-green porcelain cat with the long neck at the back door ready to carry home later. I hate the thing but I know how much Gwen adored it, so maybe I'll grow to at least tolerate it.

'It's ugly, isn't it?' she told me once when she saw me glaring at it.

'Why do you keep it?'

A devilish grin slowly crept across her face. 'Because it means I won.' I asked her what she meant but she gave me a wink and tapped her nose, indicating the conversation was over.

I make my way through her house and into the utility room, where bulging black refuse sacks are scattered across the floor. Why hasn't Paul thrown them out yet? I reach to untie one and flinch when a handful of cockroaches scuttle away to the darkness under the washing machine. I assume they're mine and thriving here. The first bag contains some of Gwen's old clothes, like her tights and underwear and stuff Paul wouldn't have been able to sell or give away. At the bottom is a pink baby blanket, a dressing gown and two matching towels with the name Connie embroidered on them in red looped lettering. I remember when I first found them, a few days after I'd inserted myself into her life. They were hidden away on the top shelf of her wardrobe in a wooden box.

'Who's Connie?' I asked casually later that day.

'The daughter Bill and I hoped to adopt,' she replied, wistfully. 'We were living in Spain when we met a young local woman who'd got herself into trouble.'

Been there and done that, I remember thinking.

'The day we were supposed to bring her home, the mother changed her mind and kept her,' she continued. 'We'd never even seen her, but the loss was immeasurable.'

By the end of the week, I was calling myself by Connie's name. And capitalising on Gwen's grief, confusion and lifelong wish to be a mum is pretty high on my list of many, many regrets. I can only hope the genuine kindness and affection I grew to have for her in our time together went a little way towards making up for the manipulation.

I hold the blanket and dressing gown to my nose but they smell of nothing more than time past. For decades, Gwen treasured them and now Paul wants to toss them out as if they don't matter. I consider what I could do with them, but I'm at a loss. I leave them next to the ornamental cat to take home with me later anyway.

The second bag contains mostly old household utility bills of Gwen's, dating back some twenty years. Deeper, there are handwritten envelopes with foreign postmarks from the 1960s. I open one and it appears they're letters Bill wrote to Gwen when they were first dating. I recall her telling me how the bank that employed him had been expanding into Munich, and he was subsequently posted there for a year. Once a fortnight he'd fly home for a long weekend. And they'd write each other long letters while they were apart. Nowadays it would be FaceTime and texts.

I know I'm intruding into their private correspondence but I've already stepped over so many lines when it comes to Gwen that

175

one more won't do any extra damage. In the first letter I read, Bill is discussing their future and how he can't wait for them to marry once he returns to the UK permanently. I notice how he always signs his letters off with the words 'Forever Yours'. No one has ever written me a love letter, or email, or even a text with words to that effect. I matter to so few people that I barely get an 'x'. Gwen only ever spoke in glowing terms to me of her husband, and it used to make me wish I'd met him. In a different universe, they'd have been my parents. I'd have been the baby girl that they'd adopted from a teenage mum. I'd have had a much better life as Connie Wright than I did as Rachel Evans.

These letters also make me wish that I had a Bill in my life, someone who loved me so completely that, even when separated by countries, I'd still feel his presence as much through his words as his person. I've tried to convince myself I'm completely self-sufficient and that I'm all I need. But deep down I wonder if I'm kidding myself. It's not like I haven't tried. However, none of my relationships survived for more than a few weeks or a handful of months. You learn from your parents' example, and Caz's was to show me it's perfectly acceptable to allow men to take advantage of you sexually, emotionally and financially. I did what she did: I lavished them in scraps of battered love and attention to make them want to stay with me. Without fail, they either became bored, took what they wanted or felt smothered and moved on. Eventually I went the opposite way and became aloof and left them before they had the chance to do the same to me. There was never any middle ground. No matter how they vanished from my life, the result was always the same. I'm alone.

It probably doesn't help my appeal that I don't need kids to complete me. The extreme, self-sabotaging ways I acted out as a teenager led to that decision. At fourteen, Caz took me to my appointment at the clinic for my first abortion, then spent the night with me at the flat, holding my hand and emptying the bucket each time I vomited. A few months later and the second time I told her I was pregnant, she rolled her eyes and gave me money to pay for a termination, then left me to my own devices. The third time, a month before my sixteenth birthday, she tried to encourage me to have it, as she had friends who would take the baby abroad and ensure I was 'well compensated for it'. 'Who are these people?' I asked. 'Couples who can't have kids?' She shrugged. 'Does it matter?'

It was the last time I fell pregnant. And that was out of choice, not circumstance or because I was scared I might make the same mistakes as Caz. It was just something that didn't appeal. I've since been told by exes that my decision to remain childless makes me 'selfish', 'self-absorbed' and even 'ungrateful', but I don't believe it makes me any of those things. If anything, it makes me selfless because I'm not bringing a child into this world who isn't one hundred per cent wanted. Over the years I've re-examined my decision, especially since I'm now approaching an age when I won't be able to change my mind. But I'm still of the same opinion.

Anyway, enough of this self-reflection. I'm here for a reason, so I pick up another letter. There's a reference in this one to a distant cousin of Gwen's, a woman called Meredith. Ahh, the elusive Meredith! She cropped up in a few conversations with Gwen over the months but I never got to the bottom of who she was in Gwen's world. Here, Bill asks Gwen if she misses her or regrets what happened. I don't have her replies so I'll never know what their problem was or if they patched things up.

When I've finished skimming through the rest, I can't bring myself to throw them away. Despite how often I lied to Gwen, I do feel a sense of loyalty to her, so I put the letters back into the bin bag to take home, along with the porcelain cat and baby stuff. I don't want anyone else intruding on her private moments.

I could do with a cigarette, so I skulk out into the garden and make my way to the fire pit in the garden. None of the neighbours can see me from here. Charred remains of paper lie in its base and I assume they're more of Gwen's bills and receipts. I shuffle them around with a bamboo cane, and underneath I spot what's left of a black-and-white photograph. I reach inside and pick it up. Pictured are two young women and the top half of a man. One girl I recognise as a much younger Gwen, and I find myself envying her natural allure. Even in this photo, you can tell she is aware of the power she has over others. It's a confidence I'll never know. The other girl has a resemblance to her and I wonder if they're related. They're standing next to one another by a rowing boat and there's a large lake behind them surrounded by hills. Both girls' expressions are positively stony. I dust off the charred edge. On the back and in faded writing, it reads, *Cousin George and daughter Meredith, August 1965, Lake District.* So Meredith *was* family. The plot thickens. I slip it into my pocket, although I'm not sure why.

Then I realise that, by moving the photo, I've exposed a second scrap that also hasn't burned completely. Closer inspection reveals it relates to a speeding fine and is dated five months ago. There's a pin-sharp image of Paul caught on camera behind the wheel of his van driving at 39 mph in a 30-mph zone. And what's this? The name attached to it is not Paul Michael, but Paul Michael Fernsby. So Michael isn't his surname but his middle name. It's then that I notice the fine wasn't sent to this address, but to a different one, somewhere in Oxfordshire. I quickly google it. But unlike that last address I searched for online, this one actually exists. I clutch the letter to my chest and feel my heart beating hard and fast against it. This is huge.

'You don't know it yet,' I whisper, 'but I'm coming for you, Paul.'

CHAPTER 39
HARRISON DOUGLAS, NEIGHBOUR

She passes the window, the second time I've seen her around here in a few minutes. Earlier, I was upstairs waking up the baby from his mid-morning nap when I clocked her standing on her tiptoes in the alleyway behind our house, trying to peer over the wall into next door's garden. Paul hasn't made it easy by attaching a wooden fence to the brick wall to keep it private.

Now she's out front, pacing up and down our row of terraced houses. If she was up to no good, she probably wouldn't be wearing trousers, a blouse and a jacket. Not exactly breaking-and-entering clobber, is it? I eye her up and down. She's not my usual type, a bit older and bit plainer than I like and not enough curves. But since we had the baby, Chantelle's got about as much interest in shagging as I have in breast pumps. So beggars can't be choosers and all that.

I shouldn't even be here today. I should be shit-faced on Carl's stag weekend with the rest of the footy team in Fuerteventura. But when half of Chantelle's colleagues went down with another new Covid variant, they called her back to work and that was my trip shafted. Now I'm on daddy duty. I pick up Ruben from his cot and put him over my shoulder along with a tea towel, as he's prone to sick burps and projectile vomiting when you least expect it. I learned that the hard way with two stained Superdry sweatshirts.

'Everything alright, luv?' I ask as I step out into the street.

She's lost in her own world and almost shits a brick in shock. I try not to laugh.

'Yes, it's fine,' she says.

'It's just that I saw you in the alley and now you're out here.'

'Oh right, well, I spotted the house on Rightmove so I thought I'd check it out before I made an appointment to view it. I don't know this side of town very well.'

'Paul is selling up?' I reply. We're not best mates or anything like that, we'll just talk about the footy or rugby if we see one another. But I told him I'd keep an eye on the house while he was working away. I thought he might've mentioned getting shot of the place though. 'I suppose it makes sense,' I add. 'He isn't around much.'

'Why, where is he?'

'He works on the rigs in the North Sea, so he's gone most of the year.'

'Are you friends?'

'I got to know him a little when he came to look after Sue.'

'Sue?'

'His mum. She used to live here.'

'And she doesn't anymore?'

'No, she died a couple of months after Paul moved in with her.'

'Oh, how sad. What happened?'

'She had Alzheimer's or something like that and was living on her own when he came back. To be honest, we didn't even know he existed until he came round to say hello. He didn't say as much, but reading between the lines, I reckon they must've had a barney back in the day. But he returned at the right time because, soon after, he had to call an ambulance a couple of times when she went proper nuts. The paramedics kept knocking her out and wheeling her off for a few days at a time.'

She shakes her head. 'That's awful. My mum had a few incidents like that with her dementia. It's horrible to watch.'

'He was out when she fell down the stairs . . . nasty business, broke her neck.' I mime pushing my head to one side like I'm hanging from a noose. 'We only found out about it later that night when he came round to tell us . . .' I stop myself when I see that her face has paled. 'Ahh, probably shouldn't be telling you all this, should I? Don't want to put you off. We could do with some fresh blood round here.' I give her a wink and her cheeks redden.

'No, not at all,' she says. 'I guess that makes sense why he's selling it. How long ago was this?'

'February the first, two years back. I remember the date because Man U were losing 5-2 to Man City. Gutted, absolutely gutted. Anyway, it's a shame, because before she died, he was right in the middle of renovating it for her. I don't know if he ever finished it though. Were there pictures of it on Rightmove, then?'

'Just a few. He's lucky to have you keeping an eye on it.'

'I haven't seen him in a few weeks. Probably back on the rigs again. But you can come in and have a look around in mine if you like. It's got the same layout, same lounge. Same bedroom.' I flash her a smile. She knows what I'm saying and I can tell she's interested, but with the worst possible timing, I feel a warm liquid trickling down the inside of my T-shirt. Ruben's vommed again, cockblocking me.

'Another time,' she says, 'when your hands aren't so full.'

CHAPTER 40

CONNIE

I reach into the canvas backpack and fumble my way around until my fingers find the bolt cutters. Soon after, the shank of the padlock attached to Paul's gate snaps in two and falls to the cobbled floor below me.

I scan the alleyway to make sure, as best I can, that nobody's watching me through the darkness. Terraced houses overlook me, and while it's still dark out here, I can't be certain I've not been spotted by an early riser. When nothing rouses my suspicion, I make my move. Opening the gate, I slip into the paved courtyard of Paul's garden, closing it quickly and using the torch on my phone to light my way.

It was two days ago when I was last here and Paul's lecherous prick of a neighbour told me about Sue, the woman before Gwen, who Paul pretended to be the son of. She also died following a fall down a staircase. I wonder how Paul met her, because she wasn't listed in Help for Homes' records. The more I learn of him, the more he repels but fascinates me. Help for Homes believes he's a charity worker who assists in drought-plagued African countries.

His neighbours think he works on the oil rigs, and he told me he works on train line repairs. He spins stories like an end-of-the-pier entertainer spins plates.

I checked online with the Land Registry and discovered that Paul Fernsby owns this house. This Sue woman must have left it to him in her will. My mind whirrs with questions. Why hasn't he sold it, when she's been dead for two years? He couldn't wait to put Gwen's place on the market. And why did he pretend to be Sue's son? Was it less effort than marrying her? Maybe that's how he saw through my relationship with Gwen, because he'd done exactly the same thing two years earlier with Sue.

Since the pub closed, I've spent much of the night wandering the streets and returning often to pass Paul's house and triple-check he's not returned. Now that I'm sure he hasn't, I get to work. His rear door is one of those modern, composite designs and way beyond my skill set to break into. But Lady Luck must be smiling upon me because the windows are not. He has yet to replace the single-pane aluminium windows that were popular in the eighties before uPVC fell into favour. I'm back to rooting around in my backpack until I locate the screwdriver. I use it to prise off the metal strip and beading around the window. Next I slip on a pair of latex gloves so I don't leave any fingerprints. Then, with light force, I insert the screwdriver between the glass and the frame. I gently lever the glass from its mounting. It weighs little and is only about half a metre square, so I place it on the ground. If Rosella could see me now, she'd be proud.

She was a girlfriend my mother had briefly back in the day: a tough-nut traveller who'd been cast out of her disapproving family, and later found herself behind bars and sharing a cell with Caz. I was thirteen when she came into my life. We bonded as she taught me how to burgle people's homes with her. Now, almost thirty years later, I have reason to again use those skills. I clock the houses around me one last time before I climb inside, reach a kitchen worktop and lower myself to the floor. I close the blind and illuminate the room with my phone. I'm in the belly of the beast.

The kitchen is small but with modern cupboards and appliances. The fridge is empty but the freezer contains a quarter-full bottle of vodka and a plastic box with four thick slices of unidentifiable pink meat. The cupboards contain only tinned foods. I assume he doesn't stay here much.

The kitchen leads into a dining room and lounge that have been knocked into one open-plan room. Both are in a state of flux. The dining room has been fitted with a modern, plain carpet but the one in the lounge is patterned and unfashionable. There's an old, 1970s-style gas fire in the lounge, but a log burner in the dining room. I shine the light against the walls. Half have been wallpapered and the rest are a dated pinky-peach emulsion. He's basically replicating everything he did at Gwen's house, here. Or maybe it's the other way round.

I begin the task in hand, to learn everything I can about the enemy before I bring him down. There's nothing in the cupboards built on either side of the chimney breast save for one framed photograph. In it, and sitting next to Paul, is an elderly woman I assume to be Sue. Her expression vacant, her eyes milky. She reminds me in part of Gwen. Neither is smiling and I wonder why he has gone to the trouble of framing it.

Next, a door under the staircase leads to a cellar. I gingerly venture partway down the stairs, shining my light to find it's empty, apart from a few paint pots, brushes and a ladder.

I head upstairs, and in the smallest of the three bedrooms I find at least a dozen cardboard boxes and files packed with paperwork. This is more like it.

The sun's early morning rays begin to light up the room so I turn off the torch. I'm still wearing my gloves and I'm careful to keep everything in order so Paul remains unaware that I've breached his privacy. But a good hour passes before anything of interest appears. It's a box crammed with handwritten letters, notes and poems. They're in envelopes and addressed to names I recognise of women Paul was paired with by Help for Homes. One by one I read them and find they fall into a rigid pattern. He tells each woman how much he has been thinking about them and how he's developing feelings for them, even though he knows he shouldn't. He tells them that he can't wait to see them again, how he loves the time they spend together, that their age difference doesn't matter and how he only wants to be with them. Three of the letters are word-for-word identical, but addressed to different names.

I assume the written word is more powerful to these women than if he just told them how he felt. A conversation can be forgotten, particularly with their conditions. But a letter can be read, re-read and pored over. It helps Paul to remain inside their heads even when they're apart, be it for a night or a few days. And the way he coos over them, it's not hard to understand why they fall for the attention. Most have likely been widowed for years and miss being the object of someone's affection. And in their vulnerable, confused state, they truly believe that in Paul, they have a second chance at love. I only realise I'm crying for them when a tear lands on a page and blurs the ink. I wonder why he's kept these letters. Does he re-read them? Are they his version of trophies? Or is it out of a twisted sentimentality?

There are more names here than the four women I think he killed before Gwen. I cross-check them again with a photo I took of the document with the names of all the women he was paired with by the charity over the years. They're all on here. Some are still alive and others died of natural causes. But these documents prove he tried to edge his way into their lives. I can only guess that they didn't fall for his charms, or they had family who stopped him in his tracks. However, I can't find any letters to or from Sue.

A brown padded envelope contains more paperwork. Inside are three marriage certificates for Eliza Holmes, Lucy Holden and Alice McKenzie. The envelope also contains different passports and driving licences using different surnames along with receipts for deed-poll name changes.

The contents of a shoebox slide about when I pick it up. I open the lid and scowl at three transparent tubs, each containing false teeth. The name of each woman is written on a lid in marker pen. The box also contains five old mobile phones. Two won't turn on but three do; in fact their batteries are almost full, which suggests Paul still uses them. None require a code to access the contents.

Each phone only contains images of him and the woman he gave that particular device to. Some are selfies taken on days out to the countryside or for lunch somewhere; others were taken in what I assume to be their gardens or houses. And what's this? Huh. He's only gone and taken every woman to Clacton-on-Sea, hasn't he? There are photos of him with Eliza on the beach and others with Lucy, eating fish and chips on the pier. I bet he planted the seed of that trip in Gwen's head.

There's something else that all these women have in common, I realise. They are all wearing the same gold band around their wedding ring finger. Among Paul's stuff I spot a small, crushed velvet ring box. I open it up and guess what I find? One after the other, each woman wore her predecessor's band. I snap the box shut.

Buried under a pile of clothes at the bottom of the wardrobe are two boxes of medication, both in plain packaging without a name attached to them. However, the tablets themselves have the word 'Omixinol' embossed on the back. A quick online search reveals it's a psychoactive substance that's illegal to possess without a licence. I'm as sure as God made little apples that Paul doesn't have one of those. And according to the Royal College of Pathologists' website, 'It is not part of routine screening so would only be identified in a toxicology report if the compound used to create it was specifically targeted.'

I press my back against the wall as I slot the pieces together. These meds explain Gwen's sudden psychotic episodes, her attack on me, and perhaps even why she 'fell' down the stairs the night she died. Paul had been drugging her like he had the wives before her. And this medication wouldn't have appeared in toxicology reports because there was no reason to look for it.

A yawn catches me unawares but I plough on. There's very little of interest for the next hour or so until the contents of another envelope raise my eyebrows. Inside are receipts from a nursing home in Oxfordshire. The account is registered in Paul Fernsby's name, but it's the name of the patient he is paying for that takes my attention.

Sue Fernsby.

Didn't Paul's creepy neighbour tell me she'd died? Yes, he was sure of it, in fact he remembered the date clearly – 1 February, two years ago – because it was the night he watched a memorable football match. This invoice says Paul was charged for the use of a private ambulance to take her to an Oxfordshire nursing home in the early hours of the next morning. And according to others, including one issued last month, he is still paying for a room for her there.

I'm still trying to get my head around this when, under this envelope, I find a photo album of Paul as a child. He was a cute lad, with an apple-cheek smile and a shock of white-blond hair. In some pictures he is riding a bike, in others he digs a moat around a sandcastle on the beach. There are two older children with him and a man I assume to be his dad, although they don't share many familiar features. A younger version of Sue is often either by Paul's side or hovering in the background. At least I assume it's her, as she looks quite like the framed photograph downstairs. In later images, Paul is older, perhaps seven or eight, and it's just him and her. He isn't looking into the lens in any of the shots and neither is he smiling. The album ends with a series of blank pages.

I close the book and bite down on my middle finger as I make sense of it. So I was wrong about two things. Firstly, Sue was, no, *is* Paul's mother after all. And secondly, she is still very much alive.

CHAPTER 41

CONNIE

I know I shouldn't have taken it, but sometimes I don't listen to common sense. Spread across the lounge carpet is all the evidence against Paul I stole from his house, arranged like the arc of a peacock's plumage. I have his phones, his passports and other ID, a dozen of the letters he wrote to his victims and their replies, copies of deed-poll name changes, the medication I suspect he fed them, and a picture of him and his mum from his photo album.

Everything else, I carefully replaced exactly as I found it, back in the boxes. I don't want him to have any idea someone has been there until he starts rooting around for something in particular. I'm also counting on him failing to notice I replaced the padlock on his back gate into the garden with a near-identical one until he can't unlock it with his key.

Walter texts to check I'm okay. He knows I was going to take a look at Paul's house but has no idea I actually broke into it or what I took. He'll only have a go at me and tell me again to go to the police. Sorry Walter, but not yet. When the next stage of my plan is over, then I'll do the right thing. Until then, I have to think of myself. So I reply, telling him I'll bring him up to speed when I clean his house tomorrow. I only started doing it on Monday. He'd been thinking about hiring a cleaner for a while, he said, and because I have more time on my hands since Gwen's death, he offered me first refusal. I'm not convinced he really does need the help as his place is always spotless. But I think he pities me, and because I have no pride, I agreed.

I was so tired on the bus rides home from Paul's place that I struggled to keep my conscience in check. I spent ages arguing the pros and cons of anonymously sending that detective Krisha Ahuja everything I'd just stolen. Even if it's enough evidence for her to look into Paul's behaviour, the best-case scenario would be an investigation, charges and a trial. But that would take more than a year. If he's found guilty, the police can seize the earnings a criminal has made from the crime they've been proven to commit. But that might take another twelve months. Can I really wait two more years to inherit Gwen's estate? No. And what if he's cleared? It'll all have been for nothing.

And that's not taking into account the many variables. I've researched them all, from Paul selling Gwen's house between now and then, to him spending the rest of her money or burying it in an obscure offshore account. It's not impossible that I could be waiting three, four or five years for forensic financial investigators to locate what's left, or I might get nothing at all.

So that leaves me with one other option, the one I've decided to take. It's a risk and I'm sweating just thinking about it. I need to calm myself down, so I make myself a roll-up. I should quit again, I think as I stand at the back door lighting it up. During my stay at HMP Bronzefield, I'd alternate between e-cigarette pens and roll-ups. We were allowed to vape in our cells but we could use tobacco when we were out exercising in the grounds. I combined the two.

When I look back on my time there, I can't complain. I made a few acquaintances, but mostly I kept myself to myself. The sentence didn't come as a great surprise. My brief had warned me that because I already had a criminal record for a similar crime a year earlier, I should expect anything up to four months. In the end, the magistrate met the guidelines in the middle. Mine was a stupid scam, I know that now, especially as I'd already inserted myself into Gwen's life by then. But it was early days in our relationship, money was tight and there was no guarantee of a pay-off.

I'd like to say my crime was complex and highly intelligent. It wasn't. It happened when I was on a date with a man I swiped left for on the app Married-But-Flirty. I've made dozens of fake profiles on morally dubious dating sites like that and met men searching for a little disingenuous fun behind the backs of their wives and girlfriends. On impulse, I stole this particular mark's credit card while he was in the pub toilets. It's never been easier to commit credit card fraud since tapping replaced chip-and-PIN as the norm. The maximum spent in any one transaction might only be £100, but that card can go a long way in a short space of time. So I used it in separate post offices to withdraw cash, netting £500 that afternoon. But when I discovered it hadn't been cancelled by morning, I got greedy and went on a mini spending spree, buying anything from groceries to toiletries and a handful of new outfits.

Usually, when these men realise they've been conned, they cancel the card and take the financial hit rather than admit to a wife or girlfriend exactly who might've stolen their card and the circumstances in which we met. But this arsehole had no choice but to confess. He and his wife ran their own company and I stupidly didn't realise that it was a business card I was spending on. She discovered the card's activity, looked through his phone, put two and two together, and once I was identified by CCTV, they insisted on pressing charges against me. The last time I was caught, I got away with a fine and a suspended sentence. This time I wasn't so lucky. And by leaving Gwen alone to serve my time, neither was she.

Fuck her.

My mum's gravelly voice comes quick and loud and out of nowhere.

Fuck Gwen. And fuck everyone but yourself.

I can hear Caz saying it so clearly, she could be standing behind me. She said it so often that apparently by the time I'd reached my second birthday, I was saying it as frequently as her. She'd even tattooed those four words along her rib cage. There were no exceptions to her mantra, not even me. But I wouldn't appreciate just what lengths she'd go to to 'fuck everyone but yourself' until I reached my early twenties and the day she had me arrested.

'No, fuck *you*,' I say. I don't want to think about her now, as there are more pressing matters than a ghost. And I wonder if she can hear me down there amidst the crackling flames of hell.

CHAPTER 42

CONNIE

Well, whoever named this place Sunny Meadows must have had a good sense of humour, because it's about as far from sunshine or a meadow as you can physically get. From the other side of the dual carriageway, I regard this nursing home from roof to road. It's a three-storey concrete eyesore, surrounded by three tower blocks that cast it in perpetual shade. Trustpilot reviewers have given it a paltry one and half stars out of five. From appearances alone, that's generous. It'd be a struggle to find a cheaper home to dump an elderly relative in than this. So it makes me wonder why Paul chose it for his mum, Sue. Surely after four murders and I assume four inheritances, he can't be short of cash?

It's my second visit to Oxfordshire in recent weeks. The last time was to visit the cemetery where Paul had Gwen buried in an unmarked plot not far from here, I think. I make a mental note to borrow flowers from someone else's grave and lay them on hers before I return home. I pat the creases out of my skirt and top before I make my way down a set of steps, along a graffiti-strewn underpass, and up another set before finally reaching double doors.

It takes a good minute after pressing the buzzer before the doors open. I head for an unmanned reception desk and push a silver bell, the kind you'd find on the concierge desk of an old hotel, then I wait again. It's only marginally more pleasant inside than it is outside. The air is stale, as if it's been trapped and recycled forever.

It takes me back to the care homes I worked at in my twenties, although none looked quite this desperate. Only now, when I look back at that period of my life, do I feel guilt. I was a horrible, selfish bitch back then. I'd use cleaning jobs at hospices and places like this to pocket the occasional ring or necklace to sell at a pawnbroker's for cash. It wouldn't be a regular occurrence, maybe once every couple of weeks, so as not to alert the managers that they had a theft problem. And when I did get caught, which happened twice, they quietly let me go, as the owners were afraid of the bad publicity a court case would give them.

I didn't question who I was robbing. I'd never met my maternal or paternal grandparents and was raised by Caz and her friends to believe elderly people were fair game. As a kid, they were a means to an end in distraction burglaries. As an adult, they weren't real people. They were unconscious, non-communicative bodies in beds, most only kept alive by ventilators. They wouldn't miss what I stole. I'm ashamed to admit that it wasn't until I reached my forties and met Gwen that my opinion changed. Once I pushed through the hazy detachment of her dementia, I discovered a human being, a woman who had lived and loved, hurt and healed, laughed and cried and who deserved my respect. I could only have dreamed of being a gifted parent like her. The more I learned about myself by being around her, the less I liked. I'm surprised I don't walk about with a stoop with the amount of shame I now carry.

I shake my head until the memories of old me disperse like dandelion heads in the breeze. I need to remain focused so I glance around the reception area. With no sign of anyone responding to the bell, I'm tempted to go behind the desk and find Sue's room number myself. Then a woman's voice sounds from behind me. 'Can I help you?' she says around a yawn.

'Hello,' I say as I turn. 'I've come to visit my aunt, Sue Fernsby.'

As the woman clocks me, she frowns, the lines across her forehead pointing down like an arrowhead. There are burst red capillary veins creeping across her cheeks. There's a ring on her wedding finger, a plain, silver band. There's something familiar about her, or at least a different version of her.

'Rachel,' she says, as if she has no doubt about who I am. Her use of my birth name takes me by surprise. The last person to use it was Paul.

'Yes?' I reply.

'You don't recognise me, do you?'

And then it hits me. 'Sammi,' I say with part-relief, part-caution. We worked together a lifetime ago, but just what does she remember about me?

'Yes!' she says with more enthusiasm than me. 'Oh my God, how long has it been?'

'I'm not sure.'

'2008, I think,' she says. 'We were working together at that home in Stratford.'

'The place with more cockroaches than patients. Wow. That was a dump, wasn't it?'

'Better than here though, right?'

I smile along with her.

'So,' she asks, 'how've you been? Married, kids?'

'No, neither,' I reply. 'You?'

'Yeah, twin boys, eleven going on twenty-one. Half the time I'm glad to be out of the house and working here, just so I can get some peace. So what really brings you here?'

The way she says 'really' means she doubts Sue is my aunt. If I continue to lie, she will see straight through me and I doubt I'll get any further than reception, no matter our shared history.

She speaks before I can think of an excuse. 'You're not up to your old tricks . . .'

'Oh God no, no, absolutely not,' I assure her. 'That was a different me.' Back in Stratford, most of us were on the take. Today, I decide to be uncharacteristically honest with her, to a point. 'It's a long story. Do you have time?'

She leads me into a private family room, orders me a tea from a vending machine and I begin to put my own spin on the events of the last few months. I explain that Gwen was a friend with no family, and that she promised to leave me her house in return for my care. I explain how Paul swooped in and came between us, and how I believe he was responsible for her death along with those of three other women.

'Holy fuck,' Sammi says when I've finished. 'That story is too crazy not to be true.'

I tell her why I haven't gone to the police – that I need more evidence against him. I need Paul to take me seriously, to see me as a threat. So I plan to take a selfie with Paul's mum to send to him, and make him aware of just how much I know about him. She looks a little unsure of my motives at first, but my face remains impassive.

'Promise me you won't stay in Sue's room any longer than five minutes, okay? Just take your picture and leave, because if you get found out, I'll get the bullet.'

'I will,' I say.

'She's in room 306 on the third floor.'

'Does Paul visit her very often?' I ask as I'm about to leave.

'Once every few weeks he'll make an appearance, but from what I've been told, he rarely pays her any attention when he's here.

He must like the view or something, because he was very insistent she had that exact room. He even pays extra for it.'

'What does the window look out on?'

'You'll see when you get there. It's both fitting and totally inappropriate at the same time.'

CHAPTER 43

CONNIE

I don't mean to sound heartless, but Paul's mum reminds me of an extra from that zombie TV show *The Walking Dead*. I stare at her from the doorway, lying there, her chest barely rising and falling. Her skin has a yellow, waxy tone and her face is gaunt and hollow-cheeked. Her eyes are closed, her mouth is open and she is toothless and missing dentures. Thin hair drapes her scalp and her frame is skeletal under that nightdress. She might be seventy or a hundred. I watch her for a few minutes, a stark reminder that any of us could become her. I'm relieved Gwen didn't suffer like this. She didn't deserve to die in the manner she did, but nobody should be forced to end their days like Sue. I'll book myself a plane ticket to a Swiss clinic before that happens to me.

I knock on the open door to alert her of my presence out of politeness rather than expectation. I pause, gaining the measure of the room. The off-white walls are bare and don't contain a single framed photograph or even a faded generic watercolour. Even if she never wakes up again, a few familiar objects might have been nice.

It seems as if Paul is as cold with his own flesh and blood as he is with the women he marries.

Time isn't on my side, so I circumnavigate the room, searching Sue's meagre possessions. Her drawers contain only nighties, spare bedsheets, towels, incontinence underwear and an unthumbed Bible. Behind me, on a shelf, I spot a cream-coloured teddy bear clutching a red love heart to its chest. I recognise it and smile to myself as an idea occurs. My plan just to take a selfie is about to take a dark detour.

But first, my attention is drawn towards an armchair in front of a window. It's positioned so that it faces out on to the view Sammi spoke of. Jesus. Now I understand what she meant. This care home overlooks a cemetery. And it takes me a moment to realise it's where I was weeks earlier – the place where Paul had Gwen buried. I squint as I stare and I can make out the plot of her unmarked grave. This can't be a coincidence.

A cold chill spreads across my chest. No, no, he didn't. I grab my phone, searching the internet for the cemetery's website. I cross-reference the names of Paul's other three victims and discover they are all buried there, in adjacent plots to Gwen's. I must have stepped over them to reach her grave. He's not just visiting his mum when he comes here; he is visiting all of them. He watches over their graves, keeping an eye on them in death as he did in life, his trophies close at hand. Every time I think I have him figured out, he moves the goalposts.

Just what am I about to get myself into by playing games with this man? It's not too late to back out. There's no shame in admitting defeat. But I just can't. I've come this far, I've got to see it through, for the sake of myself and every one of those women buried under his gaze. So I ignore common sense, regroup and slowly make my way over to Sue's open wardrobe. I reach up to the top shelf and remove a pillow. This is where they're always stored in places like this. I carry it towards a completely oblivious Sue. I turn to look at the teddy bear one more time before I lift the pillow towards my chest and then lower it. Now it's hovering just above her face. Then I gradually lower it further so that it touches the tip of her nose, her lips and forehead.

I apply more pressure until I feel her skull against the palms of my hands. She offers no resistance. Whatever basic survival instinct she once possessed has been eaten away by her dementia. Or perhaps, if a tiny shred of her old self remains locked inside, it realises death is her means of escape.

Her face is now smothered. With no resistance, it won't take long now.

Suddenly my phone rings. I turn to look again at the teddy bear and count to three before I lift the pillow back up again and take my phone from my pocket. The number has been withheld, but I know who's calling.

'Hello Paul,' I begin calmly, before he has the chance to speak. 'I think it's time we sat down and talked. Properly.'

CHAPTER 44

CONNIE

I arrive at the pub an hour early to give me the upper hand. In truth, it'll also allow me time to calm my nerves. I place the Reserved sign face down on the table and wait. This is actually happening.

I chose a village a twenty-minute bus ride away from home, so I didn't have far to travel. And it's not the first time I've been here. I visited two days earlier to check the floorplan and book a table. It had to be somewhere private enough for our conversation not to be overheard but where there was sufficient lunchtime foot-fall for us to be seen at all times. It also needed to be positioned next to the window overlooking the car park so I could see when his van pulled in. I don't want Paul to have any element of surprise. This place ticked each box. If he tries to hurt me today, I'm not going to make it easy for him.

I'm eyeing up the shelves behind the bar, which are stacked with dozens of bottles of wine. I'd kill for a glass or five of Merlot right now to take the edge off. But the sharp corners will help me keep my wits about me. I order a sparkling water instead. I'm tempted to go outside for a cigarette to calm my anxiety but I can't risk it. And it proves a wise decision, because five minutes later and approximately forty minutes ahead of time, Paul's vehicle enters the car park. My heart beats like a kettle drum when I catch sight of him making his way to the entrance.

He's dressed in a similar manner to how he was when I saw him in Gwen's house months ago, smart but casual. He doesn't scan his surroundings like I did. Instead, he saunters to the bar, pays for a bottle of beer then turns directly to me and makes his way over.

'You're early,' he says as he sits.

'And so are you,' I reply.

He looks at my chair, the table and window. 'It's where I would've sat. I told you last time, you and I are the same.'

'And I told you we are nothing alike.' But we both know there are similarities and I'm disgusted by them all. At least I want to be a better person. I doubt Paul can say the same.

'So Rachel, you got my attention with your little stunt at the nursing home.'

'I wouldn't have hurt her. I don't kill people.'

'You don't know what you're capable of until you're pushed.'

'I do, and it's not that. The plan altered when I saw the toy bear. It's one of those nanny cams parents put in nurseries to spy on the help, right?'

I don't explain how one got me fired from a hospice when the family of a patient on a life support machine caught me unclasping and pocketing a bracelet from her wrist. It was another error of judgement to add to my tally.

'So now I'm here, what do you want?' Paul asks.

'I want what's rightfully mine. Gwen's house and the money in her bank accounts.'

'That old chestnut, eh?' he sighs. 'You know that, by law, they're not rightfully yours.'

'She wanted me to have them. I cared about her, but you didn't give a damn.'

'Not strictly true,' he says. 'We had our moments. She was a game old bird. Surprisingly . . . uninhibited.'

He gives me a wink, wanting a reaction from me. But I won't bite.

'If you cared that much,' I say, 'then why did you kill her?'

He looks me up and down. 'Pass me your phone.' I hesitate, then do as he asks. 'Unlock it.' I type in my code. I assume he's now checking it to ensure I'm not recording our conversation. Eventually he slides it back and takes a swig from his bottle.

'How do you know I'm not wearing a wire?' I ask.

'Because this isn't *Line of Duty*.'

'Then I'll ask you again,' I continue. 'Why did you kill Gwen?'

He entwines his fingers and stretches them out in front of him until the knuckles crack. 'You had the pleasure of meeting my mum,' he says. 'It's taken her eight years of decline to get to where she is now. But it's still anyone's guess as to how long it'll be before she finally dies. Six months? A year? Two years? Who knows? Is that fair on her?'

'It's not fair on anyone in her condition.'

'So then you understand, what happened to Gwen was in her best interests. You know first-hand what it was like for her – pissing herself, wandering the streets, the forgetfulness, her temper tantrums.'

'There was more to her than that.'

'They were no more than glimmers. Are you really going to tell me that her accident didn't do her a favour?'

'You don't get to decide that.'

'I shouldn't, no. But until our laws on assisted suicide are over-hauled to meet a modern viewpoint, there are some people who feel obliged to take matters into their own hands.'

My eyes narrow. 'By some people, you mean you.'

'I didn't say that.'

'So let me get this right. You're saying that you've been killing women with degenerative mental conditions to spare them from future suffering?'

'They're your words, not mine.'

I sit back in my chair, my eyes burrowing into his. It wasn't what I was expecting to hear. But then I've come to expect the unexpected with Paul. I take another sip of my water and consider what he's just not quite admitted. Then I lean closer to him.

'Bullshit,' I say, slowly and carefully. 'Absolute, one hundred per cent bullshit. You are no more of a moral crusader than I am.'

Paul tilts his head ever so slightly to one side as if he is hurt by my accusation. And for a split second, I wonder if I've got it wrong and he was being genuine. Then he emits a deep laugh. 'Admit it,' he says. 'I almost had you there, didn't I?'

He finishes off his beer and stands up. Is he leaving already? No, he's going to the bar. He returns with a second bottle and a glass of red wine for me.

'Merlot, right?' he says. 'You were drinking it the night that you, me and Gwenny had dinner together.' I push it to one side. I don't trust him not to have slipped something into it. 'Incidentally,' he continues, 'why did you organise that car crash of a night? Did you really think all it'd take was an M&S Meal Deal and I'd tell you everything?'

'Walter said I should give you the benefit of the doubt. He knows better now though.'

'Oh does he?' Paul asks. 'I liked Walter. Living all alone like that, he seemed to quite enjoy the attention I gave him. Full disclosure, I've never been in a same-sex relationship, but there's a first time for everything, right?'

'He doesn't fit your criteria,' I say a little too quickly. 'He's as sharp as a pin. He's not vulnerable or gullible.'

'Not yet. But you know what the elderly are like. One funny turn can set the ball rolling, and before you know it, they're at the mercy of a stranger.'

I shake my head but I don't tell him that he disgusts me because I suspect it's what he wants to hear.

'So that's it?' he asks. 'That whole charade with my mum and the pillow was to get my attention so that you can tell me what I already know – you want Gwen's estate? Nice touch with the mice and cockroaches in her house, by the way.'

'She left it to me in her will. It's mine.'

'Mine, mine, mine,' he yawns. 'Change the record, Rachel. What do you seriously think is going to happen today? That a pang of conscience is going to make me hand it over to you, just like that?'

'If you don't, I'll go to the police and tell them everything I know about you.'

'Which is . . . ?'

I say each victim's name slowly. 'Eliza Holmes, Lucy Holden, Alice McKenzie.' I allow my words to hang there. Now it's Paul's turn not to lose eye contact with me, even when I take a sip of my water. Eventually he taps his cheek with his forefinger and breaks into a broad smile.

'What can I say?' He shrugs. 'I'm impressed. But when you think about it, what have you actually got, aside from a handful of names and a crazy theory? I'm just a man who likes his girls on the more mature side. It's no different to preferring redheads over blondes, curvy over skinny. I can marry whoever I want to because I enjoy being married. But being a widower is one of the pitfalls of my predilection. I volunteer to help the elderly in my spare time because I'm a good person. And unlike some,' he adds pointedly, 'I don't have a criminal record for conning anyone out of anything. I don't blackmail people. I haven't stolen credit cards or robbed from the infirm on their deathbeds. So why would the police believe anything you have to say?'

I pick up my phone and flick to the media section. I turn the screen and show him the evidence I took from his house. 'I have phones with photographs and videos on them, letters you wrote and proof of your name changes.'

Paul's arms and neck have tensed. He tries to hide it with a shrug of his shoulders, but he's as stiff as a board.

'So you stole from my house?' he asks.

'They're your words, not mine.'

'None of what you think you have can be used as evidence because it's all stolen material.'

'It'll be enough to get the police's attention. Different wives, identical deaths, name changes, new identities . . .'

'So what? I like to mix things up a little and change my name every now and again. It's perfectly legal. And the letters . . . well, I'm an old romantic. And why would the police be interested, when each inquest ruled those deaths as accidental?'

'There were toxicology reports for each victim, I assume?' I ask. Paul nods. 'But there'd have been no reason for the pathologist to have screened their blood for psychoactives, would there?' I flick to another image on my phone, a close-up of Paul's half-empty packets of Omixinol tablets. 'I've looked them up. The compounds used to create this particular medication can stay in the system of a dead body for up to five years. And because you buried those women, they can be exhumed and tested.'

From the corner of my eye, I watch as he very slowly curls his fingertips into his palms. I'm getting to him.

'That's assuming the police put to one side your criminal record and your own change of identity to con Gwen, and listen to you.'

'Is that a risk you're willing to take? For the sake of an estate that was never supposed to be yours?'

He takes several longer gulps from his bottle before he speaks again. 'Let's say I was to give you what you wanted. How do I know that you won't give this so-called evidence to the police anyway, out of spite or some misguided loyalty to dear departed Gwenny?'

'You don't, so you'll have to trust me.'

'Ha!' he laughs and looks around us as if waiting for the agreement of an audience. 'Did you hear that, ladies and gentlemen? Connie the con-woman is suggesting I trust her.'

'You don't have a choice.'

'We all have choices. And I'm about to give you one.' He peels the label off his bottle of Budweiser and I half expect an old Sheryl Crow song to appear on the jukebox. 'Why don't we work together?'

Pardon me? Now this I did not predict. 'You and me?' I ask, incredulously.

'Why not?'

I lean across the table. 'Because you're a killer!' I whisper. 'Why the hell would I want anything to do with you?'

Paul moves towards me, but I don't back away. We are barely inches apart. 'You have spent your life conning people,' he says. 'If we pool our experience, we could do better than we are. Especially you. Look at you, Rachel. You're an almost middle-aged spinster living in a rented house without a penny to your name. You're facing eviction and relying on food banks to feed yourself. How much shit needs to hit the fan before you pull the plug?'

I open my mouth to protest, but there's little point. I shouldn't be surprised he knows so much about me. I'm not the only one who does my homework.

'Don't cut your nose off to spite your face,' he continues. 'Think about it.'

'I don't need to,' I reply, but I can't deny there's a very small part of the old me that is tempted. I hate myself for even wanting to consider it.

We remain in a silent stalemate until, eventually, Paul shows his hand. He sits back in his chair, raises his bottle and clinks it against my glass. It cracks but doesn't break.

'Okay,' he says. 'I'll give you what you want. I'll be in touch.'

'One last question,' I ask. 'Why is your mum alive when all the others are dead?'

He purses his lips ever so slightly. If I'm not mistaken, I've hit a raw nerve.

He rests his hands on the table, and scans the rest of the pub, careful not to be overheard. 'Have you ever heard of a phenomenon called reawakening?' he asks.

'No.'

'Look it up, it's an interesting read. After years of being non-communicative and trapped in their own worlds, some dementia patients suddenly spring back to life and start talking again. Scientists reckon they tap into neural reserves for one last, brief moment of connection, and they usually die very soon after.'

'You're hoping that happens to Sue.'

'Yes. And if it does, I'm going to tell her in detail every nasty little thing I did to my girls, so that she will die knowing that it's all her fault.'

This time Paul gets the reaction he wants. His venom chills me and I feel myself pale. For the first time, I have met the real Paul. I want to ask what he means, but before I can, he turns his back on me and exits the pub, and I watch from the window as his van pulls away.

I should be feeling jubilant, like I've got one over on him. But he's left me cold and on edge. I may have won this round, but until Gwen's money is sitting in my bank account, our game is far from over.

CHAPTER 45

CONNIE

Where the hell is he? I pick my phone up and scroll through my messages again. Nothing. I check the phone isn't on silent before going through my missed calls list. Nothing. I even check my emails and junk folder. Nothing. Three days have passed since my confrontation with Paul and I haven't heard a peep from him.

How long does it take to engage a lawyer and sign everything over to me? More than seventy-two hours, I know that. But if the wheels are in motion, then why hasn't Paul messaged me with an update? It's in his best interests to keep me sweet, as I hold all the cards. I guess there's also the chance he might be calling my bluff to see if I really will go to the police with my evidence. But hoping they'll side with him over me is a big gamble for him to take. And Paul doesn't strike me as a gambling man. To pull off what he has takes research, planning and skill. Not risk. I think back to my own scams over the years, and for the most part, I've been one step ahead of the people I'm conning. At least to begin with. But Paul has been so many steps ahead of me that he's often too far in the distance for me to even focus on. Until now. Perhaps I should send him a photograph of what I have, as a reminder of who's in charge.

I look around the village pub and check I haven't missed anything. Walter recommended me to Tracy, the landlady of the Horse & Hatchet, so I have a new job cleaning here each morning. It's three hours' work, seven days a week, and I can fit it in around my dog walks and ironing. What I earn here is cash in hand and barely minimum wage and it won't keep the wolves from the door forever. But until the ownership of Gwen's estate is resolved with Paul, it'll put food in my mouth.

I put the mop and bucket in the storeroom and let myself out through the back. I check my phone again as I make my way home, but there's still nothing from Paul.

A car door opens ahead of me and I flinch. It's parked by the verge in front of my bungalow, and as the driver steps out, she looks straight at me. It takes me a second before it registers who she is.

'Hi Connie,' she says. 'How are you?'

And I don't have a good feeling about why she is here.

CHAPTER 46

DS KRISHA AHUJA

I catch sight of Connie in my wing mirror as I'm switching off the engine. A few months have passed since I last saw her. Gwen Wright's case remains in my memory, as you don't always get a successful outcome with a story like hers. And when I say 'successful', I mean her returning home alive. Not what happened next. Connie clocks me as I leave the car. I wave a static hand at her and her pace slows. I struggle to translate what she's thinking. It hangs somewhere between surprise and alarm.

'Hi Connie,' I say. 'How are you?'

'Krisha,' she says as she looks me up and down with caution. She is wearing an apron and carrying a caddy packed with cleaning products. Her hair is tied up above her head with a red scrunchie. She has lost weight and there are dark rings under her eyes. 'Keeping busy, I see,' and I point to the caddy.

'Needs must,' she replies and begins to move it behind her as if she's embarrassed. 'What are you doing here?'

'I need a word,' I say. 'Can we go inside?'

Connie hesitates for a beat too long before replying. 'Sure.'

I remove my bag from the rear seats, lock the doors and follow her up the path and into her house. When Gwen vanished, the team and I were based at Gwen's house, so it's the first time I've had reason to be inside Connie's. I don't know what I was expecting but it wasn't this. It's very small, there's a smell of stale cigarette smoke and an attempt to disguise it with lavender-scented room freshener. It reminds me of my police college digs.

It's me who asks if we can sit, and she mutters an apology for not offering sooner. She guides me to a two-seater sofa and keeps her distance in an adjacent armchair. She struggles to settle, crossing and uncrossing her legs.

'Is there a problem?' Connie asks as I place my bag by my feet. 'Is it about Mum? I assume you know that she's passed?'

'Yes,' I reply. 'And I was sorry to hear that. But let's start as we mean to go on, shall we? I know that Gwen Wright wasn't your mother. At least not biologically.' Connie opens her mouth as if about to protest but thinks better of it. 'I am a little disappointed you kept that from me when she went missing. Along with your birth name. Would you prefer me to call you Connie or Rachel?'

'Either is fine,' she says quietly. 'And for the record, I loved Gwen like a mum.'

'I'm not here to question that now. We have recently received a complaint about you regarding something else that we need to discuss.'

'About me?' she asks, perplexed. 'From whom?'

'Mrs Wright's husband, Paul Michael.'

'Paul?' she says. '*He* is complaining about *me*?'

I remove my notebook from my bag and flick through the pages to remind myself of the conversation we had when he appeared at the station two days ago. 'Mr Michael alleges that on October fourth, you broke into the property inherited by him from his late wife's estate and threatened him.'

'He said I did *what*?'

'And then again, on October twenty-eighth, you let yourself into the same house to search through his belongings.'

'They weren't his, they were Gwen's.'

'Finally, on November fourth, you illegally entered his mother's house in Oxfordshire and again, went through his private property.' I reach into my bag and remove a brown envelope containing a dozen A4 colour printouts. Each photocopy features an image of Connie in both houses on three separate dates. I pass them to her. 'They were all taken from security footage installed inside both homes, which I've viewed myself. They are dated and time-stamped. Can I ask what you were doing?'

Connie's cheeks turn a beetroot red before she clears her throat. 'I was searching for proof that Paul is a killer and I found it,' she announces. 'Before he killed Gwen, he murdered three other women in similar ways and he knows I'm on to him, which is why he's contacted you. He's trying to deflect the attention away from him.'

She waits for me to react. I think I'm about to disappoint her.

'I am aware of the allegations you've made against Mr Michael,' I reply.

'What? He's told you?'

'Yes.'

'And are you investigating him?'

'No.'

'Why? He's a killer.'

'Connie, Mr Michael said that when he began work at Mrs Wright's property back in May, you made it clear you were interested in him in a romantic capacity, engineering time to be alone with him and inviting him to dinner.'

'We had conversations, yes, but they weren't "engineered",' she huffs.

'He also agreed to go out with you for dinner, where he insists he made it clear that he wasn't interested in you in that way, despite, and I quote, "your repeated attempts to seduce him".'

'Seduce?' She lets out a sharp laugh. 'He's making this up!'

'And then, when you discovered that he and Mrs Wright were in a relationship, you turned against him and attempted to split them up out of jealousy.'

Connie shakes her head vigorously. 'Absolutely not.'

'Mr Michael told me that he agreed to meet with you recently, is that right?'

'Yes.'

'At this meeting, did you try to blackmail him and threaten to accuse him of killing his late wife and others if he didn't sign her estate over to you?'

'No, no, no, it wasn't like that at all, he's twisting what happened.'

'So that conversation categorically didn't happen? You didn't try and extort money from him?'

'Well, yes, but not extort exactly, but . . . look, Krisha, I just want what's rightfully mine.'

'And just to clarify, when you say, "what's rightfully mine", you are referring to the estate of a woman whom you had only met a year or so earlier and whom you told everyone, including me, was your mother?'

Her cheeks puff and I can tell she wants to argue the point but knows she can't. 'Once Paul signed Gwen's estate over to me, I was going to give you the evidence I'd found that proves what he did.'

'Ah yes, evidence. I assume it's the same evidence that Mr Michael mentioned has disappeared from his mother's house?'

'Yes. Did he tell you what I took?'

'He mentioned they were items of a personal nature.'

'So I assume he didn't mention it was evidence of how he chose these vulnerable women, how he pursued them, persuaded them to trust him, married them, before drugging and killing them?'

Connie doesn't give me the opportunity to respond.

'Come with me,' she says as she climbs to her feet and strides towards the door. I struggle to put my notebook back in my bag quickly enough and have to jog a little to catch her up. 'Where are we going?' I ask but she doesn't respond. We walk the length of her road, turn left at the junction and approach a row of houses. Connie marches up to a rear gate and unbolts it and I follow her into a neatly kept garden.

'Whose property are we in?' I ask cautiously.

'My friend Walter's.'

In the corner stands an old dovecote. She turns a bucket upside down, stands on it, and removes the dovecote's roof and places it on the ground. 'It's all in here,' she continues. 'Letters, mobile phone recordings, medication, fake passports and driver's licences with his different names on them. I have all of it. And I can tell you other things he did, like putting reflective film over Gwen's bedroom windows so no one could see in, a padlock on her bedroom door, and he changed the locks to the house. And I know it isn't enough on its own to prove anything and that he'll just say that she asked him to, but alongside what I've been hiding, I have enough to nail the bastard.'

She stretches her arm to put a hand inside and fumbles around. There is a hole in each side of the construction. I assume it's compartmentalised, as her hands move around it. However, her triumphant expression makes way for confusion.

'I don't understand,' she says. 'Where is it? I put it all in here myself.' She fusses some more, shaking her head and muttering.

I read Connie's criminal record before I came here. I know that for most of her life, she has conned and extorted people and served time for it. Her mother did the same. And from what Paul suggested, I suspect she was likely planning to con Gwen before he came along. She has had years to perfect this 'trying to deflect from your own behaviour by accusing someone else' routine, so if I didn't know what she was capable of, I might be convinced.

The same can't be said for Paul, though, either when Gwen vanished or during his recent appearance at the station. I didn't believe his explanation when he returned Gwen home and claimed their weekend away in Clacton-on-Sea was down to miscommunication. I also wasn't persuaded that he is being harassed or extorted by Connie, even after he showed me the footage of her breaking into his properties. And I can't deny that if what she has said about Paul changing the locks and attaching a lock to Gwen's bedroom door is true, it's highly suspicious behaviour.

'What's the problem?' I ask her.

'It's gone. Everything I found at his house and took with me. I swear, it was in this box.'

'Why did you leave it here?'

'I thought it'd be the last place Paul would look when he realised it was missing.'

Her fingertips must have connected with something because her confusion is replaced by hope. She pulls out a small electronic device, like an old MP3 player.

'Is that yours?' I ask.

'No.' She presses a button and we fall silent as the opening bars of a song play. If I'm not mistaken, it's ABBA's 'The Winner Takes It All'.

Connie's shoulders slump, despairingly. She is either a deluded fantasist, one of the most accomplished liars I have ever come across, or she is telling the truth. And I can't help but think she might be telling the truth. But without any proof to back up her claims, I'm restricted in what I can do.

'I've got photos on my phone,' she says suddenly and pulls it out to search through it. 'I don't understand,' she continues. 'They've all been deleted.'

'Connie, Mr Michael says he doesn't want to take it any further on this occasion,' I continue. 'But he has asked that we speak to you. He appreciates Mrs Wright's death has put you under extreme duress and believes you have chosen to make him the object of your anger.'

She shakes her head. 'I'm not, Krisha, I'm really not. He is a killer. He near enough admitted it.'

'Do you have any evidence at all?'

'Yes, but they're all in graves. Eliza Holmes, Lucy Holden, Alice McKenzie and Gwen. Dig up their bodies, do blood tests and I guarantee you'll find the same drug in all their systems. Omixinol. It's a psychoactive that makes their confused state even worse. Paul gave it to them all before he killed them. I'm sure of it.'

'And you saw this happen? You witnessed him giving these women that drug yourself?'

'No. But just exhume them. Please?'

'We can't just go around digging up bodies based on an accusation. There are all kinds of procedures involved in a body's exhumation.'

'I'm telling you the truth.'

'I believed you when you claimed you were Mrs Wright's daughter,' I say. 'And then I discover you have criminal convictions including fraud and theft from elderly people and had conned Gwen into believing you were her daughter to gain her trust and her money. What you have done is committed fraud. So you must see how what you're telling me appears from my perspective.'

'I know, I know,' she says, her voice shaking. 'Some of what I've done in my past is unforgivable. But Gwen's death has changed me. Honestly, it has.'

'Yet you admitted to me that, rather than bringing us your evidence and saying, "This is what I found out about Gwen's husband," you confronted him and tried to blackmail him for your own gain.'

'But Krisha, I told you, once I got what I was owed, I was going to give it all to you anyway.'

'I only have your word for that.' Christ, this is frustrating. 'Look Connie, I'm asking you to leave Paul alone. We have enough evidence to charge you with breaking and entering and possibly harassment, and if you're found guilty it will likely lead to another custodial sentence. Paul says that out of loyalty to his late wife, who was very fond of you, it's not what he wants. Do you?'

Her face begins to crumple. 'No.'

'If it continues, he's also well within his rights to look into taking out a non-molestation order forbidding you from harassing him, pestering him, communicating with him or going anywhere near his homes. And you will be arrested if you break that order. Do you understand?'

Her nod is almost imperceptible, but it's there.

I need to make her listen and understand. 'Connie,' I say firmly. 'For your own good, put Paul and Gwen's relationship behind you and start your life again. Otherwise this is not going to end well for you.'

I wish her the best and make my way to the gate, leaving her alone in her neighbour's garden. I hope she takes my advice, I really do. But something tells me she won't and that our paths will cross again.

CHAPTER 47

CONNIE

I'm shell-shocked. I collapse into the sofa, unsure of how to process everything Krisha has just told me. Where do I start? Once again Paul has turned me into the villain. How could I not have seen this coming? I'm an idiot.

If you're going to get away with multiple murders like Paul has, you must have to plan for all eventualities and have solutions in place for potential complications. And I'm a complication. But the problem I have, is that while he can think like me, I don't think like him. It didn't dawn on me that if he had a hidden camera in the room of his mother's care home, then he'd likely have them inside her old house and Gwen's place too. Once he knew I'd broken into both, he must have gone back and watched the recordings of me, then passed them on to Krisha to back up his claims I was harassing him. I handed myself to him on a plate.

One thing I don't understand is why Paul didn't show her the clip of me holding a pillow over his mum's face. I'd never have hurt her, but that evidence is more damning than anything else he has.

I'm sure that if Krisha had seen it, I'd be in a police holding cell right now and not here, licking my wounds.

How did he delete all my pictures? And leaving me an MP3 player containing that ABBA song was a particularly spiteful touch. The lyrics said it all. My cards have been played, Paul is the winner and he's taken everything from me. He cannot be beaten, he is too good at what he does. There's nowhere for me to go from here.

I must say though – and it might be wishful thinking – but there were times when I was sure Krisha was more sympathetic towards me than she was to Paul. It was as if she kept stopping short of saying what was really on her mind.

My phone suddenly vibrates with two sharp bursts, cutting through the silence. The number has been withheld but there's a blurred image. I think it's a video clip. Curiosity gets the better of me and I press play. The images are dark and grainy, but they've been recorded in a room. There's a crack in the curtains and a streetlight outside allows a little light in. Then it switches to some kind of night vision mode, the screen filling with greens, blacks and whites. There's a stationary figure, lying horizontal. Suddenly I realise what I'm looking at.

Me, in my bedroom, asleep.

This is video footage taken in my home.

Paul has been here. He's not in shot, but I know it's him. Who else would it be?

I'm too scared to blink and risk missing a second. I watch myself lying on my side in the video, facing away from the camera and towards the window. I recognise the white, patterned T-shirt I'm wearing by the logo on the back. I wore it only last night. He was here just hours ago. The camera angle is high and doesn't move but the image gets closer and closer, and as I roll over on to my back, I see my chest rising and falling. It edges its way up towards my face, which fills the screen for at least a minute. I'm not used to seeing myself sleeping; nobody is. And I'm frightened at how exposed and weak I am.

It comes to a sudden end when my body wakens with a start, and then freezes. I already know what happens next because I remember it clearly. I always do. I remain in my bed, paralysed by fear, desperately trying to decide if I have dreamed a noise or if there is actually someone there.

I want to be sick. How many times has this happened before? How many times have I lain there, scared and vulnerable, before finally plucking up the courage to turn and find myself alone? How many times have I then told myself off for letting my imagination run riot? I was right all along.

Another clip begins. This time it's footage filmed of me in the shower. Once again, it's taken from an overhead angle. I'm washing my hair, and like the first clip, it zooms in. This time it stops at my bare breasts. I feel violated, and as I watch, I find myself covering them with my elbows. A montage quickly follows: me pouring water from my kettle into a Cup-a-Soup and eating alone, on the toilet, rolling up cigarettes, dancing to music playing from my phone, crying alone in the lounge and even picking my nose. Judging by what I'm wearing, Paul has spent months capturing my every intimate moment on camera. In fact, some of this must have been filmed even before he came into my and Gwen's lives. Just how long has he had me in his sights?

I search every inch of the lounge ceiling until I find a hole, no bigger than the head of a thumb tack. It's the same in every other room of the house. I grab the long metal hook from the hallway to unhook the clip to the loft hatch. The ladder drops with alarming speed and I climb it, warily at first, until I find the light switch. The empty space is illuminated, and I continue up and walk carefully across the floorboards, looking for cameras. But there are none. Just holes with tight shafts of vertical light shining through them.

Twelve in all, sometimes two per room. Looking around, I spot next door's loft hatch. There is no firewall separating my half from the neighbour's empty house. Paul must have climbed in through that side and made his way over to mine.

That's why my pictures were deleted. He's been in my home.

I steady myself against a rafter because my whole body is trembling. I have badly underestimated Paul. He thinks that he can do whatever he pleases because he is untouchable. And what scares me the most, is that he is right.

CHAPTER 48

WALTER CLARK, NEIGHBOUR

Connie is already in tears the moment I open the front door. It's as if the weight that's constantly on her shoulders has finally crushed her. And she doesn't have to tell me that this is related to Paul, I just know.

'Come in, come in,' I say and give her a weak hug. I curse that last stroke which robbed me of my strength. Anyone who tells you getting old is a positive thing is a liar. I shuffle behind her into the lounge, and as she sits I reach for a box of tissues on the fireplace mantel. I leave them on the arm of her chair.

Despite my best attempts of late to encourage her to open up about what she has planned in the way of bringing Paul to justice, she's been reluctant to give anything away. She's palmed me off with claims that she's not discovered anything new and that as soon as she does, she'll tell me. But I don't believe her and I've done a little detective work myself.

However, today, it takes very little prompting before it all spills out and she confesses to what she's been up to. She recounts breaking into Paul's house – I don't even ask how on earth she knows how to do such a thing – and later, confronting him with the evidence she stole and demanding Gwen's house is returned to her. She even admits to how she hid evidence in my dovecote, something I'm not thrilled about but for which she apologises. She finishes by recalling the police warning to leave him alone. I'm trying my hardest to play it cool, but inside, I want to strangle her for putting herself at such risk and not going to the police first.

'I've messed it all up,' she admits. 'I shouldn't have tried to blackmail him. I was greedy.'

'You weren't greedy, you were desperate, sweetheart,' I say in the faint hope of consoling her.

'I lost my perspective. I was so worried about being evicted and being left with nothing that I panicked.'

'Are things that bad?'

She nods. 'I don't have any clients left in Italy, I can't afford the bills or rent on the bungalow. I thought that inheritance was going to solve all my problems. Then I'd give the evidence to the police, Paul would end up behind bars and that would be it. But he's still free and now I'm trapped. I'm too scared to sleep in my own bed anymore.'

'Why?'

She takes her phone from her pocket while I move my glasses from around my neck and slip them on to my nose. She plays me a video of her sleeping. I'm not sure of the relevance until the next clip of her appears in the shower. She quickly presses stop.

'He's been recording me for months,' she tells me. 'There are more like it.'

'Sweet Jesus,' I gasp. 'You need to give this to the police, you simply have to.'

'I can't,' she argues. 'The video could have been filmed by any-one for all they know. I could have done it myself to set Paul up. He's already made me out to be a stalker.'

Her stubbornness infuriates me sometimes and makes me glad I don't have kids of my own. They'd have put years on me. 'So what are you going to do then?'

'Nothing. He's won. I give up. Game over. Paul has what he wants, so that's it. I have no choice.'

I pause for thought. There's a way I can help her, but if I tell her, I can't guarantee her head is in the right place to do the right thing. I decide to keep schtum for now, until I've weighed up the pros and cons. But I do make a snap decision about something else.

'You're staying with me, here,' I say. 'This house is large enough for the two of us to muddle around in without feeling as if we're on top of one another. If you're under this roof, I'll know you're safe.'

'I can't impose on you like that,' Connie replies. But it's not an outright refusal.

'It's no imposition. You're here every day anyway to walk Oscar or to clean, so you're already a part of the furniture you polish. I'm not arguing with you on this, Connie. If you're struggling to make ends meet then there's no point in staying in a bungalow you can't afford. You need a little time to save up some money, so the spare room is yours. You'll need to clear the crap out of it first though.' She'll have her work cut out for her as I've used that room as a dumping ground for the last twenty years.

'Thank you,' she says quietly.

And for the first time in today's visit, I relax a little. Until her phone vibrates. We both glare at it and then at each other. Eventually she picks it up, and by the way the remaining colour drains from her already pallid complexion, I know she's received another message from Paul. She turns the screen so we can both see what he has sent her.

Send Walter my love, reads the caption, and my blood chills. It's followed by another video. This time it's been taken through a window, and it's of Connie walking away from her bungalow.

She holds her hand over her mouth. 'This was filmed a few minutes ago,' she whispers. 'He was in the house while I was still there.'

CHAPTER 49

CONNIE

I take a lingering look around the place I've called home for the last twenty months, and realise I won't miss it one little bit when I move out. Paul has ensured this is no longer a safe place for me. Every door and window now remains locked and repeatedly checked day and night. There's a padlock on the inside of next door's loft hatch. Yet each creak of a floorboard or clunk of a water pipe still has me on tenterhooks, frightened Paul is breaking in again.

And I know that by sending me those videos, it's how he wants me to feel. He's toying with me like a cat with an injured mouse. The predator hurts it, lets it go, plays with it, sets it free again then hurts it some more. Eventually, the cat grows bored and strikes a final, fatal blow. And I fear that's what Paul is going to do with me. I don't think he can help himself. Like the cat, it's in his nature.

I've spent all day cleaning each room from ceiling to skirting board. I don't expect to get any of my deposit back because I'm already four months in rent arrears, so the letting agency will be keeping that. I'm doing it because I feel bad for how much the owner has lost out financially by my inability to pay. I've promised myself that they'll be the last people I take advantage of. It's taken me almost forty-three years to realise I need to start leading a more honest life, but I'm finally at that point. It's like a mid-life crisis, only I'm not buying a sports car or dating a man half my age.

I reckon I'll soon be ready to move my stuff into Walter's place. It's taken days but we've finally managed to get rid of dozens of bin bags full of clutter from his spare room. I won't be able to pay my way at first, but I've told him I'll cook all our evening meals and I'll clean the house for free.

I'm a little reluctant to lose a place of my own as, Caz aside, the only time I've shared with anyone is at Her Majesty's pleasure. But needs must. And I'm sure Walter's offer isn't an entirely selfless act. He'll have company and someone to look out for him. He's in his mid-seventies, and after his strokes, there must be an underlying fear in living alone.

Walter reminds me of Gwen in many ways, as she too was a kind soul. Their behaviour couldn't be any different from my mum's, although lately I've been trying harder to focus more on the good times Mum and I spent together than the bad. They're few and far between, but one memory keeps swimming to the surface. She loved my manicures and pedicures. For a woman who only cared about her appearance when she needed to make money for her drug habit, she loved having her fingers and toenails filed and polished. I guess it was quite an intimate moment, just her and I, me gently cleaning and repairing fingers and toes that resembled my own, often in a comfortable silence. It was the closest we ever came to being a typical mother and daughter.

I remember painting them for her the night before her funeral. In truth, she didn't deserve my care, but it was my way of saying goodbye to her despite all she'd done and failed to do. The make-up artist at the funeral home had tried to hide the substantial bruising to her face and body from the fatal beating given to her by the person the police believed to have been a client when she was prostituting herself. They'd then dumped her body in a wheely bin in Walthamstow. It was a fitting end. She died as she had lived, in and as waste.

I spent about an hour with her that last day. The only sound in the room was the stick attached to the nail polish brush tapping against the side of the bottle when I dipped it in and out. I suppose that time was my final chance to get my feelings off my chest. But I didn't say a word. I didn't tell her that I hated her, that I forgave her, that I missed her or that I wished she had been a better mum. Instead, I simply painted her nails, whispered goodbye and left.

There's a sudden knock at the door, which puts the fear of God into me. Paul's face flashes into my head as fast and bright as lightning. I tell myself no, of course he wouldn't knock. He'd just appear. So I open the door, careful to keep the chain on. The caller's face is vaguely familiar. He is tall and tanned and his brow is furrowed. His smile is more hopeful than friendly.

'Connie Wright?' he begins nervously. My lack of denial gives him his answer. 'I'm sorry to bother you, but do you have a moment?'

'Who are you?'

'You called me because you were worried about my mum and said it was too late for yours.' I open the door a little further. 'I'm Jon Brown,' he adds. 'My mum's name is Fran. And two days ago, I think Paul tried to kill her.'

CHAPTER 50

CONNIE

My stomach begins the first in a series of somersaults. Now I remember where I recognise him from – his LinkedIn profile photo. That's where I learned the name of the company he works for in Dubai and found his contact details. But I didn't give him my name, so how did he find me? My phone is pay-as-you-go and unregistered. He answers my question before I can ask it.

'You didn't withhold your number when you rang,' he explains. 'And I have a mate back here who works for a telecommunications company. He pinpointed the area where the phone is most used. Then I asked around the village to see if they knew someone whose mum had died very recently of dementia, and claimed I'd lost her contact details, which is how I ended up here. I'm sorry to turn up like this.'

The whites around his hazel eyes have taken on a pinkish hue. I recognise tired and haunted when I see them, because I am both. My gut tells me that by letting Jon Brown in, I'm also inviting trouble. But I just can't close the door on him. He follows me into the lounge.

'What happened to your mum?' I ask.

'She was found in the garden, unconscious and with a head injury,' he replies.

'Is she still alive?'

'Barely. She's in a coma at Leicester General Hospital. The police think she tripped over an uneven paving stone and fell against the barbecue, knocking herself out. She was there all night until she was found in the morning. If you hadn't called me, I'd probably have thought no more of it, as she's unsteady on her feet at the best of times.'

'And you don't think that's what happened?'

He shakes his head. 'No.'

'What makes you think Paul was involved?'

'I discovered he and Mum got married last week.'

Last week? This is his fastest turnaround yet.

'The day I flew home, an ex-girlfriend who works as a junior doctor at the same hospital Mum's in noticed it in her records. She thought it was a mistake and asked me. I didn't believe it until she did a public records check and found Mum recently married a man called Paul Hayes. He came to the hospital the morning when she was first admitted – I was still on the flight over here – but he hasn't been seen since. When her doctor called him with her test results and explained she was brain stem dead and that it was only a machine keeping her alive, Paul said he wanted it turning off as soon as possible. He said he'd come in and sign the paperwork but that he didn't need to see her again. They asked about giving other family members the opportunity to say goodbye, but he told them it wasn't necessary and repeated that he wanted the machine turning off.'

'But Fran's definitely still alive?'

'For now. The hospital has given us a stay of execution for forty-eight hours, then that's it.'

My fingers form a steeple shape over my mouth. This is all too familiar. 'Can you excuse me?' I say and offer him a seat while I disappear into the kitchen. I pour myself a glass of wine and drink it in one long gulp. Something about this is off. His other victims were definitely dead before he called for help. Then it dawns on me that this might, through Jon, be the opportunity I need for my accusations against Paul to be taken seriously by the police. I pour another glass and drink half of it before I return to the lounge.

'I'm sorry, I just needed a moment,' I tell him. 'This is very personal to me and . . . a lot has happened recently that's forced me to draw a line under the Paul situation.'

'Please,' he says. 'I need to know what you know. You must have thought something was seriously wrong if you went to the trouble of tracking me down and warning me about him. I need to know who I'm up against.'

'Who found your mum?' I ask.

'Paul did. He told the paramedics he hadn't realised she'd left the house overnight. He said he checked for a pulse but couldn't locate one. Only they found it. It was very, very faint, but it was there.'

'Paul messed up,' I say. 'If he had any doubt at all that your mum was still alive, he'd have left her there for longer. He'd have only called for help if he was convinced she was dead. All the others had been gone for hours before he "found" them.'

Jon's face pales. 'The others? What others?'

I really don't want to be a part of this but I don't think I have a choice. 'I'll tell you everything I know, but you need to be aware of two things,' I say. 'I'm not going to come out of this well, and if you decide to go to the police, you have to leave my name out of it. Because if you don't, there's a very good chance Paul will try and hurt me. Do I have your word?'

'Yes,' he says without hesitation.

I start at the beginning and am completely honest as to how and why I met Gwen and what my intentions were. I recount how Paul weaved his way into her life and was responsible for her death. I tell Jon how three other women have died and how I tried to blackmail Paul into giving me what I wanted before I planned to report him to the police. And I explain how my evidence was stolen from under my nose, blowing my opportunity to get justice.

'You don't have to believe any of this,' I conclude. 'You don't know if I'm a fantasist or if I'm trying to scam you too. And I don't blame you if that's what you're thinking. All I can add is that I have no reason to lie because everything I have to lose has already gone.'

Finally, I offer him my apology. 'I'm so sorry, Jon,' I add. 'If I'd given my evidence to the police when I had it, I might've saved your mum.'

I sit back in my chair, relieved to have got it off my chest, but nervous of how he's going to react. It's a hell of a lot to take in.

'I think I need some air,' he says eventually and rises to his feet. We make our way to the back door and step outside. I light up a cigarette and he asks if I have one to spare. I light his too.

'Mum hated it when I smoked,' he recalls. 'Years ago, when I came back from a day trip to the French hypermarkets, I'd stocked up on a dozen cartons of Marlboro Lights. She found them in the shed and turned the hosepipe on them all. She'd be doing the same to me if she could see me now.'

I try, but fail, to imagine what it must have been like to have a parent who cared.

'What would you do if you were me?' he asks suddenly. 'You know this man, I don't. From what you've told me, he's holding all the cards.'

'But he doesn't, not anymore,' I say. 'Because your mum is still alive and he didn't plan for that. If it were me, I'd persuade your doctor friend to organise a toxicology report to discover what's in your mum's system. I'm sure they've already done routine blood-work, but because it's assumed her fall was an accident, they won't have tested her for everything. If Paul's used the same drugs on her as he did with the others, they will find traces of a drug called Omixinol. It's a psychoactive that she had no reason to take. Get the results fast-tracked, and if they find it in her blood, it might be enough to prompt a police investigation.' I find the direct line for DS Krisha Ahuja and he stores it in his phone. 'Don't tell her we've spoken, as I have zero credibility with her and I want your accusations to be taken seriously.'

Jon thanks me, we stub out our cigarettes and I walk him to the front door.

'I also think Paul was presumptuous when it came to your mum,' I conclude. 'He assumed with you living abroad, there was no one to look out for her. I hope it'll be his undoing.'

'I hope so too,' Jon adds quietly, and makes his way up the garden path before he stops and turns. 'You could be right when you say you might've saved Mum if you'd gone to the police sooner.' My eyes sink to the floor like a scolded dog's. 'However, I should have listened to you when you called me and done something about it. Instead, I dismissed you. Just because we let her down once doesn't mean we'll do it again.'

I hope not. I really do.

CHAPTER 51

CONNIE

I don't think it's possible to find a more characterless office than the one I am sitting in. There are about a dozen booths in here in the open-plan layout of Jobcentre Plus, all separated by clear plastic screens. They each contain a desk, a chair either side of it, and a computer. It's the kind of workplace that would have sent me and Caz running to the hills. But now I can only dream of being employed somewhere like here instead of in the unskilled manual labour roles I'm destined for.

According to his name badge, the young man sitting opposite me is called Harry. His red hair is scraped up into a man-bun and he wears two sleeves of tattoos, several of which contain clock faces. It's ironic, as people his age have no concept of how quickly time passes. And I wonder if someone his age should really be deciding if I'm deserving of the weekly £84.40 of the government's Jobseeker's Allowance I'm trying to claim?

It doesn't take long for his computer to tell him that no, I'm entitled to sod all, as I haven't paid any National Insurance for more than a decade. To his credit, Harry is sympathetic, and I get the impression that he really wants to help me back into work. But there are many objects standing in my way, like my age, my criminal record and my lack of qualifications. There are slim pickings out there for someone like me.

'Do you have any hobbies that might be able to help you find work?' Harry asks.

'No, not really.'

He's not ready to give up, bless him. 'Is there any training we could point you in the direction of, something you always wanted to do but were never in a position to explore until now?'

His question brings to the surface long-buried ambitions. As a teen, I decided beauty therapy was going to be the career that carried me away from my and Caz's grubby little world to somewhere clean. I loved looking at models like Kate Moss, Linda Evangelista and Claudia Schiffer in shoplifted *Vogue* and *The Face* magazines. I taught myself how to do my fingernails and make-up like they did theirs. I discovered how to make myself look older simply with a bit of shading or contouring. It was also how I caught the attention of unsuitable, older men. Now you'd call them paedophiles, but back then, I'd have been blamed for leading them on. The plan was to enrol in college as far away from East London as possible. And I found one some three hundred miles away in Sunderland, which, by some miracle, accepted me.

The curriculum included everything I'd need to help me become a well-rounded, highly employable therapist. I had it all planned out. Once I graduated, I'd land myself a placement at a salon or spa, and then, with practical experience under my belt, I'd find work on luxury cruise ships and liners. I'd travel the world doing a job I loved and seeing places I'd only ever watched on television. Just a few months separated me from the better life I deserved.

'I need your help.'

Caz was gasping for air when she burst through the front door of my flat, slamming it behind her. There'd been no contact between us for the best part of a month before this sudden reappearance.

'What have you done?' I asked.

I spotted a backpack under her coat as she turned. She unzipped it and removed two transparent, flour-sized bags, each containing white powder, and then a handgun. I swallowed hard.

'You've got to look after them for me,' she informed me. 'It's only for tonight. I'll be back in the morning to pick them up.'

'No, Caz,' I said. 'A stolen Nintendo or counterfeit cash is one thing, but drugs and a weapon? No. Absolutely not.'

'They don't belong to me. And the gun is a replica.'

'I don't care! Why can't you keep them with you?'

'We've already been tipped off that the police are on to us.' I didn't ask her who 'us' was, because I didn't want to know. 'If I'm caught in possession, I'm going down for a five to seven stretch, what with my record. Is that what you want?'

I shook my head and she moved towards me, clutching my hand in hers. Faint traces of baby-pink polish remained on her nails from my last manicure.

'Rach, when do I ask anything of you? I promise I'll swing by first thing to get them. You're the only person in the world I trust, you always have been. I don't say it enough, but you're the best thing I have ever done with my shitty, shitty life. And now I need you.'

I had waited all my life to hear her say she needed me. I knew I should've told her to get lost. Instead, as always, I did what was asked of me.

It was approaching 5 a.m. when the police started banging on my front door. I peered out the window, bleary-eyed, just in time to see them lining up a battering ram against the lock of the door. Warrants were flashed, searches began, officers stood watching while I protested my innocence and changed into my clothes.

The discovery of the drugs and the weapon hidden under the kitchen sink led to my arrest and questioning. I admitted that while, yes, they were in my home, they didn't belong to me. Only when I refused to name the person who'd left them there did they explain the gun wasn't a fake and had been used to fatally shoot a drug dealer in a recent robbery. I could have vomited there and then. I knew how much trouble I was in but I couldn't drop Caz in it. She was my mum and I was raised to break the law, not help it.

With bail refused, I spent nine months on remand until my case arrived at court. I hadn't heard a peep from Caz, either in person or through my brief. I pleaded guilty, hoping it might draw her out of hiding, and even on the day of my sentencing, a part of me still expected her to appear in court and admit responsibility. With all my heart, I didn't think she'd let me down. And then she did. It was only as I reached the end of the first twelve months of my four-year sentence that I learned from a new inmate and cohort of hers that it was Caz who had given the police my name to save her own skin. But by then, I was too indifferent to her to feel disappointed.

My dream of a fresh start at college in Sunderland was long dead by the time I was released on probation after two and half years. I didn't even bother to reapply. The council had repossessed my flat shortly after Caz sold all my belongings, so all I had left were the savings in my bank account I'd earmarked for college. There was enough for a deposit on another flat and to tide me over until I decided what to do next with my limited options.

It was only when I slipped my debit card into the cash machine that I discovered my account had been drained. Even the pittance I'd earned working in prison had vanished. Caz had taken it all. A study of my statements revealed she'd begun withdrawing from it the day I was sentenced. Then, every month she returned to milk her cash cow a little bit more. Now I was homeless and penniless. And twenty years later, history is repeating itself.

I shake my head at Harry's question. 'No, I've never had any career aspirations, I'm afraid.'

'That's okay,' he says. 'It was just a thought.'

One of his colleagues passes behind him and she apologises for interrupting. I glance at my phone as they talk, to see if Paul has sent me any more videos. To my relief, there's nothing. It's been a fortnight since his last message and I hope that's it between us. I also haven't heard anything from Jon Brown regarding his mum and blood tests. I'm desperate to know what's happened, but for my own safety, I can't get involved.

Harry's colleague's name badge catches my attention. Meredith. And I'm suddenly reminded of Gwen's relative of the same name. Who was she again? A second cousin or something? Later, when I'm on the Hopper heading home, the name pops up again in my head. I recall that she cropped up several times in conversations with Gwen. The last time, she was insistent I find this woman and tell her she had Tom. And then she laughed about it.

I still have the charred photo of them together that I found at the bottom of the fire pit. If I can find her, I wonder if I should give it to her. It's of no use to me. There's a good chance she might not even be alive, though. I vaguely recall Gwen telling me about a family tree Bill had started researching online before he died. I wonder how far he got? By the time I met Gwen, she wasn't capable of using a computer, but at one point I assume she did because she and Bill had a joint email address and used the same password for every online account. I open up my phone's web browser and google 'ancestry'. It's the sixth website on the opening page that accepts her email address and password: BillandGwen.

And that's where I find Meredith's full name – Meredith Sylvia Harper. She is the daughter of Gwen's mum's cousin, making her a second cousin once removed of Gwen's. She was born in 1940 and is almost a year older than Gwen, but there is no date of death. And I can't find a death certificate online either. Meredith has no social media profiles, not entirely unexpected for a woman her age, and then I realise I've overlooked the obvious. An online phone directory. I pay £2 for five credits, type in her name, and there is one Meredith S. Harper, along with her address in the Midlands.

I couldn't protect Gwen from Paul, and I couldn't get justice for her murder. But maybe passing along her message is one good thing I can do for her.

CHAPTER 52

CONNIE

I didn't imagine I'd be spending my forty-third birthday playing hide-and-seek with a ticket inspector. But that's what I'm doing onboard this train. Earlier, I stuck like Lego to the man in front of me so that I could make it through the station barriers without having to buy one. Now, I've chosen an aisle seat for this journey towards Birmingham so I can quickly disappear into the nearby toilets each time I see the inspector doing his rounds between stops. I've hidden from him twice so far, but I've just seen him going into the driver's cabin so I think I'll be okay for the rest of this journey. I hate behaving like this at my age.

I didn't mention my birthday to Walter this morning, or he'd just fuss. In fact I can't remember the last time I told anyone when it is, or received a card or present. Caz didn't raise me to acknowledge birthdays. And let's be honest, it's not like I have much to celebrate. Why would I want reminding of how little I've accomplished?

There's at least another hour to go before I reach my desti-nation, so I push in my ear pods and rest my head against my rolled-up coat on the window frame and follow the countryside as it shoots past in a blur of blues, greens and browns. I don't remember drifting off to sleep but I'm awoken by my phone vibrating. *It's Paul*, I think. He's made such a permanent scar with his secret video recordings that he's the first thing I think of every time it makes a noise. But it's Krisha's name that appears on the screen. I consider not answering it, wondering what other lies Paul has fed her. But there's no point in hiding. She'll find me eventually. It's her job.

'I've been nowhere near him,' I say quietly into the mouth-piece, before she has a chance to speak.

'Hello Connie,' she says. 'I know you haven't.'

'Oh, then what's this about?'

'Two days ago we arrested a man in connection with injuries sustained by an elderly woman in her garden, who eventually died as a result of them.'

I think my heart might be trying to beat its way out of my chest. Paul has finally been arrested. 'Fran Brown,' I say. Poor cow.

Krisha hesitates. 'It was you who put her son in touch with me,' she says as if the penny has just dropped.

'Has Paul been charged with anything yet?'

'I can't confirm anything more about an ongoing investigation,' she continues. 'Only that a man has been released on police bail. However, evidence has come to light that might be related to accusations you made when we last met.'

'What evidence?'

'Letters, photographs, videos.'

'Of Fran,' I say.

'Actually, this isn't footage involving the deceased,' Krisha says. She is treading carefully.

'Then who?'

'Others.'

'The women I told you about?' I ask excitedly. 'Where did you get it from?'

'I was hoping you might know that.'

'It was stolen from me, I told you.'

'You didn't happen to take any photographs of anything you found, or save video clips or pictures on to your phone or computer?'

'I told you that any pictures I'd taken had been deleted.'

'Before the arrest, we received an anonymous email containing a large cache of photos and video files of everything you told me that you found and took from Paul Michael's house.'

I shake my head. 'I don't understand.'

'I need you to be absolutely honest with me here, Connie. You are categorically stating that this emailed evidence didn't come from you?'

'Absolutely, but I wish it had. Maybe then you'd have believed me.'

'I am going to need to talk to you further about this.'

'What, like a police statement?'

'Normally, yes. But these circumstances are different. Should a prosecution take place, it's unlikely you'd make a credible witness. Your previous convictions and motives for appearing in Gwen's life might potentially hamper our case. But that'd be up to the Crown Prosecution Service to decide if it ever gets that far. So for now, I want to talk to you off the record about everything you've learned so far about Paul' – she corrects herself – 'about our person of interest, but the facts, not your suspicions. Anything pertinent that might help with our ongoing investigation.'

If there weren't other people in this carriage, I'd punch the air with joy. This is a massive step forwards. After all that monster put me and his victims through, is he really about to get his comeuppance? I don't even know if I want to think about this, in case it all fizzles out.

'Of course,' I tell Krisha. 'I'll be back tonight around seven-ish. Is that too late? Hello? Hello?'

It's black outside and I realise the line has gone dead because we're passing through a tunnel.

I try calling her back but realise I've run out of credit on my phone. It's hard to focus on anything else for the rest of the journey. I'm both anxious and excited. This is the best birthday gift anyone could've given me.

But Krisha's call raises several questions I can't answer. Who on earth was the anonymous sender of copies of my evidence? How did they get hold of it? And why did they start investigating Fran Brown's death first? I find her son Jon's number and use the train's wi-fi to text him on iMessage.

I've just heard about your mum, I type. *I'm so sorry.*

A few minutes pass before he replies. *You were right about the bloods. Be in touch soon.*

Soon after, the train pulls into the station at Hampton-in-Arden, a village between Solihull and Coventry and one stop away from Birmingham International Airport. I walk for ten minutes until I reach a small, terraced house on a quiet road. I stand outside a faded yellow wooden front door and check my appearance using my phone's camera. I'm inexplicably nervous.

Before I left home, I assumed this was where my journey with Gwen would come to an end. But with an investigation into Paul beginning, things might not be over just yet.

CHAPTER 53

MEREDITH HARPER

I don't get many visitors. When you reach my age, the Grim Reaper has a habit of picking off your circle of friends, one by one. It seems as if, every few months, I'm dusting off my black suit ready to attend another funeral. So when I hear a knocking at the door, I assume it's Jason the postman with a package too large to put through the letter box.

I push on the arms of the chair to help get me to my feet, then reach for the walking stick that leans against the radiator. It's a little chilly in here, I think. Winter exacerbates my sensitivity to pain and encourages small but intense muscle spasms. So when December's cold weather brings out the worst in my arthritic joints, I long to feel the sun's heat on my skin again. I've been on the NHS waiting list forever now, waiting to have both knees replaced. I'm beginning to wonder if there's any point in going ahead with it. I doubt I'll be around that much longer to enjoy new joints anyway.

Peering through the spy hole, I find a young woman outside, slight in build and height, casually dressed and with a handbag draped over her shoulder. Her face isn't familiar to me but I open the door anyway. A fortnight must have passed since I last spoke to anyone. But that's not even close to my record of ninety-three days during the last pandemic lockdown.

'Mrs Harper?' the stranger asks.

'It's Miss,' I correct her. I deliver it like it's a badge of honour when it couldn't be further from the truth. She apologises.

'I wonder if I could have a few moments of your time.'

'And who are you?'

'I'm a friend of your cousin, Gwen.'

'Gwen?' I repeat, my curiosity piqued. 'That's a name I haven't heard in an age. Well, yes, you'd better come in.'

I lead her into my modest front room. It's a three-up, two-down cottage. I outgrew it years ago and should have moved, yet still I remain.

'I'm Connie,' she says and offers her hand to shake mine. 'I was Gwen's carer.'

'Carer?' I repeat. 'Is she alright?' From her return expression and the fact she has turned up here unannounced, I can only assume she's not.

'Should we sit?' she asks.

I offer her one of my two armchairs. I don't have enough guests to justify the space a sofa takes up.

'I'm really sorry to tell you that she passed away a few months ago,' she continues.

I place my fingertips on my cheeks. 'Why did she need a carer? Did something happen to William?'

Connie contemplates the name before realising who I'm referring to. 'Oh, Bill,' she says. 'Well, I'm afraid he died about fourteen months before Gwen. I didn't know him, I only met your cousin after he passed.'

'Oh, how sad. Gwen and I lost touch such a long time ago that I know hardly anything about her life. I assume they had children, as he always wanted a large family?'

'Actually no, they didn't. From what I gather, Bill had some health issues soon after they married which meant it wasn't to be.' She clears her throat. 'Miss Harper—'

'Please, call me Meredith,' I interrupt.

'Meredith,' she continues, 'about three years ago, Gwen was diagnosed with dementia. Her doctor thinks the stress of losing Bill meant her condition rapidly escalated.'

'Oh,' I say, 'that's awful. I've seen it happen to friends and, well, it's merciless.'

'It is,' she agrees. 'But that's not what killed her.'

'Then what did?'

'A head injury, according to her inquest. At some point on the night of her death, she left her bedroom and tried to go downstairs. Unfortunately, she fell and hit her head on a radiator. By the time she was found in the morning, she was already dead. I'm afraid I didn't realise she had any family until recently, otherwise I'd have been in touch sooner.'

I pause to take a moment and absorb this news. Connie stares at me so sympathetically that I think she's about to cry.

'Where have you travelled from?' I ask.

'Avringstone in Buckinghamshire. That's where Gwen had been living.'

'The last thing I heard they were in a villa somewhere in Spain. But that was back in the mid-1990s, I think.'

'They lived in Germany too and travelled a lot, from what she told me. She mentioned your name from time to time, but when I asked about you, she'd lose her train of thought. She even called me Meredith a few times, particularly towards the end, or she'd ask me to find you. In fact the last time I saw her, she said: "Don't forget to find Meredith and tell her I have Tom.'"

I don't think Connie spots my hands gripping the arms of the chair that little bit tighter.

'She made me promise to find you and tell you that,' Connie adds. 'Do you know who Tom is?'

I shake my head. 'I'm afraid I don't.'

Disappointment crosses her face. I have a feeling there is more to her appearance than she's letting on. 'You said you were her carer. Were you live-in, or part-time?' I enquire.

'I lived in the same village as her.'

'So you weren't there the night she passed away?'

'No, but . . .' Her voice trails off.

'Is something wrong?'

'It's quite a long story. Do you have time?'

'It's all I have,' I say. 'Shall I put the kettle on?'

'Let me do it,' she says and I oblige, pointing her in the direction of the kitchen behind me. This is turning out to be a most peculiar day.

CHAPTER 54

CONNIE

As the kettle boils, I look over my shoulder and watch Meredith staring out of the window. I imagine she's gone back in time somewhere, reliving old memories and processing what I've told her so far. She looks quite content and now I'm about to ruin it. And I'm starting to doubt how far I should take this. Is it fair for me to tell a woman of her age the rest of Gwen's story? Or should I just make my excuses and leave? After all, I've done what I've come here to do: pass Gwen's message on to her cousin. If I went now, she'd be the none the wiser. But when I put myself in her shoes, I think I'd want to know. So I make my decision.

Back in the sitting room, I catch her face from a certain angle and register the resemblance between Meredith and Gwen. They share the same slim nose and defined jaw, but Meredith is smaller in frame and frailer than her cousin was. I assume she lives here alone. As far as I'm aware, she has never married and has no children and I wonder if this will be me when I reach her age. Will I too be going through the motions until death comes a-knocking? It'll probably be no more than I deserve. I haven't done much to make the world a better place, have I? Instead, I did what I did to get by and at other people's expense. At least, that's how it was. They say a leopard can't change its spots, but I'm determined to try on stripes for size.

'There's something else about Gwen's death I need to tell you,' I begin carefully. 'Something quite important, but it might be difficult to hear. I don't think it was an accident.'

Her forehead slowly crinkles. 'Do you mean she took her own life or that someone hurt her?'

'I believe that somebody hurt her. Shortly before Gwen died, she was befriended by a much younger man who took advantage of her condition and married her.'

Meredith removes the cup from her lips, mid-sip. She swallows quickly. 'Married?'

'Yes,' I reply. 'And I don't blame her, it really wasn't Gwen's fault. She wasn't thinking straight. Paul was a handsome, engaging man who lavished her with attention, which I think she really missed getting from Bill. There were many times when she even mixed the two of them up.'

I go on to fill in Meredith about the last year of Gwen's life, although I stop short of revealing anything that paints me in a bad light. And then I explain to her, as gently as I can, what happened on the night Gwen died and its aftermath. I finish by telling her about how Fran Brown became Paul's fifth wife, her suspicious death, and how I only heard about the police investigation while on my way here. 'I hope it's only a matter of time before they start looking into Gwen's so-called accident and the others,' I add hopefully. 'I read online that the specific drug he gave them can remain in the liver for up to five years.'

'I, I don't know what to say,' Meredith replies, genuinely stunned. 'I can't believe this Paul person got away with it for so long.'

I reach into my handbag and find a white envelope. I hand it to her. She opens it and removes the black-and-white photograph of herself and her cousin.

'Oh my,' she says and her bottom lip begins to quiver. 'I remember where this was taken. Loch Lomond. Our parents would book family holidays and rent the same cottage each year. We spent a fortnight by the lake every summer for over a decade.'

'I'm sorry for the scorch marks,' I say. 'Paul threw out almost all of Gwen's possessions and burned her photographs. This was the only one I could save.'

'May I keep it?' she asks. 'I lost all my own pictures in a flood back in the 1970s. This really is something quite wonderful.'

'Of course.'

I give her the moment she needs to reflect before I continue. 'I really do miss Gwen,' I conclude. 'I like to think we became more than just carer and patient. I'm supposed to keep a professional distance, but it's hard to when you spend so much time with someone. I didn't have the greatest upbringing and she was very much like a mum to me, despite her condition.' I hesitate before I tell her the next part of my story. 'And because she had no children of her own, she even rewrote her will so she could leave me her estate. I told her not to, that it was completely unnecessary, but she was very insistent.'

Meredith hesitates as if considering her words. 'I do remember that about my cousin.' She nods. 'She was very headstrong when it came to getting her own way. What Gwen wanted, Gwen always got. And what a wonderful thing for her to do for you. You must have meant so much to her.'

'It was. But unfortunately, because Paul married her, he inherited everything.'

Meredith gives me a double take. 'Can he really do that?'

'Yes. So my only hope is that if he is found guilty of killing her, something called the forfeiture rule comes into play, which prevents him from inheriting any part of Gwen's estate.'

Meredith drifts away again and I wonder where she's gone and if I'm tiring her. A minute passes before she returns. We chat for a while longer and I find out a little bit more about her. I was right to think she never married or had kids. In fact, she admits she has barely left this area in almost fifty years. I wonder what it must be like to spend more than half your life in just one place? Claustrophobic or comforting?

'If I had my time again, I'd have travelled more,' she admits. 'I'd have spent my life cruising the world's oceans.'

'It's not too late,' I reply.

She smiles as she shakes her head. 'Maybe in the next life.'

'I used to dream of doing that too,' I admit. 'Working on the liners as a beauty therapist, seeing the world.'

'You're much younger than me. It's certainly not too late for you.'

'Like you said, maybe in the next life.'

Night is starting to draw in and I need to make my way back to the train station. Meredith thanks me again for coming to see her and to deliver the news in person. She tells me I'm welcome back at any time. I'm slipping my coat back on when she asks one more question.

'I don't suppose you ever saw an ornamental cat in Gwen's house, did you?'

'Yes, she collected them, so there were quite a few. Do you mean one in particular?'

'It was quite an ugly thing, jade green in colour, a long neck and eyes—'

'—that seem to follow you around the room.'

'That's the one.'

'It's one of the few things I managed to save from the house before Paul had a chance to get rid of it.'

'It used to belong to our grandmother and I always wondered what happened to it.'

'You are welcome to it if you like.'

'I wouldn't want to put you to any trouble. You've already done so much just by coming here.'

'It's no bother, honestly. I'll make sure you get it.'

'Then thank you. Although we spent much of our lives apart, there will always be a special place inside me for Gwen. If there's anything I can do to repay your kindness, you only have to ask.'

We embrace, and as the door closes behind me and I make my way back to the station, I actually feel good about myself. I was able to do the right thing for someone else. And it's something I'd like to experience again.

CHAPTER 55

CONNIE

Trudging up the hill from the bus stop into the village doesn't get any easier with practice, and I'm absolutely shattered by the time I reach the bungalow. I spent much of the train journey back to Avringstone replaying my conversation with Meredith, but now I'm worried that I might have left an elderly woman on her own and overwhelmed by tragedy. She gave me her telephone number so I make a mental note to call and check in on her tomorrow.

I open the front door and turn the hallway lights on before my ritual begins. First, I stand, fists clenched, body tense, just listening. I stay like this for at least a minute before I am sure I'm alone. Only then do I go inside.

I've been staying at Walter's house for the last couple of nights now the box room is empty. But there are a few items I left here that I've got to move before I formally email the letting agency to tell them I'm leaving. One of them is Gwen's ugly porcelain cat that Meredith mentioned. I'm going to take it back to Walter's tonight, then tomorrow I'll parcel it up and post it to her home. I'm glad it'll have someone to appreciate it again.

With two pairs of jeans and a handful of tops now in a holdall, I make my way to the kitchen and take a half-finished bottle of wine from the fridge. I'm sure Walter will help me polish this off if he's still awake.

I turn to reach for the porcelain cat. It's been sitting on the windowsill since I took it from Gwen's house weeks ago. But something's different about its positioning, I think. In fact I swear it was facing inside the kitchen when I left this morning. I even told it to stop looking at me, a silly habit I've got into saying. Now it's facing outwards.

Someone has moved it.

Has Paul been back inside my house?

Panic accompanied by a sudden dizziness strikes me. Disorientated, I turn quickly, open a drawer and grab a breadknife, then I freeze again, listening once more for any indication he might still be here. But the house is silent.

My mind whirs with a thousand questions. Why has he been here? I look above me and the holes he drilled for his cameras to film me remain open, so it's not to re-install them. He wouldn't have come back just to turn a porcelain cat around and fuck with my head, would he? Did he come here as soon as he was released on police bail? If so, why the urgency? Does he know about the evidence the police have and does he think I gave it to them? Was he here to hurt me? Or was he looking for something in particular?

And then it hits me. Gwen's will!

That must be it. If he thinks there is a chance he is going down for murder, this might be his one last chance to ensure that if he doesn't get to keep the house, then neither do I.

I hurry into the dining room, stopping at the heavy curtains hanging over the patio doors. I feel around the hem until I locate the shape of the A4 pages that I've sewn inside. I pull the stitches apart with my fingers and flick through the document to check all seven pages Gwen and I drew up are here. They're in the name of Rachel Evans and I recall how Gwen didn't seem curious when I explained why to Reverend Eddie.

'I go by my middle name and ex-husband's surname for work,' I told him as he witnessed it. 'It's on all my documents, so I'll have to get around to changing them, I suppose.'

I slip the document back inside the curtain, temporarily folding the material back into place until I can get it out of this house and store it somewhere safer.

There are no further signs that Paul has been here when I search the rest of the house. So I'm just as confused as to what spurred it. His actions always have purpose. It's unlike him to be this careless with the cat unless he *wants* me to know he was here.

As I begin turning it back around, I notice something underneath it. I pull out a silver key, the kind that would fit into a front door. I have no idea who it belongs to or why it's here.

The flash of a memory suddenly flares and I allow it to play out. It's of the night he and Gwen came back from their trip to Clacton-on-Sea and learned the police were searching for her. The only time I heard Paul refer to one of her ornamental cats was when he claimed to have left a note under it containing Gwen's new mobile phone number. I try and recall his exact words. What did he say, now? It was something along the lines of, 'The green one in the dining room with the eyes that are always staring at something it wants you to see.'

Right now, the figurine is staring beyond the darkness of my garden and towards the houses further down the street and behind us. I follow its eyeline and then I realise.

It is staring at the rooftop of Walter's house.

I grab my keys from my pocket and realise the one to Walter's front door is no longer attached to it. It was under the cat.

Oh shit.

CHAPTER 56

CONNIE

Please be okay, please be okay, I keep saying to myself. I hope to God I've got this wrong and that I'm just a neurotic, paranoid mess. My own safety means so little to me right now that I don't even look out for cars when I'm racing hell for leather across these darkened streets to reach Walter's house. Of course he's going to be alright, there's no reason for Paul to have involved him in whatever the hell is going on between him and me. I've never wanted to be more right about anything else in my life. But there's no escaping the fact that someone – Paul – put Walter's key under the cat and turned it around so it was facing his house.

I'm wheezing by the time I reach Walter's front door, and dip into my pocket to remove the key, realising in my panic that I've left it at the bungalow. I push my face to the front window but the curtains are closed. There are no lights on inside but that doesn't necessarily mean something sinister has happened as Walter likes an early night. I pull on the door handle on the off chance it's unlocked. It is. I should be pleased about this, but now I really know I have reason for concern because, day or night, Walter keeps this place locked tighter than Fort Knox.

I step inside, but keep the door open because it's pitch black in here. The landing lamp is usually switched on for his night-time trips to the bathroom, but that's off. It takes a few attempts before I can muster enough strength to say his name. 'Walter,' I ask and wait. He doesn't answer. 'Walter,' I say a little louder. Still nothing. I try one last time, and now my voice is trembling. 'Walter, please say something?' Silence.

For once, I do the sensible thing and dial Krisha's number with the credit I bought at the train station newsagent. But it goes to voicemail. I begin to leave a hurried, garbled message about being scared Paul has done something to my friend, but before I can finish, my phone runs out of battery power. The timing couldn't be worse.

There's a sudden noise. What the hell is that? I can't immediately place it, but I know I'm not alone. Something rushes towards me and I'm about to scream when it brushes my shins and I realise it's his dog, Oscar. I clamp my hand upon my chest in a futile attempt to slow my racing heart. With my other hand, I fumble across the wall until I find the hall light switch and turn it on.

'Jesus, you scared me to death,' I say and reach down to pet him. He has a toy clamped in his jaws and he wants me to chase after him. 'I'm sorry, I can't,' I tell him. And it's only when I look at him more closely that I notice spots and streaks across his white curly fur. They're reddish-brown in colour. Like dried blood.

My stomach drops like I've fallen from the top of a bridge.

Get out now, I tell myself. *Bang on the neighbours' doors and beg them to call the police.* But what if Walter is injured and urgently needs help? I can't leave until I find him, so I pluck up the courage to make my way around the lounge, kitchen and dining room, careful not to touch anything, before I climb the stairs.

His bedroom door is ajar, which is not unusual. 'Walter?' I ask again and pray that he's been in a deep sleep and has only just heard me. I knock, but my fear makes me a little too heavy-handed and the door opens wide. The room is as gloomy as the rest of the house, and I reach to turn on the light.

Walter is here, lying on his bed and on his back, a dark bed-sheet and blanket pulled up tightly to just under his closed eyes. I'm desperate to hear him breathing, but the only sound is my pulse throbbing in my temples.

'Walter,' I say again, choking back my tears. 'Please say something, tell me Paul hasn't been here.'

I slowly make my way towards him, gently tugging his sheet until it slowly moves down his face. The material is damp. I glance at my fingertips – they're a dark red colour too. Only when I dare to look at Walter's face do I see it. His mouth is wide open, his cheeks and chin black and bloodied.

Paul has cut the tongue from Walter's mouth.

I look away before I can take anything else in and cover my own mouth with my hands. I'm immediately struck by the metallic smell of Walter's blood and I begin to retch before I back away, just as Oscar scampers into the room. I bend over to scoop him up in my arms and run down the stairs as fast as my legs will carry me, ready to scream the street down for help. But as I fling open the front door, someone is already there waiting for me.

CHAPTER 57

CONNIE

They're standing at the front door, one hand raised as if to ring the bell, when I dash across the threshold and almost knock them to the ground in my desperation to escape. I scream at the figure in the darkness before I recognise it as Krisha.

'He's dead,' I blurt out. 'Paul killed him.'

Her teeth and the whites of her eyes are illuminated by the hall light as she glares at me, like she thinks she's misheard. 'Who is?'

'Walter, my friend, he's upstairs,' I gasp. 'He's in his bed. Paul has cut his tongue out.'

She doesn't know which part of what I've just said to unpack first. 'Are you sure?' she asks and I nod frantically.

'This is all my fault,' I say.

I'm crying properly now and I feel a thick line of snot dripping from my nostrils and on to my lips. I wipe it off with my coat sleeve. My legs weaken and I can no longer hold myself up. I fall heavily to my knees like a bag of rocks but I'm still clutching Oscar. Krisha helps lift me up and escorts me to the end of Walter's drive.

She lowers me on to the lawn, holds my hands and encourages me to follow the pattern of her breathing.

Then comes her switch to police mode. 'Connie, I need you to wait here while I go inside,' she explains. 'Don't talk to anyone, don't let anyone in, and shout if you need me.'

'Please don't leave me!'

'I'm sorry, but I'll be as quick as I can.'

The door partially closes behind her and I grab a whimpering Oscar so tightly he yelps. I'm sure he's sensed something in his world has irretrievably shifted. I try in vain to calm myself as I wait for Krisha to reappear. But with every noise, light and rustle of a tree, I'm convinced Paul is about to grab me. I think back to how I started the day trying to do the right thing by visiting Meredith. Now it's ended like this, with my friend's murder. And I am to blame. I didn't kill him with my own bare hands, but I might as well have. He has paid the ultimate price for entry into my shit-show.

Through the dappled glass in the door, I spot Krisha coming down the stairs. She pushes the handle with an elbow while holding her phone to her ear. I assume she's talking to colleagues. She returns to me and confirms what I already know. But listening to it coming from her somehow makes it more undeniable and I cry even harder. She tells me that she can't offer me a hug because I was inside a crime scene and that forensics officers will need my clothes as evidence.

I don't know how much time passes before three marked police cars, an ambulance and two plain white vans pull up outside, but we haven't been waiting for long. Then it's like I'm watching a fly-on-the-wall TV documentary as officers slip into their roles, sealing off paths and roads and keeping back the neighbours who have left their homes and are craning their necks to see what the commotion and blue lights are about. I don't catch the name of the officer who

261

questions me, but I give him what he calls a 'first account' of what happened.

Next, I'm helped into the back of the ambulance and am briefly checked over by two paramedics, then driven to a police station where I'm asked to strip out of my clothes and given a white, plastic forensic suit to wear. I'm no stranger to making a police statement but this isn't like the others when I've lied to protect myself and to make their jobs harder. Two detectives help me to retrace my footsteps inside Walter's house as accurately as I can and recount what I saw. Then later, they want me to tell them everything I know about Paul.

Hours pass, and when I feel as if I'm only being held together by caffeine and nicotine, I'm driven home. The first thing I see from the car window is the forensics team wearing the same plastic suits as me, leaving the bungalow, having searched and fingerprinted it. I hear neighbours' voices from behind the tape asking me what's happened. But nothing leaves my mouth when I try to give them answers.

Back in my bedroom, I change into some sweatpants and a jumper. The uniformed officer who brought me back makes me a cup of tea and sits with me until Krisha appears. She explains how she was on her way to see me to discuss our earlier phone conversation when she received my hurried message. She knew I was staying at Walter's house which is how she found me there. I repeat what I told her colleagues at the station, about how I only recently discovered Paul had been watching me through cameras fitted throughout my bungalow but I can't show her the videos because her colleagues took my phone as evidence.

I tell her that I'm convinced Paul wanted me to be the first to find Walter's mutilated body and that I don't know if it's a threat or a promise of something to come. My train of thought meanders and I'm suddenly concerned about Oscar. I can't remember who

I gave him to. Krisha assures me he's safe and is also being treated as evidence.

'It's my fault, isn't it?' I ask her. 'If I hadn't told you what I'd learned about Paul or talked Jon Brown into getting his mum's blood tested, Paul would've left us alone.'

'I think it's more complicated than that,' she replies.

'How? It all comes back to me.'

Krisha shifts in her seat and lowers her voice. 'What I'm about to tell you is completely off the record, okay?'

'Yes.'

'The evidence you said was stolen and that later came to our attention by email, well, we believe Walter sent it.'

'Walter?' I gasp. 'How?'

'We traced the IP address of the computer through the internet provider, which was legally obliged to give us the sender's details. They belonged to Walter.'

'But I never told him where I hid them.'

'Maybe he saw you putting it in the dovecote, and when you weren't around, then he made copies of what you found?'

'And he sent it to you and that's what got him killed. It's why Paul cut his tongue out.' I hesitate before I ask my next question, unsure if I want to know the answer. 'Krisha, did he die before or after it was removed? There was so much blood.'

'There hasn't been an autopsy yet.'

'But you said someone from the coroner's office was at the crime scene. They must have told you something?'

Krisha momentarily breaks eye contact with me and I have my answer.

Bile rises quickly up my throat at the thought of what that poor man endured in his final moments. I hurry to the kitchen but I'm not quick enough to reach the sink and I vomit over the draining board and down the front of the cupboards. Krisha follows me and, without batting an eyelid, dampens two tea towels and helps me clean up the mess.

'Why was Paul on police bail when you knew how dangerous he is?' I ask.

'It's standard procedure in the early days of an investigation. We didn't have enough evidence to charge him with anything at that point.'

The brunt of my frustration is thrown unfairly in her direction. 'How about now? Is cutting out the tongue of a pensioner and killing him enough evidence?'

Krisha looks at me sympathetically. I know before she says it that her hands were tied. But it doesn't make it any easier to accept.

'I'm sorry,' I say. 'And I don't understand why Paul didn't kill me too. He's had plenty of opportunities and I've done more damage to him than Walter did.'

'Only he can tell you that. But I hope you two are never close enough to find out.'

Krisha eventually leaves just as dawn is breaking, and finally, for the first time since finding poor Walter's body, I find myself alone. Without the resources to spare an officer, an empty marked police car is parked outside the front of the bungalow. It doesn't offer much in the way of comfort though. In my bed, I barely sleep. Each time I feel myself drifting off, I wake up with a jolt, believing that Paul is standing over my bed, watching me, laughing at me, and promising me that soon, I will be next.

I might be unaware of his whereabouts, but I'm convinced that he hasn't finished with me yet.

CHAPTER 58

MEREDITH HARPER

The kettle is already on when there's a knock at the front door. I don't need to use the spy hole to see who it is. She is spot on time.

'It's lovely to see you again, dear,' I say to Connie and give her a hug. If anyone could do with one right now after all they've been through, it's her. 'Please come in.' She is carrying a large shopping bag with a wrapped, awkward-shaped object inside it.

She hangs up her coat and we make our way into the kitchen. Something about her has changed, like this version of her is mimicking the one that came just a fortnight ago. Someone has ripped an irreparable chunk from her soul. I've been there. All these years later, I remember how that feels as if it were yesterday. I'm not sure I ever quite recovered and I doubt she will either. I beckon her to sit.

'I know it's a silly question, but I'll ask it anyway,' I begin. 'How are you?'

'I'm okay,' she replies.

'Really?'

She shakes her head. All she manages to say is 'No', before her voice cracks. I lean closer to her and place my hands on hers.

'I've been watching the news so I'm aware the police are still searching for Paul. His face is everywhere, so he can't hide forever, can he?'

'I hope not. It's taken me hours to get to yours because I'm so paranoid he's following me. I changed trains three times and even hid in a café on a platform at Milton Keynes station, staring out of the window searching for his face in the crowds. And I still have a sense that he's watching me, even now.'

'It sounds like you were very careful, so I'm sure he isn't. But you can't live your life forever in fear.'

'What choice do I have?'

'You are more than welcome to stay here for as long as you like. If you don't think Paul knows about me, then he won't have any idea where you are. The house is only poky but—'

'Thank you, but no,' Connie interrupts. 'I won't risk another person being hurt because of me.'

We discuss Paul further, and the police manhunt following the murder of her friend. She explains that while the police can't publicly say they believe he's to blame for the killing without prejudicing a potential court case, they have named him as a suspect who should not be approached if spotted. Connie also tells me how they've given her a personal alarm to use in case of an emergency. I soon get the impression she wants to draw the conversation to a close, so I let her change the subject when she's ready.

'Have you had any more thoughts about who Tom was?' she asks.

'Tom?' I reply. 'You'll have to remind me. My memory isn't what it was.'

'Gwen mentioned him a few times when she was talking about you.'

'Of course, yes. But I still have no idea. By the way, is that what I think it is?' I point to the package in the bag by her feet.

'Oh yes,' she replies. 'Sorry, I've been so wrapped up in myself that I forgot about it.'

She carefully lifts the package on to the table and slides it over to me. I reach into it and untape the bubble wrap. And for the first time in almost fifty-six years, I spy my grandmother's figurine cat that was in Gwen's possession for so long. 'My, my, my. It's just as ugly as I remember it,' I chuckle. 'I assume the police have finished with it?'

'There were no fingerprints on it aside from mine and Gwen's so they gave it back to me.'

'And you're sure you don't want to keep hold of it? As a keepsake?'

'Absolutely not. Each time I look at it I think of how Paul used it to make me find Walter and I don't need reminding of that night, ever. But can I ask, if you think it's ugly, why do you want it?'

'Well, it sat on our grandmother's sideboard for years,' I recall. 'Our grandfather was a wonderful ventriloquist, and when Gwen and I were very small, he'd throw his voice and pretend it could talk. It kept us entertained for hours. So, as unpleasant as it is to look at, it brings back a lot of fond memories.'

'Then I'm glad it's going to a deserving home.'

'Thank you again. And as I said before, if there's anything I can do for you, you only have to ask.' Connie doesn't respond right away but I sense she wants to say something. 'Connie? *Is* there something I can do?'

'I feel a little awkward in asking this,' she replies. 'But I wonder if I might leave something here?'

'What is it?'

'It's . . . um . . . Gwen's will.'

'Okay. Might I ask why you want me to look after it?'

'I'm back at the bungalow as I can't stay at Walter's house after what happened, and it's likely I'll be moving around a bit soon. This is the only copy I have, so I need to know it'll be safe.'

'Can't you leave it with your solicitor?'

She drops her gaze. 'I can't afford one.'

'I could lend you some money to pay for one if you like?'

'No, but thank you. I can't take anything from you. I just need to know that someone will look after it for me and I trust you.'

I nod my head. 'Of course. Where is it?'

Inside her handbag is a white, sealed envelope that she passes to me. I immediately place it inside the bubble wrap I've just undone, seal it up, and she follows me as I place it inside the chimney breast in an out-of-sight alcove.

'It's an electric fire,' I say. 'Nothing goes up that chimney, so it'll be perfectly safe and only you and I will ever know it's here.' For the first time since her arrival, her shoulders relax.

Connie remains here for another couple of hours, and after we've said our goodbyes, I watch from behind the curtain as she crosses the road, walks up the street and then doubles back on herself. I assume she's lost her bearings until I realise she's checking that no one is following her. How terrifying to have to think like this all the time.

I return to the kitchen and look at the gift she has brought me. Already I swear he's watching me. I place him upon the fireplace, his eyes at a slight angle so he's staring at the television.

'Welcome to your new home,' I say with a smile on my face. 'It's been a long time.'

CHAPTER 59

CONNIE

My anxiety levels are through the roof today. This morning's commute on a train full of people to Meredith's house made me as nervous as hell, and the mostly empty carriages on the way home are doing the same thing. I make my way through each one, searching for somewhere I can feel safe. Eventually, I settle for a seat at the very back near a group of drunk but well-spirited young rugby players. Their green stripy kits and boots are caked in mud. They're singing songs I don't recognise and building a pyramid made of beer cans on a table. They offer me one and I politely say no, although I'm tempted. However, I need to keep my wits about me.

Meredith was right when she said I was letting my fear of Paul dictate how I live my life. But what choice do I have? As I told her, until he is in police custody, I'm unable to relax. Me staying alert at all times could literally be the difference between life and death.

I check my phone for news updates but Paul is still every bit the wanted man he was when I last looked half an hour ago. His face remains on all the major news sites. Some of the tabloids have started digging around and have discovered he has been married at least four times to women double his age and who died in accidents soon after. While they have stopped short of accusing him of anything, it's not hard to read between the lines. And the charity where he – and I, albeit briefly – volunteered has temporarily closed while managers launch an immediate investigation into their screening procedures. I keep reminding myself that in a country with more CCTV cameras than people, it's only a matter of time before he's caught.

Meredith plied me with tea all day so now my bladder is fit to burst. There's a bathroom further up the same carriage, and once I've double-checked that I've locked the door, I wipe the seat with a tissue and sit. But almost immediately, the train slows down and the chants of the rugby team fade. We must be approaching Bletchley. Now we're stopping and I can hear them leaving. I don't like this. I press my ear closer to the door and hear someone getting on: it sounds as if they're alone. My chest tenses, my breath shortens and my face feels flushed until they walk past me and into the next carriage. This toilet has suddenly become unbearably cramped, the climate control isn't working, and if I didn't know better, I'd swear the ceiling was gradually getting lower. I don't want to be in here. I don't want to be on this train. I need to get out. I quickly pull up my jeans and am moving to unlock the door when I hear the beeping of the train doors closing. Damn it, I've left it too late. I'll never get out of here quickly enough and back on to the platform.

I have no choice but to stay where I am. So I remain standing, silent, refusing to listen to the part of my brain that's telling me my behaviour is borderline insane. I try and count slowly to twenty to calm myself and it seems to work. And as the train pulls away from the platform, I prepare myself to leave. But it's the whoosh of the door that separates the first-class carriage from mine that grabs my attention now, followed by a solitary pair of feet approaching the toilet. Thump, thump, thump. They're heavy, like a man's. And they stop when they reach the door.

I spot the shadow of their footwear under the door. I freeze as the handle turns, once, then twice and then nothing. I count to five before it moves again; this time it's an aggressive yanking followed by the banging of a fist. It's Paul, I know it is. He's been following me all day, it wasn't in my head. A third bang follows, and then a fourth and a fifth and over and over again, it continues, growing faster and faster, louder and louder. The noise is unbearable and I look around and spot the emergency cord and furiously yank it. I haven't seen a guard on the train but there must be one because all trains are legally obliged to have them. A woman's voice pipes up. 'Please help me,' I shout, 'I'm locked in the toilet and someone is trying to get to me.'

'I'm on my way, luv,' she replies.

'Be careful, he's dangerous,' I continue but she doesn't reply.

Now I worry I've put her at risk too. I should have called the police instead. I grab my temporary new phone from my pocket. I have wi-fi but no phone-signal bars. It's the longest minute in memory as the banging continues and I scream at Paul to leave me alone. Eventually I hear another door open and the voice of the guard.

'Sir, can you step away from the door, please. There's someone inside who doesn't appreciate you banging on it.'

The reply is male, and it's slurred, like he's drunk. I listen carefully but it doesn't belong to Paul. 'I need to piss,' he begs.

'There's another bathroom two carriages along,' she continues.

I hear the shuffling of his feet and he's away again. I'm so embarrassed as slowly, I open the door and thank the guard. She can see how scared I am and walks me to a seat. 'He's had one too many.' She winks and I taste the tears of sweet relief on my lips. 'I can stay here for the rest of the journey if you like, luv?'

I want to say yes, but I shake my head. I remind myself that I'm a grown woman and I'm not going to be intimidated by a shadow.

We both turn our heads quickly when an alarm sounds through the speakers. It's a loud, continuous beeping and different to the one I sounded. The guard apologises as she hurries through my carriage and slips a key into a panel and resets it. Moments later, it appears again. It's so shrill that I cover my ears. Twice more she tries to stop it before picking up a handset attached to the wall and calling the driver, I assume.

I glance out the window and notice how dark and unfamiliar my surroundings are. There must only be about three stops left before I reach home. It can't come soon enough.

'Ladies and gentlemen,' the guard begins a few minutes later through the same speaker system. 'I'm afraid that due to an error with our alarm system, our next stop in Favrington will be our last.' Favrington? Where the hell is that? 'But there will be another train arriving approximately fifteen minutes after this one.'

As if I wasn't on edge enough already, her message sends me almost teetering over the brink. I'm being forced to leave this train and wait in an unfamiliar station. I clench my fists so tightly that my knuckles whiten.

I can barely see Favrington station when the train pulls in. There are hardly any lights on and I look in vain for a café or indoor waiting room but both are closed. I can only assume it isn't used much at night so they lock it up. I stand by the doors to my carriage as they open, and poke my head outside, waiting until everyone else has disembarked. I only leave when I'm convinced Paul wasn't onboard.

I cross a bridge above the track to a second platform where the next train is due and where I stand alone, but close enough to the other half-dozen passengers to shout if I need help. But that's not going to happen, I know that now. I've let my imagination run away with me and I'm ashamed of what that guard must have thought of me.

Sixteen minutes pass – I know this because I keep checking the time on my phone – before a bend in the track behind me is lit by the headlamps of another train. As it pulls into the station, the doors open and I cautiously approach them. I'm relieved when I see a handful of others already in the carriage. Once again I look at their faces to assure myself there's no Paul inside.

A 'mind the gap' announcement comes through the train's speakers and I do what I'm told and look down as I lift my foot high enough to step inside. But then, without warning, something thick and heavy moves under my chin and presses deep on my throat. Before I can push it aside, I realise it's an arm and I'm being dragged down on to the platform floor.

I see a flash of his eyes. It's Paul.

CHAPTER 60

CONNIE

I try to yell, to scream my lungs out, but his arm is placed so forcefully against my throat that nothing comes out. Not even air. He covers my body with the weight of his own to stop me moving, pressing me tight against the cold concrete. Just above us, the passengers already onboard and waiting for the train to move are so wrapped up in their gadgets and conversations that they're completely oblivious to what's happening to me below them.

And then his arms tighten even further around me, gripping me like a boa constrictor as he rocks his body, left and right, left and right, faster and faster until we pick up enough movement. Before I know it, we are rolling off the side of the platform, through the gap between it and the carriage and on to the track below. We land on our sides, both of our heads connecting hard with the steel of the tracks and the gravel scattered between them. It dazes me but I don't know about him. He rolls on top of me again, pinning me down, and both of us are no longer moving. I draw desperate breaths through my nose: all I can smell is oil, warm metal and the staleness of his skin. The panic I felt on the last train doesn't come close to what I am feeling now. I try and make sense of the madness. Is he trying to kill us both? Surely there must be an easier way.

It's only when I catch sight of the torchlight above us that I realise why we are down here: he's hiding us from the train guard who checks the platform is clear before signalling to the driver it's safe to leave. I'm suddenly aware of how loud the diesel engine is; it's almost deafening this close up as the train throbs and vibrates, making everything, including my bones, rattle. I want to scream for help, I want the guard to hear me, to look under the train before it pulls away. But their torchlight disappears as quickly as it arrived and the train exits. I can only hope there's a piece of mechanical equipment hanging low from the carriage that slices, skewers and rips Paul apart as it passes above him.

No such luck. Because moments later, the train has gone and it's just me and him. There's no time for me to think because Paul jumps to his feet and then pulls me up with him, pushing me into the wall below the platform. My chest takes the brunt of the force before he grabs my waist and throws me up on to the platform. I scramble to lift myself up and run but I'm way too light-headed and disorientated. He drags me backwards to the darkest corner of the station. We pause there for a moment – I think he's making sure no one else is here. I feel his stubble graze against my cheeks and smell the sourness of his sweat as he speaks for the first time.

'What's wrong, Rachel?' he begins. 'Cat got your tongue?'

CHAPTER 61

CONNIE

We're moving backwards again so I can't see where Paul is hauling me to. I look in every direction, desperate to spot a commuter, a straggler who may have caught a glimpse of what's happening and is processing how they can help. But to my dismay it's just the two of us.

I wish I could put up a better fight and not be this clichéd weak woman overpowered by the brute force of a man, but I'm not. The muscular arms I gawped at the day we first met are now my enemy. And the pressure he's putting on my windpipe is so hard, I think I might pass out. The last thing I want is to make this easier for him. I gasp and grunt as I desperately try and get breath in my lungs and remain conscious.

We stop again, somewhere behind the train station and hidden by what I think is a bike rack. But it's so dark it's hard to tell. I hear two car engines starting up and tyres moving on gravel as they pull away. Paul takes something from his pocket and pulls my wrists together behind me. It feels like a plastic tie and it digs into my flesh the tighter he pulls. Then we start to cross the now-empty car park that's lit by one solitary, flickering lamp. Finally, when we reach the far side, he spins me around so we are face-to-face. He holds the tip of a knife to the left side of my throat. My survival instinct kicks in and I try to move my head away from it but it's futile. His weapon glints in the lamp's glow and the serrated edge tells me it's made for hunting. I wonder why he chose this, of all weapons, and then I understand. I have been hunted down. I'm like the women he married. I'm prey.

I stare into Paul's eyes. I remember them as blue, but at this moment they are as dark as the night and unreadable.

'Do anything stupid and this will go straight through your jugular,' he says calmly. 'You'll bleed out in less than a minute.'

'What do you want from me?' I gasp. I can barely hear my own voice. Even though he doesn't respond, I know he's listening. And then we are moving again. Now he's pushing me forward, frog-marching me out of the car park and towards a country lane. The solid ground becomes a field. It's getting harder and harder to see in front of me as there are no more lights and the moon is offering only a little help. Think. *Think.* I strain wildly but my hands are tied behind me. So the best I can do with my limited options is to deliberately stumble and collide with a fence post. My breasts bear the brunt of it and have never felt pain quite like it. But I know that if I have any chance of surviving this, it's a necessary agony.

'Where are we going?' I ask as he yanks me up.

'I have something very special planned for you,' Paul replies.

My leg suddenly starts to pulse and I realise it's my temporary new phone. I want to reach for it, to slide the answer button so that even if I can't speak to the caller, they can hear I'm in trouble. But Paul has heard it too. He reaches into my pocket, grabs it, and pulls it out before hurling it into a thicket ahead. Seconds later we pass it, the partially covered illuminated screen a marker to my green mile.

I stumble on the uneven ground, this time accidentally, and when I begin to fall, he catches me and yanks me up again, but with such force that my upper back makes a cracking sound and I whimper. My reward is a punch to the back of the neck, and this time when I topple forward, he doesn't try and stop me. I land hard on my cheekbone and ear. Paul drags me to my feet again and he continues forcing me to walk. My face burns and I try to wipe away the grit and dirt by rubbing it against my shoulder. It becomes damp and I realise I'm bleeding.

There's a sudden, small bright light, and in my disorientated state, I think someone is ahead of us. Then I realise no, it's Paul's phone. There's a map on the screen.

My emotions are shooting all over the place like stray fireworks. I can't decide if the sudden swell of anger rising inside me is because I think I'm about to die, or because Paul has total control over me. 'You're a fucking coward!' I cry, my boldness and fury taking us both a little by surprise. 'You pick on the weak and the vulnerable. You wouldn't dare treat a man like this.'

'Because men don't lie like women do,' he replies.

'Of course they do,' I say. 'You're worse than all of them.'

'My lies reach the truth. People like you lie to exploit.'

'And so do you! You and I, we are the same. Remember? You told me that. I didn't want to believe it, but you were right. We are not good people.'

I feel a second punch to my neck. And now my brain is spinning like a thousand hangovers all at once. I want to pass out but I manage to stay conscious. He laughs when I retch. And then it's his turn to stumble, and to my surprise, his grip on my arm slackens.

This is my opportunity. I start to run. Only I haven't taken into account just how unstable I am and I manage a handful of steps before I topple over. Once again, I cower as Paul yanks me up but this time, there's no punishment. I think he recognises my body is failing me and that he no longer needs strength to make me do what he wants. And as we continue our journey to wherever he's taking me, I know that I don't have long to find a way out of this. But try as I might, I'm at a loss to think how. I'm utterly helpless.

'Why did you have to kill them?' I ask. 'Couldn't you have just taken their money and disappeared?'

'You still don't get it, do you, Rachel? This has never been about the money. This is about the truth.'

'Which is what?'

His laugh is gruff and humourless. 'I don't need to explain myself to you.'

'Your face is everywhere,' I continue. 'If I die, they'll know you're to blame and they'll double their efforts to track you down. But if you just leave me here and disappear, you might never be found.'

'It's already over for me. You saw to that when you told them to test Fran Brown's blood. Once they start digging up my girls, they'll find the same drugs in them all and they'll take them away from me. They'll get me in the end, but not until I've finished with you.'

The ground beneath us begins to firm and now we are stumbling along a path next to a road that gradually rises to a hump. I think it's a bridge, partially illuminated by a street lamp. A few short moments later, Paul stops me.

'What now?' I ask weakly. 'Drug me and find some stairs to shove me down? That's how you operate, isn't it?'

His arm rises too swiftly for me to turn my head and protect myself. His fist collides with my nose with a sickening crack. The pain is red hot and I drop to my knees, wanting desperately to cup it with my hands but they're still tied behind me.

'Rachel,' he sighs. 'Riling or stalling me won't work. You are where you were always meant to be.'

He raises his foot to push me backwards and my head hits the pavement. My ears ring like church bells and as he mounts me, he's talking but it's like my head is underwater. He's so muffled, I can't understand him. Now he's prising my lips apart before he shoves his fingers into my mouth and moves them around. I clamp my mouth shut, and with what little strength I have left, bite hard into his finger. 'Fuck,' he yells and punches me in the kidney with his other fist so my jaw instantly slackens. I can't close my mouth because I can't breathe through my broken bloodied nose. Then he's gripping the hinge of my jaw with one hand, locking it open, and the fingers of his other hand are back inside me and it's then I realise what he is about to do. He is trying to get a grip of my tongue.

He wants to slice it out with his knife.

CHAPTER 62

CONNIE

My body thrashes, contorting into awkward and agonising positions as I do anything I can to throw Paul off me and get his fingers out of my mouth. But it's not enough, he's far too strong for me. My tongue darts around like an eel trying to escape a predator but his fingers are long and his pinch is vice-like. He grabs the centre of it between his thumb and his forefinger and pulls it out with such speed and to a length I didn't think possible. It strains at the root and I think he might succeed in ripping it out instead of cutting it.

A cloud veers from covering the half-moon and illuminates Paul's face. White, foamy spit gathers in the corners of his mouth. The pleasure he is getting from what he's about to do to me is immeasurable. And I can't stop it. For a second, he glances at his wrist before he releases my jaw – no need to hold it open any longer, as I'm not about to bite my own tongue off – and switches hands, gripping my tongue with the recently freed one and taking in the other the knife with the serrated edge.

I'm dizzy again and I don't know if it's pain or fear of the inevitable that makes me want to pass out. One thing I do know as I feel the cool silver blade on my teeth and tongue is that this trauma is making me hallucinate. I begin thinking I can see lights flashing in the corner of my eye: perhaps this is my brain paving the way towards death.

'I won't be making this quick,' Paul crows, his voice now less muffled. I'm choking on the blood oozing down my throat from my shattered nose and fear it'll go to my lungs and I'll drown. I want to beg him not to go through with this, but with my tongue in his grasp, there's no hope of that.

There's another sharp burning sensation as the blade penetrates the side of my tongue. A part of me wants to die right now but the flashing lights are glowing brighter and what's that? There's a wailing sound too, and it's growing louder and louder. It's like a siren, and only when the slicing stops and Paul's fingers and the blade leave my mouth do I realise I'm not hallucinating. It's a siren. Help is here.

My tongue curls up in my mouth, tender and sore, but I can live with that as long as it's still attached. Paul's head turns sharply towards screeching car tyres, before beams of torchlight bounce as wildly as the figures running towards us, yelling.

Paul puts his hands under my armpits and hoists me to my feet, then shoves me against the wall with force. 'Come any closer and I'll kill her!' he yells toward the lights. His tone is not as self-assured or as menacing as it was minutes ago. This was not part of the plan. He's flustered, he's on the backfoot.

'I hear you,' comes a male voice. 'We'll stop here, just don't hurt her.'

Paul must sense that I can barely stand because one hand remains under my arm while the other holds the knife once again at the centre of my throat. I squint at a sudden beam of light.

'Stay back,' Paul warns, louder, 'or I will fuck her up.'

'We're not coming any closer,' the same officer replies.

'Get back in your cars.'

'It's Paul, isn't it?'

Paul doesn't respond.

'I'm sorry, Paul, but you know we can't do that. We can stay here and talk this through though. Connie, how are you?'

'Don't talk to her!' Paul screams. 'Focus your attention on me or I'm going to ram this fucking thing through her throat.'

The officer agrees, and as he attempts to keep Paul calm, all I can think is that they're wasting their time. This is not a hostage negotiation. They don't know what kind of man they're dealing with. And if they don't hurry up and find a way to help me, I'm going to leave here in a body bag.

'How did they know where to find us?' Paul growls in my ear. He takes a quick glance at his watch.

'I don't know,' I whisper, but I'm lying. They're here because of something I did. After Paul murdered Walter, then vanished, Krisha organised for me to wear a new style of panic alarm the force is trialling. It hangs around my neck on a cord, a pendant lying in the centre of my chest. It contains a GPS that, when pressed, alerts police that the wearer needs urgent assistance, and is traceable to within around ten metres of their location. With my hands tied behind my back, I couldn't press it, so I purposefully stumbled chest first into a fence post in the hope it would send the signal.

'How can we help you, Paul?' the officer asks again. 'What would you consider an acceptable outcome from this situation?'

'Shut up and let me think,' Paul snaps. And for a third time, he glances at his watch. Who is he waiting for?

A moment passes before the officer talks again. I assume that he is stalling, hoping for a professional hostage crisis negotiator to arrive who is better trained than him at stopping a psychopath from murdering me in front of them. The others stand behind and are discreetly whispering into their phones. The only words I catch are when one of them says frantically, 'Make it *stop*.' Make *what* stop? This situation? I'm all in favour of that, but it seems it might go without saying. Or is a sniper going to take Paul out?

'What can we do for you, Paul?' says the officer. 'What do you need from us?'

Again, Paul doesn't respond, and instead stares deep into my eyes. A sudden calmness has replaced his alarm, which puts the fear of God back into me. I wish I could predict the direction his mind is taking now. If we were the same person he thinks we are, then I'd know. I make another attempt to plead my case.

'Paul,' I begin, 'just let me—'

'Hush now,' he whispers. 'I'm not going to stab you. You know that's not my style.'

Bright, beaming white lights cut through the darkness and appear from a road ahead. I can't decide if it's a civilian car or another police vehicle. My ears are still ringing but the increasing noise coming from the engine cuts through.

Paul turns his head towards the police, a grin now spreading across his face. He presses his mouth close to my ear. 'It's time,' he whispers.

He turns his head to the police and yells, 'There's only one way you and I can reach a satisfactory conclusion to our story. And that's with her down there and not up here.'

It all happens so quickly I don't have time to process what he means until I recognise the approaching vehicle isn't a police car, but a train. And Paul has been looking at his watch because he's been waiting for it to appear.

He drops the knife, slips his hands either side of my waist, then hoists me higher against the bridge wall so that my feet are no longer touching the ground. The officers must realise what he's about to do because they rush towards us.

They are not fast enough.

With all his strength and mad determination, Paul throws me over the side of the bridge and straight into the path of the speeding train below.

PART THREE

CHAPTER 63

EIGHT MONTHS LATER – REVEREND EDDIE EDWARDS

The congregation joins me in song for the final hymn of this morning's funeral service. There are only four verses to 'Abide With Me' but I take the opportunity to perform a headcount. I stop when I reach a hundred. This is by far the largest number we've had under our roof since the Christingle service was filmed for *Songs of Praise* a decade ago. I think the newspaper and television coverage of her story has brought a lot of journalists here, alongside those who knew her and others who simply want to experience the thrill of being part of a media circus. But if it means the collection tin is full at the end of the day, then who am I to complain?

This service has been relatively short, even with the inclusion of three hymns. Last night, my timed rehearsal came in at a little over twenty minutes. Most are double that, or longer if you include readings and recollections. But though she made some friends here, little was actually known about her. That makes my role more challenging. So I brought to mind a few memories of my own and padded my words out with the usual tropes, such as 'living a vibrant and colourful life' and 'always putting her love for others above her own needs'. It's not as personal as I'd have liked, but I've done my best.

I chose not to dwell too much on the circumstances surrounding her death. Everyone knows what happened, they don't need to hear me rehashing it. Joe and Mary Lawson paid their own tribute and made sure to mention Walter. His death was just as tragic and shocking as the others, but he hasn't received half the press attention. If he's not being omitted from the newspaper stories, then he's relegated to a footnote. He deserved better and now he has it, next to Him.

The hymn draws to an end and I begin to wrap things up. I speak of God's promises and of the hope that death is not the end. Even if those listening don't necessarily agree with my belief of what happens to us next, I hope my words might still bring them a little comfort. The Lord's Prayer follows and it always delights me how so many know the words off by heart and without reading them from the Order of Service cards, especially when most have barely set foot in a church for most of their adult lives.

With perfect timing, the funeral director's four immaculately dressed pallbearers return to lift the coffin on to their shoulders and make their return journey along the aisle and out of the doors. June, our organist, accompanies us with 'Guide Me O Thou Great Redeemer' as I follow them outside and into the church grounds.

It's a short walk to the plot where she is to be buried. To my left and on the pavement outside the church grounds, three cameramen are filming us and a handful of photographers are pointing their lenses in our direction. I try to ignore them. Wreaths are removed from the lid of the coffin, and as she is lowered slowly into the ground, I begin Psalm 23, which most people here will know as 'The Lord Is My Shepherd'. Finally, I use the words that have been spoken for centuries before me, and I hope for the centuries to follow. 'Earth to earth, ashes to ashes, dust to dust: in sure and certain hope of the resurrection to eternal life through our Lord Jesus Christ.'

And with that, handshakes and fragmented conversations follow, marking the end of my role. I've been invited to join them for the wake at the Horse & Hatchet, so once I have hung up my alb and stole in the vestry, I'll make my way there.

Back inside the church, I hope my service has gone some way to remembering the person and not the manner in which she died.

Her funeral ticked a couple of boxes of firsts for me. It was the first that I have either attended or officiated that has been crowdfunded. In fact, I had never even heard of such a thing until Zainab and her daughter set up a Facebook page to promote it. More than £8,000 was raised by the villagers and others who'd read the story online, all wanting to give her the final resting place she deserved.

It's also a first because I have never buried anyone who has been buried before. But once Gwen's body had been exhumed and released by the coroner, she was brought to where she was meant to be, reunited with her husband Bill in a plot adjacent to his.

I turn my head, and through the doors I spot Connie, supported by Zainab and her daughter. She is leaning on her walking frame, taking one step at a time. She catches sight of me and offers a grateful nod. I hope I have done both her and Gwen proud.

CHAPTER 64

CONNIE

It doesn't matter where I go this morning, my phone is not leaving my sight. I know it's unlikely to ring until at least the afternoon, but I don't care. I need to have it with me. I glance at the time as I have done every few minutes since waking up at dawn. It's still not even 10 a.m. I let out a long, frustrated groan. Today is the first day of Paul Michael's trial and the uncertainty of it all is already killing me.

He has pleaded 'not guilty' to the unlawful killings of Alice McKenzie, Lucy Holden, Walter Clark, Gwen Wright and Fran Brown. And as he suspected on the night when he tried to add me to his scorecard eight months ago, it was Fran's toxicology report that got the ball rolling. It confirmed she had been drugged with Omixinol, the psychoactive medication. And once the other women's bodies were exhumed, traces were found in all but the first, Eliza Holmes. Too much time had passed for her body to have retained that vital evidence.

Paul has also pleaded 'not guilty' to attempting to murder me. Every time I replay that moment – which, as you might imagine, is many times, daily – I think of how easily I could've been another victim. Although I suppose I am a victim, of sorts, just not in the way Paul intended. If he'd had his way, I'd be six feet under with my body parts taped together.

When I was convinced he'd been following me to and from Meredith's house, it wasn't paranoia but canny intuition. Despite my best efforts to keep safe, he'd been lurking in the shadows, waiting for his moment. CCTV cameras attached to shops, doorbells and inside a passing taxi proved he had actually been following me from the moment I left Avringstone. And according to his phone records, on my return journey home, he had logged on to the train's wi-fi to look up its timetable and then Network Rail's private intranet to discover the exact positioning of bridges on our journey. Of all the jobs he told people he did, railway maintenance and track installation turned out to be the truth. So he knew many routes across the Midlands like the back of his hand. Further evidence against him included train CCTV capturing him paying two teenage girls to walk up and down pressing panic alarm buttons. When the guard and driver assumed there was a technical problem and aborted the journey, Paul had pushed the emergency exit button to ensure he was first to disembark, then waited for the rest of the doors to open and watched from a distance as I left.

While he hadn't anticipated me wearing a personal alarm or the arrival of the police, he had timed my fall to perfection, stalling the officers on top of the bridge until the train appeared. But what his research hadn't told him was which track the train would be travelling along. At night and with its glaring lights, he assumed he was throwing me on to the correct track. But he was unaware the train had switched tracks before passing Favrington. He'd inadvertently hurled me sixteen feet below on to an empty line, albeit a hair's breadth from that high-speed train.

It all happened so quickly that I remember very little about the fall itself, other than the brief, sudden weightlessness. I recall hitting the metal rails on the left side of my body, my hip and arm connecting with it first, followed by my skull. I don't know if the impact affected my vision or if I was losing consciousness, but the train's lights seemed to disappear. The last thing I recall is the deafening sound of its brakes as it screamed to a halt, followed by blackness, then nothing else.

Nine days passed before doctors in my ICU team brought me out of my medically induced coma. Regaining consciousness was a gradual process, like swimming from deep water back to the surface of an ocean. So many parts of my body felt heavy, like rocks had been attached to them. Machines beeped and ventilators whooshed all around me, tubes were stuck in my veins and down my throat and I could pee myself but I never felt wet. As they gradually lowered my medication, it took me a few days to become completely aware of my situation. Then memories of Paul's attack returned to me like I was being handed pieces of a jigsaw. I began slotting them together one by one with the help of Krisha and her colleagues. My care team explained how my shattered hip had been artificially rebuilt, that my broken femur had been repaired and two breaks in my jaw sealed. My ankle, arm and wrist were in plaster casts with metal rods jutting out each side. Other injuries added to my tally included multiple fractured ribs, two cracked vertebrae and three missing molars. How I survived or am able to walk is beyond me.

Hospital became my home for a little over six months, and today marks my eighth week of freedom since being discharged. As an outpatient, I have regular physiotherapy sessions along with regular check-ups from specialists with different areas of expertise. I'm no longer in plaster but I'm aware of the thrumming and hot jabs of pain in various parts of my body. They've put me on a low level of meds but I've been warned opioids are addictive so they won't keep me on them forever. Eventually, they'll refer me to one of those pain management clinics.

There's a long list of other after-effects from that night. I have balance issues and I'm often stumbling around like a dozy toddler. My leg muscles are weak so I need to retrain them. And for now, I'm forced to use a walker. Well, they call it a mobility rollator, but everyone knows it's actually a walking frame with wheels. But it's temporary, and if I put in the hard work with physio and exercise, I could be walking with a crutch within a month or so.

Yesterday, Dr Chambers asked if I'd given any more thought to counselling for post-traumatic stress disorder. I said no because I feel pretty much in control of my thoughts and my moods, so he threw a trauma denial diagnosis at me. Apparently it's the brain's way of putting a distance between yourself and an 'overwhelming experience'. I guess you don't get much more overwhelming than being hurled over a bridge in front of a moving train. Perhaps I might have a rethink and take him up on the offer in time. But for now, I'll pop my pills, deal with things in my own way and remain grateful to be alive. If I can survive what Paul did to me, I can survive anything.

How he thinks he might get away with any of this is still beyond me. Krisha actually left me speechless when she first told me he'd pleaded not guilty to all charges. Perhaps he thinks he has nothing to lose for the murders. But as for trying to kill me in front of six police officers? Come on now. The footage from their bodycams demonstrates his absolute intent.

I check the time again – finally, it has passed 10 a.m. Paul's day of reckoning has arrived. And so has mine. When she came around last week, Krisha warned I might be called to give evidence against him in about a fortnight. I am *dreading* it, because my testimony is going to bring out into the open every aspect of my life, past and present. Currently, no one in Avringstone knows about Rachel. They all still believe I'm Gwen's daughter Connie.

But the truth will come out the moment I stand in that witness box and am cross-examined by Paul's barrister. I bet his team are champing at the bit as they wait to expose my lies, my background and my criminal record. And I assume they'll try and shift the blame for some of Paul's actions towards me, like trying to get the jury to believe I provoked him or that I was in on his scheme to scam Gwen. The jury will neither like nor trust me, and I can't blame them. I only hope they don't punish me by disregarding the evidence against Paul.

I hear a clanking of cutlery going into a drawer and glance out of the window. Zainab's in her kitchen emptying the dishwasher. After the owner of my bungalow evicted me while I was still in hospital, Zainab offered me the annex at the end of her garden to stay in until I'm better. My temporary new home is a brick building with its own wall heaters, television, pull-out bed, kitchenette and shower room. It's tiny, but I don't have much in the way of belongings to fill it up with, so that suits me just fine. And I doubt I'll be here for much longer anyway. Zainab will likely kick me out when my court appearance causes my life to unravel like a ball of wool.

Meredith will discover my truths too. She calls me at least twice a week, and because it was too long a journey for her to attend Gwen's recent second burial, she sent a beautiful flower arrangement instead. I could always call her and pre-empt what's to come in Paul's trial. And soon it will destroy my present and follow me around for the future. It saddens me, it really does, but then I have no one to blame but myself. And Paul, of course.

There is one piece of evidence involving all his victims that will come out and that fascinates and repulses me in equal measure. Krisha told me off the record that when his victims' bodies were exhumed, each was found to be missing their tongue. But unlike

Walter's, they'd been removed post-mortem, some time between the coroner releasing the body and their funeral. With the exception of Fran Brown's, each funeral was paid for by Paul. That meant he had access to a private room at the undertaker's before they were buried. I remember when I was alone with Caz in one and painted her nails before she was cremated. And in those private rooms is when the prosecution believes Paul removed their tongues. No blood flow meant no mess, so he simply closed their jaws when he was finished, leaving no one any the wiser.

'The other tongues were found in a plastic tub in Paul's freezer,' Krisha explained to me.

I shivered as I recalled finding a solitary box of meat in there the day I broke into his house. If I'd known what it was, I'd have called the police without hesitation. To hell with my plan.

'Just what kind of man is he?' I asked.

'A criminologist we work closely with suggests he is a "process-focused killer". That's someone who drags out the suffering of their victim. In Gwen and perhaps the other women's cases, that could mean weeks of being drugged before he picked his moment to kill them.'

'He's evil.'

'It hasn't stopped him from getting fan mail.'

Now that took me aback. 'Fan mail?'

'From both sexes. A dozen letters a week, according to my friend who works at the prison. Letters, photos, gifts . . . even marriage proposals. The world is a funny place, isn't it?'

I suppose it did him no harm that his police mugshot, released to the media, was exceptionally flattering. They are usually so bad they could make David Beckham look like Shrek, but Paul's somehow captured the twinkle in his blue eyes and flattering uplighting gave him sharp cheekbones and full lips. He looked like the kind of man you'd want to take home to show off to your mother. You'd just want to keep him away from Nana.

There is a solitary light at the end of my very dark tunnel though. Because if Paul is found guilty of Gwen's murder, I am once again set to inherit her estate. But until the trial is over, the will is staying with Meredith for safekeeping. I won't lie, there was a tiny little voice in the back of my mind that has asked what happens if she tries to make a claim on it because I deceived Gwen about who I was. However, the will is in my real name. And according to what I've read online, her estate will remain in my possession because there is no proof that I coerced her into signing it.

My heart almost skips a beat at the sudden ringing of my phone. Krisha's name appears on the screen. I glare at it – why is she calling me now? Surely she should be in court for the opening statements? I pray she's not about to tell me something awful has happened and all charges against Paul have been dropped. I don't know what I'd do if that happened. Throw myself off a bridge, maybe. Save him the trouble of doing it again.

Krisha doesn't give me the opportunity to say hello. 'Paul has changed his pleas.'

I must have misheard. 'He did what?'

'His barrister has altered Paul's pleas to guilty.'

'For which charges?'

'All of them. Including your attempted murder.'

I suck in a rush of air. 'Why?'

'He didn't say.'

I'm dumbstruck. Every worst-case scenario I have spent months imagining, might not actually happen. There is a chance I can bury Rachel forever.

'So I won't have to go to court?'

'No, you won't. It's over, Connie, all bar the sentencing. You can go and get on with your life.'

I can barely get the words 'thank you' out of my mouth before a rush of emotions hits me all at once. Tears, joy, sadness, confusion . . . I want to punch one fist into the sky and another into Paul's face. I hate him, but I'm grateful he's ended this now. For whatever reason, he has decided he doesn't want to play this game anymore.

Krisha is right. It's over. This is finally over.

Almost.

CHAPTER 65

CONNIE

Looking around the room, I realise I have spent far too much of my life in buildings like this. I vowed after leaving the last time that I'd never return. Little did I know that less than a year later, here I would be again, back in prison. Only today, I'm not an inmate.

I didn't have the opportunity to experience the inside of a visitors' room during my two-and-a-half-year punishment for hiding Caz's drugs and weapon, or more recently, during my stint for credit card fraud. I used to put a brave face on it, but I remember how much it stung knowing that of the billions of people out there in the big wide world, there wasn't one single person who wanted to come check on me. The pain has dulled and settled, but it remains.

This room reminds of a school gym, with scuffed wooden floors and high windows. Only there are bars on the glass, and instead of being surrounded by pommel horses and crash mats, I have tables and plastic chairs in rows of three. It stinks of stale air, cleaning supplies, cooking meat and floor polish. I'm surprised a Category A prisoner would be allowed visitors in an open space like this just a couple of months after sentencing, but apparently so.

Coming here to face Paul one last time felt like a good idea at first. I am sick of him living rent-free in my head and this was going to be my turning point. But now an ever-growing part of me wants to get the hell out of this building. I'm kidding myself if I think I can get on with the rest of my life without formally closing this chapter. And once I do, I hope I can find a way to start making the right decisions instead of selfish, stupid ones. It won't be easy, but nothing ever is when you're me.

I was the first person allowed inside the room this morning, probably because I'm the only one in the waiting room who walks with the help of a frame. The prison officer who guided me to my table apologised as he took it away with him. Apparently, it's 'a potential weapon'. It's only now I'm without it that I'm aware of how much I've come to depend on it psychologically as well as physically. But if Paul can't see the frame, he won't be able to gloat at the ongoing extent of my injuries, ten months on.

The room gradually fills with wives, girlfriends, grandparents, teens and toddlers. More minutes pass before a second door opens and the inmates file in. Men of all ages scan the room, searching for familiar faces. There are excited yelps from children and tears from partners. And all of a sudden, Paul appears in the doorway after everyone else – more psychological games, I assume, making me wait, keeping me on my toes, wondering if he's changed his mind after accepting my request to meet him. He refused the first one three weeks ago, but then sent me an invitation for an alternate date days later. Even behind bars he's trying to control the narrative.

His lips are moving, ever so slightly, as if he is talking to some-one. But he's the only one standing there. I remember him doing the same thing a few times at Gwen's house. Talking to himself. He stops suddenly and enters the room. His eyes widen when he clocks me and a familiar wry smile spreads across his face. In an instant, I'm taken back to the railway bridge and the moment he lifted me up and hurled me over the side. Even in the light of a partial moon and solitary street light, his smile was every inch as sinister as it is now. The memory is brief but powerful enough to make a breath snag in my throat. I wish I'd brought a bottle of water with me. *You're in the driving seat here*, I remind myself. *Not him. You are free, Paul is not. He will not intimidate you.*

He takes a seat opposite me, arms folded and legs spread. Defiant yet proud. Marking his territory. Telling me who is running this show. He looks me up and down. I've made sure my own arms and legs are covered so he can't see the scars of where metal once protruded from my bones, helping them to fuse. I give him the once-over as well. We are like two scorpions circling one another, each waiting for the other to strike first. He has clearly been making the most of his time as he awaits his sentence. His biceps are more pronounced than before and his chest protrudes from under his grey sweatshirt. The casual uniform that is baggy on other inmates clings to him.

'Well, isn't this nice?' he begins. 'My stepdaughter coming to visit her old man. How have you been, Rachel?'

'Very good, actually,' I lie.

'Managing well with your walker?'

I'm unsure how he knows about it but I don't ask. 'Perfectly, thank you.'

'Do I detect a slight lisp when you speak?'

'I have no idea, do you?'

'A shattered jaw can cause a speech impediment. Makes you hiss your esses like a snake. Kind of fitting, isn't it?'

'You might want to consider getting your ears syringed while you're here,' I reply. 'I'm sure you can find the time.'

300

'I'll add it to my to-do list. You've not asked me how I am.'

'You haven't given me the chance to. Or perhaps you have and I missed it. Or maybe I just don't care.'

'Let's not kid ourselves. If you didn't care, you wouldn't be here. Remember, you practically begged me to allow you to visit.'

'Begged isn't the word I'd—'

'I'm settling in very well, thanks very much,' he interrupts. 'You know what the lads are calling me?' I shake my head. 'The Old Dear Hunter,' he laughs. 'And apparently there's also memes online of me, my head stuck on Robert De Niro's body from the movie poster. I'm a bit of a celebrity.' I don't respond. 'So what brings you to HMP Manchester? That must've taken a lot of busses.'

'Two trains, actually.'

'So you're still using trains? Interesting. I wasn't sure if I'd scared you off them. You never know who's sitting in the rear carriage, do you?'

For a second, I can taste blood in my mouth, but I know it's not real. He's triggering me. I won't allow him to see I'm flustered. 'Perhaps I should've brought you a housewarming card,' I continue. 'Do they make them for cells?'

'I'd assumed you'd know. You have more experience of these places than I do.' Touché. 'So what really brings you here?'

I don't waste any more time. 'Why did you plead guilty at the last minute?'

He yawns and stretches his arms above his head. 'It wasn't last-minute.'

'But you waited until the day you went to trial.'

'I didn't see any hurry to reach that foregone conclusion. I'm not naive.'

'Then why not do it earlier? Why put the families of your victims—'

His laugh is as brief as it is sudden.

301

'You're laughing because I called them victims?' I ask. He rolls his hand in a circular motion, beckoning me to continue. 'Why put the families of the *victims* you murdered through months of hell waiting for a trial that was never going . . .' My voice trails off as I grasp his motivation. 'Ah, okay. You wanted to make them suffer for as long as possible.'

'If you say so.'

'And me too, as I waited to testify. Keep me on tenterhooks, assuming that I'd be scared of being exposed in court for who I used to be.'

'*Used* to be? Surely you mean *remain*?'

'I'm not Rachel anymore.'

'That's funny, because I swear I saw that name on the visitor's request form. It's not in a woman's nature to change, Rachel, only to find new ways to lie.'

'So why not go ahead with the trial, even if you knew what the outcome would be? Have your day in court and have your barrister rip me to shreds in the witness box?'

'While I am a supporter of blood sports, it would've been like shooting fish in a barrel and where's the fun in that? Besides, I'm not letting a "jury of my peers" dictate whether I'm guilty or not guilty. I have no peers. I will live out the rest of my life on my terms, not those dictated by nobodies.'

'That's not true though, is it? Because with or without their verdict, you're still living your life on other people's terms. Like the judge who'll decide your sentence, the prison officers who tell you when to sleep, eat, shower and exercise. Your life is no longer in your control.'

'Oh, don't worry about me, Rachel. I still have my little freedoms.' That wry smile makes way for a gloating one. He's up to something.

'You like to think you're a step ahead of the rest of us, don't you?' I continue. 'But you got greedy and sloppy with Fran Brown. If you'd killed her straight away, they wouldn't have done blood tests or exhumed the other bodies. You might still be a free man.'

'And you might not be dangerously close to an addiction to painkillers. Like mother, like daughter, eh? Although Caz wasn't as discerning when it came to what – or who – she popped inside her, was she?'

Don't react, I remind myself. But I am curious as to how he knows so much about me. He saves me the opportunity of trying to phrase my next question. 'There are plenty of bent coppers on the dark web willing to dig out criminal and medical records for the right price.'

'You weren't working alone, were you?'

'I suppose it wouldn't harm to credit Derek at Help for Homes for that.' Ahh, Derek Reid, the strange little man I worked with there who was never without his tartan tweed flat cap. He was also a witness at Paul and Gwen's wedding. 'As the requests came in for new clients with few family members, he'd tell me. He did all my research for me for a share of the spoils. Before you even think about tittle-tattling to your copper friend about him, he's now retired and about to enjoy every moment of it. And ask yourself why that video of you holding a pillow over my mum's face has yet to see the light of day? But more importantly, who has it now.'

I try my hardest not to swallow, but my body lets me down. I know Paul's seen it.

'You keep his secret and he'll keep yours.'

I change direction without warning. 'Why did you cut their tongues out?'

He answers without a beat. 'They were dishonest.'

'In what way?'

'In every way. They'd spent their whole lives lying to the people they claimed to love.'

'According to who?'

'According to them. Listen to someone carefully enough and you'll always find a lie in their truth. I silenced them so they couldn't lie anymore.'

'When you met them, dementia was destroying their capacity to separate fact from fiction. How could they tell the truth when they no longer knew what the truth was?'

Paul suddenly becomes animated; his hands and arms move like he's about to launch into flagless semaphore. 'What you don't understand, Rachel, is that by losing their self-control and their ability to self-edit, they could no longer hide behind their masks. What was left was raw and honest. They slipped up, they revealed their truths and exposed who they really were.'

'And who were they, really?'

'Let's see, shall we. Fran Brown confessed to having had two abortions without telling her husband. Who does that? A liar. Lucy Holden left a teenage boy paralysed in a hit and run when she drove home drunk after her sister's wedding. What kind of selfish bitch behaves like that? I'll tell you again. A liar. Alice McKenzie paid her mortgage with charity money raised to help a neighbour's daughter who needed cancer treatment in California. Why? Because she's a liar. Eliza Holmes? Well, she was a delight. Turned a blind eye to her boyfriend abusing her daughters for years. She was lying to herself.'

'But they make things up,' I reply. 'People with advanced Alzheimer's and dementia don't always know what they're saying. Gwen told me she was a bronze canoeing medallist in the 1980 Russian Olympics. I've yet to find proof of that.'

'Ah, your beloved Gwen.'

'She was a kind soul who didn't deserve either of us.'

'If you believe that you're as gullible as she was. She absolutely *deserved* the both of us.'

'I'd have killed for a mother like her.'

His response is more of a cackle than a laugh. 'Then you'd have been very well matched.'

'What's that supposed to mean?'

Paul ignores my question. 'Each one of my girls lied to protect their bad decisions and poor judgement. Without tongues, they cannot talk, and therefore they cannot lie.'

I pause to think on this for a moment. He's keeping something from me. I shake my head slowly. 'No,' I say. 'I don't believe you. There's more to it than that. They were already dead when you cut them out, and dead people don't talk.'

The images of Paul muttering to himself at Gwen's house, and then again, today, in the waiting room, return. And the penny drops.

'Except they talk to you, don't they?' I gasp. 'Your victims follow you around after you kill them. They haunt you, they pick away at your conscience, reminding you of what you are and what you did to them, and the only way you can make them stop is to cut out their tongues.'

Paul's eyes lock on to mine. I'm expecting him to argue, but he doesn't. So I continue.

'You hear their voices right up until the moment you visit them in their funeral homes that one last time and remove their tongues. Walter was the exception, because by the time you killed him, the police had opened their investigation into you. It wasn't going to be long before their bodies were exhumed and tested. So you had nothing to lose doing it there and then in his bedroom.' Now I'm thinking out loud. 'But when I saw you at Gwen's house talking to

305

yourself, you'd already removed Eliza, Lucy and Alice's tongues, and it was before you'd even met Fran Brown . . .' And then it hits me.

'Shit!' I say a little too loudly. Heads turn in our direction. 'Those women . . . they weren't the first, were they? You've been doing it for years.'

CHAPTER 66

CONNIE

Paul doesn't need to admit to anything for me to know I have him bang to rights. His face doesn't flinch, his body doesn't move. His once impenetrable stare is now transparent. I need to keep up the momentum.

'So there are more victims out there who you've murdered that nobody knows about,' I say. 'But for whatever reason, you weren't able to silence them like you did the others. And now you're in here, you'll never be able to do it. For the rest of your life, you're going to have to live with their voices haunting you for what you did to them.'

Only now do I notice he has started clenching his fists so tightly that his knuckles are ashen. I sit back a little, half expecting him to launch himself across the table and finish the job he started when he dragged me off that train.

'And what about your mum?' I persist. 'Why did you dump her in that awful care home? You must hate her more than any of your "girls" to leave her there. Because I know you can afford better.'

'You wouldn't understand what a woman like her deserves,' he says slowly.

'Understand what? Bad parenting? If you've researched me like I think you have, you know better than that.' He shakes his head dismissively. 'Come on,' I say.

He clears his throat as if something is caught in it. 'What would you like me to tell you about my mum, Rachel? Should I start with how she cheated on my dad relentlessly with many, many men and women? That she'd lie to him and make him believe it was all in his imagination until it literally drove him insane? How, when he finally cracked, to punish her, he took my brother and sister with him to a multi-storey car park, threw them over the edge and then himself? Do you want me to tell you that she blamed me for what he did, telling me it was because I was such an awful son and brother, the rest of my family would rather die than be around me? What about how she'd drive me to the same car park, make me stand on that ledge and beg me to jump too? That she'd pull on my tongue and threaten to cut it off with garden shears because she believed everything that came out of my mouth was a lie? I could always tell you how it turned out my father wasn't actually my father after all. And even though she knew who he was, she refused to give me his name. Or do you want to hear how she slammed her own head into the garage wall over and over again and accused me of attacking her, all so that social services removed me from our home and put me in care for *her* safety? Are these the sorts of confessions you want from me?'

In an instant, I recognise segments of myself in him. In the pitch of his voice, the tilt of his head, the fear and loathing etched into every pore of skin on his face. In this moment, I see it. He was right, we *are* alike, and I hate him for it. We share an entrenched pain that will never heal. I'm convinced this is the first time he has admitted to anyone how badly he was wronged by the person he was supposed to trust. The good side of me, the decent side, wants to tell him that what she did to him wasn't his fault, that we are the products of our environments and that while others escape and soar high, there will be people like us who remain with one foot anchored to the past, forever struggling to leave the ground. However, I can't offer him my sympathy, not even the tiniest shred. Because I don't want him to know how similar we are. I don't want him to know that in spirit, we are linked. I don't want him to know that finally, I understand who Paul is.

'You are no better than your mum,' I goad. 'You think you have the right to punish people for their mistakes like you're judge, jury and executioner, when the truth is that you have no idea if those women were being honest with their confessions or if their minds were playing tricks on them. They might have made up those stories on the spot or they could've mixed them up with the plot of a book they once read. You were just looking for an excuse to punish and kill women that reminded you of Sue and her dementia diagnosis because it was easier to murder them than your own flesh and blood.'

I watch in awe as his cheeks hollow and he tries to suppress the urge to swallow his regret for exposing his truth. He quickly regains his composure and we both know that I am the first person to have reached his core. He begins to clap at me, slowly, his hands making large, exaggerated movements. Heads once again turn towards us and a prison guard makes his way in our direction until Paul stops. Silence follows, one that's left for me to fill.

'I assume you heard that we moved Gwen into the plot next to Bill's?' I recall. 'It was a lovely funeral, by the way. The kind she was supposed to have had.'

'Do you dream about me?' he asks suddenly. 'That night? How often do you think about it? Every minute, every hour, every day?'

I want to tell him that I don't dwell on it at all, but he'd know that would be a lie. 'What do you think?' I ask.

'I think you never stop replaying it in your head. The taste of the metal blade on your tongue, my fist connecting with the vertebrae in the back of your neck, the feeling of having me rolling on top of you under that train and pinning you down. I think that was the part you liked the most. I know I did. Seeing, tasting, feeling your fear – it got me hard. Did you feel my cock pressing into you? I bet you did. And I bet when you're replaying it, that's the part you always come back to.'

I don't react. He's trying to make me feel uncomfortable because he's desperate. He is powerless and he knows it. That's what weak men do in the last throes of an argument. All they have left is their sex to dominate when they're coming undone.

'It must have been so disappointing for you when I survived,' I add. 'Here I am. Still alive. And there you are. Locked away for the rest of your life. You failed.'

'There's more than one way to skin a cat,' he replies before he leans back in his seat. 'So is that it? Have you checked off everything on your list that you came here to say?'

'Almost,' I say. 'I'm also here to tell you I'm about to start proceedings to gain control of Gwen's estate.'

The wry grin I detest so intensely returns. 'And you're one hundred per cent sure that's going to happen are you, Rachel?'

'Absolutely.'

He leans forward again and I don't back away. He is so close I smell tea on his warm breath. In two words, he silences me.

'How's Meredith?'

I glare at him blankly. What did he just say? I hesitate too long to disguise my surprise at this curveball. How does Paul know about her? Then I recall the day he attacked me: CCTV cameras confirmed he had been following me all day. So of course he saw me enter her house. Oh Jesus, has he done something to hurt her? No, how can he, from here? Maybe he's paid someone else to do his dirty work for him? Has he had Derek kill Meredith to punish me? He sounds like a man unburdened by conscience. No, of course he hasn't. He's just trying to mess with my head. It's working. I spoke to Meredith a few days ago and she was perfectly fine. I told her I'd pick up the will when I visit her next week.

'She's keeping well, I hope?' Paul continues. 'And safe? Living on your own at her age . . . You never know who might suddenly turn up on her doorstep, unannounced.'

I don't get the opportunity to ask anything else because a bell sounds to indicate visiting time is over.

'Well, it was lovely to see you again,' Paul says as he rises to his feet. 'Don't be a stranger.'

When he reaches the door to return to his wing, he turns around and winks at me. And all I can think about is how I might have killed Meredith.

CHAPTER 67

CONNIE

'Where are you?' I yell into my phone.

I try calling Meredith for the dozenth time, but there's still no answer. I can't remember a time when I rang and she wasn't there to pick up.

My stomach is performing somersaults as I sit outside the prison gates waiting for the bus to arrive that will take me to the train station. Following Paul's deliberate mention of Meredith, I'm terrified. She rarely leaves her house. If she doesn't answer soon, I'll call Krisha, recount Paul's veiled threat and beg her to ask police colleagues in Coventry to check in on her.

My heart is jackhammering and I'm again aware of how dry my throat is. I grab a bottle of water from my handbag and take long gulps. Another thirty minutes pass and I alternate between Meredith's landline and her mobile number. The landline rings out, but the mobile keeps going straight to voicemail. All I can think of is that, by befriending her, by giving her Gwen's will to look after, I've sealed her fate like I did with Walter. I really don't know if I can live with myself if another person dies because of me.

Suddenly, as the bus pulls into Manchester Piccadilly, the phone rings in my hand. It's Meredith's mobile number.

'Meredith!' I say. 'I've been trying to get hold of you all afternoon.'

'Is everything okay?' she asks.

The sound of her voice brings me to tears. Wherever she is, it's windy, and I can hear people talking in the background. I thank God she's not in her house, lying in a pool of blood as I'd imagined.

'I was worried when you weren't answering your phones.'

'I'm absolutely fine,' she replies chirpily. 'I'm at the hairdresser's. It's been an age so I thought I'd treat myself to a wash and blow dry before you come up next week. I thought that maybe we could go out for afternoon tea. My treat, if you fancy it?'

'I'd really like that.'

I feel like an idiot. Of course she was at the hairdresser's. She mentioned it when we spoke last week. There'd be no benefit to Paul or Derek killing her. I decide not to tell Meredith that I've visited him today, or that he mentioned her by name. Scaring her is the last thing I want to do.

'I just wanted to make sure that you were alright,' I reply, calmer now.

'Oh, that's very sweet of you, but yes, I'm wonderful.'

We say our goodbyes soon after and I'm angry at myself for granting Paul the power to scare me like that. Will I ever be truly free of him, or are our lives now destined to remain entwined? I had hoped that by seeing him this last time, I was now free to get on with living. But now I'm not so sure.

Maybe Dr Chambers was right and I should think about that PTSD counselling. I naively assumed I was in control of my thoughts and my moods but Paul has proved how quickly he can creep inside my head. And while I'm at it, I might also look into cognitive behavioural therapy. From what I've read, it might go a long way to helping ensure my past doesn't dictate my future. It's time for me to embrace life instead of simply getting by at the expense of others. I know I can't change overnight, and sometimes I might get it wrong. Actually, there's no 'sometimes' about it. Of course I'm going to get it wrong, as it's hardwired into my brain to put my needs above everyone else's. But I've never tried to be the best version of myself before. And I no longer have an excuse not to.

For now, for today, I'm going to concentrate on the fact Paul is behind bars and likely will be for the rest of his life. Meredith and I are safe. And that is all that matters.

CHAPTER 68

CONNIE

Well, this feels strange. It's the first day I'm not being reliant on my walker and I'm only using a crutch. It's kind of liberating, but my brain is convinced that if I loosen my grip even slightly, I'll fall over. So I'm clutching the handle so tightly that my fingers are starting to cramp.

For a winter's day, it's refreshingly mild, so I decide to walk from Hampton-in-Arden's train station to Meredith's house. It'll also help me reach the daily steps goal my physio Zara has given me. That girl is half my age but nags me like a parent harping on at a child to finish their homework.

A mobile person might take ten minutes or so to reach Meredith's, but for me it's double that, and then some. Zara warned me there's a chance I might always need a walking aid in some form. I never quite pictured myself as a forty-three-year-old reliant on a cane for balance, but if that is the case, I can handle it. It's not the worst thing to have happened to me. I have survived my mum, I have survived myself and I've survived Paul. If none of that killed me, a stick won't either.

I think about our prison confrontation a lot, especially the part where he didn't deny killing other women before Eliza Holmes. However, he didn't admit it either. I've ummed and ahhed about telling Krisha about it, and about his friend Derek and the role he played in identifying Paul's potential victims. If there are others, I bet he knows who they are. But by pointing the finger at him, I'll be putting myself at risk of investigation, as Derek has the video Paul recorded of me holding a pillow over Paul's mum's face. So even though it doesn't sit easily with me and contradicts my new, more honest approach to life, I've decided I have little choice but to let it go.

It's time I pushed both Paul and Derek out of my head, so I think about Meredith instead. I'm really looking forward to seeing her again. We speak regularly by phone and text, but this will be the first time we'll have been together in person since before the accident.

Accident, I say to myself. I don't know why I use that word. Being deliberately thrown to what was supposed to have been my death is hardly an *accident*. But it's easier to call it that than to keep saying 'since my attempted murder'. It's nice to have people like Meredith in my corner who really care about me. She and my neighbours have been there for me at my worst and I've never been surrounded by people like that before. It's why I'm so single-minded about not screwing up my future.

I also want to see Meredith to thank her. Because not only am I picking up the will I left at her house, she has also offered to lend me the money to hire a solicitor to ensure everything is done properly. She wants to make sure all the i's are dotted and the t's are crossed. Initially I refused, because for once, I wanted to do something for myself. But I had a change of heart. This is different. I'm not trying to con her out of anything and I intend to give her back every penny as soon as Gwen's money is paid into my bank account. And she's right when she says there can't be any cutting of corners when it's something this important. If this is going to be a new start for me, then it must be done properly.

I'd like to buy her something to show my gratitude. I'm not sure what yet, perhaps a nice piece of jewellery to remember Gwen by? I make a mental note to subtly enquire if she prefers necklaces, brooches or bracelets.

There's a list of things I want to do with Gwen's money. And buying myself a car is at the top of it. Nothing flashy or expensive, a cheap runaround will do. Then I can wave goodbye to buses and trains and go where and when I please, not when a timetable dictates. Next will be headstones to mark the graves of Paul's victims Eliza Holmes, Lucy Holden, Alice McKenzie and, of course, Gwen. Regardless of what Paul claimed these women confessed to him, they were still casualties and their lives deserve to be marked. Walter and Fran were both cremated so I plan to leave some flowers in the places where their families told me their ashes had been scattered.

Finally, I'll pay to change my name by deed poll from Rachel Evans to Connie Gwen Wright. I am so far removed from Rachel that I truly believe any trace of her died the day Paul threw me over the bridge. Perhaps in some weird, sick way, he did me a favour after all.

I've also decided to keep Gwen's house and remain in Avringstone. That she was killed there doesn't put me off. There are plenty of ghosts who haunt me already, so one more won't make a difference. And eventually, I'd like to volunteer for a charity that helps families and friends of those living with dementia-related conditions. I don't know if my criminal record will stop that from happening, but I'll ask about.

I pick a bunch of yellow chrysanthemums from a bucket outside the supermarket and pay for them out of my government compensation money for being the victim of a violent crime. The cost of living, travel expenses and my inability to earn elsewhere have taken a huge chunk of the £6,782.48 I was awarded – don't ask me how they came to that figure – but I have around £1,000 left which, if I'm careful, should last me until my inheritance comes through.

And a few minutes later I arrive at Meredith's front door, my right leg pulsing, my left exhausted, but my spirits high. I knock and wait, and when there's no response, I try again. Again, nothing. That's strange. I check my phone and I definitely have the right date and time. I cup my hand to the window and try to peer inside, but the curtains are drawn. I return to the front door and after a struggle, I lower myself to my knees and look through the letter box. Nothing appears out of place in the hallway.

There's a gentle but twisting tug in my stomach, the one that has a habit of appearing when I think of Paul. His last words to me were referring to Meredith. 'You never know who might suddenly turn up on her doorstep, unannounced,' he warned.

'No,' I say aloud, shutting him down before he has the chance to spook me again. 'Stay in control.'

'Meredith?' I shout through the letter box. 'Are you there? Meredith? Can you hear me?' It's only then that I notice my hands have begun to tremble. It's happened on occasion, and my surgeon has put it down to nerve damage. But it feels different today. Ominous, even.

'Everything alright?' comes a voice from behind. I know it's not Paul, but I jump nonetheless. I turn to see a postman, an envelope in his hand and a bag across his shoulder.

'I'm not sure,' I say, and ask if he can help me to my feet. 'I think something's happened to Meredith because I've been knocking and there's no answer.'

'She moved, didn't she?' he replies breezily.

'No, she didn't. I spoke to her on Monday. She was right here, in the village.'

He shrugs. 'Well, I had a conversation with her as the removal men were loading her stuff on to the back of a lorry and taking it away.'

'What lorry?'

'It said something about house clearances on the side.'

I shake my head. 'You're mixing her up with someone else. Meredith Harper, she lives here at number 23. She has done for most of her life.'

'And that's why I know I'm right,' he continues, now defiantly. 'This has been my round since 2015. I've known her all that time.'

He is very convincing, but I don't want to believe him. 'Well, where did she say she was going?'

'Somewhere away from the village and something like "far away from this life", and then she winked at me. She didn't leave a forwarding address so I have to keep putting her mail through her door until someone redirects it.'

'There's no forwarding address at all?'

'Nope. Said she didn't need one where she was going.'

He pushes an envelope through the letter box and leaves me alone again to try to make sense of what he's said. But I can't because it makes no sense at all.

I shuffle as fast as my legs will allow along the street, my stick tapping against the paving slabs. I turn left and head into an alley and locate the back of Meredith's property. Her gate is unlocked, and scattered about the rear garden are half a dozen black bin bags. One has been ripped open by a cat or a fox and only contains cans and the remains of food packets. The back door is locked, but when I look around, I spy a rock that looks out of place. I've seen these keyholders before. I take the key out, unlock the door and make my way inside.

'Meredith?' I ask one more time, desperately hoping she replies. But my voice echoes around the deserted kitchen. I move into the sitting room and her two armchairs and television are gone. Upstairs there are no wardrobes or beds. Yet still, I'm in denial.

I call her mobile number once, twice and a third time, but it keeps going to voicemail. I try to recall our last conversation and how she hadn't answered the landline or her mobile for ages. And when she finally called me back, I remember the sound of wind blowing and people talking in the background. She said she was in the local hairdresser's, but had she already moved away from the village?

I ring her again but this time I leave a message. 'Meredith, it's Connie,' I say. 'I'm in your house, but you're not here and the postman reckons you've moved. What's going on? Call me back as soon as possible please. I'm worried about you.'

Ten minutes pass as I sit at the top of the stairs, clutching the phone, willing it to ring back. But it doesn't. And even now, surrounded by all this evidence, I still can't accept the truth because Meredith leaving makes no sense at all. Where could she have gone? Why didn't she tell me? What is moving 'far away from this life' supposed to mean? She wasn't talking about suicide, was she? No, surely not. Meredith wouldn't do that. She has no reason to. At least not that I know of . . .

Bang!

It hits me with the force of a thunderbolt. The other reason I'm here to see her: to pick up Gwen's will. A split second later and I feel the blood draining from my face.

CHAPTER 69

CONNIE

I hurry downstairs but lose my footing on the third from last step. My feet fly out from under me and down I go, *hard*, spine first on the edge of the tread. White-hot pain shoots up the right side of my back into the base of my skull and I cry out loud like an outraged child. For a long, miserable moment I don't know which part of myself to hold to make it go away. When at last it subsides just enough, I reach for my stick and get back on my feet, then hobble to the chimney breast where I watched Meredith hide Gwen's will. I feel around inside until I find the plastic bag. I drag it out, see the envelope through the bubble wrap which is still stuffed inside it. My writing is on the front, *Gwen's Will* in blue biro. I tear through the bag and the envelope and don't dare to breathe again until I have checked that it's definitely here. Then I let out the longest sigh of relief.

I tell myself off for questioning Meredith's integrity, but what else am I supposed to think when she's emptied her house and upped sticks without telling me? This must have been a gigantic upheaval for her that's taken planning. It wasn't done on a whim.

My fingers are caked in grey dust from inside the breast and there's nothing to wipe them on but the carpet. But as I do so, I lose my grip of the will and it falls to the floor. It opens on the last page. As I pick it up, I look more closely at it. No, that can't be right. The final page is missing.

Now, a second tidal wave of panic emerges as I flick through the will page by page, desperate to find it. I need this seventh page, as it's the one containing my signature, alongside Gwen's and that of our witness, Reverend Eddie. It proves that Gwen wanted to give her estate to me. It has to be here somewhere, it *has* to be. I lick my dirty fingers to get a better grip of the paper in case two pages are stuck together, but they aren't. And I know for sure that before I left it here, every page was in order, all held together with a staple. I even double-checked it on the train journey to Meredith's house.

This is the only copy I have. Without it, I have no claim over anything of Gwen's.

I search the chimney breast again, desperate to find that missing page, refusing to believe that this is deliberate. The only thing up here is more dust. I tear the rest of the house apart but find nothing. I dial Meredith again and again and leave more messages. Finally, I return to the lounge and wipe away the tears that have been streaming down my face. I catch my reflection in one of the few objects Gwen has left behind, a mirror above the fireplace. I'm broken.

I hold my head in my hands and accept the truth. Meredith, the only person in the world who knew the whereabouts of the will, has ruined it for me. That kind, humble, lonely old woman was playing a game I had no idea I was competing in. I trusted her and she took it all from right under my nose. As Gwen's only living relative, that house is now hers. *My* house. I bet that's why she's moved from here and sold all her furniture. A new life awaits her in Avringstone. That old bitch. I don't know to process this, how to feel. I can't settle on one emotion. I'm devastated beyond words, I want to cry until I'm out of tears and scream until I'm hoarse. I want to lash out but there's no one here to take it out on.

And then it catches my eye, glaring at me. The green porcelain cat that once belonged to Gwen and that I gave to Meredith is still here, perched on the windowsill, partly hidden by a curtain. I don't know how I could have missed it before now. It's been watching me this whole time, laughing at me. There's a handwritten note poking out from underneath its paws. *Look after Tom for me*, it reads.

Tom, I think. So this is the mysterious Tom. The fucking cat. She knew all along to whom Gwen was referring. What else has she been lying to me about?

All my rage and frustration come to a head in one mighty explosion. I reach for my crutch, raise it above my head and bring it crashing down on that ugly cat. It shatters into a dozen pieces on the floor. Then something inside it grabs my attention – it's another piece of paper. It's been rolled up and placed inside a hole in the base. I unroll it. It's dated three years earlier and has a crest at the top, and underneath, the words 'Appraisal Certificate'. It describes the cat's appearance, dimensions, its Chinese origins, and finally, its valuation.

I have just destroyed something worth £50,000.

Numbness takes over my body. I don't know what to do. I look at what I have just destroyed, panic and hurriedly try and piece it back together. There must be a way, surely? But no, this fucking thing is too badly damaged to be worth anything.

I scream at the top of my lungs, lift the crutch up again and continue pummelling it until all that's left are slivers of porcelain and dust, swallowed up in the pile of the carpet. And that is all that's left of me too. Shards of my new self, scattered into too many pieces to ever put back together again.

CHAPTER 70

ONE YEAR LATER –
MEREDITH HARPER

Oh my, the sun is certainly in glorious form today. It's as blistering out here as I can ever remember. And only occasionally does it vanish behind cotton-wool ball clouds. But as much as I've relished being reacquainted with these temperatures after so many years spent in the self-exile of my little cottage, I'm in need of a little respite. I prop myself up on the sun lounger with my elbows, fold over the corner of my current page and place my book cover-down upon the sand. I lower my sunglasses and take in the sights surrounding me. According to a travel blog review I read en route, El Mirador is regarded as one of Cancún's most beautiful locales, thanks to its 'white sandy beaches that lead the way towards the remarkably motionless azure sea'. You won't hear me disagreeing. It's heaven.

I turn my head to catch the attention of Luís, one of the young waiters hovering behind the bar, and wave my fingers at him. He smiles and nods his acknowledgement before trudging across the beach to reach me. The staff here are so attentive. I ask him if he wouldn't mind moving my sun lounger so that I can take shelter under the parasol. 'Of course, Senóra Harper,' he chirps, and helps me to my feet before rearranging the position of my sunbed. Nothing is too much trouble for him and I tip him a handful of pesos.

I glance out towards the sea and squint when I catch motion before the horizon. It's a pod of dolphins breaking through the water's surface and spinning through the air in an arc-like formation. I smile and raise my glass to them. It's taken me almost eighty-five years but I finally know how it feels to be free like them.

Further out is the motorboat that brought us to shore, and behind that, *The Adventurer*, the luxury cruise liner I've spent the last month of my life aboard. Most of my fellow guests are either enjoying excursions inland or have remained onboard, enjoying one of the many bars or entertainments on offer to us all. But I prefer to make the most of the beaches, as and when I can. I've wasted too much of my life cooped up indoors to spend my remaining days living that way.

It's my first time in El Mirador but the second time I've visited Cancún in the year I've been travelling. It's become one of my favourite places on earth and I now have a good number of journeys under my belt to compare it to. I've enjoyed cruises around Europe, the Bahamas and Australia. But I've decided Mexico is where my heart lies. The people, the aromas, the food, the sights and sounds . . . all of it makes my heart sing in a way I have never heard it do before.

The money from the sales of both houses barely had time to make a dent in my bank account before I made a withdrawal to pay for my first cruise around Europe. It lasted six weeks and I enjoyed it so much that I booked a second while I was still onboard the first. But the trip I'm on now is a little different. I'm four weeks into a mammoth two-hundred-and-eighty-day worldwide journey. I'll be taking in six continents, sixty-two countries and a hundred and fifteen ports. And my residency ticket means I get to keep the same cabin for this tour and the one after that. The only time I'll be away from this ship is for a few short weeks when routine maintenance work takes place between excursions. And I've already planned and paid for what I'll do then. I'll be on a shorter trip around the British Isles and Europe. It'll be like taking a holiday from a holiday.

I no longer have a permanent base back in England. At my time of life, this should terrify me. But it doesn't, which confirms in my mind that I've made the right decision. I am a million miles away from what I thought was my comfort zone, and for the very first time, life is exhilarating. I don't ever want to go back because I have everything I could ever need here. It's all done for me – my meals, washing and dry cleaning, there are onboard cabarets and singers every night along with sports to play, a spa, a library and three cinemas. I'm one of almost nine hundred passengers and the vast majority are retired, like me. We call ourselves the Silver Sailors – a community of floating expats from every corner of the globe, all from different walks of life but with the same shared sense of adventure. We aren't willing to give up the ghost just because that's what society expects of us. We plan to live our lives, not spend what's left of them reflecting on what has been and gone. Each day we meet for lunches and dinners, we take spa breaks together or exercise, or visit the mainland on excursions. I didn't realise just how gregarious I was until I woke from my hibernation. My social life hasn't been as extensive or exciting as this since my university days.

My cabin is spacious enough for me to relax and spend time alone when the mood takes me. My bedroom and bathroom are the size of the entire ground floor of my old house. I have access to doctors, a physiotherapist, masseuses and a dentist if I need them. I still use my walking stick to get me about, but my joints haven't felt as flexible in years. And I love my new knees! The surgeons at the Sheba hospital in Israel have a reputation for being some of the best in the world for good reason. And exercise, the sun and a lust for life are marvellous tools for recovery. Who wouldn't want this life?

Sometimes I take a step back from myself and wonder if this is all real, or whether I've suffered a colossal stroke and I'm actually lying in a hospital bed and this is all in my imagination. Only when I pinch myself and watch my skin redden do I accept this is my reality and will be until the day I die, God willing. It really is the perfect existence. And I have Gwen, Connie and Paul to thank for it all.

I don't like to dwell on the past anymore, but I briefly allow my mind to wander back to my Hampton-in-Arden home. I thought I'd see out my days under the same roof I'd spent most of my life under. I remember when Covid struck and my social life was obliterated by the first lockdown. By the second, I'd lost my confidence in going out and seeing other people. By lockdown number three, I was completely alone. I remained in my foxhole, not seeing anyone but the postman for weeks and weeks at a time. I'm not ashamed to admit there were occasions when I considered emptying all the pills prescribed for my various ailments and swallowing them in one go. Because the thought of living another decade like that left me empty. And then Connie turned up on my doorstep and changed everything. She gave me options and I will always be grateful to her for that, even if it wasn't what she intended for me.

I had fallen for her story, hook, line and sinker. I had no reason to doubt she was being anything other than completely honest about her relationship with Gwen. Even when she slipped in the conversation about Gwen leaving her the estate in her will, I thought nothing of it. She had looked after my cousin, so why shouldn't she be rewarded for it? And then, after what Paul tried to do to her . . . well, I thought, that money might help her until she was able to recover, return to Italy and pick up her career again as a wedding planner.

And then Paul's letter arrived.

A few hours after being charged with the murders of Gwen and those other unfortunate souls, he wrote to me. Across three detailed pages, he explained Connie wasn't who she claimed to be; that she was a career criminal and con-woman who, like him, had edged her way into Gwen's life with the sole purpose of taking her money upon her death. Only Paul wasn't willing to wait around as long as Connie was.

While he stopped short of admitting to any actual crimes, he was eager to reveal all he knew about his adversary. In a package that arrived later the same week, each of his accusations was proven with factual, tangible evidence, supplied by an unnamed associate of his. There was a copy of her criminal record, birth certificate, passport and driver's licence, and bank statements including her withdrawals from Gwen's accounts for her own use. Unless they were elaborate forgeries, together they made damning evidence. He also warned it was likely she was targeting me next.

Words like 'shocked', 'dismayed' and 'disappointed' do not do justice to how let down this left me. I wrote back to him, asking why he was contacting me with this, especially after murdering my cousin. He informed me, honestly, I suppose, that his only motive was to ensure that, like him, Connie was stopped from inheriting anything of Gwen's. He knew the evidence was weighted against him but until he was found guilty or confessed to his crimes, her estate still technically belonged to him.

But if I was to organise a lawyer of my own, he would sign everything over to me.

My answer was immediate. *No*, I wrote. *I don't want anything to do with your blood money.* That level of deception might be second nature to people like Connie and Paul, but not to me. I've led an honest life and I've hurt no one, even when I've been provoked.

I informed him by return of post that even if I did want a change, I didn't need him to do it. I had access to Gwen's will and if I made it disappear, it would go to probate and everything would end up with me anyway, being Gwen's sole surviving relative.

It's six months until my trial, and you could be waiting up to a year after that until it's in your name, he wrote back. *Do you really have all that time on your side? Why wait when it can all be yours in a couple of months? I'd already drained Gwen's bank account and changed ownership of the property into a business account in the Cayman Islands before my assets could be frozen. But you need to act quickly before it's traced and the recovery process begins.*

He made a compelling argument and set the cogs in my brain spinning. Neither Paul nor Connie deserved Gwen's money, but after what my cousin had put me through, I did. I asked myself a question I should perhaps have asked many moons ago. Where has being a decent human being got me? Unmarried, childless, with very few surviving friends and waiting to die alone. I had long known and accepted that I was one of life's also-rans . . . someone who had allowed the world to pass them by because they were too afraid to make changes by themselves. I had never lived anything close to what young people today call 'my best life'. I didn't have the foresight, ambition or access to finances to do that. But now Paul was offering me a way to completely alter my future. And the decision was mine.

So I wrote back to Paul and told him yes, I'd accept his offer. Then I set the wheels in motion, using my savings to hire a lawyer to discreetly begin what was necessary.

In the meantime, I kept from Connie what Paul had told me of her. We texted regularly and continued to speak on the phone weekly while she was recovering in hospital and then after her release. I gave her every opportunity to tell me the truth about who she was and how she and Gwen had really met, but she kept up her

329

charade. I'd ask questions about her family and background, her 'work' in Italy, her previous careers, but nothing she revealed bore any resemblance to the documents Paul had sent. If she couldn't be honest with me, she didn't deserve my honesty in return.

Nine weeks before Paul changed his plea to guilty on the day of his trial, Gwen's estate legally became mine. And the clock was ticking. My house and hers were uploaded to an online auction site in the same week, as I didn't want estate agents showing potential buyers around Gwen's and alerting Connie or her neighbours to what was happening. I also insisted on cash-only buyers to speed up the transactions. Gwen's home was immediately snapped up by a builder while mine was sold to a landlord. Then, once the money from both transactions was deposited into my account, I sold all my belongings to a house clearance company. I bought my tickets for my first cruise, and booked a driver to take me to Portsmouth, where I stayed for a few days in a four-star hotel before my ship set sail.

A week before Connie was to visit my house, our liner was navigating the Mediterranean Sea and preparing to dock in Barcelona when she began calling me, multiple times. I diverted them all to voicemail so that she wouldn't hear a foreign ringtone. *She knows what I've done*, I thought and I waited until we reached calmer waters and when the sound of the boat slicing through the waves died down. Her message sounded worried, not angry, and I realised she had yet to discover the truth. When I called her back she was completely oblivious to my location on the top deck of a ship, and that it was the wind blowing through my hair and not a hairdryer at the village salon. She was concerned when I hadn't answered straight away, which gave me a brief stab of remorse. I wondered if perhaps she did care for my well-being after all, until she reminded me she was coming to pick up Gwen's will the following week. That was what she cared about, not me. I bet I wouldn't have seen her for dust once it was back in her possession. What she did to Gwen was far worse than what I was doing to her.

Sometimes I try and imagine her face when she found my home was empty of all belongings. If it was anything like the many voice-mails she left afterwards, she will have run through a full gamut of emotions. Her reaction reminded me of the five stages of grief. To begin with, she was confused as to where I was and wanted to know why I hadn't told her I was moving. Then came the frustration as to why I hadn't called her back. Next came anger over the missing page of the will, followed by denial that I could have done such a thing. Finally, she finished with near-hysterical threats.

As the months have progressed, her calls have continued, although less so now. In some, she is angry and swears a lot; in others, her speech is slurred as if drunk and her words are more of a running commentary on her life now. She complains about how someone has stolen her handbag from the hostel she's been staying at. She sobs as she recalls how she has been arrested for shoplifting, and somehow I'm to blame. Sometimes she hurls more abuse at me and in other messages she begs me to help her financially. And in the last call I received, about six weeks ago, an operator explained the call was coming from a women's prison. I hung up. One can only assume that things took a very sharp turn in the wrong direction for Connie.

I think of Paul on occasion and how his first letter altered everything for me. He will be approaching his second year behind bars now, if you include his time on remand. There will be another thirty years to go of his sentence before he'll be able to apply for parole. But in all likelihood, he will be long dead by then, which is no more than he deserves. Regardless of his actions, I have sent him a few colourful postcards of my journeys along the way. If nothing else, they might brighten up his cell and he can see how the money has not gone to waste. I hate him for what he did to those other women. However, I cannot be angry with him for what he did to Gwen. The cruelty with which he treated my cousin is beyond belief, but it was every bit deserved. A painful, lingering death like the one she suffered couldn't have happened to a better woman.

She and I were bonded by blood and we should have been friends for life. Our mothers were first cousins and had a close relationship in childhood and as adults. However, Gwen and I didn't replicate their friendship. Neither of us had brothers or sisters and only five months separated us. In personality, we were as far apart as the continents I sail to now. I was kind and thoughtful while Gwen was spoiled and jealous of me. But we were forced to spend time together either on annual family holidays to the Norfolk Broads and Scotland, or at each other's houses during the long summer school breaks.

There was always an intense rivalry between us, and a day wouldn't pass without us bickering over something trivial. If my parents gave me a gift, she would whine until hers bought her something similar, or better. If I caught the eye of a boy, Gwen flirted like crazy until his attention was drawn to her. I dreaded her extended visits as she belittled me in front of my friends to win laughs and favour. It was as if she feared that she did not exist if she wasn't someone's priority.

I excelled both academically and at sports, and because she didn't, there were plenty of reasons for Gwen to resent me. The only things she possessed and that I lacked were good looks and confidence. I'd have to use make-up, spend time styling my hair and wear something modern to earn attention. All Gwen did was ruffle her curls, stick out her chest and wait for the opposite sex to swarm around her like bees to a honey pot.

But William was different. He was immune to her charms. We met at a party during our first year of university. I was studying chemistry and he was in the midst of a business and finance degree.

Possessing such a serious speciality, I expected him to be as equally intense. Yet he was the opposite. He was such a quick-witted boy with a knack of doing pin-sharp impressions of lecturers and friends we had in common. We became besotted by one another, and fifteen months later, he got down on one knee and proposed on New Year's Eve. Of course I said yes. I felt safe with him and I was sure I had met my soulmate, even though we had barely left our teens. Gwen had her own boyfriend at the time, but I could tell he was only there for her to pass the time with. The grass was always greener on the opposite side to Gwen.

The first time she and William met was at what was to be our final family summer holiday. I could tell immediately what was on her mind by the way she batted her eyelashes as she introduced herself to him on our arrival. But I wasn't worried. I'd never seen William so much as look at another girl on campus and there had been plenty to choose from. He had picked me, he had wanted us to spend the rest of our lives together. He and Gwen were like chalk and cheese.

'Keep your eye on that one,' my grandmother warned me. We were sitting together in the garden watching as William and Gwen played tennis.

'I don't have any reason not to trust William,' I said.

'Honesty leaves when lust arrives,' she replied.

I dismissed her comments, but gradually, her caution began to niggle. And I realised that each time I let William out of my sight, he and Gwen just so happened to be together. They'd be strolling around the gardens, they'd disappear for an hour to row across the lake, or I'd find her in the kitchen making him something to eat. I hated how she called him Bill and they began to share little in-jokes I wasn't privy to. I had little choice but to retaliate. Each evening for the rest of that fortnight, I reminded him of what a better option I was with the most sex we'd ever had in our time together. In the bedroom, the bathroom, the woods and even up against a pier by the lake, I made sure to exhaust him. Nowhere and nothing was out of bounds.

And when the holiday drew to a close, I left victorious. Gwen had failed to snare my fiancé and William and I returned to university as happy as we had ever been. We saw nothing of her until the following Easter when her family came to stay with mine. By now she had another new boyfriend, but that didn't prevent her from shamelessly flirting with William. And this time, I'd had enough. But when I confronted her about it and ordered her to stop, at least she didn't insult my intelligence by denying it or suggesting I was imagining it.

'Men like Bill don't want girls,' she hit back. 'They need women.'

'You've got no idea what he wants.'

'And you've got no idea what he needs.'

The biggest mistake I have ever made was allowing that woman to creep into my head. Because she made me panic. William and I weren't planning to marry until a couple of years after we'd graduated from university. And children weren't on the agenda until we reached our thirties. But in my sudden desperation to hang on to him, I decided to bring forward those plans. And without his agreement.

I was pregnant within weeks of flushing my remaining contraceptives down the toilet. William tried to put a brave face on it, even though I know he was both shocked and scared. Even now, guilt hardens in my chest when I think about what I did, but I knew that a family of our own would solidify what we had. And I could justify it by reminding myself I wasn't trapping him, I was only bringing forward the inevitable. We made plans to marry, and seven weeks later, our families and friends gathered at a church in Winchester, waiting to watch me walk up the aisle.

I had never been prouder of the man I was to marry as when I saw him standing by the flower-strewn altar, accompanied by his best man. My cheeks ached from how much I was grinning as my father walked me up the aisle. But as the vicar began to address us and the congregation, I realised William's excitement was not mirroring mine. *It's just nerves*, I told myself. *That's why he's not looking at you properly*. Then gradually I realised there was more to it than that. Something was wrong.

We hadn't reached the chorus of 'Give Me Joy in My Heart' when he wiped a tear from his eye with the cuff of his morning suit, mouthed an apology and began to walk away.

'William!' I yelled as the confused congregation's singing petered out. 'What are you doing?'

But he didn't answer me or so much as turn his head to look back. I clutched our unborn child as he reached the halfway point of the aisle, stopped, held his hand out, and I watched in horror as Gwen took it. The last time I ever saw either of them was as they pushed open the arched wooden doors and vanished into bright daylight.

For days afterwards, I was inconsolable, refusing to eat, unable to sleep and surviving only on caffeine. Then crippling stomach pains saw my father rush me to hospital where I miscarried our baby at eighteen weeks. And in the same week, on my twenty-first birthday, I contracted a serious internal infection that threatened my life. There was no choice but for me to undergo a hysterectomy.

In a few short days, I'd lost my husband-to-be, my baby, our future together and any chance of experiencing motherhood again.

Meanwhile, William and Gwen were uncontactable. Neither were answering their home telephone lines and our families didn't hear or see anything of them. I also discovered through the grapevine that the whole time I'd thought I'd kept them apart they were actually writing to one another and organising clandestine meetings.

It was only later I discovered that while I was losing my baby, they had taken a ferry to the Isle of Wight and were staying at the hotel that William and I had booked for our honeymoon. They also married there and, by their own choice, with no family or friends in attendance. Soon after, William transferred university courses to a college in London, and on his graduation they spent much of their first year apart with him working for a German bank in Munich. I assumed that would be the kiss of death for their relationship because without his constant attention, Gwen wouldn't be able to help herself and would search for it elsewhere. But by all accounts she didn't. Instead, they remained devoted to each other until William's death. And oh boy, did that knowledge hurt. It still does, learning from Connie that they were better suited together than he and I were. My only consolation in this sorry mess was learning that, like me, Gwen never had children. William ruined motherhood for us both.

I allowed my inability to trust another man or to give him a family to prevent me from finding love again or marrying. For many men back then, adoption was out of the question when they could create a biological child of their own. So eventually, I stopped looking for love. I remained in the first house I bought, alone, and with no distractions I should have thrown myself into my career as a chemist for a pharmaceuticals company. But without ambition or an end goal, I stayed in the same level of role without seeking promotion until I retired at seventy-five. Since then, I have wallowed in self-reflection and dwelled on wasted opportunities. If I could do it all again, I'd have changed everything.

And then Connie and Paul appeared in my world. Neither of them will ever know just how much they have done for me. And I hope that Gwen is rolling in her grave watching every penny of her savings being spent on my happiness.

It's not all bad news for Connie, though, as I didn't leave her completely empty-handed. She has Tom, our grandmother's porcelain cat. Gwen and I loved that ugly-looking thing, but it was me who Gran gifted it to as a wedding present. Mum sent all of the presents back the week after I was jilted, and when Gran died a couple of years later, I did wonder where it had gone. Gwen must have beaten me to the punch and taken it. I doubt it's worth anything, but you never know, she might get a few pounds for it at a car boot sale whenever she's released from prison again.

I return to the present when the sound of another small motorboat's engine catches my attention. It's making its way from the ship to the shore, another wave of guests ready to explore El Mirador. I had planned to catch it on its return to the ship as I have a pilates class booked this afternoon. I'll use the app on my phone to cancel it, as I'm enjoying myself too much here. I smile to myself as I think of these champagne problems.

I reflect again on how I have found my home on oceans and seas and how I intend to live and die on them. I've half joked to the crew that if I pass away en route to somewhere, they must simply throw me overboard. But if I have a suspicion my time is running out, I might just find a way of straddling the railings and disappearing under the waves on my own terms.

When Luís finishes helping the passengers from the boat and on to the beach, I beckon him over again. 'I'm sorry to be an annoyance, but do you have some matches?' He returns from the bar with a packet and I ask for his assistance to help me to the shoreline, as my feet aren't terribly stable on sand. The sea is wonderfully warm as it covers my feet and laps at my ankles. I glance down at my chipped toenails and make a mental note to see that lovely young Filipino pedicurist again after my hair appointment tomorrow. And I need to look my best because I have a date! It's my first in more than twenty years and I know that I should be nervous, but I'm feeling quite relaxed about it. Derek, a recently retired charity worker, joined the cruise back in Florida and fitted in with our group like he'd been with us for the whole journey. But he often made me the focus of his attention. When he asked me if I'd like to join him for dinner I thought he meant a group of us but it turned out it was just me. And I can't deny I was flattered. He's a quirky chap, never without a tartan flat cap on his head despite the temperature. Some of the girls have been teasing me, calling him my toyboy, which makes me chuckle. Anyway, I don't know if anything will come of it, but nothing ventured, nothing gained.

I remove from my pocket a photograph Connie gave to me of Gwen and me. It's the one Paul tried to burn, so it's already a little scorched. I strike a match. *Look at us*, I think, as the edges begin to curl. In another life, we could have been friends, or at least equals. But not in this one. Because in this one, I have won and she can burn in hell like the flames igniting our picture.

Then I drop it gently into the water and turn my back as my one last reminder of the past floats far, far away from my present and oceans from my future.

ACKNOWLEDGEMENTS

Dementia's variations are cruel and non-discriminatory and affect both the victims and their carers in almost equal measure. Like millions of other families, I've watched loved ones suffer. My grandmother, an uncle and a close family friend slowly lost every part of themselves to the disease until nothing remained. Their carers, either voluntary or paid, often go above and beyond the call of duty to make life more manageable for them. They are incredible, strong-willed people who give dignity to those who need it the most and deserve much more credit than they get. This book is dedicated to them.

While *The Stranger in Her House* and its characters are fictitious, there are elements of my story that are not. As the law in the UK currently stands, in 2024, someone with a condition such as dementia can get married. And if they don't make another will after their marriage, it revokes an existing will, allowing their new spouse to inherit everything, even if they have only been in that person's life for a short time. This means vulnerable people can be ripe for exploitation. For more information on the law now and those campaigning for reforms, please visit www.predatorymarriage.uk.

No book is ever just the work of the author. So I'd like to extend my gratitude towards my Thomas & Mercer team, including my editors Vic Haslam and David Downing, who always manage to add some spit and polish to whatever I produce. Thanks also to the eagle eye of Sadie Mayne and Freya Ward-Lowery.

I'd like to thank all you Instagrammers, TikTokers, vloggers, Tweeters, bloggers and Facebookers for your incredible support in getting the word out there about my books. Apologies if I have forgotten anyone, but on Facebook, thanks to groups including THE Book Club, and its illustrious leader/despot Tracy Fenton, along with Book Mark!, The Fiction Café Book Club and members of Psychological Thriller Readers. For the latter, I am holding a list of acknowledgements I didn't realise I was holding. IYKYK.

Thank you to my TV and film rights agent Jon Cassir, my beta readers, including Grammar Queen Kath Middleton, Rhian Molloy, Carole Watson, Mark Fearne, Louise Beech, Mary Wallace, Elaine Binder, Mandie Brown, Laura Pontin, Wendy Clarke, Denise Stevenson and Maddy Cordell. Thanks to Louise Talbot for helping me with my social worker chapter; any errors made in my description of procedure are the fault of the author.

Of course I'd like to thank my family: Elliot, my husband John, my mum Pam, and my four-legged best friend Oscar, who was still with me while this book was being written like he was for its ten predecessors. I hope he and Dad are enjoying long walks together up in the stars.

And finally, thanks to every one of you who has taken the time to buy and borrow my books. Without you, I wouldn't have a bad neck and shoulder knots from spending hour after hour hunched over this bloody keyboard. My physio thanks you, though. You're putting his kids through university. x

ABOUT THE AUTHOR

Photo © 2017 Robert Gershinson

John Marrs is an author and former journalist based in Northamptonshire, England. After spending his career interviewing celebrities from the worlds of television, film and music for numerous national newspapers and magazines, he is now a full-time author. This is his eleventh book. Follow him at www.johnmarrsauthor.com, on Twitter @johnmarrs1, on Instagram @johnmarrs.author and on Facebook at www.facebook.com/johnmarrsauthor.

Follow the Author on Amazon

If you enjoyed this book, follow John Marrs on Amazon to be notified when the author releases a new book!

To do this, please follow these instructions:

Desktop:

1) Search for the author's name on Amazon or in the Amazon App.
2) Click on the author's name to arrive on their Amazon page.
3) Click the 'Follow' button.

Mobile and Tablet:

1) Search for the author's name on Amazon or in the Amazon App.
2) Click on one of the author's books.
3) Click on the author's name to arrive on their Amazon page.
4) Click the 'Follow' button.

Kindle eReader and Kindle App:

If you enjoyed this book on a Kindle eReader or in the Kindle App, you will find the author 'Follow' button after the last page.